The *Satyrica* of Petronius

OKLAHOMA SERIES IN CLASSICAL CULTURE

Oklahoma Series in Classical Culture

SERIES EDITOR

Ellen Greene, *University of Oklahoma*

ADVISORY BOARD

The *Satyrica* of Petronius

An Intermediate Reader with Commentary and Guided Review

Beth Severy-Hoven

UNIVERSITY OF OKLAHOMA PRESS : NORMAN

This book is published with the generous assistance of
Macalester College, Saint Paul, Minnesota.

The Latin text presented is from Konrad Müller, *Petronius, Satyricon Reliquiae* (Munich and Leipzig: K. G. Saur Verlag, 2003) and courtesy of Walter De Gruyter. A few punctuation changes have been made as suggested in Gareth Schmeling, *A Commentary on the* Satyrica *of Petronius* (New York: Oxford University Press, 2011).

Library of Congress Cataloging-in-Publication Data

Petronius Arbiter, author.
[Satryricon]
The Satyrica of Petronius : an intermediate reader with commentary and guided review / Beth Severy-Hoven.
pages cm — (Oklahoma series in classical culture ; volume 50)
ISBN 978-0-8061-4438-2 (pbk. : alk paper)
1. Petronius Arbiter. Satyricon.
I. Severy, Beth. II. Title. III. Series.: Oklahoma series in classical culture ; v. 50.
PA6558.A2 2014
873'.01—dc23   2013042700

The Satyrica *of Petronius* is Volume 50 in the Oklahoma Series in Classical Culture.

The paper in this book meets the guidelines for permanence and durability of the Committee on Production Guidelines for Book Longevity of the Council on Library Resources, Inc. ∞

discipulīs meīs

Contents

Preface for Students

The *Satyrica* is one of the strangest texts to survive from the ancient Roman world. In all honesty, we do not know who wrote it or why. The ending and beginning do not survive. The main characters aspire to be like their heroes from epic and myth, but in reality they are debauched con artists. I think the novel provides a marvelous introduction to Roman literature and culture, as well as to the challenges of studying these things through imperfect, fragmentary evidence.

This book assumes that you have studied at least the equivalent of one year of college-level Latin. If you have a basic understanding of Latin grammar and syntax, everything you will need to engage this fascinating ancient text is provided: an introduction to the novel and the world that created it, selections of unadapted Latin prose, a sentence-by-sentence commentary, and a dictionary. In the commentary, glosses are provided to address unusual vocabulary or grammatical constructions, cultural issues, problems with the Latin text, and the like. Your instructor may also choose to use other features of the book, including the guided review of Latin grammar, chapter vocabulary lists, and supplemental Latin passages. I hope you enjoy your travels through this puzzling literary masterpiece.

Preface for Instructors

This book is an intermediate-level textbook for undergraduate students who are reading Petronius' *Satyrica* for the first time. It is appropriate for third- or fourth-semester undergraduate Latin courses or advanced high school Latin. At this level, students often transition from a focus on grammar to reading long passages of prose. The book provides selections of unadapted Latin text, a running commentary, and a concise review of critical vocabulary and grammar, as well as a dictionary. It thus serves as the primary text for both Latin passages and review. The *Satyrica* is an attractive text for undergraduates, since the surviving fragments of this comic novel introduce a wide range of issues, including Roman sexuality, slavery, the banquet, religious diversity, marriage, imperial politics, philosophical schools, textual transmission, and literary allusion and parody. This book will help students explore these issues through a substantive introduction to the novel and its cultural and literary landscape, as well as inset pages on specific topics such as the *atrium* house, public baths, and wall painting. The grammatical review and accompanying exercises focus on key forms and syntax and utilize current scholarship on Latin language acquisition and reading comprehension.

The number of textbooks directed toward the intermediate level in Latin has increased recently; however, only two on the *Satyrica* are currently available for classroom use. One is Gilbert Lawall's *Petronius: Selections from the* Satyricon, which is now in the third edition (1995). It provides almost all the vocabulary in a given passage on the same page as the Latin, and it glosses even simple grammatical constructions. So much information is provided that only five to fifteen lines of Latin text fit on two facing pages, and little if any work is left to students. An alternative is M. G. Balme's *The Millionaire's Dinner Party* (originally published in 1973). Although I used it multiple times to teach intermediate Latin, I finally became exasperated with the degree to which Balme modifies the original Latin text to make it both easier for beginning students and more appropriate for the British schoolboys for whom his book was originally intended. (For example, most sexual references are eliminated.) The grammatical review in the back of that book requires extensive supplementation, and passages are taken only from the dinner party of the freedman Trimalchio. My aim with this new text is to create a more complete and more authentic textbook—a *Satyrica* reader and grammatical review for the overworked intermediate-level Latin instructor and the literarily and culturally curious twenty-first-century undergraduate Latin student.

This book is divided into twelve chapters. Although all of the Latin is gathered together at the front, the passages are arranged by chapter, so that they correspond to the chapters of grammatical and lexical review in the back. This structure is meant to provide flexibility—you may choose to use, use selectively, or ignore the review material. The selected passages progressively increase in length. In the commentary, glosses are provided to address unusual vocabulary or grammatical constructions, cultural issues, textual problems, and the like. Five additional passages of original Latin are then provided from the novel without commentary, although the vocabulary for those passages is included in the dictionary.

Each chapter in the "Guided Review" summarizes key forms or syntax. The order of presentation reflects either how common the forms or constructions are (for example, participles come in the second chapter) or their presence in the corresponding passages (such as the unusual number of conditions in Niceros' story of the werewolf). This review is meant to complement, rather than replace, a student's elementary Latin textbook and a standard reference grammar such as Allen and Greenough. My intent is to contribute another voice to a student's instructional chorus, an addition to that of their other textbooks and teachers, so the tone is informal. After the grammatical review, examples and review sentences are provided, taken from earlier passages in the novel whenever possible. To engage a wide range of learning styles and interests, post-reading activities are included, from rewriting scenes as scripts to be performed or as pages from a comic book, to hunting for coordinating conjunctions, anticipating character reactions, and transforming Latin participles into *cum* clauses. I use these only selectively in my class, but I wanted to provide you with a range of resources and ideas based on suggestions from the latest research on language acquisition, such as John Gruber-Miller's edited volume *When Dead Tongues Speak: Teaching Beginning Greek and Latin* (2006). Each chapter also contains the synopsis of an irregular verb or demonstrative adjective worthy of close review and a vocabulary list, and thus forms a complete unit suitable for regular quizzes or exams. The most common Latin words in the passages are listed in the vocabulary lists of the first two chapters; the most common conjunctions, prepositions, and adverbs are collected in chapter 3; and lists for subsequent chapters are selected based on a combination of frequency and order of occurrence. All words that appear in the passages five or more times are included, as are many of the words that recur three or four times. Some words have also been added to the lists so that they can be reviewed at the same time as words with which they are frequently confused.

Each chapter (with passage and review material) is designed to take about one week of a college-level intermediate Latin course. All critical components of Latin syntax and grammar are reviewed. Even with interspersed exams and supplemental reading of other authors or the extra passages from the *Satyrica*, students should be able to complete the textbook within a semester.

Acknowledgments

The Latin text presented here is from Konrad Müller, *Petronius, Satyricon Reliquiae* (4th ed., revised, 2003), and is used courtesy of Walter de Gruyter GmBH, with a few punctuation changes as suggested in Gareth Schmeling's magisterial 2011 *Commentary on the* Satyrica *of Petronius.*

I owe many debts to the teachers who brought me to my love of the Latin language, including Mrs. Geraldine Hodges of Fort Clarke Middle School in Gainesville, Florida. But for this particular book, I am obligated just as much to my students. Christopher W. Larabee, Macalester '11, coauthored the first draft of the Latin texts and commentary with the support of funding from a Macalester College Student-Faculty Summer Collaboration grant. He also created the first vocabulary review lists. His insights as a student who had recently encountered Petronius for the first time were invaluable, and his enthusiasm and work ethic are unparalleled. This book would not exist without him. In the fall of 2009, sixteen brave intermediate Latin students used the first draft of our book as their primary text for class. They competed in spotting typographical errors, suggested worthy changes, and demonstrated extraordinary patience, and they are thus thanked individually: Brad Andres, Luke Clapp, Keith Couture, Julia Dahle, Lauren Edmundson, Tim Erkel, Natalie Foote, Anna Hardin, Neil Hilborn, Josh Kramer, Dirk Petersen, Kate Petersen, Miranda Pettengill, Julianne Ragland, Anna Renken, and Tosca Saltz. Two subsequent classes have used and improved various sections of the book as well. David Oosterhuis helped revise the first two chapters of the grammatical review. Herta Pitman was instrumental in obtaining high-quality scans of the illustrations. Readers Jean Alvares of Montclair State University and Daniel H. Garrison of Northwestern University provided invaluable suggestions for improvement, and I thank them sincerely for their diligence and professionalism in working with the manuscript. The eagle eye of copy editor Jane Lyle also made this a much better book than it would have been without her. Finally, thanks are owed to my colleagues in Classics at Macalester who encouraged me to try my hand at a textbook, and particularly to my friend Nanette Goldman, who first suggested the *Satyrica* to me for an intermediate-level course.

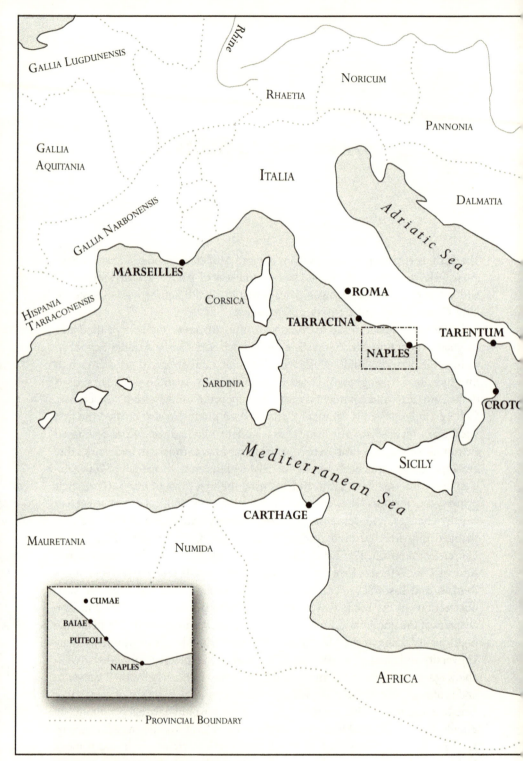

World of the *Satyrica*. Map by Jeffrey Becker.

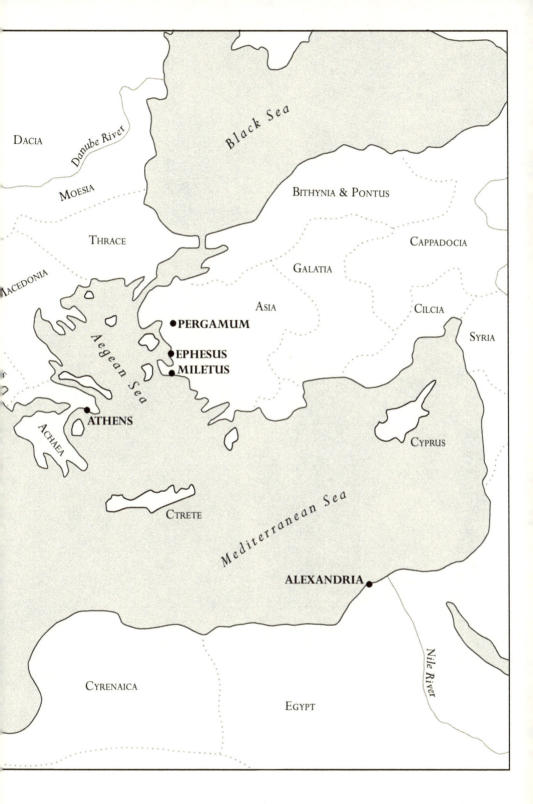

DACIA

Danube River

MOESIA

Black Sea

BITHYNIA & PONTUS

THRACE

CAPPADOCIA

MACEDONIA

GALATIA

ASIA

CILCIA

SYRIA

Aegean Sea

●PERGAMUM

●EPHESUS
●MILETUS

●ATHENS

ACHAEA

CYPRUS

CRETE

Mediterranean Sea

●ALEXANDRIA

Nile River

CYRENAICA

EGYPT

The *Satyrica* of Petronius

Introduction

The fragmentary remains of Petronius' magnum opus, the *Satyrica*, are a wild, episodic ride through a fictional ancient south Italy. In the longest surviving section, the problematic narrator Encolpius, "Crotch" in Greek, attends a dinner party hosted by the wealthy ex-slave Trimalchio; through these scenes the author communicates in no uncertain terms the degree to which money cannot buy class. The rest of the existing plot adapts a classic romantic storyline: boy meets boy, boy loses boy to a rival, boy regains boy only to be shipwrecked, and so on. Encolpius, "a *demimondaine* with upper-class breeding but no money and a taste for the gutter" (Romm 2008, 11), provides an unreliable first person account of his lover and rivals in a story also populated by such characters and caricatures as lusty priestesses, self-serving teachers, despised poets, slaves, sailors, witches, vagabonds, con artists, and everything in between. The text is one of the most puzzling to reach us from antiquity, and scholars still debate its genre, goals, original length, and form. What is not disputed is Petronius' skill with the Latin language, his mastery of characterization, and the invaluable peek he provides into the rich cultural world of early imperial Rome.

The following pages provide a basic introduction to this fascinating text to prepare you to read sections of the novel in the original Latin. You will learn how fragments of the work reached us from the ancient world, as well as current scholarly thinking about what it was called and who wrote it. After considering the narrative structure, we will explore the contexts in which it was written, including the Greek and Latin literature with which the novel constantly interacts, the historical time and political circumstances of its creation, and the social and cultural world that it inhabits and refracts. We will also pay attention to Petronius' use of Latin. The author moves from elegant prose and verse to raunchy colloquial speech to the imperfect Latin of nonnative speakers in order to color his character portraits or parody different literary styles and genres. Finally, we will consider the influence Petronius' work has had on later literature and arts, from the Italian film *Fellini Satyricon* to F. Scott Fitzgerald's *The Great Gatsby*, an early version of which was titled *Trimalchio*. Hopefully this information will help you ask good questions about what is at issue and what is at stake in various scenes, as well as appreciate being able to read in the original Latin what remains of this biting and superbly crafted story.

THE TEXT

Sadly, neither the beginning nor the end of Petronius' lengthy work survives. Even the narrative that has reached us is in fragments, some of many pages in length, others of just a line or two. It is worth considering for a moment why the text is so damaged. What happened to it after it was created almost two thousand years ago?

In Rome in the middle of the first century of the Common Era (CE), litera-ture was recorded on rolls of papyrus. All works were written by hand, and any copies for friends, buyers, or libraries also had to be handwritten. Since a work as long as the *Satyrica* would have taken up several scrolls, Petronius' work would have been a particularly expensive and rare commodity. Other authors in fact do not often mention the text. Papyrus also does not last long in most climates, so it would have had to be recopied regularly onto new material in order to survive. Before the printing press was invented in the fifteenth century, a text had to jump other technological hurdles and cultural changes in order to reach us. One exam-ple is the introduction of the codex book to the Roman world sometime in the second century. Made of animal-skin parchment and of separate pages bound together on one side, the codex was both more durable and easier to read. Petro-nius' work must have been copied into codices, because we have references to it from authors of the fifth and sixth centuries. Some even quote from parts of the text that no longer survive, so the work may well have been intact at this point.

More cultural changes were on the horizon, however, as interest in classical authors waned after the sixth century and ancient Latin texts came to be pre-served primarily in European monasteries. The content of Petronius' racy work probably did not lend itself to popularity in this milieu, or in the educational institutions of medieval Europe. Changes in standard handwriting styles also formed barriers to transmission. Dramatically different, parchment-saving styles spread quickly; within a few generations, older scripts became illegible and thus could no longer be easily copied. All of these factors in conjunction explain why our evidence suggests that only one manuscript of the *Satyrica* made it to the ninth century. Already heavily damaged, missing the beginning and end, that manuscript is the source of all that we now have, even though we do not have the document itself.

Fortunately, scholars in the court of Charlemagne and his descendants were quite interested in classical materials, and in the period sometimes known as the Carolingian Renaissance, this sole surviving copy of Petronius' work was excerpted by two or three people. What we have today is fragmentary because they *selected* passages, rather than recopying everything they found. Their manuscripts are lost, but we have their handwritten descendants, which reflect another problem of transmission—the selectivity of the excerpters. One set of copies contains lots of verse and dialogue but carefully omits any stories involving sex between men; another set records narrative regardless of the content. Since the rediscovery of the first manuscript in the early fifteenth century, the various surviving copies have been collated by scholars and published regularly, including the 1669 printing in Amsterdam of the first edition to contain everything we now have of the *Satyrica*. The Latin text used in this book, Konrad Müller's edition of 2003, reflects the most recent scholarly work done to correct the errors that inevitably creep in when a literary work has passed through dozens of handwritten copies of copies of copies.

In its most basic outline, the surviving part of the story relates the adventures of the narrator character, Encolpius, in southern Italy. Traveling with his young lover, Giton, and another companion, Ascyltos, Encolpius is posing as a student when he and his friends are invited to a dinner party. The story of the banquet hosted by the ex-slave Trimalchio forms the bulk of our surviving text. Following the party, Ascyltos makes off with Giton. A new friend, Eumolpus, helps Encolpius get him back, and the three men escape by ship. After a storm at sea, the survivors make their way to the south Italian town of Croton, where they set up an elaborate con. Encolpius meanwhile has a less than successful affair with a girl named Circe. At this point the text gives out.

In more detail, here are the elements of the story that we still have, in the order in which they are offered by our surviving manuscripts. The conventional section numbers are given in parentheses:

Encolpius ("Crotch") and another young man with a Greek name, Ascyltos ("Untroubled"), are outside a school of rhetoric run by a teacher named Agamemnon somewhere around the Bay of Naples. As the fragment begins, Encolpius is delivering a highly stylized rant about modern education in oratory, to which Agamemnon responds verbosely that parents are to blame (1–5). Ascyltos sneaks off, but Encolpius cannot break free of Agamemnon's rhetorical spell until some students pour noisily out of the school. Encolpius then loses his way to the inn where he and Ascyltos are staying. An old woman misdirects him to a brothel, where he finds the lost Ascyltos, who has been led there by a lecherous old man with designs on him (6–8). Somehow they escape.

In the next surviving section, we meet the sixteen-year-old boy Giton ("Neighbor Boy" in Greek), apparently Encolpius' lover, who is complaining that Ascyltos has been making advances toward him. Encolpius and Ascyltos stage a fight, then agree to part ways after the banquet to which they have both been invited (9–11). At a market, we hear references to what must have been an earlier episode in which our protagonists sewed what were probably stolen coins into the lining of a tunic, but then lost it. While attempting to sell an expensive stolen cloak, Ascyltos and Encolpius spy the local farmer from whom they took it; he is holding their lost gold-lined tunic. They attempt a swap and are almost dragged into court, which they are anxious to avoid, but they manage to get the right garment back, at least for now (12–15).

Next comes a substantive set of fragments that many believe should be placed earlier in the novel (16–26). It begins with a priestess, Quartilla, and her entourage interrupting the three young men during dinner. She alludes to their having witnessed a secret ritual of the fertility god Priapus, probably an event described earlier in the *Satyrica*. She swears them to secrecy and then punishes their sacrilege by making them participate in a highly sexualized and highly fragmentary banquet. The scene ends with Encolpius and Quartilla peeping on Giton as he celebrates a mock wedding night with the seven-year-old girl Pannychis ("All-Nighter" in Greek) as a ritual for Priapus.

Encolpius is worrying over his troubles when Menelaus, an assistant of the teacher Agamemnon, finds him and his friends at the baths and points out the wealthy freedman Trimalchio (from the root for "Prince" in Semitic languages), at whose house they have been invited to dine that evening (27–28). Encolpius and Ascyltos attend as young scholars, while Giton acts as their slave. Encolpius describes the entryway to the house, the slaves and how they greet the guests, the various courses of the meal and how they are presented, the host and his behavior, Trimalchio's wife, Fortunata ("Fortunate" in Latin), conversations with fellow diners, and the entertainments provided. In trying to display his learning, Trimalchio butchers accounts of Roman history and Greek myth (28–62). His pet slave boy competes with a dog for their master's attention; the host's drunken best friend Habinnas (a Semitic name) and his wife arrive from another party. After other wine-soaked antics, Trimalchio invites the group to his private bath complex. Our "heroes" try to escape, but in their stupor they get lost and are harassed by a dog until they are escorted back to the party. Trimalchio and Fortunata fight when Trimalchio flirts with a slave boy. Habinnas calms the host, who eulogizes himself, shows off his intended burial clothes, and orders trumpeters to play a dirge. The trumpets are so loud that the local firemen rush in, and Encolpius and his friends escape in the melee (63–78).

Giton leads them home, where Encolpius awakes to find Ascyltos taking advantage of Giton. They wage a mock battle, but then decide to let Giton choose his companion. Giton promptly selects Ascyltos, and they leave together. A heartbroken

Encolpius weeps by the seashore and attempts unsuccessfully to commit suicide by attacking a soldier (79–82). At a picture gallery in a temple, he meets the poet Eumolpus ("Good Singer" in Greek). Eumolpus tells a couple of colorful stories about his service as a provincial magistrate when he seduced the son of his host. Then, inspired by a painting, he launches into a verse rendering of the Fall of Troy, upon which passersby stone him (83–90). As they escape, Encolpius and Eumolpus agree to have dinner. At the baths beforehand, Encolpius sees Giton, and they return to the inn together. Eumolpus finds them later and makes his own moves on Giton, which enrages Encolpius. A battle ensues involving the innkeeper and other lodgers (90–96).

Later, Ascyltos arrives with a public official searching for a runaway slave matching Giton's description. Giton hides while the inn is searched, but eventually a sneeze gives him away (97–98). In a section that does not survive, Encolpius manages to evade Ascyltos with Giton.

Eumolpus leads the happy couple on board a ship he has previously booked. After they set sail, Encolpius recognizes the owner of the ship and a passenger, whom he and Giton must have met and offended in earlier sections of the novel. Encolpius had a relationship, potentially sexual, with the wealthy man Lichas ("Lick" in Greek), and there is a hint that Encolpius may have seduced his wife. Encolpius was also involved somehow with the lady Tryphaena ("Luxurious" in Greek), who then became enamored of Giton and was somehow publicly disgraced. She is now headed for exile in Lichas' hometown of Tarentum for reasons we do not know (99–101). After a debate about various means of escape and disguise, Encolpius and Giton shave their heads and pretend to be recaptured runaway slaves. They are recognized even so—by Giton's screams and Encolpius' generous genitalia— and put on trial. This dissolves into a mock battle until Giton threatens to castrate himself. Tryphaena sues for peace, and Eumolpus negotiates a treaty (102–109).

Eumolpus then entertains the group with a story about the fickleness of women: a dramatically devout widow from Ephesus is seduced into escapades with a new lover in her husband's tomb (110–12). After some fragments indicating further jealousies and couplings on board, a storm arises that rips the ship apart. Giton belts himself to Encolpius so they will not become separated, and they somehow make it to shore with Eumolpus and a servant. After finding Lichas' body washed up on the beach, they bury him (113–15).

The survivors hike inland until they meet a local farmer. He describes how the nearby city of Croton has fallen to legacy hunters, people who ingratiate themselves with the childless in hopes of receiving a rich inheritance. Eumolpus concocts a plan to enter the town as a shipwrecked, ailing widower who recently lost his only son. Encolpius and Giton will play his slaves while he supposedly awaits a ship bringing riches from Africa. En route to Croton, Eumolpus delivers a long poem about the civil war between Julius Caesar and Pompey. Upon their arrival, Eumolpus is showered with gifts by legacy hunters (116–24).

Meanwhile, Encolpius is courted by a maid on behalf of her lady, Circe. He becomes infatuated and promises to give up Giton for her, after which he suffers from impotence. Circe arranges for a witch to treat him, to no avail, and he composes some amusing poems on his condition. Later he appeals to the gods for help and is attended to by an old priestess, Oenothea ("Wine Goddess" in Greek). Eventually Encolpius seems to escape from her and some other lascivious old women in a series of fragmentary scenes. Circe's maid also makes a play for him (126–39).

Eumolpus enjoys the sexual services of the daughter of a legacy hunter with the physical assistance of a servant, since he has announced that he is nearly dead from illness. Encolpius and the girl's brother watch through a keyhole. In the last surviving fragments, it seems that our con artists are about to be found out as the promised ship from Africa fails to arrive. A will is read in which the beneficiaries may inherit only if they eat some of the deceased's corpse in public view. A discussion of sauces and historical precedents for cannibalism closes out what survives of the novel (140–41).

How this stretch of narrative relates to the full original text is a matter of some dispute. Using hints from some titles in our surviving manuscripts, editor Franz Bücheler suggested in 1862 that what survives of the *Satyrica* is taken from books fourteen to sixteen of an original work of twenty-four books, and later scholars on the whole have followed him. However, this means that Petronius' original text would have been a giant, eight times the length of the other Latin novel known to us, Apuleius' *Metamorphoses*. Recently Giulio Vannini has suggested that Petronius' original text came to be divided into two volumes, books one through twelve and books thirteen to twenty-four, the first of which does not survive. Thus what we have is excerpts from the second volume, save the last three books, a reconstruction that would make Petronius' novel about twice the length of Apuleius'. Gottskálk Jensson advocates for a text of eighteen books and does a lot of work reconstructing the missing storyline through the brief references in what survives. This evidence, as well as quotes in other authors and random fragments, hints that Encolpius' wanderings may include or even start in Marseilles, a Greek city on the Mediterranean coast of Gaul, from which he is a voluntary ritual scapegoat and exile. This may be where he first encounters Lichas and Tryphaena and offends Priapus, although that is unclear. We also hear about his mistreatment of a host, perhaps at the villa of someone named Lycurgus, and a close escape from a gladiatorial arena.

The name of the work is just as problematic as its state of survival. No title is provided by ancient references to the work, and you will see in much of the bibliography the name *Satyricon*, a transliteration of a Greek genitive plural used with a nominative plural *libri*, thus "Books of *Satyrica*." Similar ancient works, however, tend to have titles in the neuter nominative plural (*Aethiopica*, *Ephesiaca*, *Milesiaca*, *Sybaritica*), so scholars have recently but broadly started using the title *Satyrica* for the whole work. Whatever its original form, the title probably puns on two terms: (1) "satyr," a part-human, part-animal creature from Greek myth with an immense sexual appetite and a phallus to match; and (2) the Latin word *satura*, "medley," a Roman literary genre, predominantly in verse, which commented satirically on society, literature, and people and their foibles. Thus, the name *Satyrica* denotes a tale about raunchy satyr stuff variously and satirically treated, which describes what we can see of Petronius' story fairly well.

THE AUTHOR

Although the author is consistently referred to here as Petronius, we of course do not know exactly who this was. The single name "Petronius" is given in most medieval and later manuscripts, and we know of about six families with this name from the early Empire. Some manuscripts add an additional name, "Arbiter." This name is extremely unusual as a *cognomen*, but we hear of it as an unofficial court title in the case of an ex-consul named Petronius. The historian Tacitus describes his life and death under Nero, who was emperor from 54 to 68 CE. The name "Petronius Arbiter" in a few manuscripts suggests that someone early on identified the author of our text with this aristocrat who fell afoul of the emperor.

It is worth considering Tacitus' Petronius for a moment, since most scholars agree that he is a likely candidate to be the author of the *Satyrica*. He committed suicide in 66 CE, a not uncommon event in the later years of Nero's reign. Instead of being executed, senators and other men of the elite accused of crimes were permitted or encouraged to kill themselves, an honorable means of death that the Romans felt demonstrated ultimate self-discipline and control. (In contrast, condemned slaves were crucified.) An important conspiracy against Nero had been revealed in 65, and among those invited to end their lives in its wake were the authors Seneca the Younger and Lucan. In the following year, more were so condemned, including the brother of Seneca, who was the father of Lucan, and someone named Petronius. Here is Tacitus' account of him (*Annals* 16.17–20, translated by Michael Grant):

> Petronius deserves a brief obituary. He spent his days sleeping, his nights working and enjoying himself. Others achieve fame by energy, Petronius by laziness. Yet he was not, like others who waste their resources, regarded as

dissipated or extravagant, but as a refined voluptuary. People liked the apparent freshness of his unconventional and unselfconscious sayings and doings. Nevertheless, as governor of Bithynia and later as consul, he had displayed a capacity for business. Then, reverting to a vicious or ostensibly vicious way of life, he had been admitted into the small circle of Nero's intimates, as Arbiter of Taste: to the blasé emperor nothing was smart and elegant unless Petronius had given it his approval. So Tigellinus [the powerful head of the imperial bodyguard], loathing him as a rival and a more expert hedonist, denounced him on the grounds of his friendship with Flavius Scaevinus [one of the conspirators of 65]. This appealed to the emperor's outstanding passion—his cruelty. A slave was bribed to incriminate Petronius. No defense was heard. Indeed, most of his household were under arrest.

The emperor happened to be in Campania. Petronius too had reached Cumae; and there he was arrested. Delay, with its hopes and fears, he refused to endure. He severed his own veins. Then, having them bound up again when the fancy took him, he talked with his friends—but not seriously, or so as to gain a name for fortitude. And he listened to them reciting, not discourses about the immortality of the soul or philosophy, but light lyrics and frivolous poems. Some slaves received presents—others beatings. He appeared at dinner, and dozed, so that his death, even if compulsory, might look natural.

Even his will deviated from the routine death-bed flatteries of Nero, Tigellinus, and other leaders. Petronius wrote out a list of Nero's sensualities—giving names of each male and female bed-fellow and details of every lubricious novelty—and sent it under seal to Nero. Then Petronius broke his signet-ring, to prevent its subsequent employment to incriminate others. Nero could not imagine how his nocturnal ingenuities were known. He suspected Silia, a woman of note (she was a senator's wife) who knew all his obscenities from personal experience—and was a close friend of Petronius. For breaking silence about what she had seen and known, she was exiled.

Thus, the name Petronius Arbiter in some of our manuscripts of the *Satyrica* refers to this nickname *Elegantiae Arbiter,* Arbiter of Taste. Unfortunately, Tacitus does not identify this man as a writer, nor do Pliny (*Natural History* 37.20) and Plutarch (*Roman Questions* 19.60e) when they each allude briefly to an extravagant Petronius who reproached Nero in some fashion. Tacitus, Pliny, and Plutarch also disagree on the personal name (*praenomen*) of this Petronius. The most likely consular Petronius of this period in the historical record is one Petronius Niger, consul in 62, but none of these other sources give that *cognomen*. So Petronius may well be the right name, and someone in antiquity thought that Petronius the author was the Petronius in Nero's inner circle who crossed someone more powerful in 66 CE. We, however, cannot be sure.

Most scholars do agree, even so, that the text was written around the time of Nero, probably in the early to mid-60s. Kenneth F. C. Rose carefully pulled the evidence together in 1971 in *The Date and Author of the* Satyricon. This evidence includes references to well-known pop culture figures of the period, such as the gladiator Petraites and the lyre player Menecrates. The *Satyrica* also engages frequently with the writings of Seneca the Younger and Lucan. The text is rife with allusions to literary works, but most are by canonical authors of Greek and Latin, such as Homer, Plato, Horace, Vergil, and Ovid; on the whole, Lucan and Seneca were not taken to be among these greats in later periods of history. Since the *Satyrica* elaborately mocks these Neronian writers, it is reasonable to assume that they are contemporary rivals. Finally, the material culture described, the habits of daily life from baths to banquets, the historical events occasionally referred to—all these fit well with what we know of Italy in the mid-first century.

So we can assert with some confidence that the work is a product of Nero's time. It adds great color to the story to think of the author as the Petronius who was a consul under Nero and a celebrated hedonist of his court who fell from favor and made his suicide into subversive performance art. (Federico Fellini incorporates just such a suicide scene into his cinematic interpretation of the *Satyrica*.) But we should keep in mind that this historical figure is a bit of a construction himself, crafted by the author Tacitus, and this figure's tie to the Latin text we are reading is not straightforward. The final features that we can probably agree on about the author, however, are that (most likely) he was very well educated and had the leisure time to compose a long work. Even if he was not Tacitus' consul, the author Petronius was quite probably an aristocrat. This status is not at odds with the gritty quality of this story, which travels through the seedy underbelly of imperial Italy. This type of realism is a stylistic choice and an aesthetic effect, an effect layered within elegant Latin prose and poetry and dense allusions to elite literature. Only a similarly well read audience would get most of Petronius' humor, sophistication, and social commentary. The *Satyrica* is not a journalistic account or historical record, but a well-crafted fiction set in a world apparently distant from that of its elite author.

NARRATIVE STRUCTURE AND TECHNIQUE

In thinking about the author, we should take a moment to explore the structure of the narrative he presents to us in the surviving fragments. Although modern scholars of course do not all agree with each other, they have looked carefully at the way the story is told, and particularly at the differences among the author, narrator, and protagonist.

First, let us consider Encolpius. Who is "Crotch"? Since at least the first half of the original work is lost, we do not know how—or even if—Petronius reveals Encolpius' social status to the reader. The fact that he has a single Greek name, rather than three Latin names like Marcus Tullius Cicero, implies that he is a slave or former slave. From what we can see, he and his companions are living hand-to-mouth, sometimes by petty theft, sometimes by social posing—as scholars invited to a freedman's dinner, for example, or as a wealthy widower courted by legacy hunters. Giton plays a slave at Trimalchio's banquet, and both he and Encolpius willingly serve Eumolpus in Croton as part of their con game. Their prostitution is sometimes implied. This low status feels at odds, however, with Encolpius' apparently high level of education. Encolpius often interprets his experiences using characters and storylines from great literary works, and he knows when Trimalchio gets his history and mythology horribly wrong. He and Ascyltos and even Giton look down their noses at the (other?) freedmen at the dinner party. Is "Crotch" a well-educated slave? A freeborn citizen from a respectable Greek family down on his luck? Is Encolpius a Roman traveling under a Greek pseudonym? Is the fact that we do not know the result of a conscious decision by Petronius, or just a product of the fragmentary quality of our text?

It gets even more complicated. All of the events of the surviving novel are described by Encolpius in the first person, but in the past tense. Is there a difference between the Encolpius who is narrating and the Encolpius who experiences the story? Roger Beck makes this case in important articles of 1973 and 1975. He argues that an older and wiser narrator Encolpius is looking back on his younger, foolish self, Encolpius the protagonist. Gareth Schmeling (1994–95) concurs, describing Encolpius as an unreliable narrator confessing his disreputable past. We, as readers, then join the older Encolpius in condemning his younger self. The other surviving Latin novel, Apuleius' *Metamorphoses* of the second century CE, has just such a divided narrator. The first person protagonist witnesses something he should not and is turned into the lowest of the low—a donkey. He then experiences an epiphany toward the end of the story and becomes a religious devotee of Isis, who returns him to his human form. Once the reader has reached this point, it becomes clear that it is this older man who has been narrating the asinine adventures of his unenlightened youth. Because the *Satyrica*'s ending does not survive, we cannot know whether Apuleius' novel imitates it in this narrative closure. In both, however, we hear the story through the voices of those who are voiceless in more traditional literature—a pack animal, and if not a slave, then a quite marginal young man. It is worth considering the point of these artistic choices as you read.

The Italian scholar Gian Biagio Conte approaches the narrator from a different angle. In his influential 1996 monograph *The Hidden Author*, Conte emphasizes the gap between Encolpius and Petronius. In particular he characterizes Encolpius as being "mythomaniacal," that is, of interpreting the events of his life using heroic and tragic paradigms from high literature. For example, when Giton leaves with Ascyltos, Encolpius weeps and withdraws to the seashore to lament his loss. The scene in Latin includes verbal echoes of Achilles' lament for the slave girl taken from him in the first book of the *Iliad*. Then Encolpius expresses a mad desire to lash out and die in a way that recalls Aeneas in the second book of the *Aeneid*. Since Troy is falling and he has lost his wife, Creusa, Aeneas wants to throw himself into the heat of battle and be killed. Encolpius gives a soliloquy modeled on that of Aeneas. However, as Conte points out, the hidden author shapes the narrative so as to force the grandiose delusions of Encolpius to meet everyday reality. Thus, after his soliloquy, Encolpius arms himself in a scene extremely common in epic as the narrative switches from speech to action, but he sticks into the traditional scene *largioribus cibis excito vires*, "I keep up my strength with a rather large meal." Traditional epic has no room for such bodily concerns. Then when the armed Encolpius meets a real soldier, the centurion points to Crotch's dainty slippers, takes away his sword, and tells him to stay out of trouble.

Conte argues that Petronius' narrative is continuously moving up into epic, tragic, or other high tone and speech, then plummeting down into the realia of mundane life, including base fears and appetites. Such narrative moves are funny, but they also distance the author or orchestrator from the naive narrator Encolpius. Although a first person narrator has some claims on the reader since we see the world through his eyes and thus his illusions, the author shapes the plot around Encolpius to smash these illusions. A reader who gets the humor—who perceives the literary allusions and Encolpius' utter inability to live up to them— is an elite reader who laughs with Petronius at Encolpius and who feels a satisfying sense of superiority.

Certainly, you should watch for Encolpius' explicit and implicit allusions to epic, tragedy, and other high literature as you read from the novel and consider the effect these allusions achieve. The references do not characterize Encolpius alone, but also those he meets. For example, when Encolpius enters a temple decorated with Greek art, he is taken in by the works of the great masters, especially those depicting love stories. He shudders with the effect the images have on his soul, and he shouts out *ergo amor etiam deos tangit*, "thus love touches even the gods!" This is highly reminiscent of a scene in the *Aeneid* when Aeneas arrives in Carthage and sees the doors of a temple engraved with images of the Trojan War; he also cries out as he recognizes his own story. For Aeneas, Dido then appears and strikes up their first conversation. It is Eumolpus who begins speaking to

Encolpius at this moment. Does this signal that the aging, bald Eumolpus will be a tempting erotic distraction for our hero? Do our missing pieces of the text include their cave scene?

Eumolpus is certainly a strange character, and in a way another narrator within the *Satyrica*, although in fact we hear what Eumolpus says only through the narration of "Crotch." As mentioned earlier, "Eumolpus" means "Good Singer" in Greek, and he introduces himself to Encolpius as a poet. He delivers the longest sections of verse in the existing novel. The first, at the end of this initial encounter with Encolpius, is an account of the siege of Troy, still alluding to the second book of Vergil's *Aeneid,* and the other is an imitation/parody/revision of Lucan's *Bellum Civile* delivered on the walk to Croton. Although modern scholars agree that the poetry is not terrible, following his first recitation Eumolpus is stoned by the other people in the temple. Encolpius is constantly asking him to stop making verses. Much better received are the short stories Eumolpus tells, including a potentially autobiographical account of his seduction of a young man under his tutelage while serving in Asia Minor and the immoral parable, or perhaps dirty joke, about a widow from Ephesus. Eumolpus tries to project an image of himself as a grand, tragic figure, a tormented and austere sage, but his stories about how he exploited his young charge in Pergamum give away his true character. Watch and listen for how Petronius communicates to us through his first person narrators how disreputable and untrustworthy these narrative voices are.

HISTORICAL AND POLITICAL CONTEXTS

Authors operate not just in literary worlds, but in social and political ones as well. This is doubly true of the Romans, since our surviving authors overwhelmingly come from the political class and their dependents. Although we have already discussed the dating of the *Satyrica* to the period of the emperor Nero, it is worth exploring some of the implications of that date. For this we will need some historical context.

The Romans themselves dated the founding of their city to 753 BCE. The period we now call the Monarchy followed, with seven legendary kings to match the seven legendary hills, but information beyond the later legends is sketchy. The year 510 is when later Romans thought their ancestors rebelled against the last king and founded the *res publica*, the commonwealth or Republic. In this new system, all free, adult, male citizens voted, although the votes were weighted in favor of the elite, and they were the only officeholders. So the Roman Republic was a largely oligarchic, representative republic. Checks and balances made sure that no one person became too powerful—fear that a king would arise again was pronounced in Republican culture. Each office was held by at least two men at a time, and their terms were limited. But the oligarchic class had a stranglehold on most forms of social capital. The same men were the politicians, priests, generals, scholars, poets, lawmakers, lawyers, and judges. Just about everything was overseen by a body of former magistrates called the senate.

The history of the Republic, which lasted about five hundred years, can be told in two ways. One focuses on the military expansion of Roman control, first from the conquest of the other groups who spoke Latin in central Italy in the fifth and fourth centuries BCE, then on to peninsular Italy and the western Mediterranean in the third. These wars brought the Romans into contact with Greeks, who had long since colonized south Italy and Sicily, as well as with the Carthaginians of northern Africa, who had settlements in coastal Sicily, Iberia, and Gaul. After the defeat of Carthage and its general Hannibal in the Second Punic War (218–202 BCE), the Romans were drawn into events in the eastern Mediterranean, ruled largely by Greek-speaking kings descended from the generals of Alexander the Great. The Romans took another two centuries to gain dominance over these Hellenistic kingdoms and the remainder of the Mediterranean basin.

The other way to tell the story of the Republic is to focus on internal political developments. Two issues provoked frequent struggle: (1) Who gets to be a citizen of the Republic? (2) Who gets to be a member of the ruling oligarchic club? This story is not unrelated to the one of continuous military expansion, since those conquered by the Romans became their allies and eventually wanted partner status. The most significant tensions along these lines culminated in the revolt of the Italian allies around 90 BCE. By that time, Italians had been part of the Roman military machine for more than two hundred years. They demanded Roman citizenship, and when it was denied, they rebelled. Fighting was fierce up and down Italy for a decade until a settlement was negotiated; the Romans "won," but the Italians became Roman citizens, and their leaders could run for political office.

The last century of the Republic witnessed many tensions, including the incorporation of these Italians into the state, the governance of conquered territories carved into more and more provinces, and money from these provinces pouring into the city and disrupting traditional power structures. The elegant oligarchy of the Republic was not designed to govern vast territories, and it is not surprising that eventually powerful generals began fighting each other. The first to fight this way were the leaders in the suppression of the Italian allies, Marius and Sulla. In the next generation, Julius Caesar fought a group of opponents led by Pompey, and a generation later Caesar's right-hand man Marc Antony fought Caesar's nephew and heir, Octavian. Antony happened to have as his chief ally Cleopatra, the queen of the last surviving major Hellenistic monarchy, the Ptolemies of Egypt. So when Octavian won the war in 30 BCE, he finished the last of the Republican civil wars and the Roman conquest of the Mediterranean basin.

This was a pivotal moment in Roman history. After his victory, Octavian took the new name Augustus and became the first Roman emperor. In practice, he developed a new form of government, which we call the Principate or Empire, and in which men from an imperial family succeeded to sole rule. In name, Augustus claimed to have "restored the Republic," and offices such as the consul and provincial governors were kept, although the men who held them were appointed by the emperor. Augustus' political delicacy here was driven by the Roman cultural antipathy toward kings, made manifest in the assassination of his uncle Julius Caesar. Augustus presented himself not as a *rex*, but as a new founder of Rome in the tradition of Aeneas and Romulus, bringing peace and prosperity to a state damaged by generations of civil strife. This *Pax Romana* did not mean that the Empire was peaceful, as wars of conquest continued under Augustus and his successors, and Augustus maintained careful, autocratic control of the military. But the sense of renewal was palpable in everything from new and repaired temples, streets, and sewers to the creation of some of the most respected and influential works of Latin literature, including Livy's *History of Rome*, Vergil's *Aeneid*, and Ovid's *Metamorphoses*.

Augustus founded the Julio-Claudian dynasty of emperors, so named because although he himself had been adopted by Julius Caesar, most of his heirs were from the line of his stepson, Tiberius Claudius. The Empire was really created when Tiberius became emperor in 14 CE; Augustus was but an extraordinary individual until he passed his unusual powers on to a designated heir. Tiberius was succeeded by his grandnephew Caligula in 37, after internal power struggles had taken out most of the alternatives. Caligula's reign took a dramatic turn for the worse, and he was assassinated in 41. In the subsequent turmoil, the imperial bodyguard hailed Caligula's stuttering uncle Claudius emperor. Although he had a young son of his own, Claudius married his niece Agrippina, a great-granddaughter of Augustus, and adopted her son Nero. When Claudius died in 54, he was succeeded by Nero, the emperor under whom we believe the *Satyrica* was written.

So what do we know about this time in Roman history and life under the emperor Nero? It cannot be stressed enough that our picture of Nero is distorted at best, for a wide variety of reasons, but exploring how this happened to our historical accounts should give you a good picture of the age. By the time Nero became emperor in 54, the Empire as a political system was more than eighty years old. This was within the lifetime of few, if any, so the Republic was by now part of a nostalgic, ancient past. For those below the political elite in the social hierarchy, the transformation into the Empire probably did not change life much aside from ending the cycle of civil wars—which should not be underestimated. The story of who got to be in the club continued from the Republic. Over time, individuals or whole groups or towns outside of Italy were granted Roman citizenship. Descendants of Gauls made citizens by Julius Caesar were admitted into the senate under the emperor Claudius, to the dismay of those already there. This reveals who *was* affected by the change to the Empire—the senatorial elite. The senate continued to exist, and it held authority over the trials of senators, among other duties. But the members of the senatorial class were not responsible for the state in the same way they had been in the Republic, despite the administrative work they did for the emperor; and they thrived or not in accordance with the whims of the ruler and those closest to him. These changes clearly distressed the nonimperial elite. Perhaps as a result, senators came to take tremendous pride in their class status and privilege. Emperors who disrespected that status are routinely presented poorly in our sources, which were written on the whole by senators. Although Claudius gained few friends in the senate when he allowed prominent Gauls to become senators, Nero did far worse. In the later part of his reign, many prominent citizens were suspected of conspiring against him and were asked to commit suicide. In 59, he even had his own mother executed. The sources describe Nero as a capricious tyrant. But the sources are angry not just for these reasons, but also because of Nero's disregard for status markers. A good example is his interest in theater and performance. In many ancient Greek cultures, theater had a high social value, and actors on the whole were citizens. In Rome, in contrast, actors were largely slaves and ex-slaves, treated as part of the same suspect legal category as prostitutes and condemned criminals. When the most powerful man in Rome acted the role of Orestes onstage, where did that leave the senators? There are signs that Nero may have been popular with the people of Rome and the Empire—in the years following his death, two or three men claimed to be Nero and developed large followings, and plebeians were said to have laid masses of flowers on his tomb. Nevertheless, he was far from popular with those who wrote our surviving accounts of him.

As usual, it gets even worse. In addition to his apparent disregard for senatorial sensibilities and lethal exercises of power, Nero is also depicted poorly because he was the last of his imperial line, and because he may have played a role in an early persecution of Christians. Perhaps due to his poor treatment of senators, generals in charge of Nero's armies revolted against him in 68 CE. While these generals engaged in a fierce but brief civil war against each other, Nero fled in disgrace and killed himself. After a quick succession of three different emperors, in 69 Vespasian finally took control, a general who had been busy putting down a revolt of the province of Judea. In the wake of this crisis, historians and other writers worked hard to explain why it was appropriate for an emperor to have been overthrown and yet for Rome to still have an emperor. The answer was that Nero was a wretched individual, and that Vespasian was the man for the job; as a matter of self-preservation under the new regime, authors created and repeated stories that made Nero look bad. Nero thus begins a prominent pattern in imperial historiography—the last emperor of a dynasty is always presented as monstrous in the sources. Compare the depictions of Domitian and Commodus, the latter of *Gladiator* fame. Moreover, because Nero was the first fallen emperor, he is sometimes discussed in later periods in lieu of openly criticizing a reigning emperor. Tacitus, for example, lived under Domitian and wrote with a vengeance about the disrespectful, effeminate, and disastrous behavior of Nero. About whom is he really complaining? Finally, in subsequent centuries, the impulse to depict Nero as evil became even stronger as Christianity rose in importance. In 64 CE, during Nero's reign, a massive fire destroyed large swaths of downtown Rome. The Romans interpreted such a disaster as a sign from the gods that something was terribly wrong in their relationship; Tacitus reports that Nero blamed a new cult of "Christians" for this disruption of the *pax deorum* and had those who would not confess killed in spectacular fashion (*Annals* 15.38–44). Although scholars are highly dubious of Tacitus' account, Nero's image can never be disentangled from the persecutor of Christians who sang while Rome burned.

It is difficult to think away these negative depictions of Nero and imagine life in his court before his downfall and thorough disgracing in various retrospective historical accounts, but there are some things that we can infer. We know that literature flourished. His reign is traditionally called the Silver Age, as in lesser than the Golden Age of Augustus but nevertheless impressive. Seneca the Younger, Pliny the Elder, Lucan, Persius, Calpurnius, and Petronius are among the authors known. Although our sources are hostile, Nero seems to have been deeply interested in theater and to have been a performer himself. Theatricality is taken to extremes in Petronius' work, from the way the presentation of courses at the dinner party is transformed into drama to the mock battles of Ascyltos and Encolpius. Similarly, the *Satyrica*'s display and critique of contemporary oratorical practices belong in the early Empire. During this period, declamation became a type of public performance for adult men, not just training for students. Under an autocratic regime, rhetoric grew to have little or no role in politics, but was largely for show and in itself increasingly theatrical. It was also a particular fascination of the uncle of Nero's tutor, Seneca.

In addition, since literature, poetry, and art in general were important to Nero, we should think about them as a means of attracting imperial attention and favor. John Sullivan (1968) demonstrates this in his analysis of the lives of Seneca the Younger and Lucan. Seneca, while exiled under Claudius, composed opportunely, flattering the emperor, a prominent imperial freedman, and women of the court. Claudius' last wife, Agrippina, finally had him recalled to serve as Nero's tutor. Following Claudius' death, Seneca's savagely satiric account of his deification in the *Apocolocyntosis*, or "Pumpkinification," reveals that there was no love lost for the dead emperor as he pandered to the tastes of the new one. Seneca's nephew Lucan attracted attention as a rising poet at a young age. Coupled with his uncle's influence, he used this to segue into political success: Lucan attained senatorial status and a magistracy at the very young age of twenty (Suetonius *Life of Lucan*). In turn, when he began to fall from favor, Lucan was banned from public speaking and from publishing his poetry (Tacitus *Annals* 15.49, Dio 62.29.4). Although the sources on Nero are hostile, it cannot have been entirely fabricated that among those senators whom he invited to end their lives were many prominent authors, including Seneca, Lucan, and Petronius. In such a climate, literary rivalries were plays for power, and thus the *Satyrica*'s attacks on Seneca and Lucan suggest that its author was a player in the game.

One of these literary attacks on Lucan is illustrative. In *Satyrica* 118, Eumolpus complains about young men who turn their skill in oratory to the "easier" work of writing poetry and who leave the actions of the gods out of their poems. He then proceeds to recite 295 lines of hexameter about the civil war between Caesar and Pompey (119–24). Not only was this the subject of Lucan's epic poem the *Bellum Civile*, but for various reasons Lucan had left out the divine apparatus otherwise ubiquitous in ancient Greek and Roman epic poetry. So, although Lucan is not named directly, Petronius is clearly using Eumolpus to criticize him.

The assault on Seneca is more sustained and pervasive. Scholars have perceived numerous passages in which themes are presented from Seneca's late philosophical work, the *Moral Epistles*, and then made to appear ridiculous in context. A good example is when Eumolpus discourses at length, in typically Senecan language, on the decadence of the age—just after he has told the amusing and immoral story of his seduction of his host's son. Similarly, in *Epistle* 47, Seneca philosophically argues that slaves are human beings, subject to Fortune, and that it is not inappropriate to dine with them; in *Satyrica* 70–71, Encolpius is disgusted when the cook flops down on the couch above him at Trimalchio's sentimental, if drunken, invitation. Nor is Seneca's poetry spared. Eumolpus' other long poem, the "Fall of Troy," delivered at the temple when he first meets Encolpius (*Satyrica* 89), takes its plot from the second book of the *Aeneid*, but its meter, style, and rhetorical treatment reveal it to be imitating Seneca's tragedies. This is the performance for which passersby throw rocks at Eumolpus. Similarly, lines that Trimalchio recites and attributes to the mime writer Publilius seem really to parody the poetry of Seneca. Petronius has Trimalchio make the wrong attribution in order to compare Seneca's poetry to the base genre of mime.

Given this mocking of Seneca and Lucan and the extreme elite frustration with Nero revealed in post-Neronian writing, some scholars have tried to find parody or satirical treatment of the emperor himself in the text. Trimalchio is the most commonly advanced candidate as a stand-in for Nero, and he is even referred to by Encolpius as a *tyrannus* (41). Rose gathers evidence brought forward for the case (1971, 78):

> For example, Trimalchio's manner of dress (27.2, etc.) and favourite colours (28.4, 8) are similar to those of Nero; and his steward, like the emperor, dislikes wearing the same clothes more than once (30.11). Among Trimalchio's personal possessions is a *pyxis aurea* (29.8), an *armilla aurea* (32.4), and an astronomical design (30.4). He keeps a group of *cursores* (28.4, 29.7), he likes having a lot of cushions (32.1–2, 59.3, 78.5); he is fond of the music of water-organs (36.6), and is struck by a falling acrobat (54.1).

The list goes on in similar fashion. Rose argues importantly, however, that these points of comparison do not indicate that Petronius is mocking Nero through Trimalchio. More likely, part of the characterization of Trimalchio is that he is trying pathetically to imitate the emperor, which probably amused Nero.

Eumolpus has also been read as a portrait of the emperor. A song on the Fall of Troy is supposedly what Nero performed during the great fire of 64 (Suetonius *Nero* 38.2), and a poem on hair that Eumolpus delivers after Giton and Encolpius have shaved their heads (109) may recall a poem that Nero was said to have composed about his wife, Poppaea's, locks (Pliny *Natural History* 37.50). Since Eumolpus is a self-described poet who is quite deceived about the quality of his work, he is potentially more satiric in his gestures to Nero. In his roles as tutor and philosopher, however, Eumolpus works better as a comic imitation of Seneca. It is probably best to consider any satiric references to real historical figures as indirect and not sustained, but instead lurking in multiple characters. In terms of satirizing Nero, it is worth returning to Conte's description of our narrator as mythomaniacal, obsessed with high literature and the interpretation of his own experiences through mythic figures and stories. Nero was the most mythomaniacal person of the day, a self-styled musician and actor who performed tragedies, as well as sang and composed epics. Encolpius, the real tyrant of our text as its first person narrator, may be the funniest, and most subversive, indirect allusion to the emperor.

The ways in which the *Satyrica* may reflect the age of its creation most compellingly, however, are in what it is overall, and what it is not. Given what happened to so many authors in Nero's court, for example, it is worth considering a suggestion by B. E. Perry (1967) that Petronius' very unusual choice of form, genre, and tone may have been driven by a desire to avoid competing literarily with Nero. There is also the vast distance between the world of the characters and that of their author and intended audience. No explicit mention is made of Nero by name, and as far as we can tell the surviving text contains not a single freeborn Roman male, let alone an aristocratic one. Only female characters even have Latin names. The expected readers are not encouraged to identify with anyone. Is this degree of alienation in the text a product of life under a capricious emperor? In her influential book *Actors in the Audience,* Shadi Bartsch argues that this context also helps explain the theatricality of the work. Romans performed loyalty or admiration for Nero constantly; artifice and doublespeak were a matter of life and death for the political elite. It is intriguing to consider whether the heavy theatricality of the age and the *Satyrica*, as well as the gulf between the narrator and author, is related to the false public face required of everyone within such a system.

SOCIAL AND CULTURAL CONTEXTS

Discussions of baths, wall painting, dining rooms, tombs, the *atrium* house, and the *porticus* are provided later in this book; the following pages provide other cultural information and some Latin vocabulary that should prove useful as you begin the novel. Although it is important for you to have some knowledge of the Roman cultural habits and attitudes you will encounter in the *Satyrica*, it should be emphasized from the start that whenever we consider closely what Petronius is doing with these mores, we return to the densely literary and perhaps moralizing nature of this fascinating work. The *Satyrica* is not a historical or journalistic account that provides evidence about classes of people we tend not to meet in other elite literature. As Costas Panayotakis remarks, "modern readers of the *Satyrica* should not be deceived by the atmosphere of verisimilitude with which Petronius builds up the literary artifice of the episode at Trimalchio's house" (2009, 51), or any other episode, for that matter. Still, Petronius' characters inhabit a version of the Roman social and cultural world, and it will be useful for you to know some of its features.

The Roman banquet is an excellent case in point. Trimalchio's gathering could never be used as a guide to Italian dinner parties of the first century CE; however, in order to perceive how Petronius uses the setting of the banquet to display Trimalchio's social aspirations and failures, you need to know something about them. In ancient Italy, dining out at a restaurant was a phenomenon of the lower classes, since people sufficiently wealthy to own a dwelling equipped with a kitchen and slaves would have found it unseemly to purchase and consume foods elsewhere. Towns such as Pompeii provide ample evidence of taverns and hot food stands, but those were for working people, and the sources written by the elite of Rome associate such places with ill health and immorality. Well-to-do homeowners were still sociable, however, and they expressed this by banqueting in each other's homes. (Incidentally, the same holds true in traveling as in dining—while away from home, "respectable" people stayed at the houses of relatives, friends, or friends of friends; only lower-class or disreputable people without social contacts stayed at inns.)

Based on the architectural accommodation for it, the banquet (*convivium*) was a prominent part of ancient Italian life. Rooms for dining (*triclinia*) were often among the most elaborately decorated in a home, including use of fine and engaging frescoes, mosaics, and furniture. Although the Romans sat at a table with chairs or even stood for most meals, at a *convivium* they reclined: lying down on a couch (*lectus*) on their left side, they supported their upper body on cushions and the left elbow. They then ate and drank using only the right hand, and of course with the assistance of many slaves. Customarily about three banqueters reclined together on a *lectus*, with their heads all leaning into the center of the room. Up to three couches were arranged in a U shape so that as many as a dozen persons in total could banquet together in a room. The fourth side was left open for entertainers and for servers, who positioned small portable tables, or *mensae*, in front of the couches with dishes to be shared. Assigned positions on the couches delimited social hierarchy; the host quite literally controlled the pecking order. Guests (*convivae*) might include social superiors (who would be given the best seats), peers, and inferiors, on down to the host's former slaves. Contrary to the male-only *symposia* of the Greek world, men and women respectably dined together in Roman culture both as hosts and as guests in other houses. As Matthew Roller (2006) has explored, however, tensions surrounded the issue of whether it was appropriate for women to recline, and we have images of women seated in chairs next to dining couches.

Banquets tended to follow a sequence of events. Guests would be welcomed by slaves, remove their sandals, and rinse their feet before reclining. Then water would be poured over their hands. Three courses were considered a minimum: the *gustatio* or appetizer (eggs, beans, fresh or pickled vegetables, birds, or dormice), the *prima mensa* or main course (pork, goose, duck, rabbit, or sausage, with bread), and the *secunda mensa* or dessert (fruit, nuts, cheese, or pastries, in honey). After the *prima mensa*, an offering of meat, cake, and wine was usually made to the household gods, the *lares*. Foods were eaten with the fingers or with spoons, and guests usually brought their own napkins (*mappae*) to keep their faces clean and to take home gifts and leftovers. Shells, seeds, and anything else that could not be eaten were dropped to the floor and swept away by a slave.

Wine accompanied the meal. Since they had a very high alcohol content, ancient wines were served mixed with water—which also effectively cleaned the water. Drinking might follow dinner as well, but the goal was conviviality rather than drunkenness, which was considered vulgar. Conversation was highly prized. Our elite Roman sources valued guests who displayed wit and learning and who might deliver impromptu songs, poems, or brief treatises on history or philosophy. Entertainment might also be provided professionally, especially by musicians or poets, sometimes by dancers, although this bordered on the inappropriate, or even acrobats. As you may have now surmised, the ritual of the banquet often lasted for several hours. For a wealthy man, the banquet might take up the last third of a typical day. He conducted business in the morning, followed by a light noon meal. A visit to the baths took up some of the afternoon. Then it was time for the main meal of the day, or *cena*, known in its formal forms as a *convivium*.

Given the importance of the banquet in ancient Italian life, it should come as no surprise that social issues and tensions might be expressed through it. Banquets were a prime occasion for the display of wealth, learning, and refinement, and we read of enormous sums having been paid for tableware, delicacies, experienced chefs, and beautiful serving boys. Similarly, food and banquets occupy a prominent place in the long tradition of Roman moralizing. Some elite authors looked back with nostalgia on the simpler tables of early Rome and associated reclining at lavish *convivia* with foreign influence, effeminacy, illness, and immorality. Part of the conversation concerned the corrupting influence of wealth, unsustainable consumption, and competition that did not improve the health of the state. These become entangled with masculinity because a lack of control over one's appetites was often equated in Roman writings; that is, an unquenchable lust for food might be symptomatic of one for drink or sex or power. Food is thus a good symbol to follow in the novel for both its literary and moralizing overtones; for a rich study of this and other body metaphors in the *Satyrica*, see Victoria Rimell's *Petronius and the Anatomy of Fiction* (2002). If good company and a simple meal were the paragons of virtue, then Trimalchio is a debauched mess. Many scholars have argued that excess leads to death in the *Satyrica*, not

just in Trimalchio's *triclinium*, for example, but also in the will requiring cannibalism of Croton's legacy hunters, and in Encolpius' visit to the primitive hut of
Oenothea. Martha Malamud (2009, 283–89) insightfully reads this last scene as
a parody of one of Horace's *Satires* in which morality is found in a rustic hut
and diet. After a simple meal, the lusty old priestess treats Encolpius' impotence
by anointing and stuffing him for an ambiguously sexual or culinary feast.

Slaves are another ubiquitous aspect of the Roman world. Slave-owning
Romans considered their slaves to be part of their *familia*. A legal family unit was
defined as the eldest free male (*paterfamilias*) and those subject to his authority,
including his free and legitimate children, his slaves, and potentially his wife.
Within a large urban household, slaves had specialized jobs organized into a
social hierarchy. Work performed for the free members of the family would have
included food storage, preparation, and service; textile production and cleaning;
house maintenance and childcare. Depending upon the house, services might
also entail such things as work for the family shop or business, secretarial and
accounting tasks, management, or work as an artisan, valet or dresser, messenger,
entertainer, tutor, or guard. Legally, slaves were considered a particular type of
property, and they were not allowed to own capital of their own. Even so, many
owners allowed their slaves to keep a small private fund (*peculium*), from which
some slaves eventually bought their freedom. Slaves had even less control over
their human offspring than the products of their labor. The children of a slave
woman had the same status as their mother; they were the property of her owner,
liable to be exposed at birth or sold, lent, given, or willed out of the household
at his or her whim. Although slaves sometimes took spouses informally (*contu-
bernales*), these bonds created no legal ties between the couple or between slave
fathers and children. In fact, all the slave's familial relationships outside of that
to the owner went formally unacknowledged in the broader community.

Which is not to say that what we would call the nuclear family was not
important—in fact, Romans considered the family the most important social
structure for free people. For example, many of the topics for impromptu speaking
in oratorical training center on relationships between parents and children. As
the first Roman emperor, Augustus took special pride in his title *Pater Patriae*,
"Father of the Fatherland." There are few, if any, such relationships presented in
the world of the *Satyrica*. The only family we see together is that of Philomela and
her two children in Croton; she is prostituting them in hopes of a legacy from
Eumolpus' will. As far as we know, most if not all of the key adult characters are
childless—Trimalchio, Habinnas, Lichas, Tryphaena, Eumolpus. Who and where
are Encolpius' parents? Within the dominant Roman ideology, these people are
adrift because they have no family to provide a tie to society. This is another way
in which Trimalchio is only faking it, and faking it badly—his *familia* includes

only slaves. Is it significant to note in this context that Nero had his mother executed, and that he failed to produce an heir?

To return to the line between slave and free, what the jurist Gaius referred to as the "primary distinction in the law of persons" (*Institutes* 1.9–11) was enacted not just in terms of law and labor, but also in the realms of religion, sexuality, and discipline, among others. As discussed earlier, many homes contained shrines to household divinities, usually including deities of place, such as the *lares*, as well as the divine twin of the *pater* (father) or *dominus* (master), referred to as his *genius*. At meals and holidays, guests, members of the free family, their slaves, and freedpersons made offerings at these shrines, called *lararia*. Thus every day slaves and others enacted their dependency upon the master of the house by expressing adoration of his *genius*. Members of a household also might swear oaths by his *genius*. A *paterfamilias'* unfree dependents were carefully distinguished from the free in at least two further spheres: discipline and sex. We might generalize this by saying that slaves lacked bodily integrity. Roman authors considered physical abuse in the form of beatings or whippings appropriate for slaves but not for freeborn children. We have already discussed the variety of ways in which Romans administered capital punishment, scaled from most to least degrading and painful depending upon social status; the worst was reserved for slaves and low-class foreigners, including crucifixion and burning alive. In the same way that a slave's body was treated as penetrable by stick or lash, it was considered open to the master for sexual use as well. We hear about slave boys being kept in part as sexual pets (*deliciae*), and the law would not allow a woman dressed as a slave to be considered a rape victim. In contrast, a freeborn male citizen was able to sue someone for outrage if that person treated him like a slave in some way, including striking or flogging him, invading his home, preventing him from enjoying public amenities such as baths and theaters, dishonoring his wife, children, or slaves, or sexually penetrating his person. Freeborn citizen children wore a protective amulet, called a *bulla*, which among other things helped visibly mark them as sexually off-limits, unlike slave children.

The sexual use of male and female slaves by their masters leads us to sexual categories in Roman society, another critical cultural issue that you should consider in your reading. The Romans who left our surviving literature understood sexuality in ways that do not involve our contemporary notions of heterosexual and homosexual, or attraction to the same or opposite sex. In the dominant ideology, sexual activity was considered someone doing something to someone else, and the operative categories that arose from this were active and passive, penetrator and penetrated, or "doer" and "doee." In other words, men were considered sexually "normal" whether they penetrated women or boys or both. Any preferences a man expressed among sexual objects were considered just that—personal preferences, rather like preferring sex at night or midday, and these would not have affected his identity or status in the community. To be penetrated, or to prefer to be penetrated, however, put a man into a different, and socially suspect, category, one that assimilated him to women, who, for the most part, the Romans considered biologically trapped in the "doee" category. This distinction was hierarchical and obviously intersected with other statuses, including gender and age. "Doers" tended to be adult freeborn citizen men; "doees" were women, but also slaves, children, and noncitizens. To "be done" in any way carried some degree of shame, as it tended to effeminize or infantilize the individual. As Ellen Oliensis writes, "Penetration is the prerogative of free men, penetrability the characteristic condition of slaves and women; sexual intercourse is an enactment and reflection of social hierarchy, and conversely, social subordination always implies the possibility of sexual submission" (1997, 154). Within this rubric, men who liked to be done by other men (*cinaedi*) and women were stereotyped as sex-crazed and unable to control their desires, which indeed describes almost every female character in the surviving portion of the *Satyrica*, as well as most of the men.

The Roman habit of referring to even an adult male slave as a *puer,* or boy, reinforced on many levels a male slave's lack of manhood, bodily integrity, and independent standing in the community. As you can imagine, the transition out of slavery into freedom was thus complex, and the status of Trimalchio as a freedman is crucial to understanding Petronius' portrait of him. Among slaves with specialized and marketable skills, manumission was not uncommon; slaves either saved the money needed to purchase themselves or were freed by their owner in a will or for various reasons during the owner's lifetime. Moreover, within the Roman legal system, someone freed by a citizen became a citizen. (Which is how, ironically, Trimalchio may be one of the only Roman citizens in the whole novel.) Freedmen were thereby able to marry and produce legitimate children, own property, make contracts and wills, vote, and take legal action. Two factors continued to shape the lives of a *libertus* (freedman) or *liberta* (freedwoman) throughout their lives, however: stigmas attached to having been a slave, and continuing obligations to one's former owner. Patrons retained a claim on their former slave's labor, estate, public obedience, and sexual services. As Seneca the Elder wrote, *impudicitia in ingenuo crimen est, in servo necessitas, in libero officium,* "inchastity in the freeborn is a crime, in a slave a necessity, in the freedman a duty" (*Controversiae* 4.praef.10). Even though Trimalchio's patron is deceased, aspersions are easily cast. Since Roman authors thought that women and *cinaedi* very much enjoyed "being done," ex-slaves were easy targets for the accusation of failing to achieve full masculinity. Look closely at Petronius' presentation of Trimalchio along these lines.

Social stigmas and formal restrictions on the activities of freedmen seem to relate to their former, and in some respects continuing, lack of bodily integrity. Ex-slaves were forbidden from joining the Roman military and holding most political and religious offices, except for two priesthoods created by Augustus. The *Augustales* formed an important part of the civic community, and they are mentioned often by the freed guests at Trimalchio's house. A freedman's name eloquently encapsulated his social standing. Whereas the full nomenclature of a freeborn citizen man would include his personal name (*praenomen*), his family name (*nomen*), his father's personal name, and any names indicating a sub-branch of the family or special honors (*cognomina*), a freedman's name consisted of his former owner's name, his status as freedman of that patron, and his old slave name appended at the end. Despite his ability to have a legally recognized wife and children, the freedman's name emphasized his lack of free parentage and privileged instead his relationship to the family he had belonged to as a slave. A child born to someone who had been freed, on the other hand, began life free-born, and tombs often celebrate the accomplishment of the family in reaching this status in the next generation.

Perhaps due to the realistic quality of the *Satyrica*'s portraits of freedmen, some scholars have tried to use the text for evidence of what it was like to be a freedman in early imperial Italy. (For a good overview of this work, see Jean Andreau's "Freedmen in the *Satyrica*" [2009].) In her 2006 monograph *The Freed-man in Roman Art and Art History*, Lauren Hackworth Petersen feels compelled to start with a discussion of Petronius' Trimalchio. It is certainly worth asking whether there was a freed subculture for which we simply have little or no evidence. There are issues of concern to Trimalchio and his guests that differ from the attitudes we perceive in other literature. A good example is work—Trimalchio and his guests often boast about having risen from nothing through their labor. Interestingly, in her study *Work, Identity and Legal Status at Rome* (1992), Sandra Joshel found that about 78 percent of the funerary inscriptions in Rome that mention the profession of the deceased commemorate slaves or ex-slaves. It seems that one's occupation was of particular importance to this group of people, and thus it is good characterization for Petronius to have freedmen at the party take pride in their work. Of course, Petronius puts it in there to mock them, since elite Romans frowned upon trade and manual labor as slavish and undignified. Similarly, landownership was positively valued by the dominant group, while maritime trade was considered risky, inappropriate, and *nouveaux*. When Trimalchio boasts of his success in shipping, what are we to make of that? Finally, the notion of education we hear from most of our sources, written by the elite, is also at odds with the ideas of Trimalchio's guests. The freedmen at the party value education, but what they mean by that is learning a trade and earning one's freedom or a living. Elite education focused on public speaking and works of high literature. To refer to myth and poetry was almost a type of code that denoted membership in the elite club. Trimalchio aspires to this learning and the social status it implies, but unwittingly reveals his ignorance at every turn.

The fact that Encolpius can speak the code, however, seriously complicates our understanding of his status, which brings us to another cultural feature worthy of our consideration—ethnicity, or, more particularly, being Greek. For the Romans, the Greek language denoted both literary masterpieces such as Homer's epics and the native tongue of slaves, making it difficult to interpret what Greek symbolizes in a literary work. Roman authors suffer from a type of inferiority/superiority complex when it comes to Greek culture, a complex they frequently resolve using a historical narrative: "The Greeks were great and had their day, then they declined into weakness, effeminacy, and immorality, so we manly and virtuous Romans easily conquered them." Vergil's *Aeneid* was so popular in part because it gave the Romans their own Homeric epic while repeating this narrative of the rise, decline, and fall of Greece; at the same time, the immense cultural influence of Greece is expressed in the very need to have a Roman Homer. For many years, military conquest was a primary source of slaves, so Greek was at the same time a slavish tongue, reinforcing the sense of Roman superiority. Some elite authors worried, however, that Greek influence brought the ills that destroyed Greece upon the Romans themselves; as Horace so famously phrased it, *Graecia capta ferum victorem cepit*, "captive Greece captured her fierce victor" (*Epistles* 1.1.156).

In the *Satyrica*, most of the characters have Greek names, but what does this mean? Partly it reflects a comic interaction with a number of Greek literary works. Agamemnon and Menelaus are the brother kings who led the Greek forces at Troy, and it is amusing to have them as leaders of a questionable school of rhetoric. Amy Richlin expands on this reading of the names as literary: "the characters' peculiar names in fact are pen-names, as it were, tying them to genre fiction: the characters in Greek romances have Greek names, as do many characters in Roman comedy and some figures in Roman satire; hence, so do the characters in the *Satyrica*" (2009, 96). But the names also reflect ancient Italian practice, in that slaves were often given names from myth and epic, rather like naming a dog Ajax or Perseus. Almost all of the names in the *Satyrica*, although they are also clearly indicative of character, are names used for real people in the Roman Empire, even if some only rarely. Yet another cultural layer to the names is that the dissolute behavior of the episodes is thus characterized as Greek, as is perhaps the homoerotic central storyline. In his study of the Greek subliterary genre of Milesian Tales, Stephen Harrison describes how Greek writers themselves placed collections of pornographic stories in infamous cities such as Miletus, Sybaris, and Rhodes, creating a tradition of "malicious erotic ethnography"

(1998, 63); here the technique and tradition may be used by our Roman author to displace this decadent behavior from himself and his audience, providing a safer satirical target. The chosen locales, however, are interesting. Eumolpus' pornographic short stories, likely examples of Milesian Tales, are set very close to Miletus in Asia Minor (in Pergamum and Ephesus)—as Harrison observes, "a geographical indication symbolises literary origin" (69). Petronius' main story, on the other hand, travels through Greek places much closer to home in Italy. Is this pointed?

Let us explore some implications of these cultural attitudes and habits by looking again at the narrator character, "Crotch." He just cannot be put safely into—or refuses to stay in—any of the cultural categories that Roman authors seem to consider important. He plays at being a slave, but looks down on the wealthy freedmen at the dinner party for their lack of class and education; he sexually uses Giton and some women, but is used by others; he lacks a family except for potentially Giton, although Giton should be a pet, a *deliciae*, not someone around whom a respectable person builds his life. Encolpius exhibits ambivalence in his legal, civic, sexual, educational, and ethnic status; in an ancient Roman context, his malleability as a character compounds his unreliability as a narrator. And it makes him funny.

Similarly, the *Satyrica* certainly puts love between men at center stage, but whether the implications of this are literary, comedic, moral, ethnic, countercultural, or conservative is difficult to determine. Encolpius acts like the stock "cuckolded husband" character of stage comedy and mime, and his epic romance should end in marriage. But marriage in our other Roman sources is treated as a means to the end of legitimate children, a boring economic and civic duty largely void of the expectation of affection, let alone love or romance. For elite men, proper objects of romantic and sexual expression were mistresses and boy lovers. Does the novel feature a male couple to mock a heteronormative world? To turn the world comically on its head? To characterize Encolpius as marginal, as outside or ignorant of normal social values? To mock genres that romanticize marriage? To show how ridiculous those Greeks are?

We can also bring in potential political implications. Scholars and filmmakers have drawn attention to the similarity between this homoerotic romance and anecdotes that the later biographer Suetonius reports about Nero. It is worth quoting the episodes in full, because they reveal themes from across this account of Roman culture—banquets, moralizing, and the intersections of legal, sexual, and gender categories (*Life of Nero* 27–29, Loeb translation):

Whenever [Nero] drifted down the Tiber to Ostia, or sailed about the Gulf of Baiae, booths were set up at intervals along the banks and shores, fitted out for debauchery, while bartering matrons played the part of innkeepers and from every hand solicited him to come ashore. He also levied dinners on his friends, one of whom spent four million sesterces for a banquet at which turbans were distributed, and another a considerably larger sum for a rose dinner.

Besides abusing freeborn boys and seducing married women, he debauched the vestal virgin Rubria. The freedwoman Acte he all but made his lawful wife, after bribing some ex-consuls to perjure themselves by swearing that she was of royal birth. He castrated the boy Sporus and actually tried to make a woman of him; and he married him with all the usual ceremonies, including a dowry and a bridal veil, took him to his house attended by a great throng, and treated him as his wife. And the witty jest that someone made is still current, that it would have been well for the world if Nero's father Domitius had had that kind of wife. This Sporus, decked out with the finery of the empresses and riding in a litter, he took with him to the assizes and marts of Greece, and later at Rome through the Street of the Images, fondly kissing him from time to time. . . .

He so prostituted his own chastity that after defiling almost every part of his body, he at last devised a kind of game, in which, covered with the skin of some wild animal, he was let loose from a cage and attacked the private parts of men and women, who were bound to stakes, and when he had sated his mad lust, was dispatched by his freedman Doryphorus; for he was even married to this man in the same way that he himself had married Sporus, going so far as to imitate the cries and lamentations of a maiden being deflowered.

The episode resembles not just the relationship between Encolpius and Giton, but also Trimalchio and his *deliciae* Croesus, who gets to ride his master like a pet pony. Because of all the problems associated with the sources on Nero, it is not possible to have historical faith in the accounts of Sporus and Doryphorus. But even if we could work out the historical relationship between the stories, we probably are not looking at scenes that target or mimic each other directly. Rather, these episodes are similar because this was a good way to insult a Roman man. In these stories, Trimalchio, Encolpius, and Nero hopelessly jumble critical social categories—free and slave, male and female, doer and doee. By giving too much or inappropriate attention to their boy toys, they reveal themselves to be controlled by their lust, and thus effeminate, and they confuse the social obligation of marriage with sexual dalliances. The pattern does not reveal a parody, but rather a trope that might be employed to mock a freedman or an unreliable narrator or a dead emperor.

In terms of the *Satyrica* particularly, given dominant Roman notions of sexuality, in setting two males within what is usually a marriage-destined plot, the novel seemingly presents a confusion of recreational sex and marriage that is part of a larger picture of social disorder and decay, a decay that its participants—such as our unreliable narrator, Encolpius—cannot perceive, and that we thus never hear of directly. The question is whether we think Petronius challenges social norms or strongly and conservatively reinforces them. Or does he just invert them for comic effect? As the prominent Petronian scholar John Sullivan asks in a broader context, "is Petronius an artist or a moralist?" (1985, 1670). All we can probably say with confidence is that the author is elusive.

LANGUAGE

Another feature of early imperial culture that we should explore is the issue of how this text was experienced by its contemporaries, that is, whether it was primarily read or heard. The theatrical elements, the influence of the patterned speech of rhetoric, and the first person narration have led many scholars to argue that the text was well designed to be performed. We have discussed at length the problems with the sources on Nero, but in detailing how authors got into trouble with him, our sources reveal the variety of ways in which literary works were shared. For example, one man was banished for his *codicilli* against the priesthood and senate—these are written texts that somehow circulated (Tacitus *Annals* 14.50); but another was punished similarly for the "infamous *carmina* (songs) against the emperor" that he performed at a dinner party at a private home (14.48–49). Persius mocks literary recitals in his first satire; Nero sponsored public, semipublic, and competitive exhibitions of dramatic and literary works (Pliny *Natural History* 14.51, Dio 62.19). Tacitus states that at the palace, Nero hosted a sort of literary circle for young writers, who recited works in progress for criticism and revision after dinner (*Annals* 14.16). You would do well to consider this as you read—and you are encouraged not just to read the *Satyrica*, but to *listen* to it as well.

This leads us to the important consideration of Petronius' Latin. Although his subject matter has in many periods been considered obscene, his Latin style has been admired consistently since the fifteenth century. In keeping with the rich array of literary allusions and parodies, he does not maintain a consistent tone or style, but within a given speech or scene, Petronius' careful use of language helps create the allusion or mimicry. Hubert Petersmann (1999) analyzes such differences among passages that he characterizes as rhetorical, poetically colored, and colloquial, the last ranging from sophisticated to vulgar. Encolpius' narrative is usually lucid and flowing. He frequently uses particles near the beginnings of sentences to connect one idea or event with the next, and he employs rhetorical devices such as anaphora (repeated words or phrases), asyndeton (lists of items not joined by conjunctions), and alliteration. Konrad Müller has analyzed the prose rhythms of Petronius and shown that his sentences repeat distinctive patterns strategically (1983, 449–70).

Many have observed, however, that Encolpius' clear but elegant, rhythmic prose contrasts sharply with the speech patterns of the freedmen characters in the *Cena*. But the debate over this among scholars—as well as over what it means—is still fierce. Some of the features of these speeches are to be found in other sources for everyday speech. For example, in Cicero's letters or in Plautus' plays, we also find ellipsis (omission of words implied by a previous clause), proverbs, diminutives, and the use of the present tense in place of the future. But other patterns may go beyond colloquialism to a characterization of lower-class speech, or even nonnative speech. For example, the sound *"au"* is sometimes changed to *"o,"* as in *copones* (39.12) for *caupones* (98.1). This is a phenomenon of popular, even rustic, speech—we might compare the patrician politician Claudius, who changed his name to the more popular Clodius in the first century BCE. Some of the word endings used suggest common speech, such as the noun ending -*o* (*Cerdo, Felicio, Lucrio* at 60.8 or *cicaro* at 46.3 and 71.11) and the adjective ending -*osus* (*dignitosus* at 57.10 or *linguosus* at 43.4 and 63.1). Many more of these have been catalogued by scholars, particularly by Bret Boyce in his 1991 study *The Language of the Freedmen in Petronius'* Cena Trimalchionis.

Grammatical gender, however, better illustrates our difficulty in interpreting what all of this means. The neuter faded out in later Latin and is therefore not found in the Romance languages that spring from it. It is thus reasonable to interpret the use of masculine or feminine for the neuter in the *Cena* as an early sign of a colloquialism that would become more pronounced over time. And we get several instances of masculine for neuter (such as *caelus* for *caelum* at 39.4, 39.6, and 45.3, or *fatus* for *fatum* at 42.5, 71.1, and 77.3) or feminine for neuter. Surprisingly, however, we also find the reverse—neuter for masculine and feminine. And, although there are other sections with dialogue, almost all such gender changes in the *Satyrica* (approximately thirty) occur in the speeches of the freedmen at the *Cena*. Thus, another reasonable interpretation is that the freedmen are not just speaking colloquial Latin, but speaking Latin badly. A similar issue arises with the deponent. In later Latin the deponent gradually disappeared, but in the *Cena* we find the active sometimes used for the deponent and vice versa. Is this a sign that the deponent faded first in colloquial speech? Or do the native Greek (or Aramaic or whatever) speakers at Trimalchio's party make mistakes with active and passive? It is but one speaker who uses the demonstrative *ille* when he should use a reflexive pronoun, and he makes the error twice (38.4 and 38.16); another uses the indicative in an indirect question where we would expect the subjunctive (44.1). As someone new to the study of Latin, do you think these are types of errors you might make? On the other hand, Andrew Laird makes the important point that the editors who created our text of the *Satyrica* were influenced by this perception that the freedmen speak differently from Encolpius, and so-called "vulgarisms" in the rest of the text have often been eliminated as scribal errors (1999, 249–55). Even in the text so created, Encolpius lapses into colloquial or even vulgar style in some scenes. What does this mean? In the Commentary, forms and words that might be used to engage this controversy have been marked; see what you make of them.

The heavy use of Greek is another noteworthy feature of the *Satyrica*, again open to varied interpretation. We have already discussed the prominence of Greek names, but Greek loan words are also pervasive. One scholar of Petronius' vocabulary, Donald Swanson, estimated that almost 10 percent of the *Satyrica's* lexicon is Greek (1963, xxvi–xxvii, 224–27). The more uncommon Graecisms, however, cluster in the speeches of the freedmen, and the speech of Hermeros, Encolpius' neighbor on the dining couch, is littered with them. For a member of the educated elite, quoting a famous line in Greek or using Greek vocabulary might be like an upper-crust modern Brit elegantly sliding into French. But among ancient Italian freedmen, the use of Greek would more likely have given away a slave background and the fact that they learned Latin as a second language. In the plays of Plautus, Greek words are used most frequently by slaves and lower-class characters. Greek in the Latin speech of ex-slaves in ancient Italy might have the sociocultural resonance of Spanglish in the United States of the twenty-first century. Greek loan words used in the Latin passages you are reading are thus also marked in the Commentary.

LITERARY ENGAGEMENTS

By now you are probably beginning to appreciate that the *Satyrica* is a bit of a puzzle. We do not have most of the story, and scholars tend to disagree about how to interpret what we do have. Along these lines, having more detail about the literary quality of the text will make it easier for you to work on more of these scholarly puzzles. The *Satyrica* engages with a variety of genres that people were writing and reading in this period. A genre is a category, a type of literature whose content, form, and features are broadly recognized and expected. For example, audiences in the modern United States know what they will encounter if they begin a romance novel or a biography, a newspaper article or a comic book. Audiences of Hollywood films can easily distinguish a western from a romantic comedy, a courtroom drama from a horror flick. Although an individual book or film might mix up these genres, the point of such a work would be to play with what the reader or audience expects. The basic goal of this section is to lay out the genres of literature in Petronius' world and how the *Satyrica* may relate to them. You may have noticed, however, the frequent use of vague words, such as "engage" and "relate." That is because allusions to specific works of literature or literary genres may have a variety of effects, and this is something else that scholars disagree about in regard to the *Satyrica*. As you read, consider how these allusions work. Is the goal to parody a genre or a work? Alternatively, the *Satyrica* might demonstrate respect for a piece of literature itself, but allude to it in order to mock a character who does not understand it or who misquotes or overuses it. Or, rather than mocking a character, Petronius might be mocking another author who has tried to imitate the work in question. Just because you spot a literary allusion does not mean that you have figured out why it is there and what effect it is designed to achieve.

Epic

Long, majestic poems describing the glorious deeds of heroes and gods are referred to as epics. As early as the first millennium BCE, bards in Greece were singing such songs about the cycle of events surrounding the Trojan War. The most famous and influential of these are Homer's *Iliad* and *Odyssey*. The *Iliad* takes place in the ninth year of the war and focuses on the Greek warrior Achilles. Agamemnon, the commander of the Greek forces, insults Achilles by taking back his war prize, a slave girl. Achilles withdraws from battle and prays to his goddess mother for the Greeks to regret Agamemnon's actions. Book after poetic book describes battles, attempted negotiations, and the deaths of heroes until Achilles retakes the field in vengeance for a slain comrade. This epic ends after Achilles returns the body of a fallen Trojan prince for burial and hosts funeral games for his beloved Patrocles.

Although there are moments of allusion to the *Iliad* in Encolpius' rich imaginative life, such as when he withdraws from the playing field after Ascyltos makes off with Giton, on the whole you will find more frequent references to Homer's other epic, the *Odyssey*. The *Odyssey* describes the Greek warrior Odysseus' voyage home from the Trojan War. The beginning and end of the epic recount the misbehavior and punishment of a group of suitors in his homeland who are pursuing his loyal wife, Penelope, and harassing his son, Telemachus, while the central portion of the poem details Odysseus' ten years of struggle to reach home. Cursed by the god Poseidon, the warrior survives adventures and trials, including shipwrecks, an encounter with the monstrous Cyclops, the enchantments of the goddess Circe, and a visit to the underworld. In the last books of the poem, Odysseus arrives home disguised as a beggar, tests the loyalty of his family, punishes the suitors, and reestablishes himself as king.

We can see the interaction of the *Satyrica* with the *Odyssey* in the narrative structure, which is episodic due to the travel of the main character, and which may be driven by the vengefulness of an angry god, albeit Priapus in lieu of Poseidon. The Romans thought that Odysseus' adventures had taken place in south Italy, the location of the surviving part of Encolpius' journeys. The *Satyrica's* protagonist is also shipwrecked and threatened with emasculation by a temptress named Circe. Although we are missing some of Encolpius' story, the contrast between his base poverty and his high education may result from an abrupt reversal of fortune, just as Odysseus plays a beggar when he first arrives home. Since Odysseus himself also narrates the most fantastical of his adventures to the Phaeacians in the middle of the *Odyssey*, he may even be a model as a narrator, and an unreliable one at that. As recently as 2009, John Morgan concluded "that the novel was conceived as a comic rewriting of the *Odyssey* on an epic scale" (34).

The Greeks were not the only ones to write epics, however, and the most important literary engagement of the *Satyrica* with epic may be with Vergil's *Aeneid*. Vergil's massive poem elaborates an old Italian tale in which Aeneas, a Trojan character from the *Iliad*, survived the fall of Troy, traveled around the Mediterranean to Italy, and defeated some hostile locals before founding a new community. We have already discussed how this story gave the Romans a role in the heroic past, as well as a reason to conquer Greeks—after all, they had sacked Troy. In combining episodes of adventure at sea and a war story, Vergil was folding together the *Iliad* and the *Odyssey*, setting himself up as a Roman Homer.

Written during the early years of Augustus' rule, the *Aeneid* was immensely and immediately popular. In part this reflects the hope it offered for a people who had recently survived yet another bitter civil war. Since it was set in the distant past, the epic vicariously allowed readers from either side of the recent war to experience fierce battles and struggles, emerge victorious, and imagine a prosperous future in which Rome again would thrive. The *Aeneid* also was and is recognized as a major poetic achievement, so much so that poets in subsequent generations dwelt in its shadows. Ovid's *Metamorphoses* is one type of poetic response—epic in meter and length, it knits together hundreds of separate myths and legends, told by dozens of narrative voices, to create a history of the universe.

A couple of generations later, Lucan tried to compete in a different way by writing up recent history as epic. He composed a poem about the civil war between Caesar and Pompey, a poem with which Eumolpus interacts in some way when he spouts verses on the same topic.

As you read, consider whether or not you can see the *Satyrica* as a type of comic response to the *Aeneid*. Just like Aeneas, Encolpius traverses some of the same ground as Odysseus. Even the dinner of Trimalchio may be fitted in; based on the obsessive references to death and dying in these scenes, John Bodel (1994) argues that Encolpius' experience of the *Cena* serves as his visit to the underworld. If the *Satyrica* is a comic *Aeneid*, it is in the wrong medium (prose) and has a hero who is the opposite of the ideal man in either Greek epic or Roman culture: Encolpius lacks moral integrity, is sexually used, and is weak, fearful, often unsuccessful in his endeavors, and easily confused by his surroundings. Michael Paschalis contends that "to Petronius' select audience the *Aeneid* was the most familiar Roman literary work and one that carried the greatest weight and authority" (2011, 77). If Augustus' reign produced the *Aeneid*, is this the epic we should expect under Nero?

Drama

Various theatrical modes were popular in early imperial Rome, and we can see the *Satyrica* interacting with them on different levels. Tragedy was highly valued in Nero's court, and Encolpius evokes characters and scenes from this form of high culture in his grandiose self-delusions. Stock scenes and gags from Roman comedy are evident in episodes such as the recognition and recovery of the coin-lined tunic at the market. But particular influence can be felt from two types of street theater popular in the imperial period: mime and farce. Atellan farces, *fabulae Atellanae*, were coarse burlesques in which low-life stock characters parodied episodes from myth or domestic life in a manner very similar to later European *commedie dell'arte*. Named after a town in south-central Italy that the Romans stereotyped as the place where the "crazy, backward" people lived, these verse comedies came to be staged in Roman theaters after tragedies, although later they were replaced by Greek mimes. In mime, men and women, speaking prose and without masks, enacted scenes from everyday life, romance, or myth. Themes include abrupt changes of fortune, the concealment of adulterous lovers, lusty women, witchcraft, the interrupted or ruined party, escape in disguise, theft, and arrest. Spectacular effects were popular, such as fires or the punishment of condemned prisoners or slaves on stage; sex was also graphically presented. Mime was considered indecent and vulgar by many elite authors, although the work of some, such as Ovid, seems to have been adapted for mime.

The *Satyrica* includes a direct reference to mime in the poem with which Encolpius laments Giton's departure with Ascyltos (80.9):

> nomen amicitiae sic, quatenus expedit, haeret;
> > calculus in tabula mobile ducit opus.
> dum fortuna manet, vultum servatis, amici;
> > cum cecidit, turpi vertitis ora fuga.
>
> grex agit in scaena mimum: pater ille vocatur,
> > filius hic, nomen divitis ille tenet.
> mox ubi ridendas inclusit pagina partes,
> > vera redit facies, assimulata perit.

> *The name of friendship sticks so far as it suits;*
> > *The task of a game piece still on the board is changeable.*
> *While fortune is fair, you keep face, friends;*
> > *When it falls, you turn your masks in shameful flight.*
>
> *A troupe acts a mime on the stage: that one is called father,*
> > *This one son, another has the name of a rich man.*
> *As soon as the script has shut upon the ridiculous roles,*
> > *The true face returns, pretense perishes.*

Here Encolpius the narrator compares his life experiences with stage performances, but the moment is more than a little metatheatrical or metaliterary, since scholars tend to agree with Encolpius' assessment. Encolpius and his friends wear disguises and engage in mock duels, trials, and battles. Two scenes even involve a stage prop, as Giton and Encolpius each threaten to commit suicide with a purposefully blunted razor (94). Trimalchio is no better. His banquet is so packed with display and performance that it becomes difficult for Encolpius to distinguish the real food from the props. Trimalchio acts as the leader of a mime troupe, both directing the performance and serving as the lead actor in the banquet show, accompanied all the while by the house band. Mime may be the main source of Trimalchio's spotty knowledge of Greek myth, and the slave at the party who recites verses from Vergil's *Aeneid* mixes in lines from Atellan farce. At this level, comedy is produced by the confusion of high and low culture by the uneducated. At a deeper level, theatricality pervades the world of the *Satyrica*. Conte's notion of mythomania is at its root theatrical—Petronius' characters play at being both famous literary figures and types of real people, like slaves and widowers. Is this learned allusion, or base histrionics? Is Petronius' point that it is getting hard to tell the difference?

Satire

The title *Satyrica* clearly plays on the Latin word *satura*, mélange or mixture, a particularly Roman literary genre in which historical figures, types of people, or society is mocked. The poet Horace (65–68 BCE) was particularly influential. Targets of his two published books of *Satires* include legacy hunting, uppity freedmen, excessive banquets, bad poets and philosophers, and the law courts. His stories are largely presented in a dialogue format, thus frequently use the first person, and include a battle between Priapus the garden god and some witches (1.8) and an uncultured host so unpleasant that the narrator and his friend are forced to escape his wretched dinner party (2.8). Horace also focuses on social types and caricatures, rather than targeting specific historical individuals. The similarities to Petronius' work should be clear.

In terms of form, however, Horace and subsequent Latin satirists such as Martial and Juvenal stayed with verse, whereas Petronius' text, although it plays with poetry, may even be interpreted as hostile to it—after all, "Good Singer" gets stoned. The most well known "prosimetric" genre (mixed prose and verse) is a Roman one called Menippean satire. Varro, a first-century BCE Roman scholar, wrote *Saturae Menippae*, assorted humorous social commentaries, claiming to be imitating a third-century Cynic philosopher named Menippus, about whom almost nothing is known. Only a few fragments of Varro's work survive, but Seneca the Younger revived the form when he wrote his savagely satiric account of the deification of Nero's imperial predecessor Claudius in the *Apocolocyntosis*, "Pumpkinification." Although this prose narrative includes sections of verse that mimic tragedy and funeral laments, it is brief and targeted at a specific individual, in both of which ways it strongly differs from the *Satyrica*. Nevertheless, Petronius' work has often been labeled a Menippean satire.

It is well worth pondering what drove Petronius' preference for prose, since it is an unusual choice in his literary world. But then, given that choice, why do so many of his characters break into song? Catherine Connors (1998) has provided a nuanced analysis of Petronius' poetry and its narrative context, but scholars continue to debate this quality of the work. Is Petronius demonstrating skill with meter even though he prefers prose? Perhaps this mixed form is itself part of a satiric picture of a world gone awry, where the sacred language of epic has devolved into Eumolpus' bombast and Encolpius' pithy poems to his flaccid phallus.

Romance

What if the *Satyrica* is not a comic *Odyssey* or *Aeneid* per se, but instead is mocking other genres that make frequent and heavy allusions to epic? Gian Biagio Conte (1996) has used Encolpius' mythomania to think about other literary genres with which Petronius engages. After all, it is not just the author of the *Satyrica* who has the *Odyssey* in mind; his characters compare themselves explicitly to figures from the *Odyssey*. When Giton hides from Ascyltos under a bed, Encolpius compares him to Odysseus evading the Cyclops beneath a wooly ram. Encolpius compares the way he himself is recognized by his genitalia to the way Odysseus' nurse recognizes him by his scar. As we have seen already, Conte interprets this dense allusion to epic as part of the characterization of Encolpius, but he also takes this notion into his analysis of genre by arguing that this character and his mythomania are an allusion to a lower literary form, the Greek romance, a genre that is itself mythomaniacal in seeing references to epic and tragedy in its own narrative events.

It was proposed long ago that the *Satyrica* might be a Roman version of a Greek romance. The surviving examples of this form of popular literature share a basic plot: a respectable young man and woman are tossed about the Mediterranean in various adventures, beset particularly by erotic temptations and distractions, until finally they are reunited and live happily ever after. Does this sound familiar? Conte also draws attention to another feature of romances—that at moments of high tension, the narrative alludes to heroes of myth and speeches of high literature; as a genre, Greek romance saw itself as a descendant of the great classical genres of epic and tragedy. Conte thus takes up an argument first set out by Robert Heinze in 1899, that the *Satyrica* is so similar to the Greek romance not because it is an example but because it is a parody, and a parody on many levels. Petronius uses the stock plots of romance, but populates it with ridiculous characters, especially Encolpius, who is an anti-model of an ideal romantic hero. Encolpius is totally debauched, with the moral fiber of a twig, a coward who is particularly self-deceived about his relationship to the great mythic and literary models of old. One of Conte's main arguments is thus that the gap between the narrator and the hidden author mocks the literary aspirations of the romance itself because it encourages the educated reader to laugh at the pretensions of this lowly popular genre the same way we laugh at the pretensions of the narrator character.

Naturally, the relationship is not straightforward between this work and the Greek romances, also referred to by modern scholars as novels, a sort of picaresque prose fiction narrative. For one, most have an omniscient third person narrator, unlike the *Satyrica*. In addition, their chronological relationship to the *Satyrica* is not quite right. The surviving texts that scholars usually list as examples of the Greek novel include the potentially contemporary *Ephesiaca* of Xenophon and Chariton's *Chaereas and Callirhoe*, but the others were written much later, including Longus' *Daphnis and Chloe*, Achilles Tatius' *Leucippe and Clitophon*, and Heliodorus' *Ethiopica*. Some evidence suggests that these are well-developed examples, and thus in the Neronian period the romance may have been a recent invention, but many scholars remain unconvinced. Moreover, scholars dispute the cohesiveness of the Greek romances as a genre; such writings were referred to in antiquity only rarely, and by varied terms such as "fictions" and "stories." Since whether or not the Greek stories themselves constitute a genre remains an open question, their relationship to Petronius' *Satyrica* and Apuleius' *Metamorphoses* is vexed. Simon Goldhill insightfully asks: "Are the Roman texts to be treated as a different culture's expression of the same turn to extended prose fiction—a national version of the genre of the novel, as it were? Or are they to be seen as a different type of literature, a satiric and carnivalised refraction of the privileged forms of Roman prose, which turn only a leery eye towards the world of Greek romance?" (2008, 194).

Milesian Tales

Gottskálk Jensson argues that it is not the Greek novels that are the key referent for the *Satyrica*, but instead a class of stories called Milesian Tales, a term we do hear from ancient sources, particularly in the opening of Apuleius' novel. It originates with a lost Greek work, the *Milesiaca* of one Aristides, set in Miletus, a Greek city on the coast of Asia Minor associated with luxury and decadence. The *Milesiaca* was translated into Latin in the first century BCE. Most scholars have understood Milesian Tales to be rather pornographic short stories that conclude with an amusing twist, such as the one Eumolpus tells about the Widow of Ephesus, a city very close to Miletus. Stephen Harrison has argued, however, that the term refers to a collection of such tales put together by a first person narrator in the guise of a traveler, a distant descendant of the narrative of the Greek historian Herodotus, "a parodic version of travel literature as well as an example of malicious erotic ethnography" (1998, 71). Jensson understands Milesian Tales similarly, seeing them as "a travelogue and narrative of erotic intrigues told by an unreliable but entertaining vagabond" in the tradition of Odysseus' narration to the Phaeacians (2004, 83).

Jensson also argues that the *Satyrica* was based on a specific, but now lost, Greek text, as we know was the case with Apuleius' *Metamorphoses*. This seemed unlikely for a long time due to the mixed prose and verse form of the *Satyrica,* which was thought to be unprecedented in Greek literature. Then in 1971 a papyrus was discovered with a fragment of a Greek mixed prose and verse narrative. Referred to as the "Iolaus papyrus" (*P. Oxyrhynchus* 3010) and initially published as a "Greek *Satyricon*" (Parsons 1971), this snippet of a story reveals that it is not impossible for the *Satyrica* to have been based on a comical and raunchy Greek prosimetric narrative.

Oratory

Even if it is based on a Greek story of some form—epic, romance, or tale—the *Satyrica* engages importantly with other forms of elite composition, as well. Andrew Laird argues that "First-person fiction is closer to oratory than any other kind of writing although the connections between the two have yet to be explored in depth" (1999, 213). Oratory was the basis for the Greek and Roman educational system, since public speaking was critical in both law and politics, two major arenas of elite men. In the Roman system, practice speeches, or declamations, were of two kinds. In a *suasoria* the student's task was to persuade a famous figure from history, legend, or myth to take a certain action at a critical turning point in their story—that Agamemnon should sacrifice his daughter Iphigenia so that the winds will blow his fleet to Troy, for example (Seneca the Elder *Suasoriae* 3). This was meant to prepare the student to speak persuasively in a political setting. A *controversia* was a mock debate on a hypothetical legal case and relevant point of law, again utilizing rather fantastical circumstances. For example, here is the opening of Seneca the Elder's *Controversiae* 1.6:

> captus a piratis scripsit patri de redemptione; non redimebatur. archipiratae filia iurare eum coegit ut duceret se uxorem si dimissus esset; iuravit. relicto patre secuta est adulescentem. redit ad patrem, duxit illam. orba incidit. pater imperat ut archipiratae filiam dimittat et orbam ducat. nolentem abdicat.

> *A man captured by pirates wrote to his father about a ransom; he was not ransomed. The daughter of the pirate captain compelled him to swear that he would marry her if she let him go; he swore. Having abandoned her father, she followed the young man. He returned to his father and married her. An orphaned woman appears. The father orders his son to divorce the pirate captain's daughter and wed the orphan. When the son refuses, the father disinherits him.*

In the dialogue presentation of this *controversia*, Seneca has a cast of rhetoricians speak on behalf of the father and then the son, followed by some debate and analysis, all laced with precedents from literature and history.

Some of the *Satyrica's* engagement with oratory is overt. Encolpius and Ascyltos attend Trimalchio's dinner as students of Agamemnon, a teacher of rhetoric. Trimalchio asks him about the *controversia* he performed earlier that day, and he begins to set it out in traditional fashion: *pauper et dives inimici erant*, "a poor man and a rich man were enemies" (48). In the opening scene of our surviving text, Encolpius is complaining to Agamemnon about this training, which he says overemphasizes style and is so devoid of relevant content that students,

> cum in forum venerint, putent se in alium orbem terrarum delatos. et ideo ego adulescentulos existimo in scholis stultissimos fieri, quia nihil ex his quae in usu habemus aut adiunt aut vident, sed piratas cum catenis in litore stantes, sed tyrannos edicta scribentes quibus imperent filiis ut patrum suorum capita praecidant, sed responsa in pestilentiam data ut virgines tres aut plures immolentur, sed mellitos verborum globulos et omnia dicta factaque quasi papavere et sesamo sparsa. qui inter haec nutriunter non magis sapere possunt quam bene olere qui in culina habitant.

> *when they come into the forum, think that they have been brought to another planet. And that's why I think young men become utter dim-wits in school, because they see or hear nothing which we have in the real world, just pirates standing in chains on the shore, tyrants writing edicts for sons to lop off their fathers' heads, oracular responses to a plague that three or more virgins be sacrificed, honeyed globs of verbiage and all the words and events spiced up as if with poppy and sesame seeds. Those nourished on this stuff are no more able to acquire good taste than those who live in a kitchen are able not to stink.*

This complaint was a literary commonplace of the imperial age. Writers from Tacitus to the rhetorician Quintilian found the content of declamation impractical, if not ludicrous. Ironically, Petronius' characters use their rhetorical skills in precisely these situations. The trial of Encolpius and Giton on Lichas' ship resembles a *controversia* much more than a real trial. Before they are detected and while they are pondering their escape, Eumolpus has them imagine themselves as Odysseus in the cave of the Cyclops and propose various plans of action, mimicking a *suasoria*. In other scenes, Encolpius is shipwrecked and his young lover is kidnapped; Petronius seems to agree with Encolpius that the content of oratorical training was better suited to fiction than the forum. In this light, we might see declamation as mythomaniacal, and Conte also interprets contemporary oratorical practices as another important object of Petronian parody. The *Satyrica*'s use of prose may reflect the importance of oratory, and in the view of Laird, a great deal of the content of both Greek and Roman novels may be related to it as well: "Descriptions of nature, places, artwork, objects, and individuals, the pathologies of love and other emotions, para-philosophical disquisitions, set-piece speeches—all these elements that we tend to regard as the essential *content* of the novel are capable of evaporating into the forms and topics of conventional post-Aristotelian rhetoric" (1999, 216).

Philosophy

We can observe different types of intertextual play in the way the *Satyrica* works with the genre of philosophy. One is a direct evocation of Plato's philosophical work the *Symposium*. Both, after all, thematically focus on love and include a lengthy story about a banquet at which seven guests tell tales and one guest arrives late, drunk, and garlanded from another revel, leaning on a woman. It is important to note that our narrator, Encolpius, does not communicate any of this to us and fails to observe the similarities. So here the author is communicating with the listener or reader via a shared engagement with a revered text *around* the narrator. Averil Cameron explains Petronius' allusion to the *Symposium*:

> He is not mocking Plato. Instead, here as so often in the *Satyricon*, Petronius is subtly manipulating a famous literary passage for his audience to recognize and appreciate. He was writing for men as well read and as alert as himself, men who would see at once the absurdity and the skill of making the vulgar Habinnas play the role of the aristocratic and romantic Alcibiades. Once more Petronius casts an absurdly unheroic character in the part of a figure from serious literature. (1969, 367–68)

Eumolpus' tale about his seduction of the Pergamene boy may be read similarly as a comic inversion of the relationship between the characters Socrates and Alcibiades. In the *Symposium*, Alcibiades tells a charming story about his utter inability to attract the sexual interest of the older teacher figure; in the *Satyrica*, the mentor takes advantage of the young man until he becomes so oversexed that Eumolpus cannot keep up.

The *Satyrica* engages philosophy on a different level in the way that its characters express contemporary philosophical ideas, or the narrative may be seen to

comment on them. Within the Roman world in the first century BCE, two philosophical movements competed for the attention of the educated elite: Stoicism
and Epicureanism. The Stoic school was named after the *Stoa Poikile* or Painted
Porch in Athens where its founder, Zeno, first gathered students in the late
fourth century BCE. A holistic approach to logic, physics, and ethics, Stoicism
conceived of the universe in materialistic terms and as controlled by a divine
reason that is observable in the world as fate. Since everything is in accord with
this godly providence, the goal of the wise man is to accept whatever happens
with equanimity. This philosophy of numbness, of not feeling or expressing grief,
joy, or desire, led to the modern term "stoic," which is not far from its ancient
mark. In practice, this approach allowed individuals to pursue political and
material success, a family, and other privileges, but Stoics were supposed to struggle against becoming attached to them so that it would be possible to face their
loss without pain.

The hyperdramatic characters of the *Satyrica*, who feel every minor setback
as if it were of epic proportion, could never be described as good Stoics; nevertheless, many scholars have argued that some of them were crafted to mock the
most famous Stoic of the day, Seneca the Younger. This Seneca was the nephew
of the author of the books on rhetoric that we just explored. As noted earlier, he
served as Nero's tutor and wrote a satire of Claudius, as well as tragedies and
philosophical treatises in the form of letters and essays. Seneca used his connections to live in immense luxury, while decrying most men as ambitious, greedy,
and full of vice in their pursuit of riches, power, and sensual pleasures. His intense
tragedies also display characters who wail and lament at a high pitch—un-Stoic
in the extreme. Life tested Seneca's Stoic notion that a virtuous man does not
feel attachment to anyone or anything: he lost his wife, his son, and two nephews,
was almost executed by the emperor Caligula, was exiled by Claudius, and was
finally asked to commit suicide by Nero.

The self-proclaimed sage, poet, and tutor Eumolpus is a particularly Senecan
character. He tells a story about espousing philosophic chastity in order to serve
as the tutor of a young man—a young man whom he seduces and transforms into
a type of prostitute. We have already discussed the episode in which Eumolpus
is stoned for reciting a poem that imitates Seneca's tragedies in tone and style.
In one of his *Moral Epistles* (12), Seneca commends a freedman who staged his
funeral at banquets—the entire *Cena* can be interpreted as a comically nauseating
version of this meditation on death and loss. Worst of all, however, may be the
final scenes of the surviving novel. Using rhetorical strategies from *Moral Epistles* 17, in which Seneca urges his philosophical protégé to suffer poverty and
hunger for wisdom, a character encourages his audience to eat part of a human
corpse for money.

The *Satyrica*'s engagement with Epicurean philosophy may be different still. For Epicureans, the goal of life is pleasure. The modern use of the term denotes an indulgence in largely culinary pleasures, but that notion is quite misleading. In ancient philosophical terms, pleasure was the absence of pain, so the goal of life was to avoid pain. Since pain, grief, or loss could be experienced only by those who became attached to people or things, including family members, status, and wealth, these were to be avoided. In these terms, Stoicism and Epicureanism were quite similar; however, Epicurus (341–270 BCE) and his followers encouraged the suppression of ambitions for fame or wealth and desires for physical pleasures such as food, drink, or sex. Their ideal was a calm life in a quiet garden, eating plain foods and conversing intellectually with friends. In practice, an Epicurean lifestyle was thus different from the Stoic, and it found fewer advocates among the Roman elite.

Some scholars have seen an Epicurean critique in the *Satyrica*'s display of indulgence and emotional extremes. This notion of "Petronius the Moralist" was most stridently presented by Gilbert Highet in a 1941 article of that name. As Sullivan summarizes, Highet found Petronius to be

> not the crude Roman type of Epicurean, who regarded the philosophy of the garden as a justification for tasteful self-indulgence and the pursuit of such pleasures as one felt appropriate, but a true Epicurean who knew that the violent pleasures of luxurious food and dangerous sex had so much pain inmixed, that they were to be avoided, like politics, in the interest of *ataraxia*, the freedom from violent passions, the contentment that Epicurus himself is thought to have advocated and found. Petronius, Highet claimed, depicted the violence, misery, distress, jealousies, fears and so on, of his characters in order to further the aims of the Epicurean philosophers. (1985, 1671)

If the author of the *Satyrica* meant his story to be an elaborate example of how not to live, he does not reveal that directly anywhere in the surviving novel. Is he a social critic, comedian, philosopher, satirist, artist, some or all of the above? And here we have only scratched the surface. Croton, the south Italian town besieged by legacy hunters in the *Satyrica*, was where the mathematician Pythagoras founded his philosophical school in the late sixth century BCE. Scholars have seen evocations of the history of Livy in the battle scene on board ship and in Giton's initial refusal of Ascyltos. The literary use of letters in philosophy and elegiac poetry is parodied in Circe's epistle to the impotent Encolpius and his reply. The *Satyrica*'s literary engagements are practically innumerable and of varying intent. As Costas Panayotakis comments, "Petronius responded to the cultural polyphony of his time, and perhaps to the prolific corpus of Seneca's works or to Lucan's post-Vergilian epic, by writing *one* text which could not be given a specific generic label and encompassed a wide variety of widely differing literary genres" (2009, 60). Surveying those genres at least reveals the way the text engages with many types of storytelling and on multiple levels—high and low, oral and literary, Greek and Roman, prose and poetic—to mock, amuse, shock, characterize, and achieve effects at which we can only guess. By now you should be convinced of the high status and education of the author who composed these layers of allusion and illusion, even though they are delivered through a narrator who is questionable in about every way.

RECEPTION AND AFTERLIFE

Roman authors such as Cicero, Horace, Livy, and Ovid explicitly discuss the reception of their work and its potential life after the author's death. In some ways, Petronius' parodies and his characters' comic misuse or misunderstanding of canonical works of Greek and Latin literature comment on the problems of reception. Note the different reactions of the audience members to Eumolpus' story of the Widow of Ephesus—Lichas is outraged, the sailors laugh, Tryphaena is embarrassed. There is no guessing how a work will be received. As Plato worried, a written text travels around without its authorial parent to explain and interpret its intentions; postmodern scholars concur that literary texts have a life of their own, whatever the author may have had in mind. In the *Satyrica*, poets are stoned; Socrates' archetypal Platonic relationship is made into a dirty joke; characters mangle sublime Latin epic and apply themes from the most respected Greek tragedies to spectacularly petty moments in their own lives. Perhaps Petronius as an author mocks as a way of saying that he knows his listeners and readers will just mess it all up anyway.

We do not know what Petronius' contemporaries thought of his text, since the *Satyrica* was not mentioned much in antiquity. It never became part of the established school curriculum. The late antique literary critic Macrobius disparaged it as "narratives about imaginary lovers designed to delight the ear" (*Commentary on the Dream of Scipio* 1.2.8–9) and compared it to an unnamed work by Apuleius, presumably the *Metamorphoses*. In his novel, however, Apuleius does not refer to the *Satyrica* as a model or inspiration, and apparently the *Satyrica* did not influence any other major works of Latin literature. It was not widely copied or recopied, and only one mangled manuscript reached the ninth century. It is intriguing to note that a monastic home of an important manuscript of the *Satyrica* was Fleury, which was visited by the manuscript collector John of Salisbury in the twelfth century, an author who reveals familiarity with the *Satyrica* in his own writings. If he made a copy and took it home with him to England, the *Satyrica* may have influenced the later *Canterbury Tales*. The story of the "Widow of Ephesus" itself is repeated in a handful of medieval sources. On the whole, however, Apuleius' *Metamorphoses* was much better known and more influential in the medieval period.

When western Europeans became interested in classical materials again in the 1400s, the rediscovered Greek novels, along with Apuleius' *Metamorphoses*, began to inspire new forms of extended prose fiction. Literary scholars of the time noted the relationship to epic in terms of plot complexity and a content of "wanderings, love affairs, dangers, last minute escapes, punishment of the wicked, and so on" (Sandy and Harrison 2008, 301). Examples include everything from French and British adaptations and early novels to the rise of the Spanish picaresque, such as the classic *Don Quixote* of Cervantes. But when portions of the *Satyrica* began to be rediscovered in the same period, the reaction was mixed. On the one hand, the content was disdained. One cardinal commented that Petronius and Martial wrote works that deserved to be burned; a French scholar kept his Petronius "under lock and key . . . lest this obscene and lascivious writer corrupt anyone outside with his filthy wantonness" (quoted in Sochatoff 1979, 318). The elegance of Petronius' Latin was appreciated, even so, to the extent that in the mid-seventeenth century the authenticity of the first substantive text of the *Cena* to emerge was doubted. The "barbarisms" (that is, heavy use of Greek), misuse of cases and voices, and colloquialisms (diagnosed by their relationship to modern Italian and French) caused some scholars to decry the *Cena* as a forgery until more copies and longer passages were rediscovered. There was a flurry of work to recover as much of the text as possible and then get the entirety into print, which was achieved in 1669. Although there are debates among scholars, ever since fragments began to emerge, the influence of the *Satyrica* has been felt in European and later North American literature. This is particularly so in the development of the modern novel, from Thomas Nashe's 1594 *The Unfortunate Traveler*, "a picaresque tale with a prosimetric frame and a wide range of literary pastishe and parody" (Harrison 2009, 181), to James Joyce's *Ulysses*. On the whole, Petronius' reception has continued in this mixed vein—the *Satyrica* is treated as an immoral classic, and different readers tend toward one word or the other in this description.

The Victorian period in Britain (c. 1835–1900) provides an interesting case study. Either because of or despite the age's overt moralizing, Victorians had a particular fascination with the *Satyrica*. In his *History of European Morals from*

Augustus to Charlemagne of 1869, William Lecky called the novel "one of the most licentious and repulsive works in Roman literature" (quoted in Sullivan 1985, 1670). English translations were available—with lavish illustrations and printed by private presses that specialized in pornography. (Even so, the translator of one such text felt obliged to adapt the story so that Eumolpus seduced a girl rather than a boy in Pergamum.) Perhaps because of these associations with immorality, Petronius and his work were prominently featured in two extremely popular historical novels. British writer Edward Bulwer-Lytton's *The Last Days of Pompeii* (1834) uses Petronius' satiric, exaggerated imagery as a starting point for its image of a world gone awry and thus righteously destroyed by the eruption of Mount Vesuvius. Like the *Satyrica*, the novel uses a prosimetric structure and is set in south Italy in the first century BCE. *The Last Days of Pompeii* features hedonistic dinner parties and other events similar to Petronius' novel, even including a stoned poet. The hero and heroine of the Victorian novel, however, ultimately convert to Christianity, and thus the plot reenacts the birth of European Christendom within the early Empire. *Quo Vadis* was written in Polish in 1896 by Henry Sienkiewicz, who earned a Nobel Prize in Literature in 1905. Its main character is the nephew of Petronius, who is a prominent minor character as Nero's courtier and even gives the protagonist a copy of his work early in the novel. Petronius' contempt for the emperor is clear throughout, and his subversive suicide scene is included. His nephew of course converts to Christianity to escape the immoral decadence of the emperor. Those who chafed against Victorian morality even used Petronius as a touchstone, such as Lytton Strachey, writing to Virginia Woolf in 1912: "Is it prejudice, do you think, that makes us hate the Victorians, or is it the truth of the case? They seem to me a set of mouthing, bungling hypocrites. . . . The literature of the future will, I see clearly, be amazing. . . . To live in those days, when books will pour out of the press reeking with all the filth of Petronius" (quoted in Schmeling 1994, 166).

When the twentieth century arrived, the *Satyrica* and pornography were not uncoupled. Translations continued to be produced by private presses for its erotic content. In 1922, the artist Norman Lindsay, many of whose illustrations appear in this book, collaborated with translator W. C. Firebaugh on *The* Satyricon *of Petronius Arbiter,* "a complete and unexpurgated translation," for the New York press Boni and Liveright, famous for challenging obscenity and censorship laws. Even in the 1960s, excerpts of Paul Gillette's English "complete and uncensored reconstruction" and a "pictorial essay" of Fellini's film were both published in *Playboy.* At the same time, new strains of translation became available in England and the United States aimed at a popular or literary audience, some with content censored or adapted. This broader interest in the *Satyrica* may have been driven by Petronius' growing influence on contemporary literature, particularly with the modernist movement and the growing dominance of the novel as a literary form. Broadly defined, modernism was a social, philosophical, literary, and artistic rejection of tradition and confidence in Enlightenment thought; modernist authors self-consciously took apart, reconceived, refashioned, and parodied traditional forms of literature. You can see why Petronius' work appealed in this milieu. Massimo Fusillo argues that since "it is a subversive text that plays with the reader's expectations, genre categories, narrative roles, linguistic registers . . . at the beginning of the twentieth century . . . it became the experimental text *par excellence*" (2008, 330). Prominent examples of works so influenced include James Joyce's *Ulysses,* first published in serialized form in 1918–20. *Ulysses* obviously takes the *Odyssey* as a primary referent, but it creatively reprocesses epic in a Petronian fashion, that is, by using a low-life, urban, bodily, and bawdy setting. Fusillo describes how other early twentieth-century novels were influenced by two characteristics of Petronius' and Apuleius' novels—the picaresque, in which a first person antihero recounts episodic tales of social degradation, and the carnivalesque, which uses a plurality of voices and styles to explore grotesque, embodied, and obscene themes. Examples include Franz Kafka's *Amerika,* published posthumously in 1927; Céline's 1931 masterpiece *Voyage au bout de la nuit (Journey to the End of the Night)*; and John Steinbeck's 1935 *Tortilla Flat.* An early version of F. Scott Fitzgerald's novel *The Great Gatsby* (1925) was straightforwardly entitled *Trimalchio*; the novel's rags-to-riches protagonist, his ostentatious displays of wealth, and the wild parties fraught with class tensions reveal some of the debts to its ancient inspiration.

Other writers from this strand of modernism that critiques empty materialism were intrigued by Petronius' work. T. S. Eliot, who otherwise does not employ many allusions to classical material, used as the epigraph for his 1922 poem "The Waste Land" Trimalchio's anecdote about the Cumaean Sibyl (48.8):

> nam Sibyllam quidem Cumis ego ipse oculis meis vidi in ampulla pendere, et cum illi pueri dicerent: "Σίβυλλα, τί θέλεις"; respondebat illa: "ἀποθανεῖν θέλω."

> *Indeed I myself saw with my own eyes the Sibyl of Cumae hanging in her little jar, and when the slaves said to her, "Sibyl, what do you want?" she answered: "I want to die."*

The few mid-twentieth-century scholars who worked on Petronius also saw him as critiquing the decay caused by materialism and self-interest that lead to death, although they disagreed about his ultimate stance on whether or not there is hope for redemption. Since the association of the *Satyrica* with erotica persisted, scholars were also defending their own interest in the text when they took a moralizing stance. As William Arrowsmith summarized in 1966, "Petronius believes that perversion and also impotence are typical symptoms of a luxurious and unnatural society. . . . As constipation stands to food, so impotence stands to sexuality; both are products of *luxuria* in a society which has forgotten its cultural modalities and which cannot recover life" (309).

In addition to novels and scholarly articles, another twentieth-century medium demonstrated interest in Petronius: film. Hollywood tapped into the Victorian technique of moralizing while voyeuristically enjoying the stuff of the *Satyrica* by making a Technicolor blockbuster of the novel *Quo Vadis* in 1951 (directed by Mervyn LeRoy, starring Robert Taylor and Deborah Kerr). As is characteristic of mid-twentieth-century American cinematic interpretations of ancient Rome, *Quo Vadis* used Rome as a stand-in for European fascism and decadence in contrast to exceptional American democracy and morality. Petronius' decadent world provided perfect source material—as it did for a very different type of film later in the century, *Fellini Satyricon* (1969). A free-form adaptation of the ancient novel, this film focuses on the fragmentary quality of its inspiration. The ending is abrupt and provides no narrative closure, while the "story" unfolds as a sort of dream sequence of eight loosely connected episodes. Heavy theatrical makeup and harshly unrealistic colors help create the fantastical, dreamlike quality. Some episodes are from the *Satyrica*, such as the love triangle of Encolpius, Giton, and Ascyltos, Trimalchio's dinner party, and Lichas' ship; others are new, including scenes in a theater and a brothel, the assassination of the emperor and the start of a civil war, an aristocratic suicide, the Festival of Laughter from Apuleius' *Metamorphoses,* and Encolpius playing Theseus escaping the Minotaur. Although the film is difficult to interpret, it breaks conventions of storytelling and audience expectations about movies of ancient Rome in ways that the author of the *Satyrica* might well have appreciated. Fellini was nominated for an Academy Award for Best Director for the film.

Postmodern scholarship has witnessed an explosion of interest in Petronius. Characterized by a tendency to challenge objectivity and understand reality as socially constructed, this academic approach often explores the role of language and relationships of power in the construction of social reality. In the wake of the Cold War and movements for civil rights and women's rights, scholars have also become attracted to noncanonical works of literature, as well as questions of sexual and ethnic identity. Within such an academic framework, classicists naturally turned to the *Satyrica*. The bibliography on the *Satyrica* in multiple languages has become vast since the 1970s, and a sampling of the scholarly assessments of the text underscores these trends:

> The *Satyricon* is a radically anti-classical work, which, by its subversion
> and rejections of classical aesthetic theory with its attendant expectations,
> sets out to project a radically anti-classical world-view. (Zeitlin 1971, 633–34)

The 'Satyricon' was a work written for the amusement of the Neronian literary circle; it pandered to the tastes and snobbisms of that group; and it relied on its literary sophistication for appreciation. When morality lifts its head in the 'Satyricon', it turns out to be a parody of moralizing, whose implications are properly 'placed' by contextual irony. . . . It would seem then that taste, style, and wit in literature and art are Petronius' motives, not morality or philosophy. (Sullivan 1985, 1686)

[The *Satyrica* is] the product of an author steeped in the literary tradition who appears nonetheless deliberately to undertake to shatter the norms of stylistic, generic and topical propriety. (Boyce 1991, 1)

The interpretive polyphony behind the voices of these first-person narrators, the humiliations they suffer, the confusion about their identity and intentions, and, in Petronius, the dissolution of boundaries between theatrical self and the lived one: all of these characteristics point to a genre that not only aimed at laughter but also at transgressive play with voice, gender and class. (Bartsch 2008, 256)

Finally, it is well worth noting the contemporary reception of the *Satyrica* as a gay classic. As Helen Morales describes it, "the *Satyrica* has a privileged place in the literary history of homosexuality" (2008, 44). Lord Byron, an early nineteenth-century British Romantic poet and devout philhellene, used a Latin phrase from Eumolpus' seduction of the boy of Pergamum in letters to friends as a way to refer obliquely to sex between men (Crompton 1985, 127–28, 152). In what is now believed to be a hoax, a 1906 English translation of the *Satyrica* was attributed to a pseudonym of the recently deceased Oscar Wilde. This translation makes a fascinating cultural move by comparing Petronius and Wilde, one an extravagant aristocratic writer forced to suicide by a capricious tyrant, the other a classical scholar and celebrated aesthete who died in poverty and exile after being imprisoned for "the love that dare not speak its name." As of 2013, Petronius' work was still listed as one of the "100 Best Gay and Lesbian Novels" by *The Advocate*, a major GLBT-interest magazine in the United States. We have already discussed reasons why considering the characters gay or bisexual would be anachronistic. Nevertheless, as Petronius knew well, texts have a life of their own, and in the modern world the *Satyrica* is interestingly queer—it challenges sexual norms while giving relationships between men the cultural authority of classical antiquity.

No paperback translation into English of the *Satyrica* suitable for student use was published until William Arrowsmith's of 1960. The novel is now available in at least twenty-three different languages, including Bulgarian, Danish, Hebrew, Japanese, Russian, and Turkish. Even so, at the time of this writing, there was still no readily available student text of all the surviving Latin. Amy Richlin strikingly concludes her 2009 article "Sex in the *Satyrica*: Outlaws in Literature-land" with this challenge: "Students reading this book for a course should realize that they are part of a brief moment in history when it has been possible for a lot of people to read this text, and a much briefer moment when it has been possible for it to be taught to students. Ask yourself why that has been so, and whether this book might not be lost again" (99). Below are suggestions of scholarly works in English suitable for students who want to explore further the issues raised in this introduction, although the best next step is to read some of the *Satyrica* in Latin. Fragmentary, problematic, potentially pornographic, densely literary, elusive, debated—now it is time for you to decide for yourself whether nevertheless the *Satyrica* is worth reading.

RECOMMENDATIONS FOR FURTHER READING IN ENGLISH

Andreau, Jean. 2009. "Freedmen in the *Satyrica*." Translated by Paul Dilley. In *Petronius: A Handbook*, edited by Jonathan Prag and Ian Repath, 114–24. Wiley-Blackwell.

Arrowsmith, William. 1966. "Luxury and Death in the *Satyricon*." *Arion* 5.3: 304–31.

Bartsch, Shadi. 1994. *Actors in the Audience*. Harvard University Press.

Beck, Roger. 1973. "Some Observations on the Narrative Technique of Petronius." *Phoenix* 27: 42–61. Reprinted in *Oxford Readings in the Roman Novel*, edited by Stephen J. Harrison (Oxford University Press, 1999), 50–73.

———. 1975. "Encolpius at the *Cena*." *Phoenix* 29: 271–83.

Bodel, John. 1994. "Trimalchio's Underworld." In *The Search for the Ancient Novel*, edited by James Tatum, 237–59. Johns Hopkins University Press.

Boyce, Bret. 1991. *The Language of the Freedmen in Petronius' Cena Trimalchionis*. Brill.

Cameron, Averil. 1969. "Petronius and Plato." *Classical Quarterly* 19.2: 367–70.

Connors, Catherine M. 1998. *Petronius the Poet: Verse and Literary Tradition in the* Satyricon. Cambridge University Press.

Conte, Gian Biagio. 1996. *The Hidden Author: An Interpretation of Petronius'* Satyricon. Translated by Elaine Fantham. University of California Press.

Courtney, Edward. 2001. *A Companion to Petronius*. Oxford University Press.

Edwards, Catharine. 2007. "Dying in Character: Stoicism and the Roman Death Scene." In *Death in Ancient Rome*, 144–60. Yale University Press.

Fusillo, Massimo. 2008. "Modernity and Post-modernity." In *The Cambridge Companion to the Greek and Roman Novel*, edited by Tim Whitmarsh, 321–39. Cambridge University Press.

George, Peter A. 1966. "Style and Character in the *Satyricon*." *Arion* 5.3: 336–58.

Harrison, Stephen J., ed. 1999. *Oxford Readings in the Roman Novel*. Oxford University Press.

———. 2009. "Petronius' *Satyrica* and the Novel in English." In *Petronius: A Handbook*, edited by Jonathan Prag and Ian Repath, 181–97. Wiley-Blackwell.

Hope, Valerie M. 2009. "At Home with the Dead: Roman Funeral Traditions and Trimalchio's Tomb." In *Petronius: A Handbook*, edited by Jonathan Prag and Ian Repath, 140–60. Wiley-Blackwell.

Horsfall, Nicholas. 1989a. "'The Uses of Literacy' and the *Cena Trimalchionis*: I." *Greece & Rome* 36: 74–89.

———. 1989b. "'The Uses of Literacy' and the *Cena Trimalchionis*: II." *Greece & Rome* 36: 194–209.

Jensson, Gottskálk. 2004. *The Recollections of Encolpius: The* Satyrica *of Petronius as Milesian Fiction*. Ancient Narrative Supplementum, 2. Barkhuis.

Killeen, J. F. 1957. "James Joyce's Roman Prototype." *Comparative Literature* 9.3: 193–203.

Laird, Andrew. 1999. "Ideology and Taste: Narrative and Discourse in Petronius' *Satyricon*." In *Powers of Expression, Expressions of Power: Speech Presentation and Latin Literature*, 209–58. Oxford University Press.

Malamud, Martha. 2009. "Primitive Politics: Lucan and Petronius." In *Writing Politics in Imperial Rome*, edited by W. J. Dominik, J. Garthwaite, and P. A. Roche, 273–306. Brill.

Morales, Helen. 2008. "The History of Sexuality." In *The Cambridge Companion to the Greek and Roman Novel*, edited by Tim Whitmarsh, 39–55. Cambridge University Press.

Morgan, J. R. 2009. "Petronius and Greek Literature." In *Petronius: A Handbook*, edited by Jonathan Prag and Ian Repath, 32–47. Wiley-Blackwell.

Panayotakis, Costas. 2009. "Petronius and the Roman Literary Tradition." In *Petronius: A Handbook*, edited by Jonathan Prag and Ian Repath, 48–64. Wiley-Blackwell.

Paschalis, Michael. 2011. "Petronius and Virgil: Contextual and Intertextual Readings." In *Echoing Narratives: Studies of Intertextuality in Greek and Roman Prose Fiction*, edited by Konstantin Doulamis, 73–98. Barkhuis.

Paul, Joanna. 2009. "*Fellini-Satyricon*: Petronius and Film." In *Petronius: A Handbook*, edited by Jonathan Prag and Ian Repath, 198–217. Wiley-Blackwell.

Petersmann, Hubert. 1999. "Environment, Linguistic Situation, and Levels of Style in Petronius' *Satyrica*." Translated by Martin Revermann. In *Oxford Readings in the Roman Novel*, edited by Stephen J. Harrison, 105–23. Oxford University Press.

Plaza, Maria. 2000. *Laughter and Derision in Petronius'* Satyrica: *A Literary Study*. Almqvist & Wiksell.

Prag, Jonathan, and Ian Repath, eds. 2009. *Petronius: A Handbook*. Wiley-Blackwell.

Richlin, Amy. 2009. "Sex in the *Satyrica*: Outlaws in Literatureland." In *Petronius: A Handbook*, edited by Jonathan Prag and Ian Repath, 82–100. Wiley-Blackwell.

Rimell, Victoria. 2002. *Petronius and the Anatomy of Fiction*. Cambridge University Press.

Roller, Mathew B. 2006. *Dining Posture in Ancient Rome: Bodies, Values and Status*. Princeton University Press.

Schmeling, Gareth. 1994–95. "Confessor Gloriosus: A Role of Encolpius in the *Satyrica*." *Würzburger Jahrbücher für die Altertumswissensschaft* 20: 207–24.

Slater, Niall W. 1990. *Reading Petronius*. Johns Hopkins University Press.

Sullivan, J. P. 1968. "Petronius, Seneca and Lucan: A Neronian Literary Feud?" *Transactions and Proceedings of the American Philological Association* 99: 453–67.

———. 1985. "Petronius' *Satyricon* in Its Neronian Context." In *Aufstieg und Niedergang der römischen Welt* II.32.3, edited by Hildegard Temporini and Wolfgang Haase, 1666–86. Walter de Gruyter.

Zeitlin, Froma I. 1971. "Petronius as Paradox: Anarchy and Artistic Integrity." *Transactions and Proceedings of the American Philological Association* 102: 631–84. Reprinted in *Oxford Readings in the Roman Novel*, edited by Stephen J. Harrison (Oxford University Press, 1999), 1–49.

RECOMMENDED COMPLETE ENGLISH TRANSLATIONS

Petronius. 1965. *The Satyricon and the Fragments*. Translated by John P. Sullivan. Penguin. Reprinted in 1986.

———. 1996a. *Satyrica*. Translated and with an introduction by R. Bracht Branham and Daniel Kinney. Dent.

———. 1996b. *The Satyricon*. Translated with introduction and explanatory notes by Patrick G. Walsh. Clarendon Press.

———. 2000. *Satyricon*. Translated with notes and topical commentaries by Sarah Ruden. Hackett.

Latin Passages

An asterisk (*) marks a spot where editors tend to agree that a gap occurs in our surviving fragments; three asterisks (***) note where a lot of the story may be missing. An ellipsis (...) has been included to indicate the omission of lines of Latin text to keep the passage of a reasonable length; what happens in those missing lines is summarized in the relevant sections of the Commentary.

CHAPTER ONE: BATHS AND FIRST IMPRESSIONS
(*SATYRICA* 26–28)

26.6 venerat iam tertius dies, id est, expectatio liberae cenae, sed tot vulneribus confossis fuga magis placebat quam quies. itaque cum maesti deliberaremus quonam genere praesentem evitaremus procellam, unus servus Agamemnonis interpellavit trepidantes et "quid? vos" inquit "nescitis hodie apud quem fiat? **26.9** Trimalchio, lautissimus homo * horologium in triclinio et bucinatorem habet subornatum, ut subinde sciat quantum de vita perdiderit." amicimur ergo diligenter obliti omnium malorum et Gitona libentissime servile officium tuentem iubemus in balneum sequi. *

27 nos interim vestiti errare coepimus, immo iocari magis et circulis ludentium accedere, cum subito videmus senem calvum, tunica vestitum russea, inter pueros capillatos ludentem pila. nec tam pueri nos, quamquam erat operae pretium, ad spectaculum duxerant, quam ipse pater familiae, qui soleatus pila prasina exercebatur. nec amplius eam repetebat quae terram contigerat, sed follem plenum habebat servus sufficiebatque ludentibus. **27.3** notavimus etiam res novas. nam duo spadones in diversa parte circuli stabant, quorum alter matellam tenebat argenteam, alter numerabat pilas, non quidem eas quae inter manus lusu expellente vibrabant, sed eas quae in terram decidebant. cum has ergo miraremur lautitias, accurrit Menelaus et "hic est," inquit, "apud quem cubitum ponitis, et quidem iam principium cenae videtis." **27.5** et iam non loquebatur Menelaus, cum Trimalchio digitos concrepuit, ad quod signum matellam spado ludenti subiecit. exonerata ille vesica aquam poposcit ad manus, digitosque paululum adspersos in capite pueri tersit. ***

28 longum erat singula excipere. itaque intravimus balneum, et sudore calfacti momento temporis ad frigidam eximus. iam Trimalchio unguento perfusus tergebatur, non linteis, sed palliis ex lana mollissima factis. tres interim iatraliptae in conspectu eius Falernum potabant, et cum plurimum rixantes effunderent, Trimalchio hoc suum propin esse dicebat. **28.4** hinc involutus coccina gausapa lecticae impositus est praecedentibus phaleratis cursoribus quattuor et chiramaxio, in quo deliciae eius vehebantur, puer vetulus, lippus, domino Trimalchione deformior. cum ergo auferretur, ad caput eius cum minimis symphoniacus tibiis accessit et tamquam in aurem aliquid secreto diceret, toto itinere cantavit.

Roman Baths

FIG. 1. Norman Lindsay, "Trimalchio at Ball." From Gaius Petronius, *The Complete Works of Gaius Petronius*, translated by Jack Lindsay (Rarity Press, 1932), image insert following 16.

The Romans expended a great deal of time and money on public baths, and bathing was an important daily ritual for many. Few houses had facilities more elaborate than a wash basin. Bathing was a communal activity, and after a long morning of work, citizens tended to congregate at the baths in the afternoon. Complexes provided separate times or facilities for men and women, but different classes mixed. Of course, even without clothing, the wealthy could be identified by the number of their attendants.

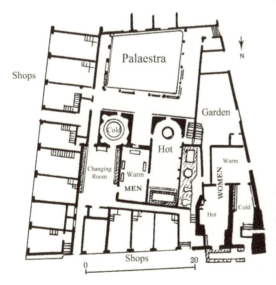

FIG. 2. Plan of the Forum Baths of Pompeii. Adapted from Pierre Grimal, *Roman Cities*, translated and edited by G. Michael Woloch (University of Wisconsin Press, 1983), 69, figure 20.

The Forum Baths of Pompeii, shown in figure 2, are a fine example of a neighborhood bath complex. Changing rooms led into chambers heated to varying temperatures; one would move from cool to warm to hot. Men also exercised in a central open space often referred to with the Greek term *palaestra*. The baths thus provided the opportunity to exercise, clean the body, see and be seen, and prepare for the evening's activities.

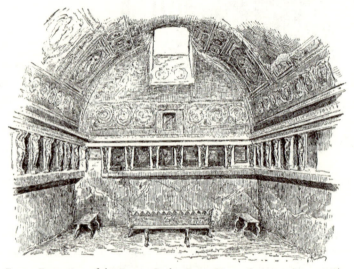

FIG. 3. Engraving of the Forum Baths. From Pierre Gusman, *Pompei: The City, Its Life and Art*, translated by Florence Simmonds and M. Jourdain (W. Heinemann, 1900), 142.

Figure 3 shows an engraving of an interior room from the Forum Baths. Note the small cubbies in the wall, presumably for storing clothing.

Baths display engineering and architectural developments characteristic of the Romans. The first true bath complexes we know of developed in southern Italy, inspired by the natural hot springs that occur in volcanic areas and a local sand that made a waterproof cement. Once artificial pools became possible, a new heating system was developed called a "hypocaust." As illustrated in figure 5, tile and stone floors were supported on piles of terracotta bricks so that air heated by a wood-burning furnace could circulate beneath—the best in ancient radiant heating. Aqueducts were also built to transport water from distant springs to the bath complexes that sprang up in towns and cities across Italy and the empire.

FIG. 4. Norman Lindsay, "The Bath." From Petronius Arbiter, *The Satyricon of Petronius Arbiter*, translated by W. C. Firebaugh (Boni and Liveright, 1922), following 162.

FIG. 5. Engraving of a hypocaust floor. From Henry Thédenat, *Pompeii: Vie publique* (Paris, 1906), 107, figure 58.

CHAPTER TWO: THE HOUSE, THE *DISPENSATOR*, AND THE SINGING *FAMILIA* (*SATYRICA* 28–31)

FIG. 6. Doorway mosaic from the House of the Tragic Poet, Pompeii. From Henry Thédenat, *Pompéi: Histoire—Vie privée* (H. Laurens, 1906), 58, figure 25.

28.6 sequimur nos admiratione iam saturi et cum Agamemnone ad ianuam pervenimus, in cuius poste libellus erat cum hac inscriptione fixus: "quisquis servus sine dominico iussu foras exierit, accipiet plagas centum." **28.8** in aditu autem ipso stabat ostiarius prasinatus, cerasino succinctus cingulo, atque in lance argentea pisum purgabat. super limen autem cavea pendebat aurea in qua pica varia intrantes salutabat. **29** ceterum ego dum omnia stupeo, paene resupinatus crura mea fregi. ad sinistram enim intrantibus non longe ab ostiarii cella canis ingens, catena vinctus, in pariete erat pictus superque quadrata littera scriptum "cave canem." et collegae quidem mei riserunt. ego autem collecto spiritu non destiti totum parietem persequi. **29.3** erat autem venalicium cum titulis pictum, et ipse Trimalchio capillatus caduceum tenebat Minervaque ducente Romam intrabat. hinc quemadmodum ratiocinari didicisset, deinque dispensator factus esset, omnia diligenter curiosus pictor cum inscriptione reddiderat. in deficiente vero iam porticu levatum mento in tribunal excelsum Mercurius rapiebat. **29.6** praesto erat Fortuna cum cornu abundanti et tres Parcae aurea pensa torquentes. notavi etiam in porticu gregem cursorum cum magistro se exercentem. praeterea grande armarium in angulo vidi, in cuius aedicula erant Lares argentei positi Venerisque signum marmoreum et pyxis aurea non pusilla, in qua barbam ipsius conditam esse dicebant. . . . *

30.5 his repleti voluptatibus cum conaremur in triclinium intrare, exclamavit unus ex pueris, qui supra hoc officium erat positus: "dextro pede!" sine dubio paulisper trepidavimus, ne contra praeceptum aliquis nostrum limen transiret. ceterum ut pariter movimus gressus, servus nobis despoliatus procubuit ad pedes ac rogare coepit, ut se poenae eriperemus: nec magnum esse peccatum suum, propter quod periclitaretur; subducta enim sibi vestimenta dispensatoris in balneo, quae vix fuissent decem sestertiorum. **30.9** rettulimus ergo dextros pedes, dispensatoremque in oecario aureos numerantem deprecati sumus ut servo remitteret poenam. superbus ille sustulit vultum et "non tam iactura me movet," inquit, "quam neglegentia nequissimi servi. vestimenta mea cubitoria perdidit, quae mihi natali meo cliens quidam donaverat, Tyria sine dubio, sed iam semel lota. quid ergo est? dono vobis eum."

FIG. 7. Norman Lindsay, "The Guilty Slave." From Petronius, *The Satyricon*, translated by W. C. Firebaugh, following 70.

31 obligati tam grandi beneficio cum intrassemus triclinium, occurrit nobis ille idem servus, pro quo rogaveramus, et stupentibus spississima basia impegit gratias agens humanitati nostrae. "ad summam, statim scietis," ait, "cui dederitis beneficium. vinum dominicum ministratoris gratia est."

31.3 tandem ergo discubuimus, pueris Alexandrinis aquam in manus nivatam infundentibus, aliisque insequentibus ad pedes ac paronychia cum ingenti subtilitate tollentibus. ac ne in hoc quidem tam molesto tacebant officio, sed obiter cantabant. ego experiri volui an tota familia cantaret, itaque potionem poposci. **31.6** paratissimus puer non minus me acido cantico excepit, et quisquis aliquid rogatus erat ut daret. pantomimi chorum, non patris familiae triclinium crederes. allata est tamen gustatio valde lauta; nam iam omnes discubuerant praeter unum Trimalchionem, cui locus novo more primus servabatur.

Fig. 8. Banquet scene. From Pierre Gusman, *Pompei: The City, Its Life and Art*, translated by Florence Simmonds and M. Jourdain (W. Heinemann, 1900), 313.

Wall Painting

FIG. 9. Reception room in the House of the Vettii, Pompeii. From August Mau, *Pompeii: Its Life and Art* (Macmillan, 1899), 332, plate VIII.

Much of what we know about wall painting in ancient Italy is due to its survival in cities that were covered by the eruption of Mount Vesuvius, such as Pompeii. In figure 9, from a room in the House of the Vettii, a thick layer of plaster underlies the paintings. The Romans used a fresco technique to paint directly onto this plaster while it was wet. At first walls were painted to look as though they were covered with expensive stone like colored marbles and porphyry—this is evident in the lower portion of this room in the dark colors and geometric patterns that resemble stone revetment. Later, fake architectural elements were added in paint, such as columns or benches, and sometimes portions of the wall were painted to look as though tapestries were hanging on them, such as the white panel in the corner of the room here. Finally, the wall was visually broken via painted illusions. Here you can see faux windows opening into elaborate architectural city-scapes "behind" the wall. Often, as here, square panels with more elaborate figural scenes were set into the center of each wall, perhaps to look like masterpiece paintings that could be bought and hung separately. These scenes often show stories from Greek myths.

The entryway and main hall of an elite house, such as the one reconstructed in figure 10, might display objects or images celebrating the homeowners, including military spoils or portraits of noble ancestors. We also have mosaic versions of Trimalchio's painted dog in Pompeii. On the whole, however, scholars argue that the way Trimalchio presents his life history in paint recalls tomb decoration more than an aristocratic house, or perhaps scenes on triumphal arches in Rome. On those monuments, images depict the emperor's victories as well as his procession into the city accompanied by the gods.

FIG. 10. Engraving of a doorway to an atrium house. From Levi W. Yaggy and Thomas L. Haines, *Museum of Antiquity: A Description of Ancient Life* (J. B. Furman and Western Publishing House, 1884), 30.

Roman Dining Rooms

FIG. 11. "Nine Guests in a Triclinium." From William Sterns Davis, *A Day in Old Rome: A Picture of Roman Life* (Allyn and Bacon, 1925), 116.

FIG. 12. Reconstruction of a summer dining room in the House of Sallust, Pompeii. From Thomas H. Dyer, *Pompeii: Its History, Buildings, and Antiquities* (Bell & Daldy, 1867), 336.

FIG. 13. Mosaic from a tabletop in a garden dining room, Pompeii. From August Mau, *Pompeii: Its Life and Art* (Macmillan, 1899), 391, figure 220.

FIG. 14. Plan of the House of Sallust, Pompeii. Adapted from John E. Stambaugh, *The Ancient Roman City* (Johns Hopkins University Press, 1988), 163, figure 12.

Many small, multipurpose rooms surround the main hall (*atrium*) and colonnaded garden of a large house in ancient Italy, as can be seen in the plan of the
House of Sallust in Pompeii in figure 14. Although these might have been used
as bedrooms, studies, storerooms, or banquet halls at different times of the year,
some houses also had rooms designed specifically for the *convivium*. In the plan
in figure 14, these are labeled with a D. Sometimes we can identify these rooms
because they have built-in dining couches, such as the one in the northern part
of the garden and shown in the engraving in figure 12. Others may be marked by
a small square mosaic set in the center of the room, the only part of the floor that
was visible when the three dining couches were set up. Many of these mosaics have
geometric patterns or scenes of still life, while others are made to look like a
floor after a banquet, with fish bones, apple cores, and other bits of trash. A few
feature skeletons or other images of death, underscoring the need to enjoy life
while it lasts.

CHAPTER THREE: TRIMALCHIO'S ENTRANCE, COMMENTS ON FORTUNATA (*SATYRICA* 32–38)

32 in his eramus lautitiis, cum ipse Trimalchio ad symphoniam allatus est posi-
tusque inter cervicalia minutissima expressit imprudentibus risum. pallio enim
coccineo adrasum excluserat caput, circaque oneratas veste cervices laticlaviam
immiserat mappam fimbriis hinc atque illinc pendentibus. . . . . **33** ut deinde
pinna argentea dentes perfodit, "amici," inquit, "nondum mihi suave erat in triclinium venire, sed ne diutius absentivus morae vobis essem, omnem voluptatem
mihi negavi. **33.2** permittitis tamen finiri lusum." sequebatur puer cum tabula
terebinthina et crystallinis tesseris, notavique rem omnium delicatissimam. pro
calculis enim albis ac nigris aureos argenteosque habebat denarios. interim dum
ille omnium textorum dicta inter lusum consumit, gustantibus adhuc nobis repositorium allatum est. . . . .

34 iam Trimalchio eadem omnia lusu intermisso poposcerat feceratque potes-
tatem clara voce, si quis nostrum iterum vellet mulsum sumere, cum subito

signum symphonia datur et gustatoria pariter a choro cantante rapiuntur. ceterum inter tumultum cum forte paropsis excidisset et puer iacentem sustulisset, animadvertit Trimalchio colaphisque obiurgari puerum ac proicere rursus paropsidem iussit. **34.3** insecutus est supellecticarius argentumque inter reliqua purgamenta scopis coepit everrere. subinde intraverunt duo Aethiopes capillati cum pusillis utribus, quales solent esse eorum qui harenam in amphitheatro spargunt, vinumque dedere in manus; aquam enim nemo porrexit. **34.5** laudatus propter elegantias dominus: "aequum," inquit, "Mars amat. itaque iussi suam cuique mensam assignari. obiter et putidissimi servi minorem nobis aestum frequentia sua facient."

34.6 statim allatae sunt amphorae vitreae diligenter gypsatae, quarum in cervicibus pittacia erant affixa cum hoc titulo: "Falernum Opimianum annorum centum." dum titulos perlegimus, complosit Trimalchio manus et, "eheu," inquit, "ergo diutius vivit vinum quam homuncio. quare tangomenas faciamus. vinum vita est. verum Opimianum praesto. heri non tam bonum posui, et multo honestiores cenabant." ...

36.7 ingerebat nihilo minus Trimalchio lentissima voce: "Carpe, Carpe." ego, suspicatus ad aliquam urbanitatem totiens iteratam vocem pertinere, non erubui eum qui supra me accumbebat hoc ipsum interrogare. at ille, qui saepius eiusmodi ludos spectaverat, "vides illum" inquit "qui obsonium carpit: Carpus vocatur. Ita quotienscumque dicit 'Carpe', eodem verbo et vocat et imperat." **37** non potui amplius quicquam gustare, sed conversus ad eum, ut quam plurima exciperem, longe accersere fabulas coepi sciscitarique quae esset mulier illa quae huc atque illuc discurreret. "uxor," inquit, "Trimalchionis, Fortunata appellatur, quae nummos modio metitur. et modo, modo quid fuit? **37.3** ignoscet mihi genius tuus, noluisses de manu illius panem accipere. nunc, nec quid nec quare, in caelum abiit et Trimalchionis topanta est. ad summam, mero meridie si dixerit illi tenebras

esse, credet. ipse nescit quid habeat, adeo saplutus est; sed haec lupatria provi-
det omnia, et ubi non putes. 37.7 est sicca, sobria, bonorum consiliorum—tantum auri vides—, est tamen malae linguae, pica pulvinaris. quem amat, amat;
quem non amat, non amat. ipse fundos habet, quantum milvi volant, nummorum
nummos. argentum in ostiarii illius cella plus iacet, quam quisquam in fortunis
habet. familia vero babae babae, non mehercules puto decumam partem esse
quae dominum suum noverit. ad summam, quemvis ex istis babaecalis in rutae
folium coniciet. 38 nec est quod putes illum quicquam emere. omnia domi nascuntur: lana, citrea, piper; lacte gallinaceum si quaesieris, invenies. ad summam, parum illi bona lana nascebatur; arietes a Tarento emit, et eos culavit in
gregem. mel Atticum ut domi nasceretur, apes ab Athenis iussit afferri; obiter et
vernaculae quae sunt, meliusculae a Graeculis fient. 38.4 ecce intra hos dies
scripsit, ut illi ex India semen boletorum mitteretur. nam mulam quidem nullam
habet quae non ex onagro nata sit. vides tot culcitas: nulla non aut conchyliatum
aut coccineum tomentum habet. tanta est animi beatitudo!" . . .

FIG. 15. Norman Lindsay, "Trimalchio." From Gaius Petronius, *The
Complete Works of Gaius Petronius*,
translated by Jack Lindsay (Rarity
Press, 1932), following 32.

CHAPTER FOUR:
THE GUESTS CONVERSE (*SATYRICA* 41–47)

41.9 ab hoc ferculo Trimalchio ad lasanum surrexit. nos libertatem sine tyranno nacti coepimus invitare * . Dama itaque primus cum pataracina poposcisset, "dies," inquit, "nihil est. dum versas te, nox fit. itaque nihil est melius quam de cubiculo recta in triclinium ire. et mundum frigus habuimus. vix me balneus calfecit. tamen calda potio vestiarius est. staminatas duxi, et plane matus sum. vinus mihi in cerebrum abiit."

42 excepit Seleucus fabulae partem et "ego," inquit, "non cotidie lavor; balniscus enim fullo est, aqua dentes habet, et cor nostrum cotidie liquescit. sed cum mulsi pultarium obduxi, frigori laecasin dico. nec sane lavare potui; fui enim hodie in funus. homo bellus, tam bonus Chrysanthus animam ebulliit. modo, modo me appellavit. videor mihi cum illo loqui. heu, eheu! **42.4** utres inflati ambulamus. minoris quam muscae sumus. muscae tamen aliquam virtutem habent, nos non pluris sumus quam bullae. et quid si non abstinax fuisset! quinque dies aquam in os suum non coniecit, non micam panis. tamen abiit ad plures. medici illum perdiderunt, immo magis malus fatus; medicus enim nihil aliud est quam animi consolatio. **42.6** tamen bene elatus est, vitali lecto, stragulis bonis. planctus est optime—manu misit aliquot—etiam si maligne illum ploravit uxor. quid si non illam optime accepisset! sed mulier quae mulier milvinum genus. neminem nihil boni facere oportet; aeque est enim ac si in puteum conicias. sed antiquus amor cancer est."

43 molestus fuit, Philerosque proclamavit: "vivorum meminerimus. ille habet, quod sibi debebatur: honeste vixit, honeste obiit. quid habet quod queratur? ab asse crevit et paratus fuit quadrantem de stercore mordicus tollere. itaque crevit, quicquid tetigit, tamquam favus. **43.2** puto mehercules illum reliquisse solida centum, et omnia in nummis habuit. de re tamen ego verum dicam, qui linguam caninam comedi: durae buccae fuit, linguosus, discordia, non homo. frater eius fortis fuit, amicus amico, manu plena, uncta mensa. . . .

43.7 et quot putas illum annos secum tulisse? septuaginta et supra. sed corneolus fuit, aetatem bene ferebat, niger tamquam corvus. noveram hominem olim oliorum, et adhuc salax erat. non mehercules illum puto in domo canem reliquisse. immo etiam pullarius erat, omnis Minervae homo. nec improbo, hoc solum enim secum tulit."

44 haec Phileros dixit, illa Ganymedes: "narratis quod nec ad caelum nec ad terram pertinet, cum interim nemo curat quid annona mordet. non mehercules hodie buccam panis invenire potui. et quomodo siccitas perseverat! iam annum esuritio fuit. aediles male eveniat, qui cum pistoribus colludunt 'serva me, servabo te.' . . .

44.15 quod ad me attinet, iam pannos meos comedi, et si perseverat haec annona, casulas meas vendam. quid enim futurum est, si nec dii nec homines huius coloniae miserentur? ita meos fruniscar, ut ego puto omnia illa a diibus fieri. nemo enim caelum caelum putat, nemo ieiunium servat, nemo Iovem pili facit, sed omnes opertis oculis bona sua computant. **44.18** antea stolatae ibant nudis pedibus in clivum, passis capillis, mentibus puris, et Iovem aquam exorabant. itaque statim urceatim plovebat: aut tunc aut numquam, et omnes redibant udi tamquam mures. itaque dii pedes lanatos habent, quia nos religiosi non sumus. agri iacent—"

45 "oro te," inquit Echion centonarius, "melius loquere. . . . **46** videris mihi, Agamemnon, dicere: 'quid iste argutat molestus?' quia tu, qui potes loquere, non loquis. non es nostrae fasciae, et ideo pauperorum verba derides. scimus te prae litteras fatuum esse. quid ergo est? aliqua die te persuadeam, ut ad villam venias et videas casulas nostras? inveniemus quod manducemus, pullum, ova: belle erit, etiam si omnia hoc anno tempestas depravavit: inveniemus ergo unde saturi fiamus.

46.3 et iam tibi discipulus crescit cicaro meus. iam quattuor partis dicit; si vixerit, habebis ad latus servulum. nam quicquid illi vacat, caput de tabula non tollit. ingeniosus est et bono filo, etiam si in aves morbosus est. ego illi iam tres cardeles occidi, et dixi quia mustella comedit. invenit tamen alias nenias, et libentissime pingit. ceterum iam Graeculis calcem impingit et Latinas coepit non male appetere. . . . **46.7** emi ergo nunc puero aliquot libra rubricata, quia volo illum ad domusionem aliquid de iure gustare. habet haec res panem. nam litteris satis inquinatus est. quod si resilierit, destinavi illum artificium docere, aut tonstrinum aut praeconem aut certe causidicum, quod illi auferre non possit nisi Orcus. **46.8** ideo illi cotidie clamo: 'Primigeni, crede mihi, quicquid discis, tibi discis. vides Phileronem causidicum: si non didicisset, hodie famem a labris non abigeret. modo modo collo suo circumferebat onera venalia, nunc etiam adversus Norbanum se extendit. litterae thesaurum est, et artificium numquam moritur.'"

CHAPTER FIVE: TRIMALCHIO'S BOWELS, THREE PIGS, AND A COOK (*SATYRICA* 47–49)

47 eiusmodi fabulae vibrabant, cum Trimalchio intravit et detersa fronte unguento manus lavit spatioque minimo interposito "ignoscite mihi," inquit, "amici, multis iam diebus venter mihi non respondit. nec medici se inveniunt. profuit mihi tamen malicorium et taeda ex aceto. spero tamen, iam veterem pudorem sibi imponit. alioquin circa stomachum mihi sonat, putes taurum. **47.4** itaque si quis vestrum voluerit sua re causa facere, non est quod illum pudeatur. nemo nostrum solide natus est. ego nullum puto tam magnum tormentum esse quam continere. hoc solum vetare ne Iovis potest. rides, Fortunata, quae soles me nocte desomnem facere? nec tamen in triclinio ullum vetui facere quod se iuvet, et medici vetant continere. vel si quid plus venit, omnia foras parata sunt: aqua, lasani et cetera minutalia. **47.6** credite mihi, anathymiasis in cerebrum it, et in toto corpore fluctum facit. multos scio sic periisse, dum nolunt sibi verum dicere." gratias agimus liberalitati indulgentiaeque eius, et subinde castigamus crebris potiunculis risum. nec adhuc sciebamus nos in medio, quod aiunt, clivo laborare. nam commundatis ad symphoniam mensis tres albi sues in triclinium adducti sunt capistris et tintinnabulis culti, quorum unum bimum nomenculator esse dicebat, alterum trimum, tertium vero iam sexennem.

Fɪɢ. 16. Norman Lindsay, "Enter Three Hogs." From Gaius Petronius, *The Complete Works of Gaius Petronius*, translated by Jack Lindsay (Rarity Press, 1932), following 48.

47.9 ego putabam petauristarios intrasse et porcos, sicut in circulis mos est, portenta aliqua facturos; sed Trimalchio expectatione discussa "quem," inquit, "ex eis vultis in cenam statim fieri? gallum enim gallinaceum, penthiacum et eiusmodi nenias rustici faciunt: mei coci etiam vitulos aeno coctos solent facere." continuoque cocum vocari iussit, et non expectata electione nostra maximum natu iussit occidi, et clara voce: "ex quota decuria es?" **47.12** cum ille se ex quadragesima respondisset: "empticius an," inquit, "domi natus?" "neutrum," inquit cocus, "sed testamento Pansae tibi relictus sum." "vide ergo," ait, "ut diligenter ponas; si non, te iubebo in decuriam viatorum conici." et cocum quidem potentiae admonitum in culinam obsonium duxit, **48** Trimalchio autem miti ad nos vultu respexit et "vinum," inquit, "si non placet, mutabo; vos illud oportet bonum faciatis. deorum beneficio non emo, sed nunc quicquid ad salivam facit, in suburbano nascitur eo, quod ego adhuc non novi. dicitur confine esse Tarraciniensibus et Tarentinis. **48.3** nunc coniungere agellis Siciliam volo, ut cum Africam libuerit ire, per meos fines navigem. sed narra tu mihi, Agamemnon, quam controversiam hodie declamasti? ego etiam si causas non ago, in domusionem tamen litteras didici. et ne me putes studia fastiditum, duas bybliothecas habeo, unam Graecam, alteram Latinam. dic ergo, si me amas, peristasim declamationis tuae." **48.5** cum dixisset Agamemnon: "pauper et dives inimici erant," ait Trimalchio "quid est pauper?" "urbane," inquit Agamemnon et nescio quam controversiam exposuit. statim Trimalchio "hoc," inquit, "si factum est, controversia non est; si factum non est, nihil est." ...

49 nondum efflaverat omnia, cum repositorium cum sue ingenti mensam occupavit. mirari nos celeritatem coepimus et iurare, ne gallum quidem gallinaceum tam cito percoqui potuisse, tanto quidem magis, quod longe maior nobis porcus videbatur esse, quam paulo ante apparuerat. deinde magis magisque Trimalchio intuens eum "quid? quid?" inquit, "porcus hic non est exinteratus? non mehercules est. voca, voca cocum in medio." **49.5** cum constitisset ad mensam cocus tristis et diceret se oblitum esse exinterare, "quid? oblitus?" Trimalchio exclamat, "putes illum piper et cuminum non coniecisse. despolia." non fit mora, despoliatur cocus atque inter duos tortores maestus consistit. deprecari tamen omnes coeperunt et dicere: "solet fieri; rogamus, mittas; postea si fecerit, nemo nostrum pro illo rogabit." **49.7** ego crudelissimae severitatis, non potui me tenere, sed inclinatus ad aurem Agamemnonis "plane," inquam, "hic debet servus esse nequissimus;

aliquis oblivisceretur porcum exinterare? non mehercules illi ignoscerem, si piscem praeterisset." at non Trimalchio, qui relaxato in hilaritatem vultu "ergo,"
inquit, "quia tam malae memoriae es, palam nobis illum exintera." **49.9** recepta
cocus tunica cultrum arripuit porcique ventrem hinc atque illinc timida manu
secuit. nec mora, ex plagis ponderis inclinatione crescentibus thumatula cum
botulis effusa sunt.

CHAPTER SIX: SACRISTIES AND
NICEROS' SCARY STORY (*SATYRICA* 60–62)

60.4 iam illic repositorium cum placentis aliquot erat positum, quod medium
Priapus a pistore factus tenebat, gremioque satis amplo omnis generis poma et
uvas sustinebat more vulgato. avidius ad pompam manus porreximus, et repente
nova ludorum commissio hilaritatem refecit. omnes enim placentae omniaque
poma etiam minima vexatione contacta coeperunt effundere crocum, et usque
ad os nobis molestus umor accidere. **60.7** rati ergo sacrum esse ferculum tam
religioso apparatu perfusum, consurreximus altius et "Augusto, patri patriae,
feliciter" diximus. quibusdam tamen etiam post hanc venerationem poma rapien-
tibus et ipsi mappas implevimus, ego praecipue, qui nullo satis amplo munere
putabam me onerare Gitonis sinum. . . .

61 postquam ergo omnes bonam mentem bonamque valitudinem sibi optarunt,
Trimalchio ad Nicerotem respexit et "solebas," inquit, "suavius esse in convictu;
nescio quid nunc taces nec muttis. oro te, sic felicem me videas, narra illud quod
tibi usu venit." Niceros delectatus affabilitate amici "omne me," inquit, "lucrum
transeat, nisi iam dudum gaudimonio dissilio, quod te talem video. **61.4** itaque
hilaria mera sint, etsi timeo istos scholasticos, ne me rideant. viderint: narrabo

tamen, quid enim mihi aufert, qui ridet? satius est rideri quam derideri." haec ubi dicta dedit, talem fabulam exorsus est:

61.6 "cum adhuc servirem, habitabamus in vico angusto; nunc Gavillae domus est. ibi, quomodo dii volunt, amare coepi uxorem Terentii coponis: noveratis Melissam Tarentinam, pulcherrimum bacciballum. sed ego non mehercules corporaliter illam aut propter res venerias curavi, sed magis quod benemoria fuit. **61.8** si quid ab illa petii, numquam mihi negatum. fecit assem, semissem habui; in illius sinum demandavi, nec umquam fefellitus sum. huius contubernalis ad villam supremum diem obiit. itaque per scutum per ocream egi aginavi, quemadmodum ad illam pervenirem: scitis autem in angustiis amici apparent. **62** forte dominus Capuae exierat ad scruta scita expedienda. nactus ego occasionem persuadeo hospitem nostrum ut mecum ad quintum miliarium veniat. erat autem miles, fortis tamquam Orcus. apoculamus nos circa gallicinia, luna lucebat tamquam meridie. venimus inter monimenta: homo meus coepit ad stelas facere, sed ego pergo cantabundus et stelas numero. **62.5** deinde ut respexi ad comitem, ille exuit se et omnia vestimenta secundum viam posuit. mihi anima in naso esse, stabam tamquam mortuus. at ille circumminxit vestimenta sua, et subito lupus factus est. nolite me iocari putare; ut mentiar, nullius patrimonium tanti facio. sed, quod coeperam dicere, postquam lupus factus est, ululare coepit et in silvas fugit. ego primitus nesciebam ubi essem, deinde accessi, ut vestimenta eius tollerem: illa autem lapidea facta sunt. qui mori timore nisi ego? **62.9** gladium tamen strinxi et matauitatau umbras cecidi, donec ad villam amicae meae pervenirem. in larvam intravi, paene animam ebullivi, sudor mihi per bifurcum volabat, oculi mortui, vix umquam refectus sum. Melissa mea mirari coepit, quod tam sero ambularem, et 'si ante,' inquit, 'venisses, saltem nobis adiutasses; lupus enim villam intravit et omnia pecora * tamquam lanius sanguinem illis misit. nec tamen derisit, etiam si fugit; servus enim noster lancea collum eius traiecit.'

62.12 haec ut audivi, operire oculos amplius non potui, sed luce clara domum fugi tamquam copo compilatus, et postquam veni in illum locum, in quo lapidea vestimenta erant facta, nihil inveni nisi sanguinem. ut vero domum veni, iacebat miles meus in lecto tamquam bovis, et collum illius medicus curabat. intellexi illum versipellem esse, nec postea cum illo panem gustare potui, non si me occidisses. viderint alii quid de hoc exopinissent; ego si mentior, genios vestros iratos habeam."

FIG. 17. Street of Tombs, Pompeii. From Pierre Gusman, *Pompei: The City, Its Life and Art*, translated by Florence Simmonds and M. Jourdain (W. Heinemann, 1900), 53.

CHAPTER SEVEN: CROESUS AND HABINNAS
(*SATYRICA* 64–65, 67)

64.5 nec non Trimalchio ipse cum tubicines esset imitatus, ad delicias suas respexit, quem Croesum appellabat. puer autem lippus, sordidissimis dentibus, catellam nigram atque indecenter pinguem prasina involvebat fascia panemque semesum ponebat supra torum ac nausea recusantem saginabat. **64.7** quo admonitus officio Trimalchio Scylacem iussit adduci "praesidium domus familiaeque." nec mora, ingentis formae adductus est canis catena vinctus, admonitusque ostiarii calce ut cubaret, ante mensam se posuit. tum Trimalchio iactans candidum panem "nemo," inquit, "in domo mea me plus amat." **64.9** indignatus puer, quod Scylacem tam effuse laudaret, catellam in terram deposuit hortatusque est ut ad rixam properaret. Scylax, canino scilicet usus ingenio, taeterrimo latratu triclinium implevit Margaritamque Croesi paene laceravit. nec intra rixam tumultus constitit, sed candelabrum etiam supra mensam eversum et vasa omnia crystallina comminuit et oleo ferventi aliquot convivas respersit. Trimalchio, ne videretur iactura motus, basiavit puerum ac iussit supra dorsum ascendere suum. non moratus ille usus est equo. . . .

FIG. 18. *Candēlābrum.* From Pierre Gusman, *Pompei: The City, Its Life and Art*, translated by Florence Simmonds and M. Jourdain (W. Heinemann, 1900), 302.

FIG. 19. *Scyphus.* From Pierre Gusman, *Pompei: The City, Its Life and Art*, translated by Florence Simmonds and M. Jourdain (W. Heinemann, 1900), 407.

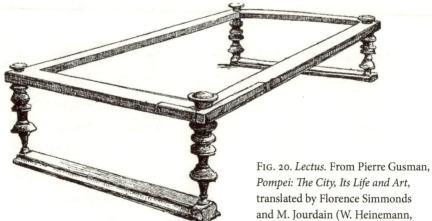

FIG. 20. *Lectus.* From Pierre Gusman, *Pompei: The City, Its Life and Art,* translated by Florence Simmonds and M. Jourdain (W. Heinemann, 1900), 294.

FIG. 21. *Mēnsa.* From Pierre Gusman, *Pompei: The City, Its Life and Art,* translated by Florence Simmonds and M. Jourdain (W. Heinemann, 1900), 396.

65.3 inter haec triclinii valvas lictor percussit, amictusque veste alba cum ingenti frequentia comissator intravit. ego maiestate conterritus praetorem putabam venisse. itaque temptavi assurgere et nudos pedes in terram deferre. risit hanc trepidationem Agamemnon et "contine te," inquit, "homo stultissime. Habinnas sevir est idemque lapidarius, qui videtur monumenta optime facere."

65.6 recreatus hoc sermone reposui cubitum, Habinnamque intrantem cum admiratione ingenti spectabam. ille autem iam ebrius uxoris suae umeris imposuerat manus, oneratusque aliquot coronis et unguento per frontem in oculos fluente, praetorio loco se posuit continuoque vinum et caldam poposcit. **65.8** delectatus hac Trimalchio hilaritate et ipse capaciorem poposcit scyphum quaesivitque quomodo acceptus esset. "omnia," inquit, "habuimus praeter te; oculi enim mei hic erant. et mehercules bene fuit. Scissa lautum novendiale servo suo misello faciebat, quem mortuum manu miserat. et, puto, cum vicensimariis magnam mantissam habet; quinquaginta enim millibus aestimant mortuum. sed tamen suaviter fuit, etiam si coacti sumus dimidias potiones supra ossucula eius effundere." **66** "tamen," inquit Trimalchio, "quid habuistis in cena?" "dicam," inquit, "si potuero; nam tam bonae memoriae sum, ut frequenter nomen meum obliviscar. habuimus tamen in primo porcum botulo coronatum et circa sangunculum et gizeria optime facta et certe betam et panem autopyrum de suo sibi, quem ego malo quam candidum; et vires facit, et cum mea re causa facio, non ploro. **66.3** sequens ferculum fuit scriblita frigida et supra mel caldum infusum excellente Hispanum. itaque de scriblita quidem non minimum edi, de melle me usque tetigi. circa cicer et lupinum, calvae arbitratu et mala singula. ego tamen duo sustuli et ecce in mappa alligata habeo; nam si aliquid muneris meo vernulae non tulero, habebo convicium. bene me admonet domina mea. **66.5** in prospectu habuimus ursinae frustum, de quo cum imprudens Scintilla gustasset, paene intestina sua vomuit; ego contra plus libram comedi, nam ipsum aprum sapiebat. et si, inquam, ursus homuncionem comest, quanto magis homuncio debet ursum comesse?" . . .

67 "sed narra mihi, Gai, rogo, Fortunata quare non recumbit?" "quomodo nosti," inquit, "illam," Trimalchio, "nisi argentum composuerit, nisi reliquias pueris diviserit, aquam in os suum non coniciet." "atqui," respondit Habinnas, "nisi illa discumbit, ego me apoculo." et coeperat surgere, nisi signo dato Fortunata quater amplius a tota familia esset vocata. **67.4** venit ergo galbino succincta cingillo, ita ut infra cerasina appareret tunica et periscelides tortae phaecasiaeque inauratae. tunc sudario manus tergens, quod in collo habebat, applicat se illi toro, in quo Scintilla Habinnae discumbebat uxor, osculataque plaudentem: "est te," inquit, "videre?" . . .

67.11 interim mulieres sauciae inter se riserunt ebriaeque iunxerunt oscula, dum altera diligentiam matris familiae iactat, altera delicias et indiligentiam viri. dumque sic cohaerent, Habinnas furtim consurrexit pedesque Fortunatae correptos super lectum immisit. "au au" illa proclamavit aberrante tunica super genua. composita ergo in gremio Scintillae incensissimam rubore faciem sudario abscondit.

CHAPTER EIGHT: SOME ENTERTAINMENT; TRIMALCHIO'S SLAVES, WILL, AND TOMB (*SATYRICA* 68–69, 70–71)

68.3 interim puer Alexandrinus, qui caldam ministrabat, luscinias coepit imitari clamante Trimalchione subinde: "muta." ecce alius ludus. servus qui ad pedes Habinnae sedebat, iussus, credo, a domino suo proclamavit subito canora voce:

"interea medium Aeneas iam classe tenebat."

nullus sonus umquam acidior percussit aures meas; nam praeter errantis barbariae aut adiectum aut deminutum clamorem miscebat Atellanicos versus, ut tunc primum me etiam Vergilius offenderit. **68.6** lassus tamen cum aliquando desisset, adiecit Habinnas: "et numquam," inquit, "didicit, sed ego ad circulatores eum mittendo erudibam. itaque parem non habet, sive muliones volet sive circulatores imitari. desperatum valde ingeniosus est: idem sutor est, idem cocus, idem pistor, omnis Musae mancipium. duo tamen vitia habet, quae si non haberet, esset omnium numerum: recutitus est et stertit. nam quod strabonus est, non curo: sicut Venus spectat. ideo nihil tacet, vix oculo mortuo umquam. illum emi trecentis denariis." **69** interpellavit loquentem Scintilla et "plane," inquit, "non omnia artificia servi nequam narras. agaga est; at curabo, stigmam habeat." risit Trimalchio et "adcognosco," inquit, "Cappadocem: nihil sibi defraudat, et mehercules laudo illum; hoc enim nemo parentat. tu autem, Scintilla, noli zelotypa esse. crede mihi, et vos novimus. **69.3** sic me salvum habeatis, ut ego sic solebam ipsumam meam debattuere, ut etiam dominus suspicaretur; et ideo me in vilicationem relegavit. sed tace, lingua, dabo panem." tamquam laudatus esset nequissimus servus, lucernam de sinu fictilem protulit et amplius semihora tubicines imitatus est succinente Habinna et inferius labrum manu deprimente. **69.5** ultimo etiam in medium processit et modo harundinibus quassis choraulas imitatus est, modo lacernatus cum flagello mulionum fata egit, donec vocatum ad se Habinnas basiavit, potionemque illi porrexit et "tanto melior," inquit, "Massa, dono tibi caligas." nec ullus tot malorum finis fuisset, nisi epidipnis esset allata. . . .

70.10 iam coeperat Fortunata velle saltare, iam Scintilla frequentius plaudebat quam loquebatur, cum Trimalchio "permitto," inquit, "Philargyre, etsi prasinianus es famosus, dic et Menophilae, contubernali tuae, discumbat." quid multa? paene de lectis deiecti sumus, adeo totum triclinium familia occupaverat. **70.12** certe ego notavi super me positum cocum, qui de porco anserem fecerat, muria condimentisque fetentem. nec contentus fuit recumbere, sed continuo Ephesum tragoedum coepit imitari et subinde dominum suum sponsione provocare "si prasinus proximis circensibus primam palmam."

71 diffusus hac contentione Trimalchio "amici," inquit, "et servi homines sunt et aeque unum lactem biberunt, etiam si illos malus fatus oppresserit. tamen me salvo cito aquam liberam gustabunt. ad summam, omnes illos in testamento meo manu mitto. Philargyro etiam fundum lego et contubernalem suam, Carioni quoque insulam et vicesimam et lectum stratum. **71.3** nam Fortunatam meam heredem facio, et commendo illam omnibus amicis meis. et haec ideo omnia publico, ut familia mea iam nunc sic me amet tamquam mortuum." gratias agere omnes indulgentiae coeperant domini, cum ille oblitus nugarum exemplar testamenti iussit afferri et totum a primo ad ultimum ingemescente familia recitavit. **71.5** respiciens deinde Habinnam "quid dicis," inquit, "amice carissime? aedificas monumentum meum quemadmodum te iussi? valde te rogo, ut secundum pedes statuae meae catellam fingas et coronas et unguenta et Petraitis omnes pugnas, ut mihi contingat tuo beneficio post mortem vivere; praeterea ut sint in fronte pedes centum, in agrum pedes ducenti. **71.7** omne genus enim poma volo sint circa cineres meos, et vinearum largiter. valde enim falsum est vivo quidem domos cultas esse, non curari eas, ubi diutius nobis habitandum est. et ideo ante omnia adici volo: 'hoc monumentum heredem non sequatur.' ceterum erit mihi curae, ut testamento caveam ne mortuus iniuriam accipiam. praeponam enim unum ex libertis sepulchro meo custodiae causa, ne in monumentum meum populus cacatum currat. **71.9** te rogo, ut naves etiam facias plenis velis euntes, et me in tribunali sedentem praetextatum cum anulis aureis quinque et nummos in publico de sacculo effundentem; scis enim, quod epulum dedi binos denarios. faciantur, si tibi videtur, et triclinia. facias et totum populum sibi suaviter facientem. **71.11** ad dexteram meam pones statuam Fortunatae meae columbam tenentem: et catellam cingulo alligatam ducat: et cicaronem meum, et amphoras copiosas gypsatas, ne effluant vinum. et unam licet fractam sculpas, et super eam puerum plorantem. horologium in medio, ut quisquis horas inspiciet, velit nolit, nomen meum legat. **71.12** inscriptio quoque, vide diligenter, si haec satis idonea tibi videtur: 'C. Pompeius Trimalchio Maecenatianus hic requiescit. huic seviratus absenti decretus est. cum posset in omnibus decuriis Romae esse, tamen noluit. pius, fortis, fidelis, ex parvo crevit; sestertium reliquit trecenties, nec umquam philosophum audivit. vale: et tu.'"

Tombs

FIG. 22. Street of Tombs, Pompeii. Postcard.

Tombs lined the streets flowing in and out of towns, since the Romans did not bury their dead within the sacred boundary of a city. The old postcard in figure 22 shows Pompeii's "Street of Tombs." Most of the monuments here are topped with a large block encased in marble and carved with images and words about the deceased. For some tombs, the large structure supporting this block features a doorway leading into underground chambers for graves and niches for ash urns. The engravings in figures 23 and 24 show these tombs from the street and what they looked like inside. Both inhumation and cremation were practiced in Roman culture, and they might both be seen within the same family complex. Many monuments were designed to serve a generation, with provision for members of the immediate family and their former slaves.

FIG. 23. Engraving of
a street scene with
tombs, Pompeii. From
Sir William Gell and
John P. Gandy,
*Pompeiana: The
Topography, Edifices
and Ornaments of
Pompeii* (Jennings
and Chapman,
1817–19), plate VII.

FIG. 24. Interior of the
altar tomb of Tyche,
Pompeii. From Henry
Thédenat, *Pompéi:
Histoire—Vie privée*
(H. Laurens, 1906),
154, figure 119.

Whole cities of the dead thus lived right outside the city gates and extended
along the road far into the countryside. The conceit of Trimalchio's epitaph that
it is chatting with a passerby is not unusual—someone walking along the road
would be a tomb's most frequent reader. We also have examples in Pompeii of the
incorporated bench that Trimalchio describes, such as the tomb of Mamia in
figure 25. The inscription runs in large block letters around the top of the seat:

MAMIAE P F SACERDOTI PUBLICAE LOCUS SEPULTUR
DATUS DECURIONUM DECRETO
TO MAMIA, DAUGHTER OF PUBLIUS, PUBLIC PRIESTESS,
[THIS] PLACE OF BURIAL WAS GIVEN BY DECREE OF THE TOWN COUNCIL

FIG. 25. The tomb of Mamia. From Pierre Gusman, *Pompei: The City, Its Life and Art,* translated by Florence Simmonds and M. Jourdain (W. Heinemann, 1900), 45.

FIG. 26. Funerary *triclinium,* Pompeii. From Pierre Gusman, *Pompei: The City, Its Life and Art,* translated by Florence Simmonds and M. Jourdain (W. Heinemann, 1900), 49.

Some tombs provided space for banquets, such as the monument in figure 26, which was built by the freedman Callistus for his former master. In addition to the funeral itself, feasts might be held here during the *Parentalia,* a holiday in February, and families also gathered to commemorate anniversaries of the deaths of loved ones.

FIG. 27. The tomb of
Tyche, Pompeii.
From Pierre Gusman,
Pompei: *The City,
Its Life and Art*,
translated by Florence
Simmonds and
M. Jourdain
(W. Heinemann,
1900), 48.

FIG. 28. Engraving of gladiator scenes from the tomb of Scaurus, Pompeii. From Pierre Gusman, *Pompei: The City, Its Life and Art*, translated by Florence Simmonds and M. Jourdain (W. Heinemann, 1900), 161.

We see incredible variation in tomb design; the decoration might include painting, columns, statues, inscriptions, and reliefs. In Pompeii alone, we find images of ships, insignia of offices, scenes of public benefaction or banqueting, and portrait busts and statues; one magistrate even had scenes from the gladiatorial games he provided memorialized in stucco on his final resting place (sketched in figures 23 and 28). The elements of Trimalchio's imagined tomb are well documented in our material evidence.

CHAPTER NINE: AN EPIC RESCUE, THE GREAT ESCAPE, AND A BETRAYAL (*SATYRICA* 72–73, 77–80)

72.2 Trimalchio "ergo," inquit, "cum sciamus nos morituros esse, quare non vivamus? sic nos felices videam, coniciamus nos in balneum, meo periculo, non paenitebit. sic calet tamquam furnus." "vero, vero," inquit Habinnas, "de una die duas facere, nihil malo" nudisque consurrexit pedibus et Trimalchionem gaudentem subsequi coepit.

72.5 ego respiciens ad Ascylton "quid cogitas?" inquam, "ego enim si videro balneum, statim expirabo." "assentemur," ait ille, "et dum illi balneum petunt, nos in turba exeamus." cum haec placuissent, ducente per porticum Gitone ad ianuam venimus, ubi canis catenarius tanto nos tumultu excepit, ut Ascyltos etiam in piscinam ceciderit. nec non ego quoque ebrius, et qui etiam pictum timueram canem, dum natanti opem fero, in eundem gurgitem tractus sum. **72.8** servavit nos tamen atriensis, qui interventu suo et canem placavit et nos trementes extraxit in siccum. et Giton quidem iam dudum se ratione acutissima redemerat a cane; quicquid enim a nobis acceperat de cena, latranti sparserat, et ille avocatus cibo furorem suppresserat. **72.10** ceterum cum algentes udique petissemus ab atriense ut nos extra ianuam emitteret "erras," inquit, "si putas te exire hac posse, qua venisti. nemo umquam convivarum per eandem ianuam emissus est; alia intrant, alia exeunt." **73** quid faciamus homines miserrimi et novi generis labyrintho inclusi, quibus lavari iam coeperat votum esse? . . .

77.7 "interim, Stiche, profer vitalia, in quibus volo me efferri. profer et unguentum et ex illa amphora gustum, ex qua iubeo lavari ossa mea." **78** non est moratus Stichus, sed et stragulam albam et praetextam in triclinium attulit. * iussitque nos temptare, an bonis lanis essent confecta. tum subridens "vide tu," inquit, "Stiche, ne ista mures tangant aut tineae; alioquin te vivum comburam. ego gloriosus volo efferri, ut totus mihi populus bene imprecetur." **78.3** statim ampullam nardi aperuit omnesque nos unxit et "spero," inquit, "futurum ut aeque me mortuum iuvet tamquam vivum." nam vinum quidem in vinarium iussit infundi et "putate vos," ait, "ad parentalia mea invitatos esse."

78.5 ibat res ad summam nauseam, cum Trimalchio ebrietate turpissima gravis novum acroama, cornicines, in triclinium iussit adduci, fultusque cervicalibus multis extendit se supra torum extremum et "fingite me," inquit, "mortuum esse. dicite aliquid belli." consonuere cornicines funebri strepitu. unus praecipue servus libitinarii illius, qui inter hos honestissimus erat, tam valde intonuit, ut totam concitaret viciniam. **78.7** itaque vigiles, qui custodiebant vicinam regionem, rati ardere Trimalchionis domum, effregerunt ianuam subito et cum aqua securibusque tumultuari suo iure coeperunt. nos occasionem opportunissimam nacti Agamemnoni verba dedimus raptimque tam plane quam ex incendio fugimus. ***

79 neque fax ulla in praesidio erat, quae iter aperiret errantibus, nec silentium noctis iam mediae promittebat occurrentium lumen. accedebat huc ebrietas et imprudentia locorum etiam interdiu obfutura. itaque cum hora paene tota per omnes scrupos gastrarumque eminentium fragmenta traxissemus cruentos pedes, tandem expliciti acumine Gitonis sumus. **79.4** prudens enim puer, cum luce etiam clara timeret errorem, omnes pilas columnasque notaverat creta, quae lineamenta evicerunt spississimam noctem et notabili candore ostenderunt errantibus viam. . . .***

79.9 sine causa gratulor mihi. nam cum solutus mero remisissem ebrias manus, Ascyltos, omnis iniuriae inventor, subduxit mihi nocte puerum et in lectum transtulit suum, volutatusque liberius cum fratre non suo, sive non sentiente iniuriam sive dissimulante, indormivit alienis amplexibus oblitus iuris humani. **79.10** itaque ego ut experrectus pertrectavi gaudio despoliatum torum * si qua est amantibus fides, ego dubitavi an utrumque traicerem gladio somnumque morti iungerem. tutius dein secutus consilium Gitona quidem verberibus excitavi, Ascylton autem truci intuens vultu "quoniam," inquam, "fidem scelere violasti et communem amicitiam, res tuas ocius tolle et alium locum quem polluas quaere."

79.12 non repugnavit ille, sed postquam optima fide partiti manubias sumus "age," inquit, "nunc et puerum dividamus." **80** iocari putabam discedentem. at ille gladium parricidali manu strinxit et "non frueris," inquit, "hac praeda, super quam solus incumbis. partem meam necesse est vel hoc gladio contemptus abscidam." idem ego ex altera parte feci, et intorto circa bracchium pallio, composui ad proeliandum gradum. **80.3** inter hanc miserorum dementiam infelicissimus puer tangebat utriusque genua cum fletu, petebatque suppliciter ne Thebanum par humilis taberna spectaret neve sanguine mutuo pollueremus familiaritatis clarissimae sacra. "quod si utique," proclamabat, "facinore opus est, nudo ecce iugulum, convertite huc manus, imprimite mucrones. ego mori debeo, qui amicitiae sacramentum delevi."

The *Atrium* House

The word *domus* denotes an urban house rather than an apartment or a country house (*villa*). The entryway (*ianua*) on the street usually led down a narrow corridor into the main hall or *atrium*, onto which other rooms opened. The roofing over the *atrium* was open in the center to allow light and air into the house. We often find a small pool or *impluvium* in the center of the *atrium*, which was used to catch rain. In larger houses, a garden was enclosed in the rear of the house. Sometimes more rooms opened onto this space, which could be made more formal by surrounding it with a covered colonnade. Due to the circle of columns, this space was referred to as the *peristylum* or peristyle: "columns around" in Greek. From the outside, the house feels closed off, with one entrance and few windows—the *domus* focuses inward.

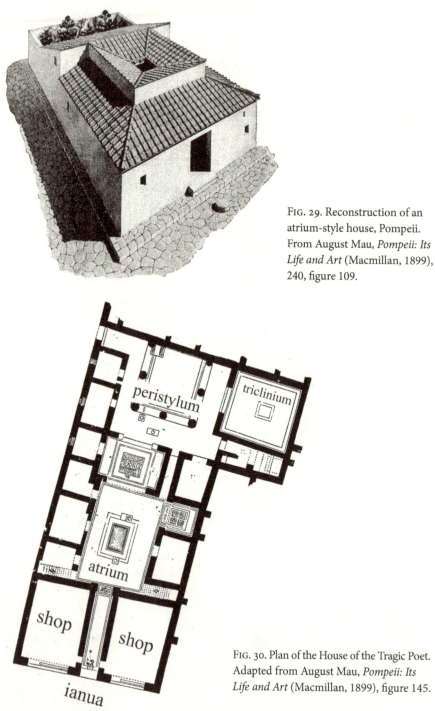

FIG. 29. Reconstruction of an atrium-style house, Pompeii. From August Mau, *Pompeii: Its Life and Art* (Macmillan, 1899), 240, figure 109.

FIG. 30. Plan of the House of the Tragic Poet. Adapted from August Mau, *Pompeii: Its Life and Art* (Macmillan, 1899), figure 145.

FIG. 31. Reconstruction of the interior of the House of the Tragic Poet, Pompeii. From Thédenat, *Pompéi: Histoire—Vie privée* (H. Laurens, 1906), 97, figure 63.

The plan and reconstruction in figures 30 and 31 show the House of the Tragic Poet in Pompeii. The famous mosaic of the dog with the words *Cave Canem* comes from the long entrance hall to this house. Note that once you are inside the *atrium*, as you are in the reconstruction, you can see all the way through to the very back of the *peristylum*. While not among the largest homes in town, the House of the Tragic Poet has a classic structure and was finely decorated.

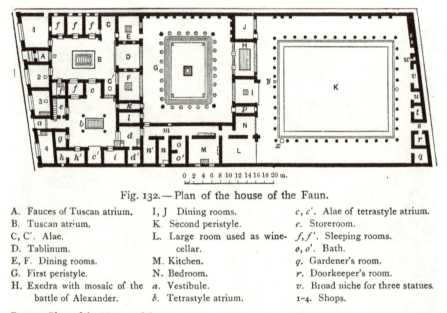

0 2 4 6 8 10 12 14 16 18 20 m.

Fig. 132. — Plan of the house of the Faun.

A. Fauces of Tuscan atrium.
B. Tuscan atrium.
C, C'. Alae.
D. Tablinum.
E, F. Dining rooms.
G. First peristyle.
H. Exedra with mosaic of the battle of Alexander.
I, J Dining rooms.
K. Second peristyle.
L. Large room used as wine-cellar.
M. Kitchen.
N. Bedroom.
a. Vestibule.
b. Tetrastyle atrium.
c, c'. Alae of tetrastyle atrium.
e. Storeroom.
f, f'. Sleeping rooms.
o, o'. Bath.
q. Gardener's room.
r. Doorkeeper's room.
v. Broad niche for three statues.
1–4. Shops.

FIG. 32. Plan of the House of the Faun, Pompeii. From August Mau, *Pompeii: Its Life and Art* (Macmillan, 1899), 282, figure 132.

Variations on this most basic arrangement are found across Pompeii. In larger houses, the rooms were larger only to a certain extent before they became unable to be roofed. So in the largest houses we find instead multiplications of the *atrium/peristylum* complex. How many of them can you identify in the largest house in town, the House of the Faun, in figure 32?

FIG. 33. Doorway to the House of the Faun, Pompeii. From Pierre Gusman, *Pompei: The City, Its Life and Art*, translated by Florence Simmonds and M. Jourdain (W. Heinemann, 1900), 289.

In plan, such a house is not dissimilar to a labyrinth, and much as with food and banquets, excessive architecture was a frequent target of Roman moralists, including Petronius' contemporary and rival Seneca the Younger. But it is unclear that this is what Petronius is getting at when his heroes have difficulty escaping Trimalchio's house. Although the House of the Faun had a small back gate for servants from the stables in the large rear garden, it very clearly had one impressive main entrance from a major street, like other large homes, as we can see from the engraving looking through the doorway in figure 33. When the slave tells Encolpius that no one leaves Trimalchio's house the way they enter, some scholars read this as a reference to Aeneas' trip to the underworld in the *Aeneid*—in book 6, the hero needs a guide to get him into Hades, and a guide to get him out a different way. Finally, even though baths were on the whole a type of public building, some homes, like this one, did provide private, heated bathing facilities.

CHAPTER TEN: ENCOLPIUS' LAMENT;
EUMOLPUS BEGINS HIS TALES OF SEDUCTION
(*SATYRICA* 80–82, 85–86)

80.5 inhibuimus ferrum post has preces, et prior Ascyltos "ego," inquit, "finem discordiae imponam. puer ipse quem vult sequatur, ut sit illi saltem in eligendo fratre libertas." ego qui vetustissimam consuetudinem putabam in sanguinis pignus transisse, nihil timui, immo condicionem praecipiti festinatione rapui commisique iudici litem. qui ne deliberavit quidem, ut videretur cunctatus, verum statim ab extrema parte verbi consurrexit et fratrem Ascylton elegit. . . .

81 nec diu tamen lacrimis indulsi, sed veritus ne Menelaus etiam antescholanus inter cetera mala solum me in deversorio inveniret, collegi sarcinulas, locumque secretum et proximum litori maestus conduxi. ibi triduo inclusus, redeunte in animum solitudine atque contemptu verberabam aegrum planctibus pectus et inter tot altissimos gemitus frequenter etiam proclamabam "ergo me non ruina terra potuit haurire? non iratum etiam innocentibus mare? effugi iudicium, harenae imposui, hospitem occidi, ut inter tot audaciae nomina mendicus, exul, in deversorio Graecae urbis iacerem desertus? et quis hanc mihi solitudinem imposuit? **81.4** adulescens omni libidine impurus et sua quoque confessione dignus exilio, stupro liber, stupro ingenuus, cuius anni ad tesseram venierunt, quem tamquam puellam conduxit etiam qui virum putavit. quid ille alter? qui die togae virilis stolam sumpsit, qui ne vir esset a matre persuasus est, qui opus muliebre in ergastulo fecit, qui postquam conturbavit et libidinis suae solum vertit, reliquit veteris amicitiae nomen et, pro pudor, tamquam mulier secutuleia unius noctis tactu omnia vendidit. iacent nunc amatores adligati noctibus totis, et forsitan mutuis libidinibus attriti derident solitudinem meam. sed non impune. nam aut vir ego liberque non sum, aut noxio sanguine parentabo iniuriae meae."

82 haec locutus gladio latus cingor, et ne infirmitas militiam perderet, largioribus cibis excito vires. mox in publicum prosilio furentisque more omnes circumeo porticus. sed dum attonito vultu efferatoque nihil aliud quam caedem et sanguinem cogito frequentiusque manum ad capulum, quem devoveram, refero, notavit me miles, sive ille planus fuit sive nocturnus grassator, et "quid tu," inquit, "commilito, ex qua legione es aut cuius centuria?" cum constantissime et centurionem et legionem essem ementitus, "age ergo," inquit ille, "in exercitu vestro phaecasiati milites ambulant?" cum deinde vultu atque ipsa trepidatione mendacium prodidissem, ponere iussit arma et malo cavere. . . .

85 *** "in Asiam cum a quaestore essem stipendio eductus, hospitium Pergami accepi. ubi cum libenter habitarem non solum propter cultum aedicularum, sed etiam propter hospitis formosissimum filium, excogitavi rationem, qua non essem patri familiae suspectus. quotiescumque enim in convivio de usu formosorum mentio facta est, tam vehementer excandui, tam severa tristitia violari aures meas obsceno sermone nolui, ut me mater praecipue tamquam unum ex philosophis intueretur. iam ego coeperam ephebum in gymnasium deducere, ego studia eius ordinare, ego docere ac praecipere, ne quis praedator corporis admitteretur in domum. ***

85.4 "forte cum in triclinio iaceremus, quia dies sollemnis ludum artaverat pigritiamque recedendi imposuerat hilaritas longior, fere circa mediam noctem intellexi puerum vigilare. itaque timidissimo murmure votum feci et 'domina,' inquam, 'Venus, si ego hunc puerum basiavero ita ut ille non sentiat, cras illi par columbarum donabo.' audito voluptatis pretio puer stertere coepit. itaque aggressus simulantem aliquot basiolis invasi. contentus hoc principio bene mane surrexi electumque par columbarum attuli expectanti ac me voto exsolvi. **86** proxima nocte cum idem liceret, mutavi optionem et 'si hunc,' inquam, 'tractavero improba manu, et ille non senserit, gallos gallinaceos pugnacissimos duos donabo patienti.'

ad hoc votum ephebus ultro se admovit et, puto, vereri coepit ne ego obdormissem. indulsi ergo sollicito, totoque corpore citra summam voluptatem me ingurgitavi. deinde ut dies venit, attuli gaudenti quicquid promiseram. ut tertia nox licentiam dedit, consurrexi * ad aurem male dormientis 'dii,' inquam, 'immortales, si ego huic dormienti abstulero coitum plenum et optabilem, pro hac felicitate cras puero asturconem Macedonicum optimum donabo, cum hac tamen exceptione, si ille non senserit.' **86.5** numquam altiore somno ephebus obdormivit. itaque primum implevi lactentibus papillis manus, mox basio inhaesi, deinde in unum omnia vota coniunxi. mane sedere in cubiculo coepit atque expectare consuetudinem meam. scis quanto facilius sit columbas gallosque gallinaceos emere quam asturconem, et praeter hoc etiam timebam ne tam grande munus suspectam faceret humanitatem meam. ergo aliquot horis spatiatus in hospitium reverti nihilque aliud quam puerum basiavi. at ille circumspiciens ut cervicem meam iunxit amplexu, 'rogo,' inquit, 'domine, ubi est asturco?'"

The *Porticus*

Fig. 34. Reconstruction of the Forum of Pompeii. From Henry Thédenat, *Pompeii: Vie publique* (Paris, 1906), 42.

To refer to a covered, colonnaded walkway, the Romans used the term *porticus*, an ancestor of the English word *porch*. Often, the term more specifically denoted a courtyard enclosed by such colonnades on all four sides. The columns give a dramatic backdrop to public buildings inside, such as the Temple of Jupiter in the forum of Pompeii reconstructed in figure 34. Providing shade in the Italian summers and cover from the rain, porticos were a prominent feature of public spaces and buildings across the Roman world. This engraving of a painting from Pompeii shows a scene of the forum. Merchants sell their wares in the central open space, and the colonnade surrounding the forum can be seen in the background.

FIG. 35. Pompeii forum scene. Engraving based on an ancient painting. From Henry Thédenat, *Pompeii: Vie publique* (Paris, 1906), 28.

In addition to enclosing markets and temple precincts, porticos are often associated with theaters. We can see this in the city of Rome, where all three permanent theaters are associated with a large portico, on down to the simple town of Pompeii, shown in figure 36. The open courtyard behind the large theater provided space for strolling before or after a performance, and the covered porches were a good place to seek shelter in the event of rain.

FIG. 36. The Theater
District, Pompeii.
From Pierre Gusman,
*Pompei: The City, Its
Life and Art*, translated
by Florence Simmonds
and M. Jourdain
(W. Heinemann,
1900), 28.

The covered interior walls of a portico were often decorated, and many porticos housed art collections. A good example is the *porticus* shown in plan and reconstructed in figures 37 and 38, the *Porticus Octaviae*. This earlier Republican monument was restored and enhanced by the first emperor's sister, Octavia, in Rome around 25 BCE. The portico abuts the Theater of Marcellus, named in honor of Octavia's son, and surrounds two old Republican temples to Jupiter and Juno. Octavia is said to have dedicated a school, library, and meeting space for the senate inside it, as well as several pieces of art, including sculptures by the famous Greek artists Phidias and Praxiteles and a statue of Cornelia, the mother of the Gracchi. The monumental entranceway to the *Porticus Octaviae* is shown reconstructed in figure 37 and is still prominent in the cityscape of modern Rome. Encolpius meets Eumolpus in a temple portico while he is engrossed in its mythological paintings, and later he notes his position in the public spaces of a town by saying that he is wandering through a *porticus*.

FIG. 37. Reconstruction of the entrance to the Porticus Octaviae. From S. B. Platner, *The Topography and Monuments of Ancient Rome*, 2nd ed. (Allyn and Bacon, 1911), 372, figure 76.

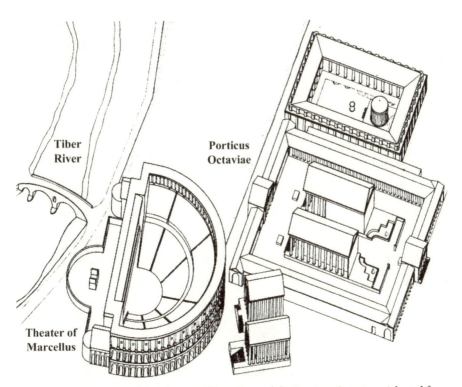

FIG. 38. Reconstruction of the Theater of Marcellus and the Porticus Octaviae. Adapted from John E. Stambaugh, *The Ancient Roman City* (Johns Hopkins University Press, 1988), 58, figure 4.

CHAPTER ELEVEN: MORE SEDUCTION;
GITON PLAYS ULYSSES; EUMOLPUS' TALE OF THE WIDOW
(*SATYRICA* 87, 97–98, 110–111)

87 "cum ob hanc offensam praeclusissem mihi aditum quem feceram, iterum ad licentiam redii. interpositis enim paucis diebus, cum similis nos casus in eandem fortunam rettulisset, ut intellexi stertere patrem, rogare coepi ephebum ut reverteretur in gratiam mecum, id est ut pateretur satis fieri sibi, et cetera quae libido distenta dictat. at ille plane iratus nihil aliud dicebat nisi hoc: 'aut dormi, aut ego iam dicam patri.' **87.3** nihil est tam arduum, quod non improbitas extorqueat. dum dicit: 'patrem excitabo,' irrepsi tamen et male repugnanti gaudium extorsi. at ille non indelectatus nequitia mea, postquam diu questus est deceptum se et derisum traductumque inter condiscipulos, quibus iactasset censum meum, 'videris tamen,' inquit, 'non ero tui similis. si quid vis, fac iterum.' **87.6** ego vero deposita omni offensa cum puero in gratiam redii, ususque beneficio eius in somnum delapsus sum. sed non fuit contentus iteratione ephebus plenae maturitatis et annis ad patiendum gestientibus. itaque excitavit me sopitum et 'numquid vis?' inquit. et non plane iam molestum erat munus. utcumque igitur inter anhelitus sudoresque tritus, quod voluerat accepit, rursusque in somnum decidi gaudio lassus. **87.9** interposita minus hora pungere me manu coepit et dicere: 'quare non facimus?' tum ego totiens excitatus plane vehementer excandui et reddidi illi voces suas: 'aut dormi, aut ego iam patri dicam.'" . . . ***

97 intrat stabulum praeco cum servo publico aliaque sane non modica frequentia, facemque fumosam magis quam lucidam quassans haec proclamavit: "puer in balneo paulo ante aberravit, annorum circa XVI, crispus, mollis, formosus, nomine Giton. si quis eum reddere aut commonstrare voluerit, accipiet nummos mille." nec longe a praecone Ascyltos stabat amictus discoloria veste atque in lance argentea indicium et fidem praeferebat. **97.4** imperavi Gitoni ut raptim grabatum subiret annecteretque pedes et manus institis, quibus sponda culcitam ferebat, ac sic ut olim Ulixes pro arieti adhaesisset, extentus infra grabatum scrutantium eluderet manus. non est moratus Giton imperium, momentoque temporis inseruit vinculo manus et Ulixem astu simillimo vicit. ego ne suspicioni relinquerem locum, lectulum vestimentis implevi uniusque hominis vestigium ad corporis mei mensuram figuravi.

97.7 interim Ascyltos ut pererravit omnes cum viatore cellas, venit ad meam, et hoc quidem pleniorem spem concepit quo diligentius oppessulatas invenit fores. publicus vero servus insertans commissuris securem claustrorum firmitatem laxavit. **97.9** ego ad genua Ascylti procubui, et per memoriam amicitiae perque societatem miseriarum petii ut saltem ostenderet fratrem. immo ut fidem haberent fictae preces: "scio te," inquam, "Ascylte, ad occidendum me venisse. quo enim secures attulisti? itaque satia iracundiam tuam: praebeo ecce cervicem, funde sanguinem, quem sub praetextu quaestionis petisti." amolitur Ascyltos invidiam et se vero nihil aliud quam fugitivum suum dixit quaerere, nec mortem hominis concupisse supplicis, utique eius quem etiam post fatalem rixam habuisset carissimum. **98** at non servus publicus tam languide agit, sed raptam cauponi harundinem subter lectum mittit omniaque etiam foramina parietum scrutatur. subducebat Giton ab ictu corpus, et retento timidissime spiritu ipsos sciniphes ore tangebat. . . . **98.4** dum haec ego iam credenti persuadeo, Giton collectione spiritus plenus ter continuo ita sternutavit, ut grabatum concuteret. ad quem motum Eumolpus conversus salvere Gitona iubet. remota etiam culcita videt Ulixem, cui vel esuriens Cyclops potuisset parcere. . . .***

110.6 ceterum Eumolpos, et periclitantium advocatus et praesentis concordiae auctor, ne sileret sine fabulis hilaritas, multa in muliebrem levitatem coepit iactare: quam facile adamarent, quam cito etiam filiorum obliviscerentur, nullamque esse feminam tam pudicam, quae non peregrina libidine usque ad furorem averteretur. nec se tragoedias veteres curare aut nomina saeculis nota, sed rem sua memoria factam, quam expositurum se esse, si vellemus audire. conversis igitur omnium in se vultibus auribusque sic orsus est:

111 "matrona quaedam Ephesi tam notae erat pudicitiae, ut vicinarum quoque gentium feminas ad spectaculum sui evocaret. haec ergo cum virum extulisset, non contenta vulgari more funus passis prosequi crinibus aut nudatum pectus in conspectu frequentiae plangere, in conditorium etiam prosecuta est defunctum, positumque in hypogaeo Graeco more corpus custodire ac flere totis noctibus diebusque coepit. **111.3** sic afflictantem se ac mortem inedia persequentem non parentes potuerunt abducere, non propinqui; magistratus ultimo repulsi abierunt, complorataque singularis exempli femina ab omnibus quintum iam diem sine alimento trahebat. assidebat aegrae fidissima ancilla, simulque et lacrimas commodabat lugenti et quotienscumque defecerat positum in monumento lumen renovabat.

CHAPTER TWELVE: THE WIDOW RELENTS; EPISTOLARY ENCOUNTERS WITH CIRCE (*SATYRICA* 111–112, 129–130)

111.5 "una igitur in tota civitate fabula erat, solum illud affulsisse verum pudicitiae amorisque exemplum omnis ordinis homines confitebantur, cum interim imperator provinciae latrones iussit crucibus affigi secundum illam casulam, in qua recens cadaver matrona deflebat. proxima ergo nocte, cum miles, qui cruces asservabat, ne quis ad sepulturam corpus detraheret, notasset sibi lumen inter monumenta clarius fulgens et gemitum lugentis audisset, vitio gentis humanae concupiit scire quis aut quid faceret. descendit igitur in conditorium, visaque pulcherrima muliere primo quasi quodam monstro infernisque imaginibus turbatus substitit. **111.8** deinde ut et corpus iacentis conspexit et lacrimas consideravit faciemque unguibus sectam, ratus scilicet id quod erat, desiderium extincti non posse feminam pati, attulit in monumentum cenulam suam coepitque hortari lugentem ne perseveraret in dolore supervacuo ac nihil profuturo gemitu pectus diduceret: omnium eundem esse exitum et idem domicilium, et cetera quibus exulceratae mentes ad sanitatem revocantur. at illa ignota consolatione percussa laceravit vehementius pectus ruptosque crines super corpus iacentis imposuit.

111.10 "non recessit tamen miles, sed eadem exhortatione temptavit dare mulierculae cibum, donec ancilla, vini odore corrupta primum ipsa porrexit ad humanitatem invitantis victam manum, deinde refecta potione et cibo expugnare dominae pertinaciam coepit et 'quid proderit', inquit, 'hoc tibi, si soluta inedia fueris, si te vivam sepelieris, si antequam fata poscant, indemnatum spiritum effuderis?

id cinerem aut manes credis sentire sepultos?

Fig. 39. Norman Lindsay, "The Ephesian Matron." From Petronius, *The Satyricon*, translated by W. C. Firebaugh, following 258.

vis tu reviviscere? vis discusso muliebri errore, quam diu licuerit, lucis commodis frui? ipsum te iacentis corpus admonere debet ut vivas.' nemo invitus audit, cum cogitur aut cibum sumere aut vivere. itaque mulier aliquot dierum abstinentia sicca passa est frangi pertinaciam suam, nec minus avide replevit se cibo quam ancilla, quae prior victa est. 112 ceterum, scitis quid plerumque soleat temptare humanam satietatem. quibus blanditiis impetraverat miles ut matrona vellet vivere, isdem etiam pudicitiam eius aggressus est. nec deformis aut infacundus iuvenis castae videbatur, conciliante gratiam ancilla ac subinde dicente:

'placitone etiam pugnabis amori?'

quid diutius moror? ne hanc quidem partem corporis mulier abstinuit, victorque miles utrumque persuasit. 112.3 iacuerunt ergo una non tantum illa nocte qua nuptias fecerunt, sed postero etiam ac tertio die, praeclusis videlicet conditorii foribus, ut quisquis ex notis ignotisque ad monumentum venisset, putaret expirasse super corpus viri pudicissimam uxorem. ceterum delectatus miles et forma mulieris et secreto, quicquid boni per facultates poterat coemebat et prima statim nocte in monumentum ferebat. itaque unius cruciarii parentes ut viderunt laxatam custodiam, detraxere nocte pendentem supremoque mandaverunt officio. 112.6 at miles circumscriptus dum desidet, ut postero die vidit unam sine cadavere crucem, veritus supplicium, mulieri quid accidisset exponit: nec se expectaturum iudicis sententiam, sed gladio ius dicturum ignaviae suae. commodaret modo illa perituro locum et fatale conditorium commune familiari ac viro faceret. 112.7 mulier non minus misericors quam pudica 'nec istud,' inquit, 'dii sinant, ut eodem tempore duorum mihi carissimorum hominum duo funera spectem. malo mortuum impendere quam vivum occidere.' secundum hanc orationem iubet ex arca corpus mariti sui tolli atque illi quae vacabat cruci affigi. usus est miles ingenio prudentissimae feminae, posteroque die populus miratus est qua

ratione mortuus isset in crucem." . . .***

129.3 cubiculum autem meum Chrysis intravit codicillosque mihi dominae suae

reddidit, in quibus haec erant scripta: "Circe Polyaeno salutem. si libidinosa

essem, quererer decepta; nunc etiam languori tuo gratias ago. in umbra voluptatis

diutius lusi. quid tamen agas, quaero, et an tuis pedibus perveneris domum;

negant enim medici sine nervis homines ambulare posse. narrabo tibi, adule-

scens, paralysin cave. **129.6** numquam ego aegrum tam magno periculo vidi:

medius iam peristi. quod si idem frigus genua manusque temptaverit tuas, licet

ad tubicines mittas. quid ergo est? etiam si gravem iniuriam accepi, homini

tamen misero non invideo medicinam. si vis sanus esse, Gitonem relega. recipies,

inquam, nervos tuos, si triduo sine fratre dormieris. nam quod ad me attinet,

non timeo ne quis inveniatur cui minus placeam. nec speculum mihi nec fama

mentitur. vale, si potes."

129.10 ut intellexit Chrysis perlegisse me totum convicium, "solent" inquit "haec

fieri, et praecipue in hac civitate, in qua mulieres etiam lunam deducunt * itaque

huius quoque rei cura agetur. rescribe modo blandius dominae animumque eius

candida humanitate restitue. verum enim fatendum est: ex qua hora iniuriam

accepit, apud se non est." libenter quidem parui ancillae verbaque codicillis

talia imposui: **130** "Polyaenos Circae salutem. fateor me, domina, saepe peccasse;

nam et homo sum et adhuc iuvenis. numquam tamen ante hunc diem usque ad

mortem deliqui. habes confitentem reum: quicquid iusseris, merui. proditionem

feci, hominem occidi, templum violavi: in haec facinora quaere supplicium. sive

occidere placet, cum ferro meo venio, sive verberibus contenta es, curro nudus ad dominam. illud unum memento, non me sed instrumenta peccasse. paratus miles arma non habui. quis hoc turbaverit nescio. forsitan animus antecessit corporis moram, forsitan dum omnia concupisco, voluptatem tempore consumpsi. non invenio quod feci. paralysin tamen cavere iubes: tamquam ea maior fieri possit quae abstulit mihi per quod etiam te habere potui. summa tamen excusationis meae haec est: placebo tibi, si me culpam emendare permiseris."

Commentary

Here you will find information about words, phrases, and unusual constructions in the order in which they appear in the passages. Traditional section numbers are also given for ease of reference. Vocabulary words are included here if they occur only once or twice in the passages, do not have close English cognates or derivatives, have not yet appeared in vocabulary lists, and are unlikely to appear in an elementary Latin textbook. Vocabulary and other glosses are in general more generous in the first few chapters. The words that appear only in the *Satyrica* are also identified. When the given passage is the only instance in which this word is found in surviving Latin texts, it is marked with the technical term "hapax legomenon," Greek for "something said once." Words that recur in the novel but not in other texts are labeled "only in the *Satyrica*." Greek loan words are noted as well, since the interaction with Greek on multiple levels is an important feature of the novel.

Some allusions to other literary works are noted, as well as cultural resonances of some terms. These are meant to be suggestive rather than exhaustive. Readers interested in more can now consult the magnum opus of Gareth Schmeling, *A Commentary on the* Satyrica *of Petronius* (Oxford University Press, 2011).

CHAPTER ONE: *SATYRICA* 26–28

Since the beginning of the *Satyrica* is lost, what has happened up to this point in the story is rather unclear. The narrator, Encolpius, presents three men traveling together: Encolpius himself; his young lover, Giton; and their companion, Ascyltos. There is an incident concerning a cloak into which they had previously sewn gold coins but lost. Encolpius and Ascyltos have been taking rhetoric lessons from a teacher named Agamemnon. And our heroes seem to have witnessed rituals in honor of the god Priapus that they should not have, and are punished for this by a priestess at a bawdy banquet. Somewhere in these events may be the troubles that Encolpius laments in the opening line of this passage.

26.6

lībera cēna: Literally a *free meal*, this term is used of a dinner provided to gladiators the evening before the games. The allusion may be to the arena or death, although the situation it refers to here is unclear.

cōnfossis: dative with **placēbat**, whereas **vulneribus** is ablative; from **cōnfodiō, cōnfodere, cōnfōdī, cōnfossus**: *dig up; stab; harm*

quōnam genere: *in just which fashion; how*; from **quīnam, quaenam, quodnam**: *which, just which, just what*

ēvītō, ēvītāre, ēvītāvī, ēvītātus: *avoid, escape*

procella, procellae, F: *storm, squall*

Agamēmnōn, Agamēmnonis, M: Agamemnon, the rhetoric teacher of Encolpius and Ascyltos. In myth, Agamemnon was the leader of the Greek forces at Troy, and after his victory he was killed by his wife, Clytemnestra, upon returning home.

trepidantes < **trepidō, trepidāre, trepidāvī, trepidātus**: *be startled by; be nervous*; present active participle in the accusative

quid?: here prepares listener for a question; *Hey!* or *Listen!*

apud quem fiat: An indirect question. You might understand **cena** or **convivium** as the subject of **fiat**, but it is more likely slang with an impersonal construction, *at whose house it is happening.*

26.9

Trimalchiō, Trimalchiōnis, M: *Trimalchio*, name combining *tri*, three, and a Semitic root for *prince*

lautissimus: Superlative form of **lautus**, the perfect participle of **lavō, lavāre, lāvī, lautus** or **lōtus** or **lavātus**: *wash, bathe*. Thus, **lautissimus** means *most polished, smartest, most elegant* (compare **lautitia, lautitiae**, below).

* Indicates a probable lacuna or gap in the text.

hōrologium, hōrologiī, N: *clock*

būcinātor, būcinātōris, M: *trumpeter*

subōrnō, subōrnāre, subōrnāvī, subōrnātus: *equip, supply; dress*

subinde (adverb): *immediately afterward; from then on; from time to time*

amicimur < **amiciō, amicīre, amicuī** or **amīxī, amictus**: *wrap around, cover, clothe*

omnium malorum: used substantively, a genitive object of a verb of remembering or forgetting

Gītōn, Gītōnis, M: Giton, the boyfriend of Encolpius. *Gitona,* "Neighbor Boy," is a Greek masculine accusative singular.

tuentem < **tueor** or **tuor, tuērī, tuitus** or **tūtus sum**: *look at, look after*

27

vestiti: perfect passive participle of **vestiō, vestīre, vestīvī, vestītus**: *dress, clothe, attire;* modifies subject

immo: here *indeed, quite so,* confirming a prior statement about the group's uplifted mood

iocari < **iocor, iocārī, iocātus sum**: *say in jest, joke.* This infinitive is dependent upon **coepimus** in the previous clause.

circulus, circulī, M: *circle; group of people*

ludentium < **lūdō, lūdere, lūsī, lūsus**: *play (with), amuse oneself,* a genitive plural of the present participle

calvus, calva, calvum: *bald*

capillātus, -a, -um: *long-haired,* thus attractive

pila, pilae, F: *ball.* Ball games were a popular form of exercise at the baths.

esse operae pretium: *to be worthy of the effort* or *of attention, to be worthwhile*

soleātus, soleāta, soleātum: *wearing slippers*

prasinus, prasina, prasinum: *green*

eam: refers back to **pilā**

follis, follis, M: *bag, sack*

27.3

spadō, spadōnis, M: *eunuch* (Greek loan word)

matella, matellae, F: *chamber pot*

lusu expellente: ablative absolute; **expellō, expellere, expulī, expulsus**: *drive out, expel.* This seems to be a technical term in the ball game *trigon,* in which three players tried to keep several balls in the air among them. The counter usually kept track of the players' hits amidst the flying balls.

vibrō, vibrāre: *wave around, hurl; vibrate, quiver*

dēcidō, dēcidere, dēcidī: *fall down, drop*

Menelāus, Menelāī, M: *Menelaus*, assistant of the rhetorician Agamemnon. In myth, Menelaus was the younger brother of King Agamemnon and the husband of Helen of Troy.

cubitum, cubitī, N: *elbow*. At a Roman banquet, diners reclined on a couch on which they rested their left elbow, while they used their right hand to eat.

ponitis: Use of the present for future tense was common in everyday speech.

27.5

concrepō, concrepāre, concrepuī: *snap, clash*

exonerō, exonerāre, exonerāvī, exonerātus: *unload, empty*

vēsīca, vēsīcae, F: *bladder*

paululum (adverb): *a little, to some extent*

adspergō, adspergere, adspersī, adspersus: *sprinkle, scatter*

*** Indicates a probable large gap in the text.

28

longum erat singula excipere: *There was no time to take up details.*

sudore calfacti: literally, *having been baked in sweat*

ad frigidam (aquam): Encolpius is describing their movement through the bath complex.

linteum, linteī, N: *linen*

pallium, palliī, N: *cloak* (Greek loan word)

lāna, lānae, F: *wool*

iātraliptēs, iātraliptae, M: *masseur, rubbing physician* (Greek loan word)

Falernum < Falernus, Falerna, Falernum: *Falernian*, from the slopes of Mt. Falernus, between Latium and Campania, and famous for vineyards. Understand as modifying an omitted **vīnum**.

rixor, rixārī, rixātus sum: *brawl, fight*

propin esse: An editor's suggestion for the unlikely *propinasse* in the manuscript. *Propin* is a contraction and transliteration of the Greek προπιεῖν, *to drink in honor of someone*, so Trimalchio interprets the spill as a toast.

hinc (adverb): *from here, hence*

28.4

involutus: describes Trimalchio

coccin(e)us, coccin(e)a, coccin(e)um: *scarlet*

gausapa, gausapae, F: *felt; fleecy wool*

lectīca, lectīcae, F: *litter*, a couch or chair carried by slaves as a means of transportation

phalerātus, phalerāta, phalerātum: *wearing medals; decorated* with **phalerae**, military medals worn by soldiers and horses (Greek loan word)

cursor, cursōris, M: *runner* who cleared a path before his master's litter or carriage

chīramaxium, chīramaxiī, N: *handcart* (Greek loan word)

dēliciae, dēliciārum, F pl.: *delights, pleasures*; often used for a favorite young slave, *pet, boy toy*

vetulus, vetula, vetulum = **vetus, veteris**: *old, aged*, with diminutive **-lus**: *little old, poor old*

lippus, lippa, lippum: *with sore eyes, blear-eyed*

dēfōrmis, dēfōrme: *misshapen, ugly*

symphōniacus, symphōniacī, M: *musician* (Greek loan word)

tībia, tībiae, F: *shinbone*, here used as a *flute*

CHAPTER TWO: *SATYRICA* 28–31

28.6

satur, satura, saturum: *sated, well-fed*

postis, postis, M: *doorpost, door*

libellus, libellī, M: *little book; notice, bit of writing*

dominicus, dominica, dominicum: *belonging to the master*, an adjective from **dominus, dominī**, M: *master, owner*

forās (adverb): *out, outside*

plāga, plāgae, F: *blow, lash*

28.8

aditus, aditūs, M: *doorway, entrance*
ōstiārius, ōstiāriī, M: *doorman*
prasinātus, prasināta, prasinātum: *wearing a green garment* (hapax legomenon)
cerasinus, cerasina, cerasinum: *cherry-colored, cherry red* (only in the *Satyrica*)
succingō, succingere, succīnxī, succīnctus: *tuck up, put on*
cingulum, cingulī, N: *sash, belt*
pīsum, pīsī, N: *pea*
līmen, līminis, N: *threshold, doorway*
cavea, caveae, F: *cage*
pīca, pīcae, F: *magpie, jay*
varius, varia, varium: *variegated, of differing colors*

29

stupeō, stupēre, stupuī: *be amazed at; be stunned*
resupīnō, resupīnāre, resupīnāvī, resupīnātus: *throw on one's back, throw down*
crūs, crūris, N: *leg, shin*
catēna, catēnae, F: *chain, fetter*
vinciō, vincīre, vīnxī, vīnctus: *bind, tie, restrain*
pariēs, parietis, M: *wall* (of a house or building)
quadrātā litterā: *in block capital letters*
dēsistō, dēsistere, dēstitī: *stop, desist from*

29.3

vēnālicium, vēnāliciī, N: *slave sale, slave market*
titulus, titulī, M: *inscription, label, tag*. These refer either to captions identifying characters in the painting or to placards carried by the slaves on the sale block.
cāducēus, cāducēī, M: *herald's staff, caduceus*
ratiōcinor, ratiōcinārī, ratiōcinātus sum: *calculate; keep accounts*
dein = deinde

dispēnsātor, dispēnsātōris, M: *highest-ranking household slave or ex-slave, chief of staff, steward*

cūriōsus, cūriōsa, cūriōsum: *careful, diligent*

dēficiō, dēficere, dēfēcī, dēfectus: *fail; desert; die out,* here indicating the end of the portico

levatum mento: modifies an understood Trimalchio, *lifted up by the chin* (**mentum, mentī**, N: *chin*)

tribūnal, tribūnālis, N: *platform, tribunal; magistrate's chair, seat of honor.* Trimalchio was entitled to this official chair because of his status as a priest of the imperial cult, a **sēvir**.

excelsus, excelsa, excelsum: *high; eminent*

29.6

praestō (adverb): *at hand, ready;* **praestō esse**: *be on hand (for), attend, aid*

cornu abundanti = cornucopia

Parca, Parcae, F: Goddess of *Fate,* one of the *Fates,* the three sisters who spun the threads of human destiny

pēnsum, pēnsī, N: *wool to be spun; work, task*

grex, gregis, M: *flock, herd; crowd*

armārium, armāriī, N: *cupboard, chest*

angulus, angulī, M: *angle, corner, nook*

aedicula, aediculae, F: *small room, shrine, closet;* (in plural) *small building*

Lār, Lares, M: *Lar,* a household god or god of a place, usually in the plural, as here

signum, signī, N: *sign, signal;* here *figure* or *statue*

marmoreus, marmorea, marmoreum: *marble, made of marble*

pyxis, pyxidis, F: *small box, jewelry box* (Greek loan word)

pusillus, pusilla, pusillum: *puny, petty*

barba, barbae, F: *beard;* accusative subject in indirect statement. Dedicating one's first beard shavings to a god was a Roman puberty rite. Nero was also said to have saved his in a precious box (Suetonius, *Nero,* 12.4).

Encolpius questions the **ātrium**-keeper about some of the paintings he sees and investigates a plaque given to Trimalchio by Cinnamus, his **dispēnsātor**. Encolpius also sees that Trimalchio has a calendar that displays all his activities and auspicious and inauspicious days of the year.

30.5

dextro pede: a reminder of how to enter the room most propitiously, for the left (**sinister**) was considered unlucky

paulisper (adverb): *for a little while*

praeceptum < **praecipiō, praecipere, praecēpī, praeceptus**: *take before; admonish, advise;* used substantively, *precept, order*

nostrum: rare genitive of **nōs** with **aliquis**, *any one of us*

pariter (adverb): *equally; at the same time*

gressus, gressūs, M: *step, footstep*

despoliatus < **dēspoliō, dēspoliāre, dēspoliāvī, dēspoliātus**: *strip, plunder;* here *stripped* of his clothes

se poenae: objects of compound verb **eriperemus**, *that we save him from punishment*

peccātum, peccātī, N: *error, mistake*

perīclitor, perīclitārī, perīclitātus sum: *be in danger*

subducta (erant) . . . sibi: *had been taken from him.* A form of the verb **sum, esse** must be understood, as is often the case. The slave was given the common task of guarding his master's clothes at the baths.

sēstertius, sēstertiī, M: *sesterce,* a small silver coin and an amount used as the base unit in accounting; genitive of value or price

30.9

in oecario: *in a little room*, based on one scholar's suggestion that this is a transliteration of the Greek οἰκάριον, a little *oikos* or house

aureus, aureī, M: a *gold coin* worth 100 **sēstertiī**

iactūra, iactūrae, F: *loss;* subject of the clause

nēquissimus, nēquissima, nēquissimum: *most worthless*

vestimenta . . . cubitoria: *clothing suitable for wearing to dinner, dress clothes*

natali meo: understand **diē**, that is, *on my birthday*

cliēns, clientis, M or F: *client* of a **patrōnus**, a dependent of a wealthier or more powerful person. (It would seem that even Trimalchio's **dispēnsātor** has clients!)

Tyrius, Tyria, Tyrium: *Tyrian, Phoenician; purple* (from a famous and expensive Tyrian dye)

lota: variant of the perfect passive participle of **lavō, lavāre**, *wash*

quid ergo est?: a common phrase in colloquial Latin, usually rhetorical: *What then? What does it matter?*

31

intrassemus: contracted form of pluperfect subjunctive **intrāvissēmus**
spissus, spissa, spissum: *thick, coming thick and fast*
bāsium, bāsiī, N: *kiss*
impingō, impingere, impēgī, impāctus: *fasten to, force against, press*
ministrātor, ministrātōris, M: *assistant, helper;* here *server*

31.3

discumbō, discumbere, discubuī, discubitum: *recline, take one's place* (at the
    table or in bed)
Alexandrīnus, Alexandrīna, Alexandrīnum: *from Alexandria,* a city in northern
    Egypt (see map), a place the Romans associated with sexual and other forms
    of excess
nivātus, nivāta, nivātum: *cooled with snow*
parōnychium, parōnychiī, N: *hangnail, inflammation of the fingernail;* **parōny-
    chia . . . tollere**: *remove the hangnails, give a pedicure* (Greek loan word)
subtīlitās, subtīlitātis, F: *fineness; exactness*
obiter (adverb): *along the way, in passing*

31.6

non minus: modifies **acido**, which in turn modifies **cantico** (**canticum, canticī,**
    N: *song; singing tone*)
quisquis aliquid rogatus erat ut daret: The previous phrase goes with this also, which
    generalizes the impulse to sing; literally, *anyone asked that he give something.*
pantomīmus, pantomīmī, M: *pantomime actor,* someone who performed
    scenes mutely with music and choral accompaniment (Greek loan word).
    Pantomime was a popular form of entertainment but was considered morally
    questionable by some members of the Roman elite.
gustātiō, gustātiōnis, F: *appetizer course*
locus . . . primus: identifies Trimalchio's location in the hierarchy of seating
    (see figure 40); **novo more** underscores that the host usually occupied a
    different spot, **summus in imo**, next to the guest of honor

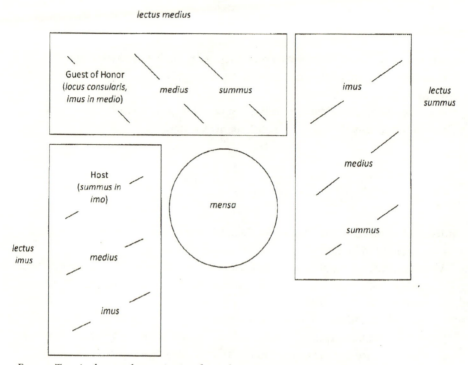

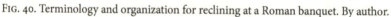

FIG. 40. Terminology and organization for reclining at a Roman banquet. By author.

CHAPTER THREE: *SATYRICA* 32–38

Appetizers are served, featuring a bronze donkey with saddlebags bearing black and green olives, platters with Trimalchio's name and the weight of the silver inscribed on them, and dormice. On a grate above ember-colored pomegranate seeds and Syrian plums "sizzle" precooked sausages.

32

symphōnia, symphōniae, F: *musical troupe, band* (Greek loan word)
cervīcal, cervīcālis, N: *pillow, cushion*
exprimō, exprimere, expressī, expressus: *press out, force* or *squeeze* an accusative from an ablative person or thing

imprudentibus: *those unsuspecting* or *unwary,* that is, guests unfamiliar with or unprepared for their host's humorous appearance

coccin(e)us, coccin(e)a, coccin(e)um: *scarlet*

adrādō, adrādere, adrāsī, adrāsus: *shave closely*

vestis, vestis, F: *clothing, dress, covering*

cervīx, cervīcis, F (often in plural with same meaning as singular): *neck, nape*

lāticlāvius, lāticlāvia, lāticlāvium: *with a broad purple stripe* (such as tunics worn by members of the senatorial class); *senatorial*

immittō, immittere, immīsī, immissus: *send, guide; insert;* here *put on, wrap around*

mappa, mappae, F: *napkin*

fimbriae, fimbriārum, F pl.: *fringe, tassels*

Trimalchio's jewelry is described, including a gold-plated ring, a solid gold ring studded with iron stars, and gold and ivory bracelets.

33

pinna, pinnae, F: *feather; quill,* here used as a *toothpick*

perfodiō, perfodere, perfōdī, perfossus: *dig through, stab, pierce*

nōndum (adverb): *not yet*

suave erat: impersonal construction

absentivus: probably = **absēns, absentis** (hapax legomenon)

morae vobis: double dative: *as a delay for you*

33.2

permittitis: present used colloquially for either future or imperative

tabula, tabulae, F: *board, tablet; painting;* here *game board.* The game is similar to backgammon.

terebinthinus, terebinthina, terebinthinum: *of the terebinth* or *turpentine tree,* a dark, hard wood

tessera, tesserae, F: *token, game piece; die*

calculus, calculī, M: *pebble; game piece*

habebat: Either the **puer** or the game itself serves as subject.

dēnārius, dēnāriī, M: *denarius,* a silver coin worth 4 **sēstertiī**

omnium textorum dicta: Most editors agree that *the sayings of all the weavers* makes little sense unless it is an otherwise unknown idiom for *common chatter* or *foul language*. **omnia tesserariorum dicta** is one suggested correction, which would restore the text to *all the sayings of dice-players*.

The dish is described, namely pastry peacock eggs with cooked birds inside.

34

eadem omnia: Trimalchio wants to catch up on eating *all the same things* that the guests have been enjoying while he played his game.

facere potestātem: here *grant authority* or *give permission*

quis = **aliquis** (after **sī**, **nisi**, **num**, and **nē**, the **ali** drops away from **aliquis, aliquid**: *some, any*)

mulsum, mulsī, N: *mead, honeyed wine*. Common with the first course of a meal.

sūmō, sūmere, sūmpsī, sūmptus: *take up; wear; begin; eat*

paropsis, paropsidis, F: *dish* (Greek loan word)

colaphus, colaphī, M: *punch, slap* (Greek loan word)

obiūrgō, obiūrgāre, obiūrgāvī, obiūrgātus: *scold*

rūrsus (adverb): *back*

34.3

supellecticārius, supellecticāriī, M: *slave in charge of household furniture*

purgāmenta, purgāmentōrum, N pl.: *filth, trash*

scōpae, scōpārum, F pl.: *broom*

ēverrō, ēverrere, ēverrī, ēversus: *sweep out*

ūter, ūtris, M: *bag, skin*

quales: a relative adjective, *which sort, the kind that*, referring back to **utrēs** and serving as the subject of **solent**

harēna, harēnae, F: *sand*, flooring of the gladiatorial arena or amphitheater; *arena*

spargō, spargere, sparsī, sparsus: *scatter, sprinkle*

dedere = **dedērunt**: alternate form of the third person plural perfect active indicative

34.5

aequum: here used substantively, *fairness, equality*; an allusion to an old notion that war is an equalizer

suam: Petronius characterizes the freedmen at the party in part by having them speak Latin poorly. As nonnative speakers, they overcorrect irregular verbs, use nouns with the wrong genders, and commit similar errors. How does Trimalchio use **suus, sua, suum** incorrectly here?

obiter (adverb): *along the way, in passing*

pūtidus, pūtida, pūtidum: *stinking, rotten*

aestum < **aestus, aestūs**, M: *agitation, anxiety; heat*; modified by **minorem**

34.6

vitreus, vitrea, vitreum: *glass, made of glass,* although glass was not used commercially for wine export in this period

gypsātus, gypsāta, gypsātum: *covered* or *sealed with gypsum, plastered*

pittacium, pittaciī, N: *small bit of cloth; label* (Greek loan word)

Falernum Opimianum (vinum): *Falernian,* from the slopes of Mt. Falernus, famous for their high-quality vineyards, and *from the consulship of Opīmius,* 121 BCE, a legendary vintage

ēheu (interjection): *alas!*

homunciō, homunciōnis, M: *poor little guy, mere human*

tangomenas faciamus: A mysterious phrase repeated once more in the *Satyrica,* meaning *let's drink our fill* or something similar. The first word may be from the Greek word for *soak.* It also fits into a line of hexameter and so may be a quotation.

bonum: understand **vinum**

Trimalchio waxes poetic, and a slave brings out a silver skeleton, which he puts into a variety of lewd poses. The first course is brought out, a platter with different foods symbolizing the twelve signs of the zodiac. Trimalchio orders his slave "Carver" to carve the various meats so that they can be served, a pun that Encolpius' neighbor will need to explain to him.

36.7

nihilō minus: *nonetheless*
suspicor, suspicārī, suspicātus sum: *mistrust, suspect*
totiēns (adverb): *so often, so many times*
ērubēscō, ērubēscere, ērubuī: *blush, grow red*
eum quī suprā mē accumbēbat: Later in the novel we learn that this man is a
    freedman named Hermeros. It is not unusual that the guests do not know
    each other and that they have not been introduced.
ēiusmodī: ēius modī, *of that type*
obsōnium, obsōniī, N: *shopping items, groceries, food* (Greek loan word)
carpō, carpere, carpsī, carptus: *pick, cut to pieces, carve*
quotiēnscumque (adverb): *as often as, however often*

37

quicquam, cūiusquam (pronoun): *anything*
quam + superlative adjective = *as* (adjective) *as possible*
accersō, accersere, accersīvī, accersītus: *summon, call*
scīscitor, scīscitārī, scīscitātus sum: *ask, consult*
nummos modio metitur: literally, *she counts coins by the bushel,* a proverbial
    phrase in Greek and Latin describing someone who has a lot of money
modo, modo: The repetition is colloquial and for intensity.

37.3

ignoscet < **ignōscō, ignōscere, ignōvī, ignōtum:** *overlook, forgive, pardon* (one
    forgiven in dative); future used as a polite imperative. Also polite is the
    use of the third person subject **genius tuus** instead of a second person
    verb ending.
genius, geniī, M: *guardian spirit* of a man (**iūnō, iūnōnis,** F, for a woman); *nat-
    ural inclination; talent, wit*
nec quid nec quare: *neither how nor why,* highly colloquial. Compare the Eng-
    lish *without rhyme or reason.*
caelum, caelī, N: here as in *the top, top of the world*

topanta, N pl.: *everything, all in all* (Greek loan word; hapax legomenon)

merīdiēs, merīdiēī, M: *midday, noon*

tenebrae, tenebrārum, F. pl: *darkness, night*

saplūtus, saplūta, saplūtum: *exceedingly rich* (Greek loan word; hapax legomenon)

lupātria, lupātriae, F: *she-wolf, whore,* from the Latin word **lupus**, *wolf* or *prostitute,* and a Greek ending (hapax legomenon)

37.7

siccus, sicca, siccum: *dry; thirsty; solid, firm;* here *thrifty*

pica pulvināris: Literally, *a magpie of the pillow.* An English equivalent would be an idiom about henpecking.

fundus, fundī, M: *ground, soil; farm, estate*

mīlvus, mīlvī, M: *kite, bird of prey*

quantum milvi volant: proverbial expression for distance or size

ōstiārius, ōstiāriī, M: *doorman*

quisquam, quidquam (pronoun): *anyone, anything*

familia: a topic raised by Hermeros, but left out of the rest of his sentence grammatically, although the **decumam partem** is part of the **familia**

babae (interjection): *great! wonderful!,* an expression of surprise and admiration derived from Greek. The repetition is colloquial. Compare *holy moly* or *ai caramba!*

mehercules: *by Hercules* (a common exclamation used by men)

quīvīs, quaevīs, quidvīs: *anyone, whoever you wish*

babaecalus, babaeculī, M: *tycoon, fat cat,* slang for a *rich man* (from Greek loan words; hapax legomenon)

in rutae folium coniciet: Literally, *into a rue leaf he will throw,* the meaning of which is unclear. Some argue that **rutae folium** is a proverbially small space, but few editors concur. Consider how hard it may be to explain the English idiom "he's rolling in dough" in two thousand years.

38

nec est quod: *nor is it the case that*

citreus, citrea, citreum: *citrus, of citrus wood*

piper, piperis, N: *black pepper,* very popular and usually imported from India

lacte gallinaceum: *chicken's milk,* a common idiom for something rare or unusual

parum (adverb): *too little, insufficiently;* modifies *bona*

ariēs, arietis, M: *ram*

cūlō, cūlāre, cūlāvī, cūlātus: *shove, thrust(?)* (hapax legomenon); a verb apparently from **cūlus, cūlī,** M: buttock

mel, mellis, N: *honey*

apis, apis, F: *bee*

vernāculus, vernācula, vernāculum: *of home-born slaves, home-born*

meliusculae: Diminutive of **melior**, the comparative of **bonus**. This series of diminutives gives the passage a colloquial tone.

38.4

bōlētus, bōlētī, M: *mushroom.* Mushrooms do not grow from a seed (**sēmen**); nor were they imported to Italy from India.

mūla, mūlae, F: *mule*

onager, onagrī, M: *wild ass*

culcita, culcitae, F: *mattress, cushion, pillow*

conchȳliātus, conchȳliāta, conchȳliātum: *purple*

tōmentum, tōmentī, N: *pillow stuffing*

CHAPTER FOUR: *SATYRICA* 41–47

Encolpius' informant confides information about the other guests, all of whom seem to be wealthy or formerly wealthy freedmen. Trimalchio explains the puns created by the foods on the zodiac dish brought out earlier. Another course is brought in: a roast boar that, when gutted, releases live birds into the *triclinium*. Trimalchio frees one of his servants and gives him the freedman's cap formerly worn by the boar.

41.9

ferculum, ferculī, N: *food tray, dish; course*

lasanus, lasanī, M: *chamber pot* (Greek loan word)

* The manuscripts have **convivarum sermones** here, *conversation among the guests*. Something like this must complete the sentence, but most editors agree that the text is corrupt.

Dāma, Dāmae, M: *Dama*, a common male slave name

pataracinum, pataracinī, N: *large drinking cup(?)*. The text may be corrupt (hapax legomenon).

rēctā (adverb): *by a direct route, straight*

mundus, munda, mundum: *neat, fine, sharp*

balneus = **balineum** or **balneum**. Either the speaker gets the gender wrong, or the neuter is starting to disappear in colloquial speech. Look for several examples in this chapter.

vestiārius, vestiāriī, M: *clothes-seller,* that is, something welcome in cold weather. The neuter may be intended, which means the *warm cloak* itself.

staminatas: with **dūcere** seems to mean drinking unmixed wine or drinking in large quantities, although the text may be corrupt (hapax legomenon)

matus, mata, matum: *drunk*

42

cōtīdiē (adverb): *daily*

balniscus, balniscī, M: *bath* (hapax legomenon)

fullō, fullōnis, M: *fuller, launderer,* referring to the harsh beating that professional cleaners gave clothes in order to launder them

cor, cordis, N: *heart; mind*

pultārius, pultāriī, M: *cooking pot,* here used as a large drinking cup

laecasin: Transliteration of Greek λαικάζειν, a present infinitive that expresses in a crude form *to have sex;* this is what the speaker tells the cold to do.

Chrȳsanthus, Chrȳsanthī, M: *Chrysanthus,* Greek name referring to the chrysanthemum

ēbulliō, ēbullīre, ēbullīvī: *babble about; bubble up;* **animum ēbullīre**: *give up the ghost*

heu (interjection): *oh! ah!*

42.4

minoris . . . pluris: genitive of value or worth

mūsca, mūscae, F: *fly*

bulla, bullae, F: *bubble*

quid si . . . fuisset: quid + pluperfect subjunctive = a wish that cannot be fulfilled; thus, *if only he had not been . . . , if only he had not . . .*

abstinax, abstinācis: *self-restrained, abstemious* (hapax legomenon)

mīca, mīcae, F: *crumb, morsel*

plures: *the dead,* a euphemism

fatus: Either the speaker gets the gender of **fatum** wrong, or he is personifying the concept.

42.6

efferō, efferre, extulī, ēlātus: *carry out; carry out to the grave, bury*

vitalis lectus: literally, *couch of life,* a euphemism for a funeral bier

strāgula, strāgulae, F: *covering, cloth,* especially a *shroud* or other covering for a corpse

manū mittere: *to send from one's hand, to release from control, to free (a slave), manumit*

quid si non . . . accepisset: see **quid si . . . fuisset** above

mīlvīnus, mīlvīna, mīlvīnum: *rapacious, like a bird of prey*

neminem . . . facere: Subject of **oportet;** understand *for women.* The double negative **neminem nihil** is emphatic.

nihil boni: Remember that **nihil** is a noun, *nothing [of] good, nothing good.*

puteus, puteī, M: *well; pit*

cancer, cancrī, M: *crab; cancer, disease, sore*

43

Philerōs, Philerōtis, M: *Phileros,* man's name meaning "Lover of Desire" in Greek, a common slave name

vivorum: Verbs of remembering and forgetting take a genitive object.

queror, querī, questus sum: *complain; lament*

ās, assis, M: *as, bronze coin, penny;* the base unit of the Roman monetary system (**dēnārius** = **decem assēs,** ten **assēs,** although soon after it was introduced it was revalued at sixteen **assēs**)

quadrāns, quadrantis, M: *quarter,* the smallest Roman *coin,* worth a quarter of
   an **ās**
stercus, stercoris, N: *manure, dung*
mordicus (adverb): *by biting, with the teeth*
favus, favī, M: *honeycomb,* something that grows proverbially quickly

43.2

centum: that is, 100,000 **sēstertiī**
linguam caninam comedī: *I eat the tongue of a dog.* This is an unknown proverbial phrase, perhaps a reference to the painful truthfulness of Cynic
   (doglike) philosophers or to the plant "dog's tongue," whose scent supposedly aided hearing.
bucca, buccae, F: *cheek; mouth*
ūnctus, ūncta, ūnctum: *anointed; sumptuous, extravagant*

Phileros explains how Chrysanthus made his money through winemaking and
then willed it out of the family because of a dispute with his brother.

43.7

quot (indeclinable interrogative adjective): *how many?* Modifies **annos.**
corneolus, corneola, corneolum: *hard as horn, tough*
corvus, corvī, M: *raven.* The reference is to Chrysanthus' hair, which has not
   yet grayed with age.
ōlim (adverb): *once, once upon a time; at times;* **ōliōrum**: invented genitive plural
   (hapax legomenon), *time of times, once upon a times ago*
salāx, salācis: *fond of leaping; salacious, lustful, horny*
pullārius, pullāriī, M: *chicken-keeper;* slang for *pederast*
Minerva, Minervae, F: *Minerva,* goddess of wisdom and technical arts; thus,
   skill or *trade,* here in a sexual context; genitive of description. "Jack of all
   trades" is a similar idiom in English.
secum tulit: that is, when he died

44

Ganymēdēs, Ganymēdis, M: *Ganymedes,* man's name. In Greek myth, Ganymedes was a Trojan prince abducted by Zeus to serve as his cup bearer
and lover.

annōna, annōnae, F: *crop, grain; price of grain*

mordeō, mordēre, momordī, morsus: *bite*

bucca, buccae, F: *cheek; mouthful*

siccitās, siccitātis, F: *dryness, drought*

ēsurītiō, ēsurītiōnis, F: *hunger, famine*

aedīlis, aedīlis, M: *aedile,* a magistrate responsible for public works and markets,
including monitoring the supply and price of grain. We might expect the
dative here with the jussive subjunctive **eveniat.** The accusative may be
used for the dative in colloquial Latin, or the curse may be parenthetical:
The aediles—may it turn out badly for them— . . .

pīstor, pīstōris, M: *miller, baker*

Ganymedes laments the lack of courage in contemporary politicians and gets
nostalgic for one particularly formidable politician named Safinius. After this inter-
lude he returns to lamenting the price of bread and cursing the current *aedile.*

44.15

attineō, attinēre, attinuī, attentus: *hold; pertain to, concern*

pannus, pannī, M: *rag, worn cloth*

casula = casa, casae, F, *house, cottage,* with diminutive ending

meos: modifies an understood group of people close to the speaker, *my friends
and family* or *me and mine*

frūnīscor, frūnīscī, frūnītus sum: *enjoy,* an archaic and colloquial variant of
fruor that takes either an accusative or ablative object. This hortatory
subjunctive expresses the strength of the speaker's next claim.

iēiūnium, iēiūniī, N: *fast, fast day* in honor of a deity

Iuppiter or **Iovis, Iovis,** M: *Jupiter* or *Jove,* king of the gods and a storm god

pilus, pilī, M: *hair; a bit, trifle;* genitive of value or worth; **nōn pilī facere:** *to
make someone out to be not worth a hair, to consider worthless*

44.18

anteā (adverb): *before, previously,* a formal version of **ante**, the more common and colloquial form

stolātus, stolāta, stolātum: *wearing a* **stola**, the formal dress of Roman matrons; *ladylike*

clīvus, clīvī, M: *hill, incline; uphill struggle*

urceātim: adverb made out of the word for bucket: *by the pitcher, "bucketously"* (hapax legomenon)

plovō, plovere, plovuī: *rain*

ūdus, ūda, ūdum: *wet*

mūs, mūris, M or F: *mouse*

pedes lanatos: *wooly feet,* a proverbial phrase that seems here to denote being slow to punish the guilty

45

Echīōn, Echīonis, M: *Echion,* one of Trimalchio's dinner guests; in Greek myth, the name of King Pentheus' father and of an Argonaut

centōnārius, centōnāriī, M: *clothes seller* or *someone who uses rags to put out fires, fireman*

loquere < loquor, loquī, locūtus sum: Echion makes a common error of non-native speakers: he overcorrects and creates an active infinitive form even though **loquor** is deponent. Most classical authors would use an imperative rather than an infinitive after **oro**, as well. Echion makes *many* similar errors.

Echion, more optimistic about the state of things than Ganymedes, goes on to rave about the upcoming gladiatorial games that the magistrate Titus will put on. Echion also mocks someone named Glyco for being a cuckold and gossips about a feast being prepared by Mammea, a politician, before going back to his discussion of gladiators. Then he notices Agamemnon, the rhetoric teacher.

46

argūtō, argūtāre, argūtāvī: *argue childishly*

fāscia, fāsciae, F: *ribbon, band; type;* here used idiomatically, *you are not of our stripe*

pauper, pauperis: *poor, not wealthy*

fatuus, fatua, fatuum: *silly; tasteless*

mandūcō, mandūcāre, mandūcāvī, mandūcātus: *chew, eat*

depravavit < **dēprāvō, dēprāvāre, dēprāvāvī, dēprāvātus:** *distort, corrupt.* Take **omnia** as its object.

satur, satura, saturum: *sated, well-fed.* Take with **unde**, *from which we may become satisfied.*

46.3

cicarō, cicarōnis, M: *small boy(?)* (only in the *Satyrica*)

quattuor partes dicit: *he says his four parts;* that is, *he can divide by four*

servulus, servulī, M: Diminutive of **servus.** This phrase may be proverbial, about a student's relationship to a teacher, rather than indicating the legal status of the boy.

vacō, vacāre, vacāvī, vacātum: *be empty; be without; be at leisure; be free from;* here used impersonally

tabula, tabulae, F: *board, tablet;* here *wax tablet* or *abacus*

ingeniōsus, ingeniōsa, ingeniōsum: *clever, talented, ingenious*

filum, filī, N: *thread; style* (of speech), *character* (of a person); ablative of description

morbōsus, morbōsa, morbōsum: *sickly; crazed;* **morbōsus in:** *crazy about*

cardēlis, cardēlis, F: *goldfinch*

quia (conjunction): Here *that*. In later Latin, the accusative and infinitive construction of indirect statements comes to be replaced more and more with **quia, quod,** or **quoniam** and the indicative. This occurs only a few times before Petronius, who thus provides some evidence of the construction's origin in colloquial speech.

mustēlla, mustēllae, F: *weasel*

nēnia, nēniae, F: *ditty, little song; trifles, playthings*

pingō, pingere, pīnxī, pictus: *paint, depict*

Graeculis: understand **litteris**

calx, calcis, F: *heel, hoof; a kick* (the corresponding English idiom is *boot*). Echion is indicating that the child has moved from Greek studies to Latin, a normal progression for schoolboys.

"Even if his teacher is mostly proud of himself and doesn't stay on topic. Indeed, he knows his letters, but he doesn't want to work. There's another, unlearned, but diligent, who teaches more than he knows. He's accustomed to come to the house on holidays, and he's content with whatever you'll give him."

46.7

libra rubricata: The opening words in an official copy of a law were written in red, so *reddened books* came to mean *law books.* **libra** (n. pl.) for **librōs** (m. pl.) is another of Echion's many grammatical errors.
domūsiō, domūsiōnis, F: *private usage, household use*
haec res: that is, the law
inquinō, inquināre, inquināvī, inquinātus: *defile, contaminate*
resiliō, resilīre, resiliī: *spring back from, shrink from, resist*
artificium, artificiī, N: *trade, skill, profession*
tōnstrīnum, tōnstrīnī, N: *barbering, trade of the barber*
praecō, praecōnis, M: *herald, public crier*
causidicus, causidicī, M: *pleader, advocate*
illi auferre non possit: Assume **nihil** or **nemo** as the subject of **possit**; **illi** is dative with compound verb **auferre.**
Orcus, Orcī, M: *Orcus, god of death; the underworld; death*

46.8

Prīmigenius, Prīmigeniī, M: *Primigenius,* name meaning "Firstborn"; a common name among freedmen and slaves
Phileronem: popular form of **Philerotem**
famēs, famis, F: *hunger*
labrum, labrī, N: *lip; mouth*
abigō, abigere, abēgī, abāctus: *drive away*
onus, oneris, N: *burden, load*

adversus (preposition + accusative): *opposite to, against, compared with.* Norbanus is a prominent local politician, whom Echion implies that Phileros is beginning to rival.

thēsaurus, thēsaurī, M: *storehouse, treasure* (Greek loan word)

CHAPTER FIVE: *SATYRICA* 47–49

47

dētergeō, dētergēre, dētersī, dētersus: *wipe off*
frōns, frōntis, F: *forehead, brow*
spatium, spatiī, N: here *space; interval, moment of time;* ablative absolute
venter, ventris, M: *belly, stomach*
mālicorium, mālicoriī, N: *pomegranate rind,* noted elsewhere as a laxative
taeda ex aceto: *pinewood boiled in vinegar*
pudor, pudōris, M: *shame, modesty*
imponit: Take **venter** as the subject.

47.4

sua re causa facere: *relieve oneself, do one's business.* A known phrase, although the literal sense is unclear.
pudeatur > pudet, pudēre, puduit (impersonal): *it shames, it causes shame.* It is unclear whether this shows an increasing fluidity between active and deponent forms in colloquial Latin, or whether Petronius is characterizing Trimalchio as a nonnative speaker.
vetare: One editor suggests eliminating this word, with humorous results.
dēsomnis, dēsomne: *sleep-deprived, sleepless* (hapax legomenon)
forās (adverb): *out, outside*
lasanus, lasanī, M: *chamber pot* (Greek loan word)
minūtal, minūtālis, N: *bit, piece,* here a reference to sponges or some other form of toilet paper

47.6

anathӯmiāsis, anathӯmiasis, F: transliteration of the Greek term ἀναθυμίασις, *a rising of vapors, an exhalation upward*

flūctus, flūctūs, M: *wave, turbulence, disorder*

castīgō, castīgāre, castīgāvī, castīgātus: *correct; reprove; restrain*

crēber, crēbra, crēbrum: *numerous, frequent*

pōtiuncula, pōtiunculae, F: diminutive of **pōtiō, pōtiōnis**

quod aiunt: *as they say,* marking the proverbial character of **in medio . . . clivo laborare**

commundō, commundāre, commundāvī, commundātus: *clean thoroughly*

sūs, suis, M: *pig, hog*

capistrum, capistrī, N: *muzzle, halter*

tintinnābulum, tintinnābulī, N: *bell*

bīmus, bīma, bīmum: *two-year-old*

nōmenclātor or **nōmenculātor, nōmenclātōris,** M: *name-reminder, name-sayer,* a slave who reminds his master of people's names and who announces courses at a banquet. Here he is giving the ages of the pigs.

trīmus, trīma, trīmum: *three-year-old*

sexennis, sexenne: *six-year-old*

47.9

petauristārius, petauristāriī, M: *acrobat, trapeze artist*

intrasse = contracted **intrāvisse,** a perfect active infinitive

in circulis: *in circles* of people, *in groups, for crowds in the street*

portentum, portentī, N: *portent, sign; abnormal event; trick, marvel*

facturos = **factūrōs esse.** Take **porcos** as the subject.

discutiō, discutere, discussī, discussus: *smash, shatter; dispel, put aside*

penthiacum, penthiacī, N: *hash.* The term seems to refer to the mythical dismemberment of Pentheus, the king of Thebes, who refused to recognize Dionysus as a god (hapax legomenon).

rūsticus, rūstica, rūsticum: *of the country, rustic, plain, coarse,* here used substantively

vitulus, vitulī, M: *calf; veal*

aēnum, aēnī, N: *bronze vessel, copper pot*

natu: ablative supine of **nāscor, nāscī, nātus sum;** describes the manner in which the pig is **maximum**

decuria, decuriae, F: *group of ten; squad, division*. Trimalchio's slaves are organized into numbered divisions, and he is asking the cook to which one he has been assigned.

47.12

emptīcius, emptīcia, emptīcium: *obtained by purchase, bought*
Pānsa, Pānsae, M: *Pansa*, a well-known Roman cognomen
vide: as in *see to it* or *watch carefully that*
decuriam viatorum: *heralds' division*, a formal title for a group of messengers at the disposal of Roman magistrates on official business
potentiae: that is, of Trimalchio
culīna, culīnae, F: *kitchen*
obsōnium, obsōniī, N: *shopping items, groceries, food*; here the pig (Greek loan word)

48

mītis, mīte: *ripe; calm, mild*
illud . . . bonum faciatis: **illud** refers to the **vinum**. Take the phrase as the subject of the impersonal verb **oportet**, *that you do it justice, that you do it right.*
suburbānum, suburbānī, N: *estate* or *farm near the city*
cōnfīnis, cōnfīne: *adjoining*
Tarracīniensēs, Tarracīniensium, M pl.: *inhabitants of* **Tarracīna**, a town on the southwest coast of Italy (see map)
Tarentīnus, Tarentīna, Tarentīnum: *Tarentine, from the city of* **Tarentum** in south Italy, about 300 miles from **Tarracīna** (see map). Is Trimalchio exaggerating? Is his geography poor? Is he mentioning good wine regions without regard for geography?

48.3

agellus, agellī, M: *little field, plot*
contrōversia, contrōversiae, F: *debate, controversy, subject for a debate*

declamasti = contracted **dēclāmāvistī**, from **dēclāmō, dēclāmāre**, *declaim*. Both **dēclāmō** and **contrōversia** are technical terms referring to rhetorical exercises and entertainment in which opponents deliver speeches on a hypothetical case (**causa**).

fastiditum < **fastīdiō, fastīdīre, fastīdīvī, fastīdītus**: *disdain, despise*. Understand **esse**.

bybliothēca, bybliothēcae, F: *collection of books; a library, study* (Greek loan word)

peristasis, peristasis, F: *theme, topic* treated by a speaker (Greek loan word). The one that Agamemnon reports is quite typical.

48.5

dīves, dīvitis: *rich, wealthy*

Trimalchio goes on to ask Agamemnon some leading but muddled questions about Odysseus, Homer, and the Cumaean Sibyl. He is interrupted by the return of the pig.

49

efflō, efflāre, efflāvī, efflātus: *breathe out, puff out*

repositōrium, repositōriī, N: *large serving dish, portable stand* for serving courses and meals

percoquō, percoquere, percoxī, percoctus: *cook thoroughly*

tanto quidem magis, quod: *indeed so much more (we began to wonder), because . . .*

intueor, intuērī, intuitus sum: *look at; consider*

49.5

dēspoliō, dēspoliāre, dēspoliāvī, dēspoliātus: *strip*

tortor, tortōris, M: *torturer*

rogamus mittas: The omission of **ut** in an indirect command is colloquial.

49.7

crūdēlis, crūdēle: *cruel*
piscis, piscis, M: *fish*
praetereō, praeterīre, praeterīvī or praeteriī, praeteritus: *go past, skip; escape
    notice of; overlook*
palam (adverb): *openly, publicly*; (preposition + ablative) *in the presence of*

49.9

culter, cultrī, M: *knife*
venter, ventris, M: *belly, stomach*
plagis < plāga, plāgae, F: *blow, lash, cut, slit*; modified by crescentibus
pondus, ponderis, N: *weight; burden*
inclīnātiō, inclīnātiōnis, F: *leaning, inclination*
thumatulum, thumatulī, N: *thyme-seasoned sausage* (only in the *Satyrica*)

CHAPTER SIX: *SATYRICA* 60–62

The cook is rewarded for his participation in the practical joke, and Trimalchio
spectacularly botches history and mythology in an account of the origin of
Corinthian bronze ware. He also tells a tale about a glass blower who made bottles
that did not shatter. One of Trimalchio's slaves reads his master the news from
all over his estates. More entertainment ensues as an acrobatic act begins, but it
is cut short when one of the performers falls on Trimalchio. Trimalchio frees
the acrobat so that no one can say that a slave harmed him. More poetry is recited
before Ascyltos and Giton are chastised by one of the other freedmen for laughing
at the poor verse. Performers come in to recite Homer, and then garlands are
delivered to the guests through panels that open in the ceiling.

60.4

FIG. 41. Engraving of Priapus. From Richard Payne Knight, *A Discourse on the Worship of Priapus* (T. Spilsbury, 1786), plate V, figure 2.

placenta, placentae, F: *flat cake* (Greek loan word)

quod medium: referring to the **repositorium,** *the middle of which*

Priāpus, Priāpī, M: *Priapus,* a Roman fertility god known for his enormous phallus, which he is commonly (**more vulgato**) depicted holding up his tunic to reveal (see figure 41). He often holds fruit in the pocket he thus creates with his tunic.

gremium, gremiī, N: *lap*

pompa, pompae, F: *procession,* often sacred in nature, here used of the edible representation of a god, so perhaps *display* or *splendid array*

commissiō, commissiōnis, F: *beginning,* especially of public games

vexātiō, vexātiōnis, F: *shaking, tossing*

crocus, crocī, M: *saffron,* a spice made from crocuses. The Romans sprinkled it for its fragrance at sacred occasions and at the theater.

ūsque (adverb): *all the way; continuously*

60.7

ferculum, ferculī, N: *food tray, dish; course*

Augustus, Augustī, M: *Augustus,* honorific name of the first emperor; generic term for an emperor

fēlīciter + dative = common acclamation or veneration of the current emperor

mappa, mappae, F: *napkin,* often brought by the guests and used to carry home favors

nullo: modifies **satis**, *insufficiently,* which together modify **amplo**

mūnus, mūneris, N: *service, duty, munificence,* especially of a magistrate or public figure

onerō, onerāre, onerāvī, onerātus: *load, burden, pile on,* although there may be a pun here with **honōrō, honōrāre**, *respect, adorn with honor*

Three slave boys bring out statuettes of the household gods, including the Lares, personifications of Gain, Luck, and Profit, and an image of Trimalchio, the last of which Encolpius feels obliged to kiss after everyone else does. (A brief prayer was part of a common ceremony between the main course and dessert at Roman dinner parties.)

61

Nīcerōs, Nīcerōtis, M: *Niceros,* a name meaning "Victory-Lover" or "Victory of Love" in Greek

convictus, convictūs, M: *socializing, a social event*

muttiō, muttīre, muttīvī, muttītus: *mutter, mumble,* make the sound *mu*

ūsū venīre: *to happen* (to someone in the dative) *in the course of life*

lucrum, lucrī, N: *profit, gain; wealth*

dūdum (adverb): *a short time ago; once*

gaudimōnium, gaudimōniī, N: derived from **gaudium, gaudiī**, N: *joy, delight;* perhaps *delightishness* (hapax legomenon)

dissiliō, dissilīre, dissiluī: *fly apart, burst*

61.4

viderint: Future perfect indicative of **videō, vidēre**. The tense indicates that the task of seeing about this or considering this is deferred for now, and with this verb the future perfect can even approach the imperative: *Let them see. They'll see.*

mihi: dative with compound verb **aufert**

satius = **melius**

haec ubi dicta dedit: an archaic and thus archaizing formula found in several authors, including in Vergil's *Aeneid* when Aeneas reports the speech of his wife, Creusa's, ghost (2.790)

exōrdior, exōrdīrī, exorsus sum: *commence.* The same verb is used to describe Aeneas launching into his account of the fall of Troy (*Aeneid* 2.2).

61.6

vīcus, vīcī, M: *row of houses; street; ward*

angustus, angusta, angustum: *narrow, close*

Gavilla, Terentius: *Gavilla, Terentius,* personal names

cōpō, cōpōnis, M: *innkeeper;* colloquial form of **caupō, caupōnis**

Melissa, Melissae, F: *Melissa,* a woman's name that means "bee" in Greek

Tarentīnus, Tarentīna, Tarentīnum: *Tarentine, from the city of* **Tarentum** in south Italy, well known for honey

bacciballum, bacciballī, N: *round berry? little pearl?* A **bāca** is a berry or pearl, but the meaning of the compound word is unknown; it must be meant as complimentary, if potentially crude (hapax legomenon).

venerius, veneria, venerium: *related to the goddess Venus, sexual, venereal*

benemōrius, benemōria, benemōrium: an editor's conjecture for a corrupt text; *having good moral qualities, well-mannered(?)* (hapax legomenon)

61.8

negatum: understand **est**

sēmis, sēmissis, M: *half; half an* **ās,** *small coin*

dēmandō, dēmandāre, dēmandāvī, dēmandātus: *hand over, entrust*

fallō, fallere, fefellī, falsus: *mislead, cheat.* Niceros creates a nonstandard perfect passive form out of the perfect active stem.

contubernālis, contubernālis, M or F: *military comrade, army buddy;* informal *spouse* of a slave. Earlier in the passage, Niceros refers to her as someone's

uxor. Either this is a different partner of Melissa or the speaker is being loose regarding the differences between these legal categories.

supremum diem obire: euphemism for *to die*

per scutum per ocream: Literally *by shield by greave*, perhaps soldier or gladiator slang. Compare the English phrase *by hook or by crook*. Asyndeton (leaving out the conjunction) is colloquial.

egi aginavi: **agināre** is otherwise unknown in literature but may mean *to scheme*. "I hustled, I bustled" might be a similar English idiom.

62

Capuae: Using the locative form to express the place to which one is going is unusual but not unknown.

scrūta, scrūtōrum, N pl: *frippery, trash*

scītus, scīta, scītum: *neat, excellent*

expediō, expedīre, expedīvī, expedītus: *put in order, settle; put up for sale*

mīliārium, mīliāriī, N: *milestone*. A Roman mile was 1,000 (**mille**) feet.

apoculō, apoculāre: *leave, get out(?)*. The precise meaning is unclear, but the verb is probably related to **cūlus**, *buttocks* or *anus*; thus the idiom resembles the English *haul ass* (only in the *Satyrica*).

gallicinium, galliciniī, N: *cockcrow*, about two hours after midnight in Roman timekeeping

monimentum = monumentum. Funerary monuments lined the roads in and out of ancient Italian towns.

stēla, stēlae, F: *stele, block of stone; tombstone* (Greek loan word)

facere: either slang, *to do one's business* (compare **sua re cause facere**, 47.4), or *to make for, head for*

cantābundus, cantābunda, cantābundum: *chanting, singing*

62.5

comes, comitis, M or F: *companion*

exuō, exuere, exuī, exūtus: *take off; disrobe*

anima in naso esse: Historical infinitive. The phrase is proverbial for being near death, when the soul would leave the body through the mouth or nose.

circummingō, circummingere, circumminxī: *urinate around*

nolite: The imperative of **nōlō, nōlle** is used to express a negative command; **putare** completes that command, while **iocari** is an indirect statement.

ut mentiar, nullius patrimonium tanti facio: ut mentiar is a result clause; **tanti** is a genitive of value, while **nullius** is possessive. The idea is that Niceros would find no one's patrimony large enough to make him lie.

ululō, ululāre, ululāvī, ululātus: *howl, ululate*

primitus = primum

lapideus, lapidea, lapideum: *stony, stone*

qui: Either Niceros incorrectly uses the relative for the interrogative pronoun **quis** or this is an interrogative adjective modifying **ego.**

mori < **morior, morī, mortuus sum**; another historical infinitive

62.9

matauitatau: Either the text is corrupt or this is a magical incantation of nonsense words such as *abracadabra.*

umbra, umbrae, F: *shade; shadow, ghost*

in larvam: *like a ghost*

bifurcum, bifurcī, N: *crotch*

sērō (adverb): *late, too late*

pecus, pecoris, N: *herd of cattle; flock of sheep*

* In the lacuna must be the verb, something like **cecīdit,** *he slaughtered.*

lanius, laniī, M: *butcher; executioner*

lancea, lanceae, F: *light spear* or *lance*

62.12

copo compilatus: *pillaged innkeeper.* The phrase may refer to Aesop's Fable 196, in which an innkeeper is cheated out of a fine suit of clothes by a guest who terrifies him into running away by claiming to be a werewolf, or it may be an allusion to a popular mime or farce.

bōs, bovis, M: *ox, bull.* Niceros uses an incorrect nominative form.

versipellis, versipellis, M: from **versō, versāre, versāvī, versātus:** *spin, twist* and **pellis, pellis,** F: *skin, pelt*

viderint: See above, 61.4.

exopīnissō, exopīnissāre: *think, believe.* Niceros combines the Latin base **opīnō, opīnāre,** *think* or *believe,* with the Greek verbal suffix -ιξω (hapax legomenon).

CHAPTER SEVEN: *SATYRICA* 64–65, 67

In response to Niceros, Trimalchio tells his own scary story about witches. Encolpius observes in a drunken stupor that where he once saw one lamp, he can now see several. Trimalchio and another guest amuse themselves by imitating actors and performers of various sorts.

64.5

nec non: Double negative words cancel each other out here, *nor was he not.*
tubicen, tubicinis, M: *trumpeter*
dēliciae, dēliciārum, F pl.: *delights, pleasures;* (often of a favorite slave) *pet, boy toy*
Croesus, Croesī, M: *Croesus,* the name of a famously wealthy king of Lydia
lippus, lippa, lippum: *with sore eyes, blear-eyed*
catella, catellae, F: *puppy*
pinguis, pingue: *fat*
fāscia, fāsciae, F: *ribbon, band*
sēmēsus, sēmēsa, sēmēsum: *half-eaten*
torus, torī, M: *bed, couch*
recusantem: modifies **catellam**
sagīnō, sagīnāre, sagīnāvī, sagīnātus: *fatten, feed, cram*

64.7

Scylax, Scylācis, M: *Scylax,* dog's name meaning "Puppy" in Greek
praesidium, praesidiī, N: *protection, guard; bodyguard*
catēna, catēnae, F: *chain, fetter*
calx, calcis, F: *heel, hoof; a kick*
candidus, candida, candidum: *white,* thus from refined and expensive white flour

64.9

properō, properāre, properāvī, properātus: *speed up; be quick, rush*
canino . . . ingenio: *canine nature, doggy inclination*
taeter, taetra, taetrum: *offensive, hideous*
lātrātus, lātrātūs, M: *barking*
Margarīta, Margarītae, F: *Margarita*, a name meaning "Pearl" in Latin; the name of Croesus' puppy
cōnsistō, consistere, constitī: *stop, pause; stand*
comminuō, comminuere, comminuī, comminūtus: *break into pieces, crush*
oleum, oleī, N: *olive oil*
respergō, respergere, respersī, respersus: *sprinkle, splash*
iactūra, iactūrae, F: *loss*, here in ablative
dorsum, dorsī, N: *back* of the body
ascendere: **puerum** is the object of **iussit** and the subject of the infinitive **ascendere.**

Trimalchio orders drinks to be prepared for the slaves, and another course, chicken and goose eggs, is served.

65.3

valvae, valvārum, F pl. : *folding doors, double doors*
lictor, lictōris, M: *lictor*, public attendant or bodyguard of a magistrate or priest
cōmissātor, cōmissātōris, M: *reveler*
māiestās, māiestātis, F: *majesty, dignity; authority*
praetor, praetōris, M: *praetor*, a high-ranking magistrate often in charge of courts
stultus, stulta, stultum: *foolish, silly*
Habinnas, Habinnae, M: *Habinnas*, a man's name possibly of Semitic origin
sēvir, sēvirī, M: *priest of the imperial cult*, a post usually held by freedmen. The office entitled Habinnas to be attended by a **lictor.**
lapidārius, lapidāriī, M: *stonemason, stonecutter*

65.6

umerus, umerī, M: *shoulder, upper arm*

praetorio loco: the place of honor in the hierarchical arrangement of a Roman banquet, also referred to as the **locus consulāris**, the end spot on the middle couch (see figure 40 above at 31.6)

caldam: understand **aquam**

65.8

scyphus, scyphī, M: *cup, goblet* (Greek loan word)

quomodo acceptus esset: Habinnas is clearly coming from another party, and Trimalchio is asking about his rival's hospitality.

Scissa, Scissae, F: *Scissa*, a woman's name meaning "Shrill" in Latin

novendiāle, novendiālis, N: *ninth-day festival, funeral feast* held on the ninth day of mourning

vīcēnsimārius, vīcēnsimāriī, M: presumably the *collector of the* **vīcēsima**, a 5 percent tax levied on the manumission of slaves (hapax legomenon)

mantissa, mantissae, F: *sauce; trouble, fuss(?).* The text may be corrupt.

dīmidius, dīmidia, dīmidium: *half of*

ossuculum, ossuculī, N, diminutive of **os, ossis**, N: *bone, skeleton.* Libations would be poured at many stages of the funeral ceremony.

66

sangunculum, sangunculī, N: *blood sausage* or perhaps *blood sauce* (hapax legomenon)

gizeria, gizeriōrum, N pl.: *giblets*

bēta, bētae, F: *beet*

autopȳrus, autopȳra, autopȳrum: *whole meal, whole grain* (Greek loan word)

de suo sibi: an idiom, *made of nothing but itself,* thus *pure*

mea re causa facio: again, the idiom *relieve myself, do my business*

66.3

ferculum, ferculī, N: *food tray, dish; course*

scriblīta, scriblītae, F: *cheese cake, cheese tart* (Greek loan word)

mel, mellis, N: *honey*

excellente: colloquial for **excellēns**

Hispanum: Most scholars agree that this must be a type of **vinum**. The dish seems to be a tart with warm honey over which Spanish wine has been poured.

ūsque (adverb): *all the way; continuously*

tangō, tangere, tetigī, tāctus: here *wash, anoint*

cicer, ciceris, M: *chickpea, garbanzo bean*

lupīnum, lupīnī, N: *lupine seed, legume, bean.* Sausages, giblets, beets, coarsely refined bread, garbanzos, and lupines are all referred to in other sources as foods for those who cannot afford better.

calva, calvae, F: *nut* with a smooth shell, perhaps *hazelnut*

arbitratu: that is, *as many as you want, at your discretion*, as opposed to **singulī, singulae, singula**: *one at a time, one each*

alligō, alligāre, alligāvī, alligātus: *bind, tie*

vernula, vernulae, M or F: a diminutive form of **verna, vernae**: *home-born slave*, perhaps affectionately, *little home-born slave, little pet*

convīcium, convīciī, N: *noise, outcry; altercation; abuse*

domina: Becomes a term for *wife* in the first century CE. Perhaps she has helped Habinnas, with his poor memory, recall all of the dishes at Scissa's party.

66.5

in prospectu: It is unclear whether this means simply *in sight* during the whole meal, or on some form of menu and thus *in our sights*.

ursīna, ursīnae, F: *bear meat*

frūstum, frūstī, N: *bit, scrap*

Scintilla, Scintillae, F: *Scintilla*, woman's name from the Latin word for *spark* or *flame*

lībra, lībrae, F: *pound*

aper, aprī, M: *wild boar*

sapiō, sapere, sapīvī: *have the flavor of, taste like*

comest = **comesset**, the imperfect subjunctive, contracted colloquially

"At last we had soft cheese in wine and a snail each, and a morsel of tripe, and liver on little plates, and garnished eggs and turnips and mustard and another crappy dish, but enough of that."

67

nosti: colloquially contracted **nōvistī**
atquī (conjunction): *but yet; however*
apoculō, apoculāre: *leave, get one's ass out of there(?)* (see above at 62)
quater (adverb): *four times*

67.4

galbinus, galbina, galbinum: *chartreuse, yellow-green*
cingillum, cingillī, N: *woman's belt, sash*
cerasinus, cerasina, cerasinum: *cherry-colored, cherry red* (only in the *Satyrica*)
periscelis, periscelidis, F: *anklet* (Greek loan word)
tortus, torta, tortum: *twisted, plaited*
phaecasia, phaecasiae, F: *slipper* (Greek loan word)
sūdārium, sūdāriī, N: *handkerchief, towel*
ōsculor, ōsculārī, ōsculātus sum: *kiss*
est te . . . vidēre: **est** = **potest** or **licet**. This is a common phrase used in greeting
　　someone not seen recently.

The women begin comparing their jewelry, and Habinnas complains about how
expensive women make everything.

67.11

saucius, saucia, saucium: *wounded; smashed; drunk*
cohaereō, cohaerēre, cohaesī, cohaesum: *stick together; be in agreement*
gremium, gremiī, N: *lap; bosom*

CHAPTER EIGHT: *SATYRICA* 68–69, 70–71

The *triclinium* is prepared for another course. Trimalchio makes some commen-
　　tary and "witty" jokes.

68.3

ministrō, ministrāre, ministrāvī, ministrātus: *serve, wait on*

lūscinia, lūsciniae, F: *nightingale*. Imitating birds and other natural sounds may have been a common form of entertainment.

canōrus, canōra, canōrum: *musical, singsong*

medium: understand **mare**; a quote from Vergil's *Aeneid* (5.1), an extremely popular epic poem

classis, classis, F: *fleet* of ships; ablative of means

praeter (preposition + accusative): *past, in front of, beyond; in addition to; except.* The object is **clamorem.**

errantis barbariae = genitive of description; **barbaria, barbariae**, F: *foreign country; rudeness, barbarity* (Greek loan word)

adiectum . . . deminutum: Describe **clamorem** as *raised* and *lowered*. Irregularity in volume is a mark of poor delivery in public speaking.

Ātellānicus, Ātellānica, Ātellānicum: *Atellan*. Associated with *Atellan farce*, a form of low comedy that the Romans associated with the town of Atella in south Italy, a place where they thought the "rustic" and "backward" people lived.

68.6

lassus, lassa, lassum: *tired, exhausted*

aliquandō (adverb): *sometime or other; ever*

circulātor, circulātōris, M: *peddler; traveling performer*

ērudiō, ērudīre, ērudīvī, ērudītus: *educate, teach*

mūliō, mūliōnis, M: *mule driver*

desperatum: accusative used adverbially: *desperately*

sūtor, sūtōris, M: *shoemaker*

mancipium, mancipiī, N: *movable property*, especially a *slave*

vitium, vitiī, N: *fault, defect; weakness, vice*. When slaves were for sale, they were legally required to carry placards listing their **morbi** (diseases) and **vitia.**

omnium numerum: that is, *complete in all respects, the top, numero uno*

recutītus, recutīta, recutītum: *circumcised*

strabōnus, strabōna, strabōnum: *squinty-eyed, cross-eyed*

Venus: We have a couple of other mysterious references to Venus being cross-eyed.

ideo nihil tacet vix oculo mortuo umquam: The obscurity of the phrase and its similarity to one in Niceros' story (62.10) lead some scholars to suspect that the text is corrupt. The original may be something like **ideo nihil latet vix oculo umquam**, *thus nothing almost ever escapes his eye.*

69

nēquam (indeclinable adjective): *worthless, bad, good for nothing*

agaga, agagae, M: *pervert? pimp?* (hapax legomenon)

curabo: What she threatens to see happen follows in the subjunctive.

stigma, stigmatis, N: *mark, brand* (Greek loan word)

Cappadox, Cappadocis, M: *a Cappadocian*, someone from central Asia Minor. Other Latin authors associate Cappadocians with brute strength, greed, and sexual prowess.

dēfraudō, dēfraudāre, dēfraudāvī, dēfraudātus: *rob, cheat*; here *deny*

parentō, parentāre, parentāvī, parentātus: *honor with a funeral service, celebrate at the* **Parentālia**, *pay last respects; avenge.* The implication may be that the man in question has no family to look after his body after death, so he may as well get as much as he can now.

zēlotypus, zēlotypa, zēlotypum: *jealous* (Greek loan word). The slave in question seems to be procuring for his master Habinnas for profit. Note that although sex with slaves and prostitutes was legal for men in ancient Italy, this does not mean that the practice was free of spousal jealousy and contempt.

69.3

sic me salvum habeatis: a type of prayer to the unnamed powers that be

dēbattuō, dēbattuere: *thump, beat, bang, bonk*

vīlicātiō, vīlicātiōnis, F: *task of overseeing a farm, job as steward* (**vīlicus**) *of a country estate*

sed tace, lingua, dabo panem: probably a proverbial saying to mark that a subject was being dropped, but otherwise unknown

fictilis, fictile: *clay, terracotta*

tubicen, tubicinis, M: *trumpeter*

succinō, succinere: *chime in, accompany*

īnferior, īnferius: *lower* (as opposed to *upper*), modifies **labrum**, *lip*

69.5

harundō, harundinis, F: *reed, cane*
quassus, quassa, quassum: *shattered, broken*
choraulēs, choraulae, M: *flute player, flautist* for dancers (Greek loan word)
lacernātus, lacernāta, lacernātum: *wearing a cloak*
flagellum, flagellī, N: *whip, riding crop*
fata: that is, *scenes* or *episodes* in the lives of **mulionum**, *mule drivers*, perhaps a
     reference to mime
tanto melior: a common expression of praise, like "bravo"
Massa, Massae: Perhaps a Semitic name, although it is also a feminine noun in
     Latin meaning a *lump* or *pile*, often of cash. Here it is used as a slave's name.
caliga, caligae, F: *army boot*
epidīpnis, epidīpnidis, F: *extra course* at the end of a meal, *dessert* (Greek
     loan word)

The dish brought out includes pastry birds stuffed with raisins and nuts, quinces
with spines attached to look like sea urchins, and something that Encolpius
describes as even more monstrous—a fattened goose apparently garnished with
birds and fish, but in reality all sculpted out of pork. Two slaves get into a fight,
and other slaves smear perfume on the guests' feet.

70.10

saltō, saltāre, saltāvī, saltātus: *dance*
Philargyrus, Philargyrī, M: *Philargyrus*, man's name meaning "Silver-Lover"
     or "Fond of Money" in Greek
prasiniānus, prasiniāna, prasiniānum: *supporting of the Greens*, one of the
     chariot-racing teams
Menophila, Menophilae, F: *Menophila*, "Moon-Lover," a well-attested Greek
     woman's name
quid multa?: *why a lot?* A common phrase to indicate that the speaker is trying
     to make a long story short.

70.12

ānser, ānseris, M: *male goose, gander*. In the most recent course, "geese" made
   of pork were served.
muria, muriae, F: *brine, pickling juice*
fēteō, fētēre: *have an offensive smell, stink*
Ephesum tragoedum: Ephesus was a town in central Greece with a large theater. It is unclear whether this is a reference to a tragedian from there or a
   playwright with the name *Ephesus*.
spōnsiō, spōnsiōnis, F: *bet*
si prasinus . . . palmam: The slave challenges his master to pay up if this condition is met. Understand a verb such as **capiet**.

71

diffundō, diffundere, diffūdī, diffūsus: *spread, extend; cheer up, gladden*
servi homines sunt: strikingly similar to a claim made by Seneca in his *Moral
   Epistles* (47.1 and 47.10)
lac, lactis, N: *milk*. The reference may be to the common practice of employing
   or owning wet nurses, who would nurse both the free and slave babies of
   a household. The masculine form found here is rare but attested.
me salvo: A common aside that makes no logical sense here. It may be so cliché
   that Trimalchio does not even notice.
fundus, fundī, M: *farm, estate*
lēgō, lēgāre, lēgāvī, lēgātus: *bequeath, leave in a will*. The Romans demonstrated
   great concern for their wills, which were seen as one's last and most honest
   evaluation of friends and family members.
contubernalem: As a slave wife, she could be left to someone as property.
Carion, Carionis, M: *Carion*, a common Greek slave name referring to Caria, a
   region in southern Asia Minor
īnsula, īnsulae, F: *island; city block, apartment building* (urban island)
vīcēsima, vīcēsimae, F: *twentieth (5%) tax* levied on the manumission of slaves.
   Here Trimalchio says that he is leaving Carion enough to pay the tax on
   his freedom.
strātus, strāta, strātum: *covered, spread with a cloth*

71.3

nūgae, nūgārum, F pl.: *nonsense, trivia, trash* (as opposed to serious matters)
ingemēscō, ingemēscere, ingemēscuī: *groan, sigh*

71.5

quid dicis: a common colloquial phrase for getting someone's attention
catella, catellae, F: *puppy*
fingō, fingere, finxī, fictus: *shape, model, form, fashion*
Petraites, Petraitis, M: *Petraites*, the name of a prominent gladiator during the reign of Nero. Gladiatorial games were held at funerals.
in fronte . . . in agrum: a well-known formula for describing the dimensions of a burial plot by its frontage along the road (**in fronte**) and its depth away from the road (**in agrum**)

71.7

genus . . . poma: **genus** here in apposition to the noun, instead of with the genitive
cinis, cineris, M: *ashes; ruin, death*; (in plural) *cremated remains*
poma, vinearum: Funerary gardens with orchards and vineyards are well documented.
largiter (adverb): *in abundance, plentifully*; here used substantively as *an abundance*
hoc monumentum heredem non sequatur: Such a common prohibition on tombstones, it could be abbreviated HMHNS.
erit . . . curae: an impersonal construction
cacō, cacāre, cacāvī, cacātus: (colloquial) *defecate*; here in accusative supine form, a means of expressing purpose when used with a verb of motion

71.9

vēlum, vēlī, N: *sail*
tribūnal, tribūnālis, N: *platform, tribunal; magistrate's chair, seat of honor*

praetextātus, praetextāta, praetextātum: *wearing the* **toga praetexta** (worn by magistrates and boys); *crimson-bordered*

ānulus, ānulī, M: *ring*

sacculus, sacculī, M: *little bag, sack*. The image is intended to commemorate Trimalchio's public benefaction, which he goes on to remind his listeners about.

epulum, epulī, N: *banquet, feast*; here a public one given by a priest or other prominent citizen

bīnī, bīnae, bīna: *two each, two to everyone*. The banquet may have cost two **dēnāriī** a head, or there may have been a distribution of cash.

sibi suāviter facere: *to enjoy oneself*

71.11

columba, columbae, F: *dove*, a bird sacred to Venus

cingulum, cingulī, N: *sash, belt*

cicarō, cicarōnis, M: of uncertain meaning, perhaps *small boy* (only in the *Satyrica*)

gypsātus, gypsāta, gypsātum: *covered* or *sealed with gypsum, plastered*

unam . . . fractam: refers to one of the **amphorae**

hōrologium, hōrologiī, N: *clock*, in this case probably a sundial

velit nolit: an aside, whether **velit** or **nolit**

71.12

C: abbreviation of male personal name **Gaius**

C. Pompeius: The name of the man who freed Trimalchio. Upon manumission, an ex-slave took his former master's name.

Maecenatianus: An added name indicating that Trimalchio was formerly owned by one Maecenas. The most famous Maecenas was a close friend of Augustus known for his sponsorship of the arts and lavish lifestyle.

sēvirātus, sēvirātūs, M: *office of a* **sēvir**, a priest in the imperial cult

decuria, decuriae, F: *group of ten; squad, division; town council; social club*. Various assistants to magistrates were organized into **decuriae**, such as scribes, lectors, runners, and auctioneers. This line of the epitaph does not have parallels in surviving inscriptions, unlike most of the other phrases.

nec umquam philosophum audivit: Many epitaphs list vices avoided by the deceased, but more may be going on in this rejection of philosophy.

vale: The pretext that the tombstone is talking to passersby was common in funerary inscriptions.

CHAPTER NINE: *SATYRICA* 72–73, 77–80

"When Trimalchio said these things, he began to weep copiously. And Fortunata was weeping. And Habinnas was weeping, and at last the whole household, as if asked to a funeral, filled the *triclinium* with their lamentation."

72.2

sic nos felices videam: Expresses a wish: *So let me see us happy*. This may be a common colloquialism; compare 61.2. A hortatory subjunctive follows.

meo periculo: *at my risk*, a reference to a belief that a hot bath after a meal is unhealthy

paenitet, paenitēre, paenituit (impersonal verb): *cause regret, displease*

furnus, furnī, M: *oven; bakery*

72.5

Ascyltos or **Ascyltus, Ascyltī**, M: *Ascyltos*, the Greek name of our narrator Encolpius' companion; **-on** is a Greek accusative singular

catēnārius, catēnāria, catēnārium: *chained*

piscīna, piscīnae, F: *fish pond; pool*. The main room or *atrium* of a Roman house had an opening in the ceiling to provide light and air, and a pool in the middle of the room caught falling rain. This may be what Ascyltos encounters, but actual fish ponds were a fad in the early Empire.

natō, natāre, natāvī, natātus, *swim*

gurges, gurgitis, M: *abyss, whirlpool*

72.8

ātriēnsis, ātriēnsis, M: *slave of the* atrium, *butler*
iam dūdum: *some time ago, long since*
lātrō, lātrāre, lātrāvī, lātrātum: *bark*

72.10

algēns, algentis: *cold*
ūdus, ūda, ūdum: *wet*
alia . . . alia: Supply via or iānua in the ablative.

73

quid faciamus: Deliberative subjunctive, *What should we do?* We might expect
    the imperfect tense in a narrative about the past, but Encolpius uses the
    present.
miserrimi et . . . inclusi: Both modify the subject (nōs).
novi: modifies generis, which is in turn describing the labyrintho by which
    our heroes are inclusi
lavari: Take this infinitive as the subject of coeperat.

The party guests continue their drunken revelry and games in Trimalchio's bath,
then they move to a new dining room. A rooster crows, and Trimalchio, after
performing a number of superstitious rituals to avert the bad omen, offers a tip
to whoever brings him the rooster. When the rooster is brought to him, he has
it cooked and eats it. Trimalchio then sends out the slaves who are currently
serving and calls in a new group. After a quarrel with Fortunata over his flirtations
with a slave boy, Trimalchio waxes poetic about his house and tells the tale of
his life, all with a great deal of melodrama. He finally announces that an astrolo-
ger told him he has thirty years, four months, and two days to live. Trimalchio
thus begins to think about his funeral and gives an order to a slave to bring out
some materials that have been prepared for it.

77.7

Stichus, Stichī, M: *Stichus*, a common slave name
vītālis, vītāle: *vital, alive, life-giving;* **vītālia, vītālium**, N pl.: *grave clothes, shroud* (euphemism)
gustus, gustūs, M: *tasting; taste; small portion*
os, ossis, N: *bone*

78

strāgula, strāgulae, F: *covering, cloth,* especially a *shroud* for a corpse
iussit: Take Trimalchio as the subject. The abrupt shift in subject is why editors believe that some text must be missing.
lāna, lānae, F: *wool*
mūs, mūris, M or F: *mouse*
tinea, tineae, F: *moth*
aliōquin (adverb): *otherwise, for the rest*
combūrō, combūrere, combūssī, combūstus: *burn*
imprecor, imprecārī, imprecātus sum: here *pray over, bless*

78.3

ampulla, ampullae, F: *small bottle, flask*
nardum, nardī, N: *nard,* an oil scented with the root of the spikenard (Greek loan word)
futurum: understand **esse**
vīnārium, vīnāriī, N: *wine flask*. Trimalchio is equipping the guests to pour libations at his mock funeral.
parentālia, parentāliōrum, N pl.: *Parentalia,* an annual festival in honor of dead relatives

78.5

ācroāma, ācroāmatis, N: *entertainment; actor* (Greek loan word)
cornicen, cornicinis, M: *horn blower*
fulciō, fulcīre, fulsī, fultus: *prop up, support*
cervīcal, cervīcālis, N: *pillow, cushion*
strepitus, strepitūs, M: *noise, crash, bang*
libitīnārius, libitīnāriī, M: *undertaker*

78.7

vigil, vigilis, M: *night watchman, fireman*
secūris, secūris, F: *axe*
verba dare + dative = *deceive, cheat; give the slip to*
raptim (adverb): *hurriedly; suddenly*

79

fax, facis, F: *torch*
praesidium, praesidiī, N: *protection, guard; bodyguard, escort.* Of course, our
heroes do not have an escort, unless Encolpius is referring to Giton in a
comically exaggerated fashion.
occurrentium: genitive plural of the present participle of occurrō, occurrere,
occucurrī, occursus: *run up to, meet, encounter*
obfutura < obsum, obesse, obfuī, obfutūrus: *be against, be harmful to*; modifies imprūdentia, imprūdentiae, F: *ignorance*, a second subject
scrūpus, scrūpī, M: *sharp stone*
gastra, gastrae, F: *large-bellied jar* (Greek loan word)
ēminēns, ēminentis: *projecting*
cruentus, cruenta, cruentum: *gory, bloody; bloodthirsty*

79.4

pīla, pīlae, F: *pillar*
crēta, crētae, F: *chalk*

līneāmentum, līneāmentī, N: *line; feature*
spissus, spissa, spissum: *thick, dense*

Our heroes make it back to their lodgings, but find that their landlady, having
passed out drunk, does not hear their demands to be let in. Trimalchio's retinue
comes by, however, making so much noise that it awakens her and everyone
else. Our heroes fall into bed.

79.9

grātulor, grātulārī, grātulātus sum: *be glad, rejoice, congratulate; give thanks to*
mero < **merus, mera, merum:** *pure, unmixed.* Understand **vino.**
volūtō, volūtāre, volūtāvī, volūtātus: *roll around;* (passive) *wallow, luxuriate;* here
    used euphemistically

79.10

expergīscor, expergīscī, experrēctus sum: *wake up; be alert*
pertrectō, pertrectāre, pertrectāvī, pertrectātus: *handle; examine in detail*
gaudio despoliatum torum: Ovid uses similar language in *Heroides* 10.9–12
    when he has Ariadne lament her bed abandoned by Theseus.
* A lacuna is suspected because Encolpius' next sentence is a condition without
an apodosis.
uterque, utraque, utrumque: *each, both* (i.e., Giton and Ascyltos)
trāiciō, trāicere, trāiēcī, trāiectus: *throw across; pierce.* In early Roman law, a
    husband who found his wife in bed with another man was allowed to kill
    either or both of them. Encolpius presents himself as a cuckolded hus-
    band, a theme also popular in mime.
tutius < **tūtus, tūta, tūtum:** *safe; cautious;* modifies **consilium**
verber, verberis, N: *whip; flogging; lash, slap, blow*
trux, trucis: *savage, fierce*
res tuas ocius tolle: language characteristic of an announcement of divorce;
    ōcius (adverb): *rather swiftly; immediately*

79.12

manubiae, manubiārum, F pl.: *spoils, money* from the sale of military booty or
   robbery

80

parricīdālis, parricīdāle: *parricidal, murderous*
praeda, praedae, F: *plunder, spoils; prey*
incumbis < **incumbō, incumbere, incubuī, incubitum**, *lean on, lie down*, but
   punning on **incubō, incubōnis**, M: a spirit that guards buried treasure or
   settles itself on sleepers and suffocates them
partem: direct object of **abscidam**
vel (adverb): *even, actually*
abscīdō, abscīdere, abscīdī, abscīsus: *cut off, chop off*
intortus, intorta, intortum: *twisted*
pallium, palliī, N: wool *cloak* (Greek loan word)
proelior, proeliārī, proeliātus sum: *battle, fight*
gradus, gradūs, M: *step, gait; stance*

80.3

flētus, flētūs, M: *crying*
suppliciter (adverb): *suppliantly, humbly*
Thēbānus, Thēbāna, Thēbānum: *Theban, of Thebes*, here referring to the city in
   Greece where the two sons of Oedipus dueled to their deaths
taberna, tabernae, F: *inn; hut*
utique (adverb): *anyhow, at least; especially*
facinus, facinoris, N: *deed, act; crime*
opus est: *there is a need* (+ ablative of thing needed)
nūdō, nūdāre, nūdāvī, nūdātus: *uncover, lay bare, strip*
mucrō, mucrōnis, M: *edge, point; sword*

CHAPTER TEN: *SATYRICA* 80–82, 85–86

80.5

vetus, veteris: *old, aged; well-established*
cōnsuētudō, cōnsuētudinis, F: *custom, habit; social ties; sexual intercourse*
pignus, pigneris, N: *pledge, security*
praeceps, praecipitis: *steep; swift, hasty*
festīnātiō, festīnātiōnis, F: *hurry, haste*
līs, lītis, F: *quarrel, dispute; lawsuit*
cunctatus < **cunctor, cunctārī, cunctātus sum**: *hesitate, delay; be in doubt.* Understand **esse.**
ab extrema parte verbi: that is, from the moment Encolpius finished speaking

Encolpius falls into despair and contemplates taking his own life. Some poetry is recited.

81

Menelaus . . . antescholanus: the rhetoric teacher Agamemnon's assistant
dēversōrium, dēversōriī, N: *inn, cheap lodgings*
sarcinulae, sarcinulārum, F pl.: *small bundles.* **collegi sarcinulas** is another phrase characteristic of divorce proceedings.
lītus, lītoris, N: *seashore, beach.* In the *Iliad*, Achilles withdraws to the seashore upon losing his lover, Briseis, and both Ariadne and Dido are abandoned on the seashore.
condūcō, condūcere, condūxī, conductus: *bring together; rent, hire*
triduum, triduī, N: *three-day period, three days*
redeunte . . . contemptu: ablative absolute
verberō, verberāre, verberāvī, verberātus: *flog, whip, beat*
plānctus, plānctūs, M: *beating*
ruīna, ruīnae, F: *fall, collapse, catastrophe*; ablative of means
hauriō, haurīre, hausī, haustus: *draw up; engulf, swallow*
effugi iudicium: This begins a series of feats that Encolpius briefly recounts, none of which are part of the surviving novel. The list may give us a

glimpse into the missing stories, but Encolpius in a rant is perhaps not to be trusted.

harēna, harēnae, F: *sand; arena*

imposui: here *impose upon, trick, cheat*

occidi: This verb is sometimes used as a euphemism for engaging in sex, so what event this refers to is entirely unclear.

mendīcus, mendīcī, M: *beggar*

Graecae urbis: Countless Greek cities in southern Italy have been proposed, most commonly Puteoli, but here Encolpius may just be underscoring his isolation by calling the city foreign or Greek.

81.4

stupro liber, stupro ingenuus: stuprum, stuprī, N: *immorality; illicit sex.* **liber** implies that Ascyltos was not always free but earned his freedom through **stuprum;** however, **ingenuus** means "freeborn." Such phrases make it diffi-cult to determine Ascyltos' actual legal status, not to mention the challenge of extracting truth from a vicious verbal attack.

tessera, tesserae, F: *token, game piece; die; ticket.* The notion may be that Ascyltos' favors were won in a dice game. Alternatively, tickets were distributed by patrons or magistrates for food, gifts, admission to the games, or even brothels, so the charge may be that Ascyltos serviced those who received his patron's **tessera.**

venierunt < **vēneō, vēnīre, vēniī, vēnitum:** *go up for sale, be sold*

conduxit: The subject is the understood antecedent of **qui** (something like **aliquis**).

die togae virilis stolam: A boy's coming-of-age ceremony was called the **diēs togae virīlis,** *day of the man's toga,* while the **stola** was a respected matron's garment.

opus muliebre: *woman's work, woman's role,* usually in a sexual sense

ergastulum, ergastulī, N: *prison, chain gang*

conturbō, conturbāre, conturbāvī, conturbātus: *confuse; disturb*

solum, solī, N: *bottom, floor; sole; foundation, source, basis;* the object of both **conturbavit** and **vertit**

secūtulēia, secūtulēiae, F < **sequor:** *one who persistently follows; sycophant? stalker? groupie?* (hapax legomenon)

tāctus, tāctūs, M: *touch, contact*

adligō, adligāre, adligāvī, adligātus: *bind, tie*

attrītus, attrīta, attrītum: *worn away, rubbed off; wasted; shameless*

noxius, noxia, noxium: *harmful; guilty*

parentō, parentāre, parentāvī, parentātus: *honor with a funeral service, celebrate at the* **Parentālia**; *pay last respects; avenge*

82

latus, lateris, N: *side, flank; body, person*

cingō, cingere, cinxī, cinctus: *encircle, surround, gird.* Greek has a third voice, called the "middle," which is reflexive in nature, and sometimes the Latin passive is used as though it were a middle voice: *I gird myself/my body.*

militiam: here in the sense of *military service* or *military skill*

prōsiliō, prōsilīre, prōsiluī: *jump forward, rush out*

furō, furere: *rage, rave*

attonitus, attonita, attonitum: *thunderstruck*

efferō, efferāre, efferāvī, efferātus: *make wild, brutalize; exasperate*

capulus, capulī, M: *hilt, handle*

dēvoveō, dēvovēre, dēvōvī, dēvōtus: *vow, sacrifice; consecrate; curse*

miles: Soldiers may well have served as informal police in Roman cities, although Encolpius reveals that it may have been hard to tell them apart from imposters or con men out to fleece the unwary.

planus, planī, M: *con man, grifter*

grassātor, grassātōris, M: *tramp; bully, hoodlum*

commīlitō, commīlitōnis, M: *comrade in arms, fellow soldier*

centuria, centuriae, F: *military company, squad* within a **legiō, legiōnis**, M, the basic unit of the Roman military

ēmentior, ēmentīrī, ēmentītus sum: *invent, fabricate; tell a lie*

phaecasiātus, phaecasiāta, phaecasiātum: *wearing* **phaecasiae**, *slippered.* Fortunata is described as wearing **phaecasiae** in 67. Soldiers wore **caligae**, *boots.*

ponere iussit: understand **me**

malo: ablative of separation

Denied his revenge, Encolpius wanders into a temple precinct filled with paintings. He particularly identifies with mythological scenes of frustrated love. He then meets an older poet by the name of Eumolpus, who explains that he is poorly dressed because powerful, immoral men work against the success of those who are morally upright and of a literary mind. He then apparently launches into a tale of his younger days.

85

quaestor, quaestōris, M: *quaestor,* magistrate in charge of the treasury or an assistant to a provincial governor

stīpendium, stīpendiī, N: *military pay; military service*

Pergami < Pergamum, Pergamī, N: *Pergamum,* a city in the Roman province of Asia (see map); locative case. The provincial setting is significant—the narrator of the tale has a lot of power as an aide of the Roman governor, but the cultural milieu is Greek.

cultus, cultūs, M: *refinement; high style of living*

fōrmōsus, fōrmōsa, fōrmōsum: *shapely, beautiful,* especially in reference to young men as sexual objects

rationem: here *plan*

quotīescumque (adverb): *as often as, however often*

usu: here in a sexual sense

excandēscō, excandēscere, excanduī: *grow hot; burst into a rage*

trīstitia, trīstitiae, F: *sadness; severity, sternness*

unum ex philosophis: that is, someone who had only Platonic relationships with young men

intueor, intuērī, intuitus sum: *look at; consider*

gymnasium, gymnasiī, N: *gymnasium, exercise ground, school,* an important part of Greek male rituals of daily life (Greek loan word)

praecipiō, praecipere, praecēpī, praeceptus: *take before; admonish, advise; teach*

85.4

dies sollemnis: that is, a holiday

artō, artāre, artāvī, artātus: *compress; limit, curtail*

pigritia, pigritiae, F: *laziness;* modified by **recedendi**

ut ille non sentiat: In the ideology of ancient Greek pederasty, the young man's modesty and masculinity required that he not enjoy the physical part of the relationship. In part, the notion was that if he began to enjoy the passive role in sex, his ability to mature into an active adult male might come into question. Also, a young man was in danger of acquiring a reputation for being too eager and too easy, essentially a slut. Watch how the characterization of the ephebe develops along these lines.

columba, columbae, F: *dove*, a bird sacred to Venus. Gifts of this sort from the older to the younger man are a regular feature of pederastic courtship in Greek culture.

bene mane: *early in the morning*

86

idem liceret: that is, the same opportunity arose
tractō, tractāre, tractāvī, tractātus: *touch, caress*
indulgeō, indulgēre, indulsī, indulsus (+ dative): *grant, concede to*
sollicito < sollicitus, sollicita, sollicitum: *stirred up; anxious, restless*; refers to the ephebe
citrā (preposition + accusative): *on this side of, before, just short of*
ingurgitō, ingurgitāre, ingurgitāvī, ingurgitātus: *pour in; gorge, stuff*
asturcō, asturcōnis, M: *horse of the Asturian breed, fine stallion*. Asturia is a region in Spain, but these horses were bred in many places.
Macedonicus, Macedonica, Macedonicum: *Macedonian, from* or *of Macedonia*, a region in the northern Balkans, home of Alexander the Great

86.5

lactēns, lactentis: *milky; tender, juicy*
papilla, papillae, F: *nipple, breast*
basio: ablative of means
inhaereō, inhaerēre, inhaesī, inhaesum: *cling to, remain attached to*
munus suspectam faceret humanitatem meam: Remember that Eumolpus is trying not to be suspected by the youth's parents of seducing him.
spatior, spatiārī, spatiātus sum: *stroll, walk*
amplexus, amplexūs, M: *embrace, caress*

CHAPTER ELEVEN: *SATYRICA* 87, 97–98, 110–111

87

satis facere + dative = *make amends, make reparation, satisfy a debt.* Understand **me** as the subject of the infinitive.
distentus, distenta, distentum: *distended, bulging*

87.3

improbitās, improbitātis, F: *wickedness, depravity*
extorqueō, extorquēre, extorsī, extortus: *wrench, wrest; extort*
irrēpō, irrēpere, irrēpsī, irrēptum: *creep in, sneak in*
indēlectātus, indēlectāta, indēlectātum: *not delighted, displeased*
nēquitia, nēquitiae, F: *worthlessness; wickedness*
queror, querī, questus sum: *complain; lament*
trādūcō, trādūcere, trādūxī, trāductus: *bring across; make a show of; disgrace, degrade*
cēnsus, cēnsūs, M: *census; income bracket, wealth*
fac: *Do it* has the same euphemistic quality in modern English.

87.6

dēlābor, dēlābī, dēlāpsus sum: *slip, fall*
maturitatis: genitive of description
annis: ablative of description; modified by **gestientibus** < **gestiō, gestīre, gestīvī**: *be delighted; be eager*
sōpītus, sōpīta, sōpītum: *asleep, sleepy*
utcumque (adverb): *however; whenever; one way or another*
anhēlitus, anhēlitūs, M: *panting, heavy breathing*
trītus, trīta, trītum: *worn, worn down, worn out*
rūrsus (adverb): *back*

87.9

pungō, pungere, pupugī, pūnctus: *prick, poke*

Encolpius and Eumolpus chat about the paintings, and Eumolpus starts reciting some of his poetry, which entices the crowd to stone them until they flee the scene. Encolpius and Eumolpus band together in the face of this adversity. Eventually, Encolpius runs into Giton at the baths and finds out that Ascyltos has been treating him like a slave. Encolpius rescues Giton and learns from Eumolpus that Ascyltos is coming after him. After Eumolpus and Encolpius have a spat over Giton's affections, Eumolpus storms out in order to turn his companions in for a reward.

97

stabulum, stabulī, N: *stable; humble lodging; brothel*
praeco cum servo publico: City officials have become involved because runaway slaves were of public concern.
fax, facis, F: *torch*
fūmōsus, fūmōsa, fūmōsum: *smoky, smoking*
quassō, quassāre: *shake, wave*
crispus, crispa, crispum: *curly-haired*
mollis, molle: *soft, tender,* often with the connotation of *effeminate*
discolor, discolōris: *of different colors*
lanx, lancis, F: *dish, platter*
indicium, indiciī, N: *evidence, proof; information*
fidēs: that is, a guarantee of payment

97.4

grabātus, grabātī, M: *cot* (Greek loan word)
annectō, annectere, annexuī, annexus: *tie, connect*
īnstita, īnstitae, F: *band, strap, rope*

sponda, spondae, F: *bed frame; bed, sofa*

culcita, culcitae, F: *mattress*

Ulixes = Ulysses, Latin name for Odysseus, who in the *Odyssey* escaped from the cave of the blinded Cyclops by holding on to the underside of a ram (**ariēs, arietis**, M). The scene also recalls the adultery theme popular in mime, where a bed under which the adulterer hides is a stage prop.

scrūtor, scrūtārī, scrūtātus sum: *scrutinize, look closely*

vinculum, vinculī, N: *binding, fetter; cord*

astus, astūs, M: *cunning; trick*

vestīgium, vestīgiī, N: *trace, track, vestige, outline, footprint*

97.7

Ascyltos: Greek nominative singular. When slaves ran away, under Roman law the owner had a right to search other people's property to retrieve them.

viātor, viātoris, M: in a legal sense, a *summoner* or *process-server*, probably the **praeco** from 97.1

quo: *to the degree that, in that*; introduces a relative clause explaining why the **spem** is **pleniorem**

oppessulō, oppessulāre, oppessulāvī, oppessulātus: *bolt, bar*

foris, foris, F: *door;* (plural) *double doors*

commissūra, commissūrae, F: *joint, hinge*

secūris, secūris, F: *axe*

claustra, claustrōrum, N pl.: *lock, bolt*

97.9

preces < **prex, precis**, F: *prayer, request.* Take as the subject.

satia: imperative

quaestiō, quaestiōnis, F: *inquiry,* here in the technical sense of a *judicial investigation* (into the escape of the "slave" Giton)

āmolior, āmolīrī: *remove, dispose of*

98

languidē (adverb): *weakly, without energy*
caupō, caupōnis, M: *innkeeper*
harundō, harundinis, F: *reed, cane*
subter (preposition + accusative): *underneath, beneath*
forāmen, forāminis, N: *hole, opening, crack*
ictus, ictūs, M: *blow, strike, hit*
scinīphēs, scinīphum, M pl.: *insects, bedbugs* (Greek loan word)

Eumolpus enters and proclaims his betrayal of Encolpius, who begs the poet to spare him and tries to convince him that Giton has fled into the crowd.

98.4

plenus: here *full*, as in *finished with*; **spiritus** is genitive
sternūtō, sternūtāre, sternūtāvī: *sneeze violently*
grabātus, grabātī, M: *cot* (Greek loan word)
salveō, salvēre: *be in good health, be well,* what you would say to someone who has just sneezed
culcita, culcitae, F: *mattress, cushion*
ēsuriō, ēsurīre: *be hungry, starve*

Somehow, Encolpius and Giton escape from Ascyltos, whom we do not meet again in the extant novel. The reunited pair manage to convince Eumolpus to get over his anger and travel with them. The trio board a ship, which after setting sail they discover belongs to Lichas, an old enemy of Encolpius. After a scheme to hide their presence on the ship, Lichas discovers them, and a dispute breaks out that rapidly grows violent. Eumolpus manages to mediate a truce, and the various parties begin to feast in celebration.

110.6

Eumolpos: a Greek nominative form
perīclitor, perīclitārī, perīclitātus sum: *be in danger*

levitās, levitātis, F: *lightness, levity; fickleness*
adamō, adamāre = ad + amō, amāre
peregrina libidine: that is, lust for a stranger
se = Eumolpus. The narrator has slipped into indirect discourse.
saeculum, saeculī, N: *generation, lifetime, era*
ōrdior, ōrdīrī, ōrsus sum: *begin*. The verb lends an epic tone to the story, as
    Vergil uses it to describe Aeneas taking up the tale of the fall of Troy in
    the *Aeneid*.

111

Ephesus, Ephesī, M: *Ephesus*, a city on the coast of Asia Minor (see map), not
    far from Miletus, thus evoking the genre "Milesian Tales"
sui: objective genitive, *to the spectacle of herself*
passis . . . crinibus: *with hair undone*, a common feature of women in mourn-
    ing, as is breast-beating
plangō, plangere, plānxī, plānctus: *beat; beat one's breast, lament*
hypogaeum, hypogaeī, N: *underground burial vault* (Greek loan word)

111.3

inedia, inediae, F: *not eating, fasting, starvation*
propinquus, propinquī, M: *a relative, someone close*
magistrātus, magistrātūs, M: *magistrate, local official*
complōrō, complōrāre, complōrāvī, complōrātus: *mourn (together)*

CHAPTER TWELVE: *SATYRICA* 111–112, 129–130

111.5

affulgeō, affulgēre, affulsī: *shine; appear*
cōnfiteor, cōnfitērī, cōnfessus sum: *confess, acknowledge*

imperātor, imperātōris, M: here *commander, leader*
latrō, latrōnis, M: *thief, bandit*
crucibus affīgī: that is, *to be crucified*
sepultūra, sepultūrae, F: *burial*. Part of the punishment of crucifixion was delay of burial and mutilation of the corpse, both considered horrific.
īnfernus, īnferna, īnfernum: *lower; infernal, of the underworld*. The soldier at first takes the widow for a ghost.

111.8

unguis, unguis, M: *fingernail*
cēnula, cēnulae, F: diminutive of **cena**
ne persevēraret . . . domicilium: typical expressions of consolation found across ancient literature
supervacuus, supervacua, supervacuum: *superfluous*
nihil profutūro gemitu: **nihil** is the object of **profutūro**, *about to yield nothing in profit, going to be of no use.*
dīdūcō, dīdūcere, dīdūxī, dīductus: *draw apart, open*, here as in *tear apart*
eundum esse: The narrator is now indirectly reporting what the soldier says.
exulcerō, exulcerāre, exulcerāvī, exulcerātus: *make sore, wound; exasperate*
ignota < **ignōtus, ignōta, ignōtum**: *unknown, strange*, even to the point of *ignoble* or *base*; modifies **consolatione**, whereas **percussa** modifies the subject, the **matrona**

111.10

muliercula, mulierculae, F: Diminutive of **mulier**. It is unclear whether this refers to the **ancilla** or the **matrona**.
refecta < **reficiō, reficere, refēcī, refectus**: *make again; repair; refresh*. Modifies the subject.
prōsum, prōdesse, prōfuī, prōfutūrus (+ dative): *be of use, benefit, profit*
sepeliō, sepelīre, sepeliī, sepultus: *bury*
id cinerem . . . sepultos: quote from Vergil, *Aeneid* 4.34, in which Dido's sister Anna tries to persuade her to abandon her love for her dead husband and yield to her attraction for Aeneas

cinis, cineris, M: *ashes; ruin, death;* (in plural) *cremated remains.* Take **cinerem** and **manes** as the subjects of **sentire**.

mānēs, mānium, M pl.: *spirits of the dead*

commodum, commodī, N: *convenience, advantage; a good* or *useful thing*

corpus: subject

112

plērumque (adverb): *generally, mostly; often*

impetrō, impetrāre, impetrāvī, impetrātus: *accomplish, achieve, bring about that* (+ **ut** + subjunctive)

īnfācundus, īnfācunda, īnfācundum: *ineloquent*

placitone . . . amori: Vergil, *Aeneid* 4.38, more of Anna's speech to Dido

placitus, placita, placitum: *pleasing; acceptable*

utrumque < **uterque, utraque, utrumque**: *each, both;* in this case, both to eat and to have sex

112.3

per facultates: *within his means, according to his means*

coemō, coemere, coēmī, coemptus: *buy up*

cruciārius, cruciāriī, M: *crucified man*

mandō, mandāre, mandāvī, mandātus: *hand over, consign; bury*

112.6

circumscriptus: as in *encircled* or *entrapped*

dēsideō, dēsidēre, dēsēdī: *sit idle*

supplicium: For a soldier to desert his post might indeed lead to capital punishment.

ius dicere: *to pronounce* or *administer judgment*

ignāvia, ignāviae, F: *laziness, idleness*

pereō, perīre, perīvī or **periī, peritum**: *pass away, die, be lost, be ruined*

112.7

misericors, misericordis: *sympathetic, merciful*
nec: an archaic use of this word for **nē** or **nōn**, making her statement sound like
    a prayer
sinō, sinere, sīvī, situs: *allow*
impendere: a pun, both *to hang, suspend*, and *to pay out, expend*
arca, arcae, F: *chest, box*; here *coffin*
qua ratione: that is, *how*

After Eumolpus' tale, a storm suddenly brews, capsizing the ship and leaving
Encolpius and Giton stranded on the shore. Later they also find Eumolpus, alive
but ill and madly writing poetry, and his hired man. They also discover Lichas'
body, which Encolpius mourns, despite their enmity. The group then travels to
Croton, a town full of nothing but legacy hunters desperate to get written into
the wills of the well-to-do. Eumolpus decides to join in by pretending to be a
rich old widower who has recently lost his son in order to attract the favors of
those who would want to be in his good graces. Meanwhile, Encolpius meets a
beautiful woman named Circe, with whom he is immediately smitten and for
whom he vows to give up Giton. Impotence prevents them from consummating
their lust for one another.

129.3

Chrȳsis, Chrȳsis, F: *Chrysis*, a name from the Greek word for gold; Circe's maid
cōdicillī, cōdicillōrum, M pl.: *writing tablets; notes, letters.* Latin poetry is full
    of love letters, from courtship to break-ups; however, the topic of impotence
    here is unique.
Circē, Circae, F: *Circe*, name of the witch who turned Odysseus' men into swine
Polyaenus or **Polyaenos, Polyaenī,** M: *much praised* in Greek, a common epi-
    thet of Odysseus in both the *Iliad* and *Odyssey*
paralysin < **paralysis, paralysis,** F: *paralysis, numbness* (Greek loan word);
    accusative singular

129.6

medius: either *in your middle, the middle part of you*, or as in *half, halfway*
tubinices: *trumpeters*, who often played at funerals
triduum, triduī, N: *three-day period, three days*
speculum, speculī, N: *mirror*

129.10

convīcium, convīciī, N: *noise, outcry; altercation; abuse*
mulieres . . . lunam deducunt: probably a reference to witches, who are said to
    draw down the moon to make potions

130

ad mortem: *with penalty of death*
dēlinquō, dēlinquere, dēliquī: *do wrong, commit an offense; fall short, be wanting*
reus, reī, M: *defendant, the accused*, a legal term
proditionem < **prōditiō, prōditiōnis**, F: *betrayal; treason*. This begins a short
    list of Encolpius' crimes, reminiscent of his account in 81. Scholars debate
    whether these are delusions of grandeur, euphemisms for sexual escapades,
    or actual events from the missing parts of the novel.
memento: singular imperative of the defective verb **meminī, meminisse**, *remember*

Supplemental Latin Text

A BOAR HUNT AND A FREEDMAN'S CAP (*SATYRICA* 40–41)

40 "sophos" universi clamamus et sublatis manibus ad cameram iuramus Hipparchum Aratumque comparandos illi homines non fuisse, donec advenerunt ministri ac toralia praeposuerunt toris, in quibus retia erant picta subsessoresque cum venabulis et totus venationis apparatus. necdum sciebamus, quo mitteremus suspiciones nostras, cum extra triclinium clamor sublatus est ingens, et ecce canes Laconici etiam circa mensam discurrere coeperunt. **40.3** secutum est hos repositorium, in quo positus erat primae magnitudinis aper, et quidem pilleatus, e cuius dentibus sportellae dependebant duae palmulis textae, altera caryotis altera thebaicis repleta. circa autem minores porcelli ex coptoplacentis facti, quasi uberibus imminerent, scrofam esse positam significabant. et hi quidem apophoreti fuerunt. **40.5** ceterum ad scindendum aprum non ille Carpus accessit, qui altilia laceraverat, sed barbatus ingens, fasciis cruralibus alligatus et alicula subornatus polymita, strictoque venatorio cultro latus apri vehementer percussit, ex cuius plaga turdi evolaverunt. parati aucupes cum harundinibus fuerunt et eos circa triclinium volitantes momento exceperunt. inde cum suum cuique iussisset referri Trimalchio, adiecit: "etiam videte, quam porcus ille silvaticus lotam comederit glandem." statim pueri ad sportellas accesserunt, quae pendebant e dentibus, thebaicasque et caryotas ad numerum divisere cenantibus. **41** interim ego, qui privatum habebam secessum, in multas cogitationes diductus sum, quare aper pilleatus intrasset. postquam itaque omnis bacalusias consumpsi, duravi interrogare illum interpretem meum, quod me torqueret. at ille: "plane etiam hoc servus tuus indicare potest; non enim aenigma est, sed res aperta. hic aper, cum heri summa cena eum vindicasset, a convivis dimissus est; itaque hodie tamquam libertus in convivium revertitur." damnavi ego stuporem meum et nihil amplius interrogavi, ne viderer numquam inter honestos cenasse.

41.6 dum haec loquimur, puer speciosus, vitibus hederisque redimitus, modo Bromium, interdum Lyaeum Euhiumque confessus, calathisco uvas circumtulit et poemata domini sui acutissima voce traduxit. ad quem sonum conversus Trimalchio "Dionyse," inquit, "liber esto." puer detraxit pilleum apro capitique suo imposuit. tum Trimalchio rursus adiecit: "non negabitis me," inquit, "habere Liberum patrem." laudavimus dictum et circumeuntem puerum sane perbasiamus.

ECHION, UNCUT (*SATYRICA* 45–46)

45 "oro te," inquit Echion centonarius, "melius loquere. 'modo sic, modo sic,' inquit rusticus; varium porcum perdiderat. quod hodie non est, cras erit: sic vita truditur. non mehercules patria melior dici potest, si homines haberet. sed laborat hoc tempore, nec haec sola. non debemus delicati esse, ubique medius caelus est. tu si aliubi fueris, dices hic porcos coctos ambulare. et ecce habituri sumus munus excellente in triduo die festa; familia non lanisticia, sed plurimi liberti. et Titus noster magnum animum habet et est caldicerebrius: aut hoc aut illud, erit quid utique. nam illi domesticus sum, non est mixcix. **45.6** ferrum optimum daturus est, sine fuga, carnarium in medio, ut amphitheater videat. et habet unde: relictum est illi sestertium trecenties, decessit illius pater. male! ut quadringenta impendat, non sentiet patrimonium illius, et sempiterno nominabitur. iam Manios aliquot habet et mulierem essedariam et dispensatorem Glyconis, qui deprehensus est, cum dominam suam delectaretur. videbis populi rixam inter zelotypos et amasiunculos. Glyco autem, sestertiarius homo, dispensatorem ad bestias dedit. hoc est se ipsum traducere. quid servus peccavit, qui coactus est facere? magis illa matella digna fuit quam taurus iactaret. sed qui asinum non potest, stratum caedit. **45.9** quid autem Glyco putabat Hermogenis filicem umquam bonum exitum facturam? ille milvo volanti poterat ungues resecare; colubra restem non parit. Glyco, Glyco dedit suas; itaque quamdiu vixerit, habebit stigmam, nec illam nisi Orcus delebit. sed sibi quisque peccat. sed subolfacio, quia nobis epulum daturus est Mammea, binos denarios mihi et meis. quod si hoc fecerit, eripiet Norbano totum favorem. scias oportet plenis velis hunc vinciturum. et revera, quid ille nobis boni fecit? **45.11** dedit gladiatores sestertiarios iam decrepitos, quos si sufflasses cecidissent; iam meliores bestiarios vidi. occidit de lucerna equites, putares eos gallos gallinaceos; alter burdubasta, alter loripes, tertiarius mortuus pro mortuo, qui habebat nervia praecisa. unus alicuius flaturae fuit Thraex, qui et ipse ad dictata pugnavit. ad summam, omnes postea secti sunt; adeo de magna turba 'adhibete' acceperant, plane fugae merae. 'munus tamen,' inquit, 'tibi dedi': et ego tibi plodo. computa, et tibi plus do quam accepi. manus manum lavat. **46** videris mihi, Agamemnon, dicere: 'quid iste argutat molestus?' quia tu, qui potes loquere, non loquis. non es nostrae fasciae, et ideo pauperorum verba derides. scimus te prae litteras fatuum esse. quid ergo est? aliqua die te persuadeam, ut ad villam venias et videas casulas nostras? inveniemus quod manducemus, pullum, ova: belle erit, etiam si omnia hoc anno tempestas depravavit: inveniemus ergo unde saturi fiamus. **46.3** et iam tibi discipulus crescit cicaro meus. iam quattuor partis dicit; si vixerit, habebis ad latus servulum. nam quicquid illi vacat, caput de tabula non tollit. ingeniosus est et bono filo, etiam si in aves morbosus est. ego illi iam tres cardeles occidi, et dixi quia mustella comedit. invenit tamen alias nenias, et libentissime pingit. ceterum iam Graeculis calcem impingit et Latinas coepit non male appetere, etiam si magister eius sibi placens fit nec uno loco consistit. scit quidem litteras, sed non vult laborare.

46.6 est et alter non quidem doctus, sed curiosus, qui plus docet quam scit. itaque feriatis diebus solet domum venire, et quicquid dederis, contentus est. emi ergo nunc puero aliquot libra rubricata, quia volo illum ad domusionem aliquid de iure gustare. habet haec res panem. nam litteris satis inquinatus est. quod si resilierit, destinavi illum artificium docere, aut tonstrinum aut praeconem aut certe causidicum, quod illi auferre non possit nisi Orcus. **46.8** ideo illi cotidie clamo: 'Primigeni, crede mihi, quicquid discis, tibi discis. vides Phileronem causidicum: si non didicisset, hodie famem a labris non abigeret. modo modo collo suo circumferebat onera venalia, nunc etiam adversus Norbanum se extendit. litterae thesaurum est, et artificium numquam moritur."'

THE FALL OF THE ACROBAT (*SATYRICA* 53–54)

53.11 petauristarii autem tandem venerunt. baro insulsissimus cum scalis constitit puerumque iussit per gradus et in summa parte odaria saltare, circulos deinde ardentes transilire et dentibus amphoram sustinere. mirabatur haec solus Trimalchio dicebatque ingratum artificium esse. ceterum duo esse in rebus humanis quae libentissime spectaret, petauristarios et cornicines; reliqua acroamata tricas meras esse. "nam et comoedos," inquit, "emeram, sed malui illos Atellaniam facere, et choraulen meum iussi Latine cantare."

54 cum maxime haec dicente eo puer * Trimalchionis delapsus est. conclamavit familia, nec minus convivae, non propter hominem tam putidum, cuius etiam cervices fractas libenter vidissent, sed propter malum exitum cenae, ne necesse haberent alienum mortuum plorare. ipse Trimalchio cum graviter ingemuisset superque bracchium tamquam laesum incubuisset, concurrere medici, et inter primos Fortunata crinibus passis cum scypho, miseramque se atque infelicem proclamavit. **54.3** nam puer quidem qui ceciderat circumibat iam dudum pedes nostros et missionem rogabat. pessime mihi erat, ne his precibus per ridiculum aliquid catastropha quaereretur. nec enim adhuc exciderat cocus ille qui oblitus fuerat porcum exinterare. itaque totum circumspicere triclinium coepi, ne per parietem automatum aliquod exiret, utique postquam servus verberari coepit, qui bracchium domini contusum alba potius quam conchyliata involverat lana. **54.5** nec longe aberravit suspicio mea; in vicem enim poenae venit decretum Trimalchionis quo puerum iussit liberum esse, ne quis posset dicere tantum virum esse a servo vulneratum.

ASCYLTOS AND GITON
GET PUT IN THEIR PLACE (*SATYRICA* 57–58)

57 ceterum Ascyltos, intemperantis licentiae, cum omnia sublatis manibus eluderet et usque ad lacrimas rideret, unus ex conlibertis Trimalchionis excanduit— is ipse qui supra me discumbebat— et "quid rides," inquit, "vervex? an tibi non placent lautitiae domini mei? tu enim beatior es et convivare melius soles. ita tutelam huius loci habeam propitiam, ut ego si secundum illum discumberem, iam illi balatum clusissem. **57.3** bellum pomum, qui rideatur alios; larifuga nescio quis, nocturnus, qui non valet lotium suum. ad summam, si circumminxero illum, nesciet qua fugiat. non mehercules soleo cito fervere, sed in molle carne vermes nascuntur. ridet. quid habet quod rideat? numquid pater fetum emit lamna? eques Romanus es: et ego regis filius. 'quare ergo servivisti?' quia ipse me dedi in servitutem et malui civis Romanus esse quam tributarius. et nunc spero me sic vivere, ut nemini iocus sim. **57.5** homo inter homines sum, capite aperto ambulo; assem aerarium nemini debeo; constitutum habui numquam; nemo mihi in foro dixit: 'redde quod debes.' glebulas emi, lamellulas paravi; viginti ventres pasco et canem; contubernalem meam redemi, ne quis in capillis illius manus tergeret; mille denarios pro capite solvi; sevir gratis factus sum; spero, sic moriar, ut mortuus non erubescam. tu autem tam laboriosus es, ut post te non respicias? in alio peduclum vides, in te ricinum non vides. **57.8** tibi soli ridicli videmur; ecce magister tuus, homo maior natus: placemus illi. tu lacticulosus, nec mu nec ma argutas, vasus fictilis, immo lorus in aqua, lentior, non melior. tu beatior es: bis prande, bis cena. ego fidem meam malo quam thesauros. ad summam, quisquam me bis poposcit? annis quadraginta servivi; nemo tamen sciit utrum servus essem an liber. et puer capillatus in hanc coloniam veni; adhuc basilica non erat facta. **57.10** dedi tamen operam ut domino satis facerem, homini maiesto et dignitoso, cuius pluris erat unguis quam tu totus es. et habebam in domo qui mihi pedem opponerent hac illac; tamen— genio illius gratias— enatavi. haec sunt vera athla; nam ingenuum nasci tam facile est quam 'accede istoc.' quid nunc stupes tamquam hircus in ervilia?"

58 post hoc dictum Giton, qui ad pedes stabat, risum iam diu compressum etiam indecenter effudit. quod cum animadvertisset adversarius Ascylti, flexit convi-cium in puerum et "tu autem," inquit, "etiam tu rides, cepa cirrata? io Saturnalia, rogo, mensis december est? quando vicesimam numerasti? * quid faciat crucis offla, corvorum cibaria? curabo, iam tibi Iovis iratus sit, et isti qui tibi non imperat. **58.3** ita satur pane fiam, ut ego istud conliberto meo dono; alioquin iam tibi depraesentiarum reddidissem. bene nos habemus, at isti nugae. plane qualis dominus, talis et servus. vix me teneo, nec sum natura caldicerebrius, sed cum coepi, matrem meam dupundii non facio. recte, videbo te in publicum, mus, immo terrae tuber: nec sursum nec deorsum non cresco, nisi dominum tuum in rutae folium non conieci, nec tibi parsero, licet mehercules Iovem Olympium clames. curabo, longe tibi sit comula ista besalis et dominus dupunduarius. **58.6** recte, venies sub dentem: aut ego non me novi, aut non deridebis, licet barbam auream habeas. Athana tibi irata sit, curabo, et ei qui te primus 'deuro de' fecit. non didici geometrias, critica et alogas menias, sed lapidarias litteras scio, par-tes centum dico ad aes, ad pondus, ad nummum. ad summam, si quid vis, ego et tu sponsiunculam: exi, defero lamnam. iam scies patrem tuum mercedes perdidisse, quamvis et rhetoricam scis. ecce 'qui de nobis longe venio, late venio? solve me.'

58.9 "dicam tibi, qui de nobis currit et de loco non movetur; qui de nobis crescit et minor fit. curris, stupes, satagis, tamquam mus in matella. ergo aut tace aut meliorem noli molestare, qui te natum non putat; nisi si me iudicas anulos buxeos curare, quos amicae tuae involasti. Occuponem propitium. eamus in forum et pecunias mutuemur: iam scies hoc ferrum fidem habere. vah, bella res est volpis uda. **58.12** ita lucrum faciam et ita bene moriar ut populus per exitum meum iuret, nisi te ubique toga perversa fuero persecutus. bella res et iste, qui te haec docet, mufrius, non magister. nos aliter didicimus, dicebat enim magister: 'sunt vestra salva? recta domum; cave, circumspicias; cave, maiorem maledicas.' at nunc mera mapalia: nemo dupondii evadit. ego, quod me sic vides, propter artificium meum diis gratias ago."

ENCOLPIUS SINGS TO HIS MISBEHAVING MEMBER (*SATYRICA* 132.7–11)

132.7 quod solum igitur salvo pudore poteram, contingere languorem simulavi, conditusque lectulo totum ignem furoris in eam converti, quae mihi omnium malorum causa fuerat:

> ter corripui terribilem manu bipennem,
> ter languidior coliculi repente thyrso
> ferrum timui, quod trepido male dabat usum.
> nec iam poteram, quod modo conficere libebat;
> namque illa metu frigidior rigente bruma
> confugerat in viscera mille operta rugis.
> ita non potui supplicio caput aperire,

>sed furciferae mortifero timore lusus
>ad verba, magis quae poterant nocere, fugi.

132.9 erectus igitur in cubitum hac fere oratione contumacem vexavi: "quid dicis" inquam "omnium hominum deorumque pudor? nam ne nominare quidem te inter res serias fas est. hoc de te merui, ut me in caelo positum ad inferos traheres? ut traduceres annos primo florentes vigore senectaeque ultimae mihi lassitudinem imponeres? rogo te, mihi apodixin non defunctoriam redde." **132.11** haec ut iratus effudi,

>illa solo fixos oculos aversa tenebat,
>nec magis incepto vultum sermone movetur
>quam lentae salices lassove papavera collo.

Guided Review

CHAPTER ONE: NOUN/ADJECTIVE DECLENSIONS AND TENSES OF THE INDICATIVE

You will have a much easier time reading a Latin novel if the case and function of a noun and the person and number of a verb come to you instantly and effortlessly. A full passage of literature provides so much for your brain to be thinking about that it should not be asked to pause over these basic forms. If you cannot automatically recognize the case endings of the first three declensions and the active and passive personal endings of verbs in the present and perfect indicative, this is where your review time is best spent.

	The First Declension Built around the vowel -*a*- Largely feminine		*The Second Declension* Built around the vowel -*o*- Largely masculine or neuter			
	feminine (& masculine)		*masculine (& feminine)*		*neuter*	
Nominative	-a	-ae	-us *or* -er	-ī	-um	-a
Genitive	-ae	-ārum	-ī	-ōrum	-ī	-ōrum
Dative	-ae	-īs	-ō	-īs	-ō	-īs
Accusative	-am	-ās	-um	-ōs	-um	-a
Ablative	-ā	-īs	-ō	-īs	-ō	-īs

Note that only the second declension has a separate vocative form, and only in the masculine singular: all masculine singulars with a nominative in **-us** have the vocative **-e**, while those with **-ius** have **-ī**.

The Third Declension
Built around either no vowel (consonant stems) or the vowel -i- (i-stems)
All three genders are widely found

| | consonant stems | | | | i-stems | | | |
	masculine & feminine		neuter		masculine & feminine		neuter	
Nominative	(varies)	-ēs	(varies)	-a	(varies)	-ēs	(varies)	-ia
Genitive	-is	-um	-is	-um	-is	-ium	-is	-ium
Dative	-ī	-ibus	-ī	-ibus	-ī	-ibus	-ī	-ibus
Accusative	-em	-ēs	(varies)	-a	-em	-ēs or -īs	(varies)	-ia
Ablative	-e	-ibus	-e	-ibus	-e	-ibus	-ī	-ibus

Note that third declension adjectives decline like i-stem nouns and have the -ī in the ablative singular of the masculine/feminine as well as the neuter.

| | The Fourth Declension | | | | The Fifth Declension | |
| | Built around the vowel -u- | | | | Built around the vowel -e- | |
	Largely masculine or neuter				Largely feminine	
	masculine (& feminine)		neuter		feminine (& masculine)	
Nominative	-us	-ūs	-ū	-ua	-ēs	-ēs
Genitive	-ūs	-uum	-ūs	-uum	-eī	-ērum
Dative	-uī	-ibus	-uī or -ū	-ibus	-eī	-ēbus
Accusative	-um	-ūs	-ū	-ua	-em	-ēs
Ablative	-ū	-ibus	-ū	-ibus	-ē	-ēbus

Note that in the fifth declension -eī becomes -ēī if the noun's stem ends in a vowel (e.g., diēī). Note too that all neuters, regardless of declension, share the same two traits: the nominative and accusative forms are the same, and the nominative and accusative plural forms end in a short -a.

As Latin authors often do, Petronius will frequently use Greek endings when declining Greek names. These will be pointed out in your notes, as with **Gitona**, a Greek accusative form found in chapter 1.

An Overview of Latin Cases

The **nominative** is the "name" of a noun. It is used for the subject of a finite verb and the nouns or adjectives connected to the subject. If the verb in a sentence is a linking verb, the predicate noun will also be in the nominative (**servus est Cinnamus**, *Cinnamus is a slave*; note that both words are nominative). Nominatives are also the subjects of historical infinitives.

The **genitive**, at its heart, expresses the source or origin of another noun. It is therefore essentially adjectival, in that it is used to modify a noun with another noun. The most common usage of this sort is to demonstrate possession. Instead of saying **vinum merum,** *pure wine,* for example, we could say **vinum Gaii,** *Gaius' wine, the wine of Gaius.* It is also used for material (**pallium gausapae,** *a cloak of wool*) or to express a partitive idea (**scyphus vini,** *a cup of wine,* i.e., not *all* the wine, just a portion of it). The genitive also is used when a noun is the object of another noun with a verbal sense (**amor vini,** *a love of wine,* i.e., one *loves* wine). Certain adjectives and verbs also simply take the genitive.

Nouns in the **dative** are indirectly affected by the action of the verb in a sentence. The subject may give the direct object to an indirect object in the dative (**Marcus puellae rosam dat,** *Marcus gives the girl a rose*). The verb may take place for the advantage (or the disadvantage) of or simply in reference to the person in the dative (**puella formosa est Marco,** *the girl is beautiful to Marcus*). The dative may be used with a form of the verb **sum, esse** to express possession (**huic nomen Marcus est,** *for him the name is Marcus, his name is Marcus*). Certain adjectives and verbs also simply take the dative.

The **accusative** marks the limit of the action of the verb. In a transitive sentence this means that the accusative receives the action of the verb; it is the direct object. An accusative can limit the duration of time in which an action takes place (**tres horas,** *for three hours*) or the extent of space that it covers (**tria milia passuum,** *for three miles*). Prepositions that take the accusative generally have a sense of movement toward, into, or through their accusative object. Another important and quite common use of the accusative is as the subject of an infinitive in an indirect statement or noun clause. An old means of forming adverbs was to use the neuter singular accusative of adjectives. This survives in common adverbs such as **multum, prīmum,** and **vērum** and the comparative adverbs in -**ius.** Many authors also borrow the accusative of respect from Greek.

The **ablative** is a largely adverbial case. It has four basic senses. One is movement from a place; hence the prepositions that signify *from* or *out of* take the ablative. The use of the ablative to express cause is an outgrowth of this sense, as is the ablative of personal agent. Another sense is locative or static. This includes the uses with prepositions that signify *in* or *on;* in these cases there is no movement. Out of this sense come the ablative expressions of time, which express when the verb takes place. The third sense is the sociative; the action of the verb takes place *with* the noun in the ablative. This might be *with a friend* or *with a feeling.* A person may simply exist **magno naso,** *with a big nose.* This notion that the ablative can be used to express information or details associated with the main clause leads to the ablative absolute. The fourth and final sense is the instrumentative. This expresses the tool or means by which the action takes place. Certain adjectives and verbs also simply take the ablative.

The **vocative** case is used to directly address a noun. It is often set apart by commas. In Latin only second declension masculine singular nouns that end in -**us** have separate vocative forms (-**us** becomes -**e**, as in **amicus/amice**; -**ius** becomes -**ī**, as in **Gaius/Gaī**). Some Greek names retain their Greek vocative forms. Otherwise the vocative is always identical to the nominative.

Latin also preserves remnants of the old **locative** case. In general, the locative was absorbed into the ablative case, but the names of cities, towns, and small islands, as well as a few common nouns like **domus**, *home*, retained separate forms (**domī**, *at home*). For singular nouns of the first and second declensions, the locative resembles the genitive (hence **Ephesī**, *in Ephesus*); for all others it resembles the ablative, although third declension singular nouns occasionally show a form that resembles the dative instead.

Case	Primary Use	Other Uses	Helpful English Words
Nominative	Subject	Predicate Nominative	
Genitive	Possession	Material Partitive (also called "of the whole") Objective Description	*'s, s', of* *for* (with Objective)
Dative	Indirect object	Reference Advantage or disadvantage Possession Agent (with gerundives)	*to* (but not *toward*) *for* (as in *for the benefit of*)
Accusative	Direct object	Place to which Duration of time Extent of space Subject of indirect statement	*to* (as in *toward*) *for* (as in extent, duration)
Ablative	Adverbial	Place from which Place where Accompaniment, manner Means, agent Time when, time within which Description Ablative absolute	*from, out of* *in, on, at* *with* *by*
Vocative	Direct address		*o*
Locative	Place where		*in, at* (only for names of cities, towns, and small islands; **domus, rūs, humus**)

Adjectives

A Latin adjective agrees with the noun it modifies in case, number, and gender, *not* in ending. Adjectives tend to follow the nouns they modify within a sentence.

For most adjectives, the comparative is formed by adding the endings -**ior** (M/F), -**ius** (N), and -**iōris** (genitive) to the stem and declining like a third declension noun. For the superlative, the first/second declension adjective endings -**issimus, -issima, -issimum** are added to the stem of most adjectives.

Verbs

Latin speakers have three different verb **moods** to use in expressing themselves. The indicative mood is used to express statements of fact or ask questions of fact, to discuss events that will happen, are happening, or have happened. (In contrast, the imperative is used to give commands, and the subjunctive to present an action as nonfactual, that is, possible, probable, hoped for, aimed at, doubtful, unachieved, or the like.)

Latin has six indicative **tenses,** which each express some combination of two notions: the time of the event and its aspect, that is, whether it is simply happening, in progress, repeated or habitual, or completed. The present and perfect are by far the most common tenses; together they make up about 85 percent of the finite verbs in surviving Latin texts. The present and perfect thus deserve the most attention and are placed first here. The imperfect and future follow in frequency, with the pluperfect and future perfect following much further behind (Mahoney 2004, 102).

Finally, Latin verbs each have a **voice;** that is, they are active or passive. An active verb communicates an action that the subject performs, while a passive verb describes something that is experienced by or done to the subject. Voice is thus the critical difference between *I killed a lion* and *I was killed by a lion.* Remember that some Latin verbs use passive forms but have active meanings. Since these verbs "put down" their active forms, we call them deponent, from **dēpōnō, dēpōnere**.

Present Indicative An action in the present time being performed once or repeatedly: e.g., vocō, *I call, I am calling.*

First conjugation (*call*)	Second (*hold*)	Third (*do*)	Third -**iō** (*take*)	Fourth (*hear*)	Deponent (*follow*)
ACTIVE					
vocō	habeō	agō	capiō	audiō	sequor
vocās	habēs	agis	capis	audīs	sequeris/sequere
vocat	habet	agit	capit	audit	sequitur
vocāmus	habēmus	agimus	capimus	audīmus	sequimur
vocātis	habētis	agitis	capitis	audītis	sequiminī
vocant	habent	agunt	capiunt	audiunt	sequuntur

PASSIVE

vocor	habeor	agor	capior	audior	
vocāris/vocāre	habēris/habēre	ageris/agere	caperis/capere	audīris/audīre	
vocātur	habētur	agitur	capitur	audītur	
vocāmur	habēmur	agimur	capimur	audīmur	
vocāminī	habēminī	agiminī	capiminī	audīminī	
vocantur	habentur	aguntur	capiuntur	audiuntur	

Perfect Indicative A completed action, which thus describes the present, e.g., vocāvī, *I have called,* or an action of the past simply performed once, e.g., vocāvī, *I called.*

ACTIVE

vocāvī	habuī	ēgī	cēpī	audīvī	secūtus sum
vocāvistī	habuistī	ēgistī	cēpistī	audīvistī	secūtus es
vocāvit	habuit	ēgit	cēpit	audīvit	secūtus est
vocāvimus	habuimus	ēgimus	cēpimus	audīvimus	secūtī sumus
vocāvistis	habuistis	ēgistis	cēpistis	audīvistis	secūtī estis
vocāvērunt/	habuērunt/	ēgērunt/	cēpērunt/	audīvērunt/	secūtī sunt
vocāvēre	habuēre	ēgēre	cēpēre	audīvēre	

PASSIVE

vocātus sum	habita sum	actum sum	captus sum	audīta sum
vocātus es	habita es	actum es	captus es	audīta es
vocātus est	habita est	actum est	captus est	audīta est
vocātī sumus	habitae sumus	acta sumus	captī sumus	audītae sumus
vocātī estis	habitae estis	acta estis	captī estis	audītae estis
vocātī sunt	habitae sunt	acta sunt	captī sunt	audītae sunt

Note that in the perfect system the passive is composed of a form of the verb **sum** and a perfect passive participle. The participle by definition modifies the subject, which it will thus match in case, number, and gender. In the examples, different genders are used for each verb to illustrate.

Imperfect Indicative An action in the past performed repeatedly or still being performed: e.g., vocābam, *I used to sing, I was singing, I sang often, I kept on singing.*

ACTIVE

vocābam	habēbam	agēbam	capiēbam	audiēbam	sequēbar
vocābās	habēbās	agēbās	capiēbās	audiēbās	sequēbāris/ sequēbāre
vocābat	habēbat	agēbat	capiēbat	audiēbat	sequēbātur
vocābāmus	habēbāmus	agēbāmus	capiēbāmus	audiēbāmus	sequēbāmur
vocābātis	habēbātis	agēbātis	capiēbātis	audiēbātis	sequēbāminī
vocābant	habēbant	agēbant	capiēbant	audiēbant	sequēbantur

PASSIVE

vocābar	habēbar	agēbar	capiēbar	audiēbar
vocābāris/	habēbāris/	agēbāris/	capiēbāris/	audiēbāris/
vocābāre	habēbāre	agēbāre	capiēbāre	audiēbāre
vocābātur	habēbātur	agēbātur	capiēbātur	audiēbātur
vocābāmur	habēbāmur	agēbāmur	capiēbāmur	audiēbāmur
vocābāminī	habēbāminī	agēbāminī	capiēbāminī	audiēbāminī
vocābantur	habēbantur	agēbantur	capiēbantur	audiēbantur

Future Indicative An action in the future performed once or repeatedly, e.g., vocābō, *I shall call, I shall be calling.*

ACTIVE

vocābō	habēbō	agam	capiam	audiam	sequar
vocābis	habēbis	agēs	capiēs	audiēs	sequēris/
					sequēre
vocābit	habēbit	aget	capiet	audiet	sequētur
vocābimus	habēbimus	agēmus	capiēmus	audiēmus	sequēmur
vocābitis	habēbitis	agētis	capiētis	audiētis	sequēminī
vocābunt	habēbunt	agent	capient	audient	sequentur

PASSIVE

vocābor	habēbor	agar	capiar	audiar
vocāberis/	habēberis/	agēris/	capiēris/	audiēris/
vocābere	habēbere	agēre	capiēre	audiēre
vocābitur	habēbitur	agētur	capiētur	audiētur
vocābimur	habēbimur	agēmur	capiēmur	audiēmur
vocābiminī	habēbiminī	agēminī	capiēminī	audiēminī
vocābuntur	habēbuntur	agentur	capientur	audientur

Pluperfect Indicative An action in the past that has been completed, that is, an action completed by a time in the past, e.g., vocāveram, *I had sung.*

ACTIVE

vocāveram	habueram	ēgeram	cēperam	audīveram	secūtus eram
vocāverās	habuerās	ēgerās	cēperās	audīverās	secūtus eras
vocāverat	habuerat	ēgerat	cēperat	audīverat	secūtus erat
vocāverāmus	habuerāmus	ēgerāmus	cēperāmus	audīverāmus	secūtī eramus
vocāverātis	habuerātis	ēgerātis	cēperātis	audīverātis	secūtī eratis
vocāverant	habuerant	ēgerant	cēperant	audīverant	secūtī erant

PASSIVE

vocātus eram	habita eram	actum eram	captus eram	audīta eram
vocātus erās	habita erās	actum erās	captus erās	audīta erās
vocātus erat	habita erat	actum erat	captus erat	audīta erat
vocātī erāmus	habitae erāmus	acta erāmus	captī erāmus	audītae erāmus
vocātī erātis	habitae erātis	acta erātis	captī erātis	audītae erātis
vocātī erant	habitae erant	acta erant	captī erant	audītae erant

Future Perfect Indicative An action that will have been completed by a time in the future, e.g., vocāverō, *I shall have sung.*

ACTIVE

vocāverō	habuerō	ēgerō	cēperō	audīverō	secūtus erō
vocāveris	habueris	ēgeris	cēperis	audīveris	secūtus eris
vocāverit	habuerit	ēgerit	cēperit	audīverit	secūtus erit
vocāverimus	habuerimus	ēgerimus	cēperimus	audīverimus	secūtī erimus
vocāveritis	habueritis	ēgeritis	cēperitis	audīveritis	secūtī eritis
vocāverint	habuerint	ēgerint	cēperint	audīverint	secūtī erunt

PASSIVE

vocāta erō	habitus erō	actum erō	captus erō	audīta erō
vocāta eris	habitus eris	actum eris	captus eris	audīta eris
vocāta erit	habitus erit	actum erit	captus erit	audīta erit
vocātae erimus	habitī erimus	acta erimus	captī erimus	audītae erimus
vocātae eritis	habitī eritis	acta eritis	captī eritis	audītae eritis
vocātae erunt	habitī erunt	acta erunt	captī erunt	audītae erunt

Contraction in the Perfect System

Verbs built on the perfect active stem sometimes contract. Verbs with -āvī and -ōvī lose the **v**, and the two surrounding vowels contract. So, for example, **amaverim** may appear as **amarim,** or **novisti** as **nosti.** Perfects in -ivi also drop the **v**, but the vowels do not contract except before **st** and **ss: audiveram** becomes **audieram, audivisti** becomes **audisti, abivit** becomes **abiit,** and **abiverunt** becomes **abierunt.** Such contraction occurs with the perfect infinitive and subjunctive forms as well, as we will review in later chapters. We find these forms most often in archaic and colloquial Latin, and thus frequently in the speeches of characters in the *Satyrica.* The first few such contractions are noted in the Commentary.

Post-Reading Activities

1. Skim the passages in the next chapter. In the first section (28.6–29), identify the subject and direct object (if there is one) of each sentence. In the second section (30.5), give the person and number of the finite verbs.

2. We now know that we are headed to a banquet. What happened at a Roman dinner party? What people, events, and objects might we expect to meet? What are these words in Latin?

3. The following sentences summarize the events of the passage in the first chapter. Put them into the correct order and then transform the sentences into a coherent narrative by adding conjunctions, making some sentences into subordinate clauses, adding details to help the reader understand the story, and so forth.

Trimalchio et servi pilis ludebant.

servus interpellavit.

iatraliptae vinum bonum effuderunt.

intravimus balneum.

symphoniacus in aurem Trimalchionis cantavit.

Trimalchionem spectabamus.

Trimalchio vesicam exonerare voluit.

Trimalchio domum latus est.

servus nobis de Trimalchione dixit.

iatraliptae rixabantur.

de malis nostris deliberabamus.

Trimalchio manus lavit.

Irregular Verb: **sum, esse, fuī, futūrus**, *be, exist*

INDICATIVE

Present	sum	sumus
	es	estis
	est	sunt
Imperfect	eram	erāmus
	erās	erātis
	erat	erant
Future	erō	erimus
	eris	eritis
	erit	erunt
Perfect	fuī	fuimus
	fuistī	fuistis
	fuit	fuērunt/fuēre

Irregular Verb: **sum, esse, fuī, futūrus** (*continued*)

INDICATIVE

Pluperfect		fueram	fuerāmus
		fuerās	fuerātis
		fuerat	fuerant
Future perfect		fuerō	fuerimus
		fueris	fueritis
		fuerit	fuerint

SUBJUNCTIVE

Present		sim	sīmus
		sīs	sītis
		sit	sint
Imperfect		essem	essēmus
		essēs	essētis
		esset	essent
Perfect		fuerim	fuerimus
		fueris	fueritis
		fuerit	fuerint
Pluperfect		fuissem	fuissēmus
		fuissēs	fuissētis
fuisset		fuissent	

INFINITIVE

Present	esse
Perfect	fuisse
Future	futūrus, -a, -um esse

PARTICIPLE

Future	futūrus, -a, -um

Vocabulary

ad (preposition + accusative): *to, toward*

aliquis, aliquid: *some; any*

alius, alia, aliud (gen. s. **alterīus**, dat. s. **alterī**): *another, other, different*

bonus, bona, bonum: *good*

coepī, coepisse, coeptus: (only in perfect) *begin*

corpus, corporis, N: *body; corpse*

cum (conjunction): *when, since, although;* (preposition + ablative) *with*

dīcō, dīcere, dīxī, dictus: *say, speak*

diēs diēī, M: *daytime; a day*

dō, dare, dedī, datus: *give; grant*

domina, dominae, F or **dominus, dominī**, M: *master, owner*

domus, domī or **domūs**, F: *house, home*

ego, mihi (dat.), **mē** (acc. and abl.): *I, me*

et (conjunction): *and, even; however, but;* **et . . . et**: *both . . . and;* (adverb) *even; also*

faciō, facere, fēcī, factus: *make, do*

familia, familiae, F: *household slaves, household*

fiō, fierī, factus sum: *be made; become, happen;* used as passive of **faciō**

habeō, habēre, habuī, habitus: *have, hold*

homō, hominis, M or F: *a human being, person*

in (preposition + abl.): *in, on;* (+ acc.) *into*

inquam: *I say* / **inquit**: *he says, she says, one says;* defective verb used to introduce direct speech

intrō, intrāre, intrāvī, intrātus: *enter, penetrate*

iubeō, iubēre, iussī, iūssus: *order, bid, ask*

lautus or **lōtus, lauta, lautum**: *washed; elegant*

manus, manūs, F: *hand; gang, group*

meus, mea, meum: *my, belonging to me*

mulier, mulieris, F: *woman; wife*

nēmō, nēminis, M or F: *no one, nobody*

nihil (indeclinable) N: *nothing*

nōn (adverb): *not, no, by no means*

nox, noctis, F: *night*

omnis, omne: *all, every*

pēs, pedis, M: *foot*

pōnō, pōnere, posuī, positus: *put, set, place*

possum, posse, potuī: *be able*

puer, puerī, M: *boy; slave*

quam (adverb): *how? how much?; than, as* (in comparisons); *as . . . as possible* (with superlatives)

quidem (adverb): *indeed; at least; of course; for example*

sed (conjunction): *but, but also*

servus, serva, servum: *slave*

sī (conjunction): *if*

sum, esse, fuī, futūrus: *be, exist*

suus, sua, suum: *his own, her own, its own, their own* (owned by subject)

trīclīnium, trīclīniī, N: *dining room*

tū, tibi (dat.), **tē** (acc. and abl.): *you* (sing.)

ūnus, ūna, ūnum (gen. s. **unīus**, dat. s. **unī**): *one, single, only*

veniō, venīre, vēnī, ventum: *come, arrive*

videō, vidēre, vīdī, vīsus: *see;* (passive) *seem*

volō, velle, voluī: *wish, want; be willing*

CHAPTER TWO: PARTICIPLES

Latin loves participles, that is, adjectives made out of verbs. Participles make up nearly a quarter of the verb forms found in surviving classical Latin (Mahoney 2004, 103). They make Latin Latin, allowing the writer to collapse several events concisely into one sentence. English speakers use verbal adjectives far less frequently, and we often must expand a Latin participle into a dependent clause to express them in English. The English subordinating conjunctions *if, when, since,* and *although* help capture some of the implicit concepts found in Latin participles.

Like other adjectives, a participle agrees with the noun it is modifying in case, number, and gender, and thus it has recognizable adjective endings. But, like other verbs, a participle also has a voice and tense, and if active can take a direct or indirect object. Latin has four participle forms: the present active, perfect passive, future active, and future passive. The tense of the participle denotes the temporal relationship between the participle event and the main verb; that is, the present participle describes something happening at the same time as the main verb, the perfect an action completed before the main verb, and the future something that will happen later than the main verb. All the forms will be reviewed here, but the present active and perfect passive are the most common in Latin texts.

iubeō, iubēre, iussī, iūssus: *order, bid, ask*

	ACTIVE	PASSIVE
Present	iubēns, iubentis	—
	ordering	
Perfect	—	iūssus, -a, -um
		ordered
Future	iūssūrus, -a, -um	iubendus, -a, -um
	about to order	*about to be ordered*

Present Active Participle

The present active participle is formed by adding **-ns, -ntis** to the present stem. For i-stem verbs, **-ie** precedes the participial ending. The present active participle is then declined as a third declension adjective. The nominative singular for all three genders in all conjugations is:

vocāns	habēns	agēns	capiēns	audiēns
calling	*holding*	*doing*	*taking*	*hearing*

Declension of Present Active Participle

	SINGULAR		PLURAL	
	M/F	N	M/F	N
Nominative	vocāns		vocantēs	vocantia
Genitive	vocantis		vocantium	
Dative	vocantī		vocantibus	
Accusative	vocantem	vocāns	vocantēs	vocantia
Ablative	vocantī/e		vocantibus	

Note that unlike other third declension adjectives, participles sometimes have a short **-e** for their masculine or feminine ablative singular ending. When the participle is modifying a noun that is expressed, the ending is usually the adjectival ending **-ī**; however, when the participle is used substantively, that is, like a noun, the ending is usually **-e**.

> servus lancem purgans in triclinium venit.
> *The slave cleaning the tray came into the dining room.*
> *While cleaning a tray, the slave came into the dining room.*

> servo lancem perganti pretium dedit.
> *To the slave cleaning the tray he gave a prize.*
> *He gave a prize to the slave who was cleaning the tray.*

Perfect Passive Participle

The perfect passive is a first and second declension adjective made out of the fourth principal part of a verb. The nominative singular for all three genders in all conjugations is:

vocātus, -a, -um   habitus, -a, -um   actus, -a, -um   captus, -a, -um   audītus, -a, -um
called   *held*   *done*   *taken*   *heard*

> servus lancem purgatam mensae imposuit.
> *The slave placed the cleaned tray on the table.*
> *After the tray had been cleaned, the slave placed it on the table.*
> *Since it had been cleaned, the slave placed the tray on the table.*

> servus monitus triclinium discedit.
> *The warned slave leaves the dining room.*
> *Since he has been warned, the slave leaves the dining room.*
> *The slave, who has been warned, is leaving the dining room.*

Future Active Participle

The future active participle is a first and second declension adjective built from the last principal part, but with -**ūr** added between the stem and the ending. The -**ūr** makes the fut*ure* active. English does not have future participles, so this notion can be difficult for English speakers to conceptualize. Understand that the modified noun will do or intends to do this action in the future.

vocātūrus, -a, -um   habitūrus, -a, -um   actūrus, -a, -um   capturus, -a, -um   audītūrus, -a, -um
about to call   *going to have*   *about to act*   *intending to take* *about to hear*

> servus lancem mensae impositurus captus est.
> *The slave about to place the tray on the table was grabbed.*
> *Before he placed the tray on the table, the slave was grabbed.*
> *The slave who was intending to place the tray on the table was grabbed.*

Future Passive Participle

The future passive is a first and second declension adjective built from the present participial stem, that is, the stem used to create the present active (ironically). The tense and voice are changed by the addition of -**nd** to the stem. Note also that the future passive participle can denote a sense of obligation—the modified noun will experience or should suffer this action in the future. An "agenda" is a list of *things to be done* to the point of *things needing to be done*. The passive periphrastic construction combines the future passive participle with a form of the verb **sum, esse** to make a finite verb that expresses obligation or necessity: **Carthago delenda est,** *Carthage must be destroyed.* This construction is reviewed again in a later chapter.

vocandus, -a, -um	habendus, -a, -um	agendus, -a, -um
about to be called	*to be held*	*needing to be done*
capiendus, -a, -um	audiendus, -a, -um	
about to be taken	*having to be heard*	

lancem purgandam iecit.
He threw the to-be-cleaned tray.
He threw the tray which needed to be cleaned.

Participles of Deponent Verbs

Despite the normal rule that DEPONENT VERBS HAVE PASSIVE FORMS BUT ACTIVE MEANINGS, deponents have all four participles, so sometimes this rule is disobeyed.

precor, precārī, precātus sum, *beg, request, entreat*

	ACTIVE	PASSIVE
Present	precāns, precantis *begging*	—
Perfect	precātus, -a, -um *having begged*	—
Future	precatūrus, -a, -um *about to beg*	precandus, -a, -um *about to be begged*

Thus, a deponent's present participle is active in both form and meaning. The perfect is the only form to follow the rule for deponents—it is passive in form and active in meaning. And deponents have both a future active and a future passive participle in both form and meaning.

Translating Latin Participles into Subordinate Clauses

As noted earlier, Latin participles are far more flexible and common than their equivalents in English. If your task is to translate into English, a dependent clause is thus often the best way to capture the nuances of the Latin participle. *When, since,* and *although* are particularly good subordinating conjunctions for capturing the Latin semantic range. In turn, a relative clause makes it clear who is performing the action of an active participle or suffering a passive one:

Gitona servile officium tuentem iubemus in balneum sequi.
We order Giton, performing a servile role, to follow us into the bath.
We order Giton, who is performing a servile role, to follow us into the bath.
We order Giton, since he is performing a servile role, to follow us into the bath.

digitos paululum adspersos in capite pueri tersit.
He dried his lightly sprinkled fingers on the head of a slave boy.
He dried his fingers, which had been lightly sprinkled, on the head of a slave boy.

A temporal clause is useful for communicating the time relationship between the participle and the event in the main clause. For example, since the present participle expresses something going on at the same time as the main verb, *while* is a particularly good English conjunction for introducing such a clause. Remember, however, that Latin lacks a present passive or perfect active participle. Thus, when an event is described that occurred before the main verb, the participle must be passive. Similarly, authors describing an event contemporaneous with the main verb may only use the active voice.

Falernum plurimum rixantes effuderunt.
The fighting men spilled much Falernian wine.
While they were fighting, the men spilled a lot of Falernian wine.

digitos paululum adspersos in capite pueri tersit.
He dried his lightly sprinkled fingers on the head of a slave boy.
After his fingers were lightly sprinkled, he dried them on the head of a slave boy.

Substantive Use of the Participle

Like other Latin adjectives, participles are often used substantively; that is, the noun that they are modifying is not always present in the sentence. You may need to supply in your mind an unstated **vir, fēmina, hominēs, rēs,** or similar words in order to understand the full idea denoted simply by the participle in Latin:

servus interpellavit trepidantes.
A slave interrupted the hesitating ones/those hesitating/the hesitators/the hesitating people.

sufficiebat pilas ludentibus.
He was supplying balls to those playing/to the players/to the ones playing.

Ablative Absolute

The ablative absolute is a common way for a Latin writer to express a condition or conditions under which the main verb occurs. In its simplest form, an ablative absolute consists of a noun and a participle modifying it, both in the ablative, although to this base may be added adverbs, objects, other adjectives, and the like. Latin prose writers tend to sandwich all the other words associated with the ablative absolute between the noun and the participle modifying it, just as they do with other participles. Syntactically, an ablative absolute has no grammatical relationship to words that are found elsewhere in the sentence—it is in a grammatical sense *absolutely* separate. Since the nouns in the ablative absolute do not occur in the main clause, they do not have a case based on their role in the clause. The ablative is used not only as the case of last resort, but because the notion here is adverbial, and the ablative absolute is thus a natural extension of the basic uses of the ablative case.

> exonerata ille vesica aquam poposcit.
> *His bladder having been unburdened, he demands water.*
> *After his bladder is unburdened, he demands water.*

> discubuimus pueris aquam in manus infudentibus.
> *We reclined while boys poured water onto our hands.*

Roman Money

By the early imperial period, the Romans had standardized denominations of coins in bronze, silver, and gold. For accounting, the **sēstertius** was used as the basic unit, abbreviated HS; in texts, however, this usually denotes a thousand such coins. The main coins referred to in the *Satyrica* are the gold **aureus, aureī**, M; the silver **dēnārius, dēnāriī**, M; the silver **sēstertius, sēstertiī**, M; and the bronze **ās, assis**, M. During the reign of Nero, a legionary in the Roman army was paid a little more than half a **dēnārius** a day, and a skilled laborer might earn one **dēnārius** a day.

1 aureus = 25 dēnāriī = 100 sēstertiī = 400 assēs

Pre-Reading Review Sentences

Consider the participles in the following sentences. What nouns do they modify? What are their tenses and voices? How could they be expressed using subordinate clauses?

1. hoc dicto Trimalchio inquit, "Canis intrantes salutabat."

2. locutus haec Trimalchio inquit, "Canis intraturos salutabat."

3. his auditis Trimalchio inquit, "Fer matellam ludenti."

4. his auditis Trimalchio dixit, "Fer matellam ludentibus."

5. motus his Trimalchio inquit, "Rixantes vinum effuderunt."

6. locuto Trimalchione inquit, "Rixa facta vinum effuderunt."

7. dicturus ista Trimalchio inquit, "Rixaturi vinum effuderunt."

8. servus Agamemnonis interpellavit trepidantes.

9. videmus senem calvum, tunica vestitum russea, inter pueros capillatos ludentem pila.

10. Trimalchio unguento perfusus tergebatur, non linteis, sed palliis ex lana mollissima factis.

Post-Reading Activities

1. We have not yet met Trimalchio, but Petronius has told us much about him. What have we learned, and how has the author communicated that information?

2. Sketch the wall painting that Encolpius describes in the entryway to Trimalchio's home. Be a *pictor curiosus* and label the elements carefully.

3. What rooms of the Roman house have we encountered so far? What are their functions? Who tends to be in them? With what other rooms or room types are you familiar? Do you know of any other characteristic features of a Roman house?

4. In the first paragraph of the passage in chapter 3 (32–33), identify all of the participles, their case, number, and gender, their tense and voice, the noun they are modifying, and any objects they have.

Irregular Verb: **volō, velle, voluī**, *wish, want, be willing*

INDICATIVE

Present	volō	volumus
	vīs	vultis
	vult	volunt
Imperfect	volēbam	volēbāmus
	volēbās	volēbātis
	volēbat	volēbant

Irregular Verb: **volō, velle, voluī** (*continued*)

INDICATIVE

Future	volam	volēmus
	volēs	volētis
	volet	volent
Perfect	voluī	voluimus
	voluistī	voluistis
	voluit	voluērunt/voluēre
Pluperfect	volueram	voluerāmus
	voluerās	voluerātis
	voluerat	voluerant
Future perfect	voluerō	voluerimus
	volueris	volueritis
	voluerit	voluerint

SUBJUNCTIVE

Present	velim	velīmus
	velīs	velītis
	velit	velint
Imperfect	vellem	vellēmus
	vellēs	vellētis
	vellet	vellent
Perfect	voluerim	voluerimus
	volueris	volueritis
	voluerit	voluerint
Pluperfect	voluissem	voluissēmus
	voluissēs	voluissētis
	voluisset	voluissent

INFINITIVE

Present	velle
Perfect	voluisse
Future	—

PARTICIPLE

Present	volēns, volentis

Vocabulary

accipiō, accipere, accēpī, acceptus: *take, receive*
afferō (adferō), afferre, attulī, allātus: *bring, carry*
agō, agere, ēgī, actus: *do, perform; drive*

alter, altera, alterum (gen. s. **alterīus,** dat. s. **alterī**): *one (of two), the other, second, next*
amīca, -ae, F and **amīcus, -ī, M:** *friend*
amō, amāre, amāvī, amātus: *love, like*

aqua, aquae, F: *water*

argenteus, argentea, argenteum: *made of silver*

auferō (abferō), auferre, abstulī, ablātus: *take away*

balineum or balneum, -ī, N: *bath, bathing place*

caput, capitis, N: *head; top; main point*

cēterum (adverb): *but, still, for the rest, otherwise*

cocus, cocī, M: *cook*

effundō, effundere, effūdī, effūsus: *pour out*

ferō, ferre, tulī, lātus: *carry, bear, endure*

iaceō, iacēre, iacuī: *lie, rest, recline*

iaciō, iacere, iēcī, iactus: *throw; set down; build*

iactō, iactāre, iactāvī, iactātus: *throw, toss; toss out, mention, brag about*

īdem, eadem, idem: *the same; also, likewise*

impōnō, impōnere, imposuī, impositus: *place on, set on* (+ dative)

inveniō, invenīre, invēnī, inventus: *find, come upon*

ipse, ipsa, ipsum (gen. s. ipsīus, dat. s. ipsī): *self, that very, precisely* (emphasizes noun)

lectus, lectī, M: *couch, bed*

magis (comparative adverb): *more; rather*

medius, media, medium: *middle, middle of*

mehercules: *by Hercules* (a common exclamation used by men)

mīles, militis, M: *soldier*

minus (adverb): *less; not, by no means*

modo (adverb): *only; just now; in a moment*

monumentum, monumentī, N: *reminder; memorial; monument*

mortuus, mortua, mortuum: *dead*

nōlō, nōlle, nōluī: *be unwilling, not want to*

nōs (nom. and acc.), nostrum (partitive gen.), nōbīs (dat. and abl.): *we, us*

noster, nostra, nostrum: *our, belonging to us*

nunc (adverb): *now*

pānis, pānis, M: *bread*

plānē (adverb): *clearly, certainly, quite*

prīmō or prīmum (adverb): *first, at first*

prīmus, prīma, prīmum: *first, foremost, front*

putō, putāre, putāvī, putātus: *consider, weigh, imagine, think*

rapiō, rapere, rapuī, raptus: *seize, carry off*

rēs, reī or rēī, F: *thing, matter, situation, job*

sciō, scīre, scīvī or sciī, scītus: *know; know how to*

sīc (adverb): *thus, so, in this way; yes*

soleō, solēre, solitus sum: *be accustomed, usual*

sōlus, sōla, sōlum (gen. s. sōlīus, dat. s. sōlī): *only, sole, alone; lonely*

tollō, tollere, sustulī, sublātus: *take up, lift, raise*

tuus, tua, tuum: *your, of yours* (sing.)

vērus, vēra, vērum: *true, real, fair*

vester, vestra, vestrum: *your, of all of you*

vīnum, vīnī, N: *wine*

vōs (nom. and acc.), vestrum (partitive gen.), vōbīs (dat. and abl.): *you* (pl.)

CHAPTER THREE: STRATEGIES FOR READING LATIN

Reading a novel is a very different task from learning grammatical principles and vocabulary. You will draw on the information you have learned from that exercise, and continue to build upon it, but the goal now is to understand what the author is trying to say at the level of the sentence, the scene, and the work as a whole. After all, grammar is not the end game—grammar is used by native speakers unconsciously and is but a tool for expressing thoughts clearly and effectively. When you make the shift from learning grammar to using it to understand literature, it can help to think consciously about strategies that will make the process easier. Please note that these are suggestions with which you should experiment. Some will match your learning style and personality well and thus feel natural; others you may find quite frustrating. The point is to find techniques that work for you and help you become a better reader.

In any language, a strong reader has certain characteristics. These include an ability to skip inessential words, guess from context, read in chunks, and continue reading even when difficulties arise with a particular word or phrase. Good readers tolerate uncertainty, use a range of clues to predict what will come next, and are generally flexible (Wallace 1992, 58–59).

Reading in Latin Word Order

Keep in mind that an author in any language expects his or her words to be perceived by the listener or reader in the order in which they are set out. This is particularly challenging for English speakers learning Latin, because meaning in English is derived from a very restrictive and specific word order. Sometimes beginning students cope with this difference by employing a "hunt and peck" tactic, looking for a subject and verb and ignoring the original order of the words. But an author writes with the intention of being understood, and thus an author crafts a sentence so that information is revealed when needed to create a desired effect. Moreover, despite the use of cases in Latin, which does allow for some flexibility of word order, Latin sentences are not a free-for-all. Latin authors follow basic patterns and avoid ambiguous constructions that may mislead readers—the patterns are merely different than in English.

Arch Composition

Latin sentences are carefully structured. One way of thinking about this is through what B. Dexter Hoyos (1993) calls "arch composition." A sentence is made up of a series of phrases and clauses, the first and last words of which tend to be fundamental. The first and last words of a phrase, clause, or sentence form a signal to the reader—you know when a clause starts and when it ends. For example, consider the following sentence:

> nec tam pueri nos, quamquam erat operae pretium, ad spectaculum duxerant, quam ipse pater familiae, qui soleatus pila prasina exercebatur.
> *Not so much the boys drew our attention to the scene, although that was worthy of attention, as much as the master himself, who, clad in slippers, was exercising with a green ball.*

nec tam pueri nos is the first part of the main clause, but it is interrupted by the subordinate clause **quamquam erat operae pretium**. That clause, sign-posted by the subordinating conjuction **quamquam** and the predicate nominative **pretium**, is completed before the main clause resumes, **ad spectaculum duxerant**. The main clause is thus framed by the initial conjunctions **nec** and **tam** and the subject (**pueri**) at the beginning and the verb at the end (**duxerant**). More-over, an observant reader knows from **tam** that more is probably coming, namely a **quam** correlating with it—and indeed, **quam** is the next word. The **quam** phrase gives us what did draw our attention, since it was not the boys. Finally, a relative clause completes the sentence, framed neatly by the relative pronoun and a finite verb. We might mark the sentence's arches like this:

[{nec tam pueri nos (quamquam erat operae pretium) ad spectaculum duxe-rant} quam ipse pater familiae] (qui soleatus pila prasina exercebatur).

Or diagram the sentence like this:

quamquam erat operae pretium

nec tam pueri nos   ad spectaculum duxerant,

quam ipse pater familiae

qui soleatus pila prasina exercebatur.

An important consequence of arch composition is that even though arches may be embedded within one another, words from within an arch (that is, a clause or phrase) tend not to escape its bounds. Just because adjectives agree with the nouns they modify does not mean they can be placed anywhere in a complex sentence. A noun and any adjectives that modify it will be located in the same clause, that is, within the same arch. Another arch may come between, but if so, that arch will *both begin and end* so that the reader knows that the author has returned to the first arch and is prepared for the noun that the dangling adjec-tive modifies.

horologium in triclinio et bucinatorem habet subornatum [ut subinde sciat {quantum de vita perdiderit}].
He has a clock in the dining room and a trumpeter so that from these he immediately knows how much of his life he has lost.

In this example, the main clause comes first. **subornatum** might modify either **horologium** or **bucinatorem**, but it comes as the last word, as far away from **horologium** as possible, and rather soon after **bucinatorem**. A reader will assume without thinking that it is the trumpeter who is equipped, rather than the clock. **ut** marks a transition to a purpose clause, concluded by **sciat**. **quantum** then introduces the indirect question expressing what he may know, a clause also concluded by a verb.

Conjunctions

If arches are not for you, a different way of thinking about this is to give conjunctions the attention they deserve. Conjunctions are all too often ignored—they are little words that do not decline or conjugate and thus do not receive much attention in a textbook or classroom. But conjunctions form the logical framework on which an expression is built; they serve as signposts marking for the reader the nature of the intersection ahead. There are two types of conjunctions. **Coordinating conjunctions** join two parallel things together. They might join words, phrases, clauses, or even sentences, but whatever the two items joined, they are syntactically and functionally equivalent. The most common coordinating conjunctions are:

et	at
ac	sed
-que	aut
nec/neque	-ve

et, ac, and **-que** are copulative; that is, they simply join things together like a plus sign. **nec** does this, too, but in a negative way. All four of these conjunctions therefore set up some form of parallel—the items being joined together are the same in some fashion. **at** and **sed**, on the other hand, form a contrast between the two items joined together. When you see one or the other, you know that things are being contrasted, and they should therefore differ in some significant way. In turn, **aut** and **-ve** present the joined items as alternatives. An author thus communicates a lot using these little words, and a little attention paid to them will be rewarded with a great deal of comprehension in return.

    Subordinating conjunctions subordinate one event or idea to another. A subordinate clause cannot stand alone as a sentence. Subordinating conjunctions, relative pronouns, or interrogatives mark the beginning of a subordinate clause, most of which end with a finite verb. A subordinate clause is thus a distinct chunk of a sentence easily marked off for the reader by the signposted frame of a subordinating conjunction and a finite verb. Relative and interrogative pronouns are reviewed in the next chapter, but some subordinating conjunctions are:

ut, nē
temporal: **dum, cum, dōnec**

causal: **quia, quoniam, cum, quod**
contrasting: **quamquam, cum**

Whether you are more comfortable visualizing arches or focusing on conjunctions, you can see how even a complex Latin sentence is always presented to a reader in manageable chunks. The ability to spot these meaningful groups of words is a useful and learnable skill—it just requires practice.

Word Order Patterns

Other patterns are observable in Latin sentences, and awareness of them helps the reader perceive the author's meaning while reading in order (see Ahern 1991 and Markus and Ross 2004):

- If no new nominative subject is expressed, the subject is usually the same as the subject of the preceding sentence. The nominative demonstrative **ille** or **illa** is often used to mark a shift in subject if it is clear to whom it refers.

- An object tends to *precede* its verb, whether that verb is finite, infinitival, or participial in nature. This is in direct contrast to English word order, and thus it is worthwhile for you to learn to expect it.

- In general, major grammatical elements (such as the subject, indirect object, and direct object) tend to be placed at or near the beginning of a sentence, particularly if they refer to people.

- Genitives are regularly placed *after* the nouns they modify.

- Adverbial elements, including adverbs and adverbial phrases, are regularly placed *before* the verbs or other words they modify.

- In questions, verbs tend to be placed first.

- Copulative or linking verbs are generally placed *between* subjects and predicate nominatives or predicate adjectives.

- When a form of **sum, esse** is expressing the simple existence of the subject, it tends to come before its subject and often first in a sentence.

- In an ablative absolute, the noun and participle tend to form the frame, and any other words in the clause (objects, adverbs, prepositional phrases) tend to fall *between* them.

Expectations

Another strategy for English speakers tackling Latin word order is to think consciously about what a reader might expect after even just the first few words of a sentence. For example, if the first word is in the accusative, you know that the verb is active and transitive. Good readers have an unconscious habit of creating an expectation of the shape of the rest of the sentence as it unfolds. Consider this start to a sentence: **cum vocāns**. This sentence has at least three main elements. Since **cum** is not followed by an ablative, it is a subordinating conjunction introducing a dependent clause. The subject of that clause is modified by the nominative participle **vocāns**, an active participle that may have a direct object. Then a main clause must follow. So just from these two words we know a great deal about the sentence.

This method recognizes the arch construction technique used by Roman authors and described above. Think about a sentence that begins **virum qui canem**. First the relative clause will be concluded by an active verb that has **canem** as the object and **qui** as the subject. Then the overall arch of the sentence, the sentence with **virum** as a direct object, will be concluded, again probably by a finite verb. A reader going in order notices these signposts, anticipates what is coming, and perceives the sentence in the manageable chunks defined by the two ends of the arch (adapted from Markus and Ross 2004, 93):

- An ACCUSATIVE/DIRECT OBJECT raises the expectation of an active verb and a subject.

- A NOMINATIVE/SUBJECT raises the expectation of a verb and possibly a direct object.

- A COORDINATING CONJUNCTION (**et, -que**) raises the expectation of a second syntactic equivalent (i.e., another noun, another clause, etc.).

- A SUBORDINATING CONJUNCTION (**cum, quod**) or RELATIVE PRONOUN (**quī, quae, quod**) raises the expectation of a dependent clause in addition to the main clause.

- An INFINITIVE raises the expectation of a verb that governs it.

- A SĪ-CLAUSE (if-clause) raises the expectation of an apodosis (then-clause).

- A COMPARATIVE word or phrase raises an expectation of something to which it is compared.

- A PREPOSITION raises the expectation of its object.

Visualization

Many Roman writers conceived of literature as something that generated images in the mind's eye. Thus, not only will visualizing the action help you follow the scene, but it is what the author expects you as the reader to do. The *Satyrica* is particularly vivid, with physical descriptions of characters, objects, and actions;

visualizing the setting and events should not be a challenge once you develop the habit. Imagine a passage as a script for a movie, and let the scene play out in your mind as you read. Pictures are a good mediation between reading Latin and translating into English. Moreover, as you see the events unfold, can you imagine what will happen next?

Gleaning from Context

Good reading involves educated guessing—using hunches from many sources to infer meaning. To guess or infer, you must get what you can from words on your initial reading but focus overall on the big picture. You may guess at the meaning of a word by using clues including context, English cognates, related Latin words, and the like. You might extrapolate a meaning for a word you know already but from other contexts. Circumlocution—expressing an idea in a number of different ways—may help you pick up on a meaning not yet found in your mental dictionary. Paraphrasing can be useful when you are having difficulty with the details. Can you describe in your own words the main thrust of the paragraph? You may also guess at a form, inferring that an unknown noun ending in -**us** is a fourth declension nominative plural because you have a plural verb and no other subject. Some students are very detail-oriented and like to look up everything in a grammar or dictionary, but such students are sometimes not the best *readers*. Try out these techniques and your guessing skills once in a while to strengthen your reading skills.

Finally, remember that Latin texts from antiquity were not written for twenty-first-century college students. The cultural, literary, historical, and linguistic knowledge that Petronius assumed of his audience is vast. The *Satyrica* is a sophisticated text that mocks a number of other authors and genres. The many layers of meaning will emerge only slowly, with multiple readings, upon discussion with classmates and your instructor, after research into idiomatic phrases, literary allusions, and the like. This is why we read together as a class—the meaning is much more than what the words say. In preparing for class, you should read a passage at least twice, and as with all literature be looking for what the author may be communicating between the lines.

Pre-Reading Review Exercises

1. Without looking up any vocabulary or forms, mark the arches that create the structure of the following sentence. How do you know when an arch begins or ends?

> non potui amplius quicquam gustare, sed conversus ad eum, ut quam plurima exciperem, longe accersere fabulas coepi sciscitarique, quae esset mulier illa quae huc atque illuc discurreret.

2. What do you expect of the following sentences based on these first few words?

> rettulimus
> ego experiri
> pueris
> ne has
> aquam enim
> laudatus propter

3. The underlined words below are ambiguous in their form; for example, **viri** may be genitive singular or nominative plural, and **causa** may be nominative or ablative singular. Identify the first word in the sentence that helps dispel the ambiguity, and explain how it does so.

> i. <u>horologium</u> in triclinio et bucinatorem habet subornatum, ut subinde sciat quantum de vita perdiderit.

> ii. "non tam <u>iactura</u> me movet," inquit, "quam neglegentia nequissimi servi."

4. Underline the coordinating conjunctions in the following passages. Are parallels, antitheses, or alternatives being presented by them? What items do they join together? Circle the subordinating conjunctions and relative pronouns. Where do the subordinate clauses end? How do you know? What other types of clauses or meaningful groups of words can you distinguish?

> i. nec amplius eam repetebat quae terram contigerat, sed follem plenum habebat servus sufficiebatque ludentibus.

> ii. his repleti voluptatibus cum conaremur in triclinium intrare, exclamavit unus ex pueris, qui supra hoc officium erat positus: "dextro pede!" sine dubio paulisper trepidavimus, ne contra praeceptum aliquis nostrum limen transiret.

Post-Reading Activities

1. In Latin, rewrite the passage in which Encolpius' informant evaluates the relationship of Trimalchio and Fortunata in such a way that their roles are reversed; that is, transform comments about her so that they are about him and vice versa. Does the passage still make sense? What gender stereotypes—ancient or modern—are revealed?

2. What are the main events of sections 32–34 in this chapter? How does the narrator transition from one to the next? Find the conjunctions, phrases, and sentences that give structure to the passage and help the reader navigate the scene.

3. In English, rewrite the passages in this chapter as scenes for a movie. Include stage directions, camera angles, costume notes—anything that helps you express how you visualize the events.

4. How would you characterize the speech patterns of Encolpius' informant, Hermeros? How is his language different from Encolpius' narration, for example? Use specific examples to explain your observations.

Demonstrative Adjective: **hic, haec, hoc,** *this*

SINGULAR			
	Masculine	Feminine	Neuter
Nominative	hic	haec	hoc
Genitive	huius	huius	huius
Dative	huic	huic	huic
Accusative	hunc	hanc	hoc
Ablative	hōc	hāc	hōc

PLURAL			
	Masculine	Feminine	Neuter
Nominative	hī	hae	haec
Genitive	hōrum	hārum	hōrum
Dative	hīs	hīs	hīs
Accusative	hōs	hās	haec
Ablative	hīs	hīs	hīs

Vocabulary

ā or **ab** (preposition + ablative): *from, away from; by, at the hands of*

ac (conjunction): *and, and in particular; than, as*

aliquot (indeclinable adjective): *some, several*

an (conjunction): *or, whether* (introduces the second part of a two-part question or an indirect question)

ante (conjunction): *before, in the past, in front;* (preposition + accusative): *before*

at (conjunction): *but*

atque (conjunction): *and also, besides, indeed*

aut (conjunction): *or*

autem (conjunction): *but, on the other hand, however* (marking a contrast); *moreover; now* (transitioning or picking up after aside)

circā: (adverb) *around, in the vicinity;* (preposition + accusative) *around, about, near*

dē (preposition + ablative): *from, out of; concerning*

deinde (adverb): (of time) *then, afterward;* (of place) *from there, from that place*

diū: *for a long time;* **diūtius** (comparative): *for a longer time*

dum (conjunction): *while, as long as, until*

enim (conjunction): *for instance; yes, indeed; for, because*

ergō (adverb): *therefore; as I was saying*

etiam (adverb and conjunction): *also, besides; yet, still*

ex or **ē** (preposition + ablative): *out of, from*

hodiē (adverb): *today, nowadays*

iam (adverb): *now, already, by then, soon, next*

inter (preposition + accusative): *between, among; during, within*

interim (adverb): *meanwhile; sometimes*

ita (adverb): *thus, so, in this manner*

itaque (adverb): *and thus, and so; therefore, accordingly*

nam (conjunction): *for; yes; on the other hand*

nē (conjunction): *that . . . not, lest; that*

nē . . . quidem (adverb): *not . . . even*

nec (adverb): *not;* (conjunction): *and not, nor*

nisi (conjunction): *if not, unless, except*

per (preposition + accusative): *through*

postquam (conjunction): *after, when*

-que (enclitic conjunction): *and* (connects attached word or phrase to preceding word or phrase)

quia (conjunction): *because*

quid (adverb): *how? why?;* (pronoun) *what?*

quoque (adverb): *too* (follows word it emphasizes)

sine (preposition + ablative): *without*

sīve (conjunction): *or if, or*

sōlum (adverb): *only, barely, merely;* **nōn sōlum . . . sed etiam:** *not only . . . but also*

statim (adverb): *at once*

super (adverb): *above, besides, in addition*

suprā (adverb): *above, earlier, before; beyond, more*

tam (adverb): *so, so much, to such a degree*

tamen (adverb): *yet, nevertheless, still*

tamquam (conjunction): *as, just as, as much as; as if*

ut: (conjunction + indicative) *as, when;* (conjunction + subjunctive) *in order that, that*

vērō (adverb): *in truth; certainly; even; however*

vērum (adverb): *yes, truly; but; yet, still*

CHAPTER FOUR: "QU" WORDS (RELATIVES AND INTERROGATIVES) AND IMPERSONAL VERBS

"Qu" words, such as **quī** and **quis**, are "wh" words in English, such as *who*. In both languages, the similarities and differences between the relative and interrogative pronouns are a challenge to nonnative speakers. Relatives relate additional information about a noun in another clause. Interrogatives (from **inter** and **rogō, rogāre**, *ask*) are how you interrogate someone, that is, how you ask a question.

Relative Pronoun

	SINGULAR			PLURAL		
	M	F	N	M	F	N
Nominative	quī	quae	quod	quī	quae	quae
Genitive	cuius	cuius	cuius	quōrum	quārum	quōrum
Dative	cui	cui	cui	quibus	quibus	quibus
Accusative	quem	quam	quod	quōs	quās	quae
Ablative	quō	quā	quō	quibus	quibus	quibus

Interrogative Pronoun

	SINGULAR		PLURAL		
	M/F	N	M	F	N
Nominative	quis	quid	quī	quae	quae
Genitive	cuius	cuius	quōrum	quārum	quōrum
Dative	cui	cui	quibus	quibus	quibus
Accusative	quem	quid	quōs	quās	quae
Ablative	quō	quō	quibus	quibus	quibus

In the paradigms, differences between the relative and interrogative pronouns are underlined. To make matters worse, the forms of the relative pronoun are used as the interrogative adjective (*which?*). Since so many forms are the same, a reader must determine from context whether the "*qu*" is relative or interrogative. If the form introduces a question, then it is interrogative. Be certain that the "*qu*" *introduces* the question and is not just found within it, because you may well find a relative clause in a sentence that asks a question. Remember also that a question may be indirect; that is, it may be being reported within a sentence that does not end with a question mark.

Relative Clauses

A relative clause is a type of subordinate clause that provides more information about a noun previously mentioned. In both English and Latin, it begins with a relative pronoun that stands in for and points back toward that earlier noun, the antecedent. The Latin relative pronoun (**quī, quae, quod**) takes its gender and number from the antecedent, so it is always clear what noun is being further described. The Latin relative pronoun then takes a case based on the job it is doing in its own clause. For example, the antecedent may be the subject of the main

clause and thus in the nominative, while in the relative clause the pronoun is
the object of a preposition:

super limen cavea pendebat aurea in qua pica varia intrantes salutabat.
*Above the threshold a cage was hanging, golden, in which a multicolored mag-
pie was greeting those entering.*

In Latin prose, the relative clause usually ends with the clause's verb. In most
relative clauses, the verb is in the indicative mood because some fact about the
antecedent is being communicated. In Latin, however, an author may use the
subjunctive mood instead to communicate that it is the type of thing the antecedent would do or the sort of person or thing the antecedent is, rather than that
the antecedent has actually done something. This is called a Relative Clause of
Characteristic, because it characterizes rather than relaying facts. Compare:

Trimalchio est qui vinum bonum heri praestitit.
Trimalchio is the one who served good wine yesterday.

Trimalchio est qui vinum bonum praestet.
Trimalchio is the kind of person who would serve good wine.

Uses of quod

quod is the neuter nominative and accusative singular of the relative pronoun.
Since the accusative may also be used in an adverbial sense, over time **quod** became
a simple conjunction, *that,* or one with a causal sense, *because.* Like **quia** and
quoniam, which also mean *because,* **quod** takes the indicative when the writer
or speaker is inserting a reason, and the subjunctive when the reason belongs
to someone else and is just being repeated:

ego non illam propter res venerias curavi, sed magis quod benemoria fuit.
*I did not care for her on account of the matters of Venus, but more because
she was well mannered.*

non illam propter res venerias curavit, sed magis quod benemoria esset.
*He did not care for her for Venereal reasons, but supposedly more because she
was well mannered.*

Impersonal Verbs

Impersonal verbs have as their understood subject an abstraction—one, it, an idea under discussion, an infinitive phrase or subjunctive clause. Such verbs regularly occur only in the third person singular and infinitive forms, and thus these are the forms given for them in the dictionary. The most common impersonal verbs in Latin include:

> **licet, licēre, licuit**: *it is permitted, one is permitted, one may, one is allowed*
> **necesse est, necesse esse**: *it is necessary*
> **oportet, opertēre, oportuit**: *it is right, it is proper*

> pati necesse est multa mortales mala. (Naevius)
> *To suffer many ills is necessary for mortals. / It is necessary for mortals to suffer many ills.*

> quid me oportet facere? (Plautus)
> *What is it right that I do? / What is it proper for me to do?*

Pre-Reading Review Sentences

In the sentences below, determine whether the underlined words are interrogative or relative. If the word is relative, circle the antecedent.

1. I drank the wine <u>that</u> Trimalchio provided.
2. Where are the jars on the spouts of <u>which</u> the labels were hung?
3. <u>Whom</u> did you see at the party?
4. Where is the boy with <u>whom</u> you were sitting?
5. <u>Which</u> dining room did you use?
6. I asked him <u>what</u> they ate.
7. Did Trimalchio offer the wine <u>that</u> I prefer?
8. I cannot say <u>which</u> party was best.
9. video pallium <u>quod</u> excidit.
10. <u>quod</u> pallium video?
11. <u>quis</u> dicit?
12. <u>quid</u> dicit?

13. Trimalchio nescit quid habeat.

14. quocum de Fortunata dicebas quae est mulier Trimalchionis?

Post-Reading Activities

1. Complete each of the following sentences to summarize the chapter:

Dama vult . . .
Seleucus est homo qui . . .
Phileros dicit de . . .
Ganymedes est tristis quod . . .
Echion est vir qui . . .

2. Perform the monologues of the speaking characters in this chapter as a skit in class. Students should prepare with an emphasis on meaning and character development.

3. Look over the irregular verbs from this and the previous chapters to determine how the imperfect, perfect, and pluperfect tenses of the Latin subjunctive mood are formed, both active and passive.

4. Is the boy whom Echion describes his slave or his son?

Irregular Verb: **faciō, facere, fēcī, factus,** *make; do*

	Active			Passive	
			INDICATIVE		
Present	faciō	facimus	*Present*	fiō	fīmus
	facis	facitis		fīs	fītis
	facit	faciunt		fit	fiunt
Imperfect	faciēbam	faciēbāmus	*Imperfect*	fiēbam	fiēbāmus
	faciēbās	faciēbātis		fiēbās	fiēbātis
	faciēbat	faciēbant		fiēbat	fiēbant
Future	faciam	faciēmus	*Future*	fiam	fiēmus
	faciēs	faciētis		fiēs	fiētis
	faciet	facient		fiet	fient
Perfect	fēcī	fēcimus	*Perfect*	factus sum	factī sumus
	fēcistī	fēcistis		factus es	factī estis
	fēcit	fēcērunt/fēcēre		factus est	factī sunt

Irregular Verb: **faciō, facere, fēcī, factus** (*continued*)

	Active			Passive	
			INDICATIVE		
Pluperfect	fēceram	fēcerāmus	*Pluperfect*	facta eram	factae erāmus
	fēcerās	fēcerātis		facta erās	factae erātis
	fēcerat	fēcerant		facta erat	factae erant
Future	fēcerō	fēcerimus	*Future*	factum erō	facta erimus
perfect	fēceris	fēceritis	*perfect*	factum eris	facta eritis
	fēcerit	fēcerint		factum erit	facta erunt
			SUBJUNCTIVE		
Present	faciam	faciāmus	*Present*	fīam	fīāmus
	faciās	faciātis		fīās	fīātis
	faciat	faciant		fīat	fīant
Imperfect	facerem	facerēmus	*Imperfect*	fierem	fierēmus
	facerēs	facerētis		fierēs	fierētis
	faceret	facerent		fieret	fierent
Perfect	fēcerim	fēcerimus	*Perfect*	factus sim	factī sīmus
	fēceris	fēceritis		factus sīs	factī sītis
	fēcerit	fēcerint		factus sit	factī sint
Pluperfect	fēcissem	fēcissēmus	*Pluperfect*	facta essem	factae essēmus
	fēcissēs	fēcissētis		facta essēs	factae essētis
	fēcisset	fēcissent		facta esset	factae essent
			INFINITIVE		
Present	facere		*Present*	fierī	
Perfect	fēcisse		*Perfect*	factus, -a, -um esse	
Future	factūrus, -a, -um esse		*Future*	—	
			PARTICIPLES		
Present	faciēns, facientis		*Present*	—	
Perfect	—		*Perfect*	factus, -a, -um	
Future	factūrus, -a, -um		*Future*	faciendus, -a, -um	

Vocabulary

accēdō, accēdere, accessī, accessum: *approach*
annus, annī, M: *year*
aureus, aurea, aureum: *golden, of gold*
auris, auris, F: *ear*

caelum, caelī, N: *the heavens, sky*
caldus, calda, caldum: *warm*
canis, canis, M or F: *dog*
crēdō, crēdere, crēdidī, crēditus: *trust, believe*

crēscō, crēscere, crēvī, crētum: *come into existence, spring forth; grow, increase*

discō, discere, didicī: *learn*

duo, duae, duo: *two* / **trēs, tria:** *three* / **centum** (indeclinable): *hundred* / **mīlle** (s.), **mīlia, mīlium** (pl.): *thousand*

eō, īre, īvī or **iī, itum:** *go, walk*

fors, fortis, F: *chance, accident*

fortis, forte: *brave, strong*

grātia, grātiae, F: *charm; service, favor, kindness;* **grātiās agere:** *thank, express gratitude*

lavō, lavāre, lāvī, lautus or **lōtus** or **lavātus:** *wash, bathe*

libenter (adverb): *willingly, with pleasure*

littera or **lītera, -ae,** F: *letter of the alphabet;* (in plural) *letter, epistle; literature*

locus, locī, M: *place, spot*

medicus, medicī, M: *doctor*

mittō, mittere, mīsī, missus: *send; throw; dismiss*

nārrō, nārrāre, nārrāvī, nārrātus: *tell, relate*

nōscō, nōscere, nōvī, nōtus: *get to know, learn;* (in perfect) *know, have learned*

oblīvīscor, oblīvīscī, oblītus sum: *forget*

optimus, optima, optimum: (superlative of **bonus**) *very good, best, excellent*

pars, partis, F: *part*

placeō, placēre, placuī, placitus: (+ dative) *please, satisfy, pleasure*

plēnus, plēna, plēnum: *full*

plūs, plūris: (comparative of **multus**): *more;* **plūs** (adverb): *more*

pōscō, pōscere, popōsci: *ask for, request*

prōclāmō, prōclāmāre, prōclāmāvī, prōclāmātus: *yell; exclaim, cry out that*

quārē (adverb): *how, by what means; why; why? for what reason?*

quīdam, quaedam, quiddam (pronoun): *a certain person, a certain one, a certain thing*

quisque, quaeque, quodque: *each*

quisquis, quidquid or **quicquid:** *whoever, whatever, anyone who, anything that*

rīdeō, rīdēre, rīsī, rīsus: *laugh at, deride; smile*

rogō, rogāre, rogāvī, rogātus: *ask, ask for*

serviō, servīre, servīvī or **serviī, servītum:** *be a slave, be obedient, serve*

servō, servāre, servāvī, servātus: *watch over, keep, preserve, protect*

sibi (dat.), **sē** (acc. and abl.): *oneself, himself, herself, itself, themselves* (third person reflexive)

tōtus, tōta, tōtum (gen. s. **tōtīus,** dat. s. **tōtī**): *the whole, all, the entire*

vultus, vultūs, M: *face, expression, look, appearance*

CHAPTER FIVE:
THE SUBJUNCTIVE MOOD, CUM CLAUSES

In Latin, the indicative mood of verbs is used to make statements of fact or to ask direct questions about facts. The subjunctive mood is associated with what is less certain—ideas, hopes, things subject to conditions, intentions, desires, fears, and possibilities. The subjunctive has a few independent uses, which you will encounter in the passages and which are reviewed in the final chapter. More often it is found in subordinate clauses, including clauses of purpose, result, or fear, indirect questions and commands, conditions, and **cum** clauses. In Latin, the indicative mood has six tenses, but the subjunctive only four—it has no future tenses. The present, imperfect, perfect, and pluperfect subjunctive tenses express different relative temporal relationships depending upon the particular construction being used. There is no one way to understand each of them or translate them into English; the meaning of the Latin subjunctive mood is always contextual.

Present Subjunctive The present subjunctive in both active and passive is formed like the present indicative. The only change is the signature vowel. The first conjugation changes from -**a** to -**e**, while the other conjugations feature an -**a**.

First Conjugation	Second	Third	Third -**iō**	Fourth
a → e	e → ea	i → a	i → ia	i → ia
(active forms)	(passive forms)	(deponent forms)	(active forms)	(passive forms)
vocō, vocāre	habeō, habēre	sequor, sequī	capiō, capere	audiō, audīre
vocem	habear	sequar	capiam	audiar
vocēs	habeāris/habeāre	sequāris/sequāre	capiās	audiāris/audiāre
vocet	habeātur	sequātur	capiat	audiātur
vocēmus	habeāmur	sequāmur	capiāmus	audiāmur
vocētis	habeāminī	sequāminī	capiātis	audiāminī
vocent	habeantur	sequāntur	capiant	audiantur

Imperfect Subjunctive The imperfect subjunctive is one of two subjunctive tenses formed from an infinitive, in this case the present active infinitive. This is the case even for deponent verbs, for which an active form is created just to be used in the imperfect subjunctive. Active and passive personal endings are simply added to the present active infinitive form; for deponents, passive endings are used, but the meanings remain active.

First Conjugation (active forms)	Second (passive forms)	Third (deponent forms)	Third -**iō** (active forms)	Fourth (passive forms)
vocārem	habērer	sequerer	caperem	audīrer
vocārēs	habērēris/habērēre	sequerēris/sequerēre	caperēs	audīrēris/audīrēre
vocāret	habērētur	sequerētur	caperet	audīrētur
vocārēmus	habērēmur	sequerēmur	caperēmus	audīrēmur
vocārētis	habērēminī	sequerēminī	caperētis	audīrēminī
vocārent	habērentur	sequerentur	caperent	audīrentur

Perfect Subjunctive—Active The perfect active subjunctive is formed by adding the following endings to the perfect active stem: **-erim**, **-eris**, **-erit**, **-erimus**, **-eritis**, **-erint**. This is nearly identical to the future perfect indicative, which differs only in the first person singular ending, **-erō**.

First Conjugation	Second	Third (deponent)	Third -**iō**	Fourth
vocāverim	habuerim	secūtus/a/um sim	cēperim	audīverim
vocāveris	habueris	secūtus sis	cēperis	audīveris
vocāverit	habuerit	secūtus sit	cēperit	audīverit
vocāverimus	habuerimus	secūtī/ae/a simus	cēperimus	audīverimus
vocāveritis	habueritis	secūtī sitis	cēperitis	audīveritis
vocāverint	habuerint	secūtī sint	cēperint	audīverint

Perfect Subjunctive—Passive The perfect passive subjunctive is formed similarly to the perfect passive indicative. The perfect passive participle, or fourth principal part, is used along with a corresponding form of the verb **sum, esse**. For the perfect indicative, the present indicative of **sum** is used; for the perfect subjunctive, the present subjunctive of **sum** is used.

First Conjugation (masculine forms)	Second (feminine forms)	Third (neuter forms)	Third -**iō** (masculine forms)	Fourth (neuter forms)
vocātus sim	habita sim	actum sim	captus sim	audītum sim
vocātus sīs	habita sīs	actum sīs	captus sīs	audītum sīs
vocātus sit	habita sit	actum sit	captus sit	audītum sit
vocātī sīmus	habitae sīmus	acta sīmus	captī sīmus	audīta sīmus
vocātī sītis	habitae sītis	acta sītis	captī sītis	audīta sītis
vocātī sint	habitae sint	acta sint	captī sint	audīta sint

Pluperfect Subjunctive—Active The pluperfect active subjunctive is the other subjunctive tense formed from an infinitive. Active personal endings are added to the perfect active infinitive. Resulting verbs of four or more syllables are sometimes contracted colloquially, such as **laudāssem** for **laudāvissem**.

First Conjugation	Second	Third (deponent, masculine)	Third -**iō**	Fourth
vocāvissem	habuissem	secūtus essem	cēpissem	audīvissem
vocāvissēs	habuissēs	secūtus essēs	cēpissēs	audīvissēs
vocāvisset	habuisset	secūtus esset	cēpisset	audīvisset
vocāvissēmus	habuissēmus	secūtī essēmus	cēpissēmus	audīvissēmus
vocāvissētis	habuissētis	secūtī essētis	cēpissētis	audīvissētis
vocāvissent	habuissent	secūtī essent	cēpissent	audīvissent

Pluperfect Subjunctive—Passive You should be able to form the pluperfect passive subjunctive based on the pattern of the perfect passive indicative, perfect passive subjunctive, and pluperfect passive indicative. To the fourth principal part is added the imperfect subjunctive of **sum**.

First Conjugation (masculine forms)	Second (feminine forms)	Third (neuter forms)	Third - **iō** (feminine forms)	Fourth (neuter forms)
vocātus essem	habita essem	actum essem	capta essem	audītum essem
vocātus essēs	habita essēs	actum essēs	capta essēs	audītum essēs
vocātus esset	habita esset	actum esset	capta esset	audītum esset
vocātī essēmus	habitae essēmus	acta essēmus	captae essēmus	audīta essēmus
vocātī essētis	habitae essētis	acta essētis	captae essētis	audīta essētis
vocātī essent	habitae essent	acta essent	captae essent	audīta essent

Sequence of Tenses

In most subordinate clauses calling for the subjunctive, a system referred to as the Sequence of Tenses is used. This system enables the tense of a subjunctive verb to express a particular temporal relationship between that verb and the event in the main clause.

Indicative (verb in main clause)		Subjunctive (subordinate clause)	Temporal Relationship
Primary tenses	Present Future	Present	same time as or after main verb
	Future perfect Perfect ("have" or "has")	Perfect	before main verb
Secondary tenses	Imperfect Perfect (simple past) Pluperfect	Imperfect	same time as or after main verb
		Pluperfect	before main verb

The tenses of the indicative are categorized into primary and secondary sequences, that is, into present or future action and the past. Within each sequence are found two tenses of the subjunctive, one that denotes an action completed before the main clause event, and another to describe a simultaneous or subsequent event. There are many ways to remember the various patterns. For example, the two subjunctive tenses found in secondary sequence are those built from infinitive forms (imperfect and pluperfect). The two subjunctive tenses that denote simultaneous or subsequent action are those built on the present stem (present and imperfect), while those used to describe an action prior to the main verb use the perfect stem (perfect and pluperfect). The system may seem complicated, but it is expressive. The order of the sometimes multiple events in a Latin sentence is always clear.

cum Clauses

The subordinating conjunction **cum**, *when, since, although*, is used to introduce clauses that describe various circumstances surrounding the main clause. If the relationship between the two events is strictly temporal, then the indicative is sometimes used in both clauses, at least in the present tense. But the notion of *when* quickly shades into *because*, and such circumstantial or causal clauses usually employ the subjunctive, as well as temporal clauses in the past. Finally, a **cum** clause may also denote a contrast between the two events. The presence of the word **tamen**, *nevertheless*, in the main clause often helps indicate that the subordinate clause is concessive, that is, that **cum** should be understood as *although*. In **cum** clauses using the subjunctive, the Sequence of Tenses is deployed to clarify the time relationship between the events in the dependent and the main clause. Note that **cum** clauses may precede or follow the main clause just like other subordinate clauses in Latin.

cum deliberaremus, servus interpellavit.
When we were deliberating, a slave interrupted.

cum deliberassemus, servus interpellavit.
After we had deliberated, a slave interrupted.
Since we had deliberated, a slave interrupted.
Although we had deliberated, a slave interrupted.

cum deliberaverimus, servus interpellit.
After we deliberate, a slave interrupts.

cum deliberamus, servus interpellit.
While we are deliberating, a slave interrupts.

cum deliberamus, servus tamen interpellit.
Although we are deliberating, a slave nevertheless interrupts.

Dama cum pataracina poposcisset, "dies" inquit, "nihil est."
After Dama had requested a drink, he said, "a day is nothing."

Dama cum pataracina posceret, "dies," inquit, "nihil est."
While Dama was requesting a drink, he said, "a day is nothing."

Pre-Reading Review Sentences

Prepare to translate the following sentences. When do events in subordinate clauses take place relative to events in the main clause? Be ready to explain the differences between nearly identical sentences in terms of both form and meaning.

1. cum te videam, felix sum.

2. cum te viderim, felix sum.

3. cum te viderem, felix eram.

4. cum te vidissem, felix eram.

5. cum te viderim, tamen felix sum.

6. Trimalchio, cum lusum nondum finiisset, noluit in triclinium ire.

7. Trimalchio, cum lusum finiret, noluit in triclinium ire.

8. lusu non finito, Trimalchio noluit in triclinium ire.

9. cum lusus non finitus esset, Trimalchio noluit in triclinium ire.

10. nos errare coepimus, cum subito videmus senem calvum.

11. cum has miraremur lautitias, accurrit Menelaus.

12. sequimur nos admiratione iam saturi et cum Agamemnone ad ianuam pervenimus.

13. cum conaremur in triclinium intrare, exclamavit unus ex pueris, "dextro pede!"

14. cum intrassemus triclinium, occurrit nobis ille idem servus.

15. in his eramus lautitiis cum ipse Trimalchio ad symphoniam allatus est.

Post-Reading Activities

1. In the review sentences above, rewrite sentences 1, 2, 3, 4, 6, and 7 in Latin by replacing the **cum** clause with a participial phrase.

2. Explain why the subjunctive Sequence of Tenses will be particularly useful in perceiving the nuances of clauses of fearing.

3. Retell the story of the three pigs from the point of view of the **cocus maestus**.

4. Skim the passage in the next chapter. Who tells a story, and what is it about?

Demonstrative Adjective/Pronoun:
is, ea, id, *this, that, the; he, she, it, they*

SINGULAR

	Masculine	Feminine	Neuter
Nominative	is	ea	id
Genitive	eius	eius	eius
Dative	eī	eī	eī
Accusative	eum	eam	id
Ablative	eō	eā	eō

PLURAL

	Masculine	Feminine	Neuter
Nominative	eī / iī	eae	ea
Genitive	eōrum	eārum	eōrum
Dative	eīs / iīs	eīs / iīs	eīs / iīs
Accusative	eōs	eās	ea
Ablative	eīs / iīs	eīs / iīs	eīs / iīs

Vocabulary

ad summam: *in short, in sum, to get to the point*

adhūc (adverb): *thus far; still; in addition*

albus, alba, album: *white; bright*

bellus, bella, bellum: *pretty, fine*

coniciō, conicere, coniēcī, coniectus: *throw together, cast, toss*

cūro, cūrāre, cūrāvī, cūrātus: *care for, pay attention to*

deus, deī (nom. pl. **dī** or **diī,** dat./abl. pl. **dīs** or **diīs**), M: *god, deity*

dūcō, dūcere, dūxī, ductus: *lead, guide*

exinterō, exinterāre, exinterāvī, exinterātus: *disembowel, gut, clean*

expectō, expectāre, expectāvī, expectātus: *await, wait for; long for; wait expectantly*

fābula, fābulae, F: *story*

hilaritās, hilaritātis, F: *cheerfulness, mirth*

ignōscō, ignōscere, ignōvī, ignōtum: *overlook, forgive, pardon* (one forgiven in dative)

ingēns, ingentis: *monstrous, vast, enormous*

iste, ista, istud (gen. s. **istīus,** dat. s. **istī**): *that, that particular, that very; that despicable*

loquor, loquī, locūtus sum: *speak,* especially in ordinary conversation

mēnsa, mēnsae, F: *a table; a course* (of a meal)

multus, multa, multum: *many*

nanciscor, nanciscī, nactus sum: *get, obtain*

nāscor, nāscī, nātus sum: *be born, originate; occur*

nōtō, nōtāre, nōtāvī, nōtātus: *mark, note, observe*

numquam (adverb): *never*

occidō, occidere, occidī, occāsum: *fall; be ruined*

occīdō, occīdere, occīdī, occīsus: *kill, murder*

oculus, oculī, M: *eye*

pater, patris, M: *father*

porcus, porcī, M: *pig*

post (conjunction): *after, behind, later;* (preposition + accusative) *behind, after*

prō (preposition + ablative): *before, in front of; on behalf of; instead of*

sanguis, sanguinis, M: *blood*

sequor, sequī, secūtus sum: *follow*

teneō, tenēre, tenuī, tentus: *hold, grasp; comprehend*

timeō, timēre, timuī: *fear, be afraid of*

umquam (adverb): *ever, at any time*

ūsus, ūsūs, M: *use, using; enjoyment; custom; benefit; need*

ūtor, ūtī, ūsus sum: *use, enjoy* (+ ablative)

vestīmentum, vestīmentī, N: *clothing*

vir, virī, M: *man, hero, husband, lover*

vīs, vīs (dat. vī, acc. vim, abl. vī; plural: vīrēs, vīrium), F: *power, strength, force*

vīvō, vīvere, vīxī, victum: *live, be alive, survive*

vīvus, vīva, vīvum: *alive, lively*

vocō, vocāre, vocāvī, vocātus: *call, name, summon*

CHAPTER SIX: CONDITIONS

Conditions are "if/then" statements:

> If you learn Latin, you are smart.
> If you learned Latin, you were smart.

> If you learn Latin, you will be smart.
> Should you learn Latin, you would be smart.

> If you were learning Latin, you would be smart.
> If you had learned Latin, you would have been smart.

Conditions in Latin are best conceived of in three categories. First are simple statements of fact about the present or past, such as the first two examples above. If the condition (called the *protasis*) is or was met, then the second part (called the *apodosis*) occurs or occurred. As you might guess, for such statements of fact, the indicative mood is used. Another type of condition involves the future, and thus a prediction, as in the middle two sentences. A Latin speaker is able to express the likeliness that the condition will be met or that the result will come about by sliding from the indicative (more likely) to the subjunctive (less likely). Finally, some conditions are statements about what might be happening but in fact are not, or might have happened but did not, as you can see in the last two sentences. These statements about things that were possible but did not actually happen—statements about what is contrary to fact—require the subjunctive.

Given the tenses that exist in the Latin subjunctive, they are deployed to create these various types of conditions in a logical way. Since there is no future subjunctive, the present is used to discuss unlikely future conditions, often referred to as the *future less vivid*. The *future more vivid* condition of course uses the future or future perfect indicative. This leaves three subjunctive tenses to describe conditions that are contrary to fact: the imperfect, perfect, and pluperfect. To communicate about something that might have been happening now but is not, Latin uses the imperfect, the tense remaining that is closest to the present and that is built on the present infinitive. To discuss something that might have happened in the past but did not, Latin speakers put their verbs into the pluperfect, the other tense built on an infinitive form. Note that contrary-to-fact conditions thus use the subjunctive tenses from secondary sequence. The perfect subjunctive is not generally used in conditions.

Please note that although the formulae below look nice and tidy, reality is not. Someone might want to communicate the idea that although a particular condition is unlikely to be met, if it in fact *is* met, the stated consequence is very likely to occur. Similarly, we might want to say that something might have happened in the past but did not, and that that is affecting something now rather than something in the past. Mixed conditions are therefore not uncommon—a protasis is sometimes employed from one type of condition and an apodosis from another. The most common combinations are included in the chart below. Finally, sometimes the condition is implied rather than expressed, and you must figure out from context that what you are looking at is in fact an apodosis, but without its **sī** clause.

One last reminder about conditions is in order. Remember that following **sī, nisi, num,** and **nē** you will find **quis** or **quid** instead of **aliquis** or **aliquid**.

Conditions	Latin		English	
	protasis/ **sī** *clause*	*apodosis*	*protasis/ if clause*	*apodosis*
Simple or factual	present or any past tense of the indicative	present or any past tense of the indicative		
Future more vivid or more likely	future perfect or future indicative	future indicative	—	will
Future less vivid or less likely	present subjunctive	present subjunctive	should	would
Mixed future	present subjunctive	future indicative	should	will
Present contrary to fact	imperfect subjunctive	imperfect subjunctive	were	would
Past contrary to fact	pluperfect subjunctive	pluperfect subjunctive	had	would have
Mixed contrary to fact	pluperfect subjunctive	imperfect subjunctive	had	would

Simple or Factual

si illam obiisti, noluisti de manu illius panem accipere.
If you met her, you did not want to accept bread from her hand.

si illam obis, non vis de manu illius panem accipere.
If you meet her, you do not want to accept bread from her hand.

Future More Vivid

si illam obieris, noles de manu illius panem accipere.
If you meet her, you will not want to accept bread from her hand.

Future Less Vivid

si illam eas, nolis de manu illius panem accipere.
Should you meet her, you would not want to accept bread from her hand.

Mixed Future

si illam eas, noles de manu illius panem accipere.
If you should meet her, you will not want to accept bread from her hand.

Present Contrary to Fact

si illam obires, nolles de manu illius panem accipere.
If you were meeting her, you would not want to accept bread from her hand.

Past Contrary to Fact

> si illam obisses, noluisses de manu illius panem accipere.
> *If you had met her, you would not have wanted to accept bread from her hand.*

> noluisses de manu illius panem accipere.
> *You would not have wanted to accept bread from her hand.*

Mixed Contrary to Fact

> si illam obisses, nolles de manu illius panem accipere.
> *Had you met her, you would not want to accept bread from her hand.*

Pre-Reading Review Sentences

What type of condition is found in each? How do you know? What does that type of condition express? Be ready to explain the differences between nearly identical sentences.

1. lacte gallinaceum si quaesieris, invenies.

2. lacte gallinaceum si quaeras, invenias.

3. lacte gallinaceum si quaereres, invenires.

4. vinum, si non placet, mutabo.

5. vinum, si non placuisset, mutavissem.

6. vinum, si non placeat, mutem.

7. pantomimi chorum, non patris familiae triclinium crederes.

8. si vixerit, habebis ad latus servulum.

9. si non didicisset, hodie famem a labris non abigeret.

10. si quis vestrum voluerit sua re causa facere, non illum pudeat.

11. postea si fecerit, nemo nostrum pro illo rogabit.

12. non mehercules illi ignoscerem, si piscem praeterisset.

Post-Reading Activities

1. Complete the following conditions from the point of view of one of the characters we have met so far in the *Satyrica*. See whether your classmates can guess who you are from the four sentences.

> si Trimalchio moriatur, . . .
> si aedilis fuissem, . . .
> si Trimalchio aliam fabulam narraverit, . . .
> si centum denarios haberem, . . .

2. Rewrite Niceros' story as a one-act play in Latin and perform it for the class or create a storyboard or set of illustrations with Latin captions to summarize the events, like a comic book.

3. Scholars have observed that Niceros' self-deprecating preamble to his tale echoes the way the character Aristophanes opens his speech in Plato's *Symposium* (189a–193e). Read this part of the *Symposium*. Do you agree with this assessment? If so, what do you think Petronius is getting at with the allusion?

4. Skim the passage from the next chapter in Latin to find the major characters and how they interact with each other.

Irregular Verb: **ferō, ferre, tulī, lātus,** *bear, carry, endure*

	Active			Passive	
			INDICATIVE		
Present	ferō	ferimus	*Present*	feror	ferimur
	fers	fertis		ferris/ferre	feriminī
	fert	ferunt		fertur	feruntur
Imperfect	ferēbam	ferēbāmus	*Imperfect*	ferēbar	ferēbāmur
	ferēbās	ferēbātis		ferēbāris/ferēbāre	ferēbāminī
	ferēbat	ferēbant		ferēbātur	ferēbantur
Future	feram	ferēmus	*Future*	ferar	ferēmur
	ferēs	ferētis		ferēris/ferēre	ferēminī
	feret	ferent		ferētur	ferentur
Perfect	tulī	tulimus	*Perfect*	lātus sum	latī sumus
	tulistī	tulistis		lātus es	latī estis
	tulit	tulērunt/tulēre		lātus est	latī sunt
Pluperfect	tuleram	tulerāmus	*Pluperfect*	lātus eram	latī erāmus
	tulerās	tulerātis		lātus erās	latī erātis
	tulerat	tulerant		lātus erat	latī erant
Future	tulerō	tulerimus	*Future*	lātus erō	latī erimus
perfect	tuleris	tuleritis	*perfect*	lātus eris	latī eritis
	tulerit	tulerint		lātus erit	latī erunt
			SUBJUNCTIVE		
Present	feram	ferāmus	*Present*	ferar	ferāmur
	ferās	ferātis		ferāris/ferāre	ferāminī
	ferat	ferant		ferātur	ferantur
Imperfect	ferrem	ferrēmus	*Imperfect*	ferrer	ferrēmur
	ferrēs	ferrētis		ferrēris/ferrēre	ferrēminī
	ferret	ferrent		ferrētur	ferrentur

Irregular Verb: **ferō, ferre, tulī, lātus** (*continued*)

	Active			Passive	
			SUBJUNCTIVE		
Perfect	tulerim	tulerimus	*Perfect*	lātus sim	latī sīmus
	tuleris	tuleritis		lātus sīs	latī sītis
	tulerit	tulerint		lātus sit	latī sint
Pluperfect	tulissem	tulissēmus	*Pluperfect*	lātus essem	latī essēmus
	tulissēs	tulissētis		lātus essēs	latī essētis
	tulisset	tulissent		lātus esset	latī essent
			INFINITIVE		
Present	ferre		*Present*	ferrī	
Perfect	tulisse		*Perfect*	lātus, -a, -um esse	
Future	lātūrus, -a, -um esse		*Future*	—	
			PARTICIPLES		
Present	ferēns, ferentis		*Present*	—	
Perfect	—		*Perfect*	lātus, -a, -um	
Future	lātūrus, -a, -um		*Future*	ferendus, -a, -um	

Vocabulary

amplius (comparative adverb): *any further; besides; more; more than*

amplus, ampla, amplum: *large; strong*

anima, animae, F: *air, wind; breath; life, soul*

animus, animī, M: *intellect, mind, thought; courage, will*

audiō, audīre, audīvī, audītus: *hear, listen to*

botulum, botulī, N: *sausage*

clārus, clāra, clārum: *loud; bright, manifest; famous*

collum, collī, N: *the neck*

cōnsurgō, cōnsurgere, cōnsurrēxī, cōnsurrēctum: *stand up, rise*

dērīdeō, dērīdēre, dērīsī, dērīsus: *deride, mock; laugh off*

exeō, exīre, exīvī or exiī, exitus: *pass, cross, avoid, exceed; go out, depart*

gladius, gladiī, M: *sword*

gustō, gustāre, gustāvī, gustātus: *taste, eat; dine; overhear*

lūdō, lūdere, lūsī, lūsus: *play (with), amuse oneself*

lūdus, lūdī, M: *game, play, diversion, joke*

lūsus, lūsūs, M: *game, play, amusement*

mālum, mālī, N: *apple, fruit*

malus, mala, malum: *bad*

mālus, mālī, F: *apple tree*

mentior, mentīrī, mentītus sum: *invent, fabricate; lie, act deceitfully*

mōs, mōris, M: *custom, practice, manner*

nēsciō, nēscīre, nēscīvī or nēsciī, nēscītus: *not know, be ignorant of; not know how to*

nūllus, nūlla, nūllum (gen. s. **nūllīus**, dat. s. **nūllī**): *no, none, not at all*

paene (adverb): *nearly, almost*

petō, petere, petīvī or petiī, petītus: *make for, go to; seek, strive after; ask for, beg*

pōmum, pōmī, N: *piece of fruit*

propter (preposition + acc.): *near, next to; on account of, because of*

sinus, sinūs, M: *curve, fold; fold of a tunic or toga, pocket; lap; crotch*

suāvis, suāve: *sweet, pleasant, agreeable*

uxor, uxōris, F: *wife, mate*

CHAPTER SEVEN:
INDIRECT QUESTIONS, REFLEXIVES, AND INTENSIVES

A direct question quotes the exact words of the speaker: *"Where were you?" "Why are you walking so late?" "Who is she?"* An indirect question reports the question or passes it along without using the speaker's own words and without quotation marks: *He asked where you were. She wondered why you were walking so late. I know who she is.* Indirect questions are thus dependent clauses embedded into sentences of asking, doubting, knowing, wondering, and the like.

Indirect questions are introduced by an interrogative, and their verbs are subjunctive. In addition to the interrogative pronoun and adjective reviewed in chapter 4, common interrogative adverbs include:

quam, *how?*
quārē, *for what reason? why?*
quōmodo, *in what way? how?*
ubi, *where? when?*
(**utrum**) . . . **an/annōn**, *(whether) . . . or/or not?*

The tense of the subjunctive used for the verb in an indirect question is selected based upon the Sequence of Tenses, detailed in chapter 5 and presented again below. At the heart of this sequence is the notion that subordinate clauses with verbs in the perfect or pluperfect tense are describing events that happened *before* the main verb, and subordinate clauses with verbs in the present or imperfect tense are referring to events taking place *at the same time as or even after* the main verb.

Main Clause		Subordinate Clause
Indicative Mood		Subjunctive Mood
	Primary Sequence	
present, future, future perfect	→	present → same time as or after
perfect using "have" or "has"		OR
		perfect → before main verb
	Secondary Sequence	
imperfect, simple perfect,	→	imperfect → same time as or after
pluperfect		OR
		pluperfect → before main verb

horologium in triclinio habet ut sciat quantum de vita perdiderit.
He has a clock in his dining room so that he knows how much of his life he has lost.

horologium in triclinio habebat ut sciret quantum de vita perdidisset.
He used to have a clock in his dining room so that he knew how much of his
*   life he had lost.*

hinc quemadmodum ratiocinari didicisset pictor cum inscriptione reddidit.
Here how he had learned to keep accounts the painter rendered with an inscription.

hinc quemadmodum ratiocinari didicerit pictor cum inscriptione reddit.
Here how he learned to keep accounts the painter is rendering with an inscription.

hinc quemadmodum ratiocinari discat pictor cum inscriptione reddit.
Here how he is learning to keep accounts the painter is rendering with an inscription.

Third Person Reflexives

A reflexive pronoun marks that the person doing this job in the sentence (direct object, indirect object, etc.) is the same person as the subject. For the first person and second person in Latin, this is straightforward, because the regular first and second person pronouns are used:

dum versas te, nox fit.
While you are turning yourself around, it becomes night.

dum verso me, nox fit.
While I am turning myself around, it becomes night.

dum versamus nos, nox fit.
While we are turning ourselves around, it becomes night.

The third person is a little more complicated. Note the distinction between the following two sentences:

Caesar eum amat.   *Caesar loves him.*
Caesar se amat.   *Caesar loves himself.*

In English, a speaker attaches the enclitic *-self* to the pronoun in order to make it point back to the subject. Latin uses a different pronoun to differentiate between the reflexive (the second example) and a neutral third party (the first example). Here are the forms of the third person reflexive:

Genitive	suī
Dative	sibi
Accusative	sē
Ablative	sē

There are a few observations worth making. Since this pronoun indicates that this is the same person as the subject, there is never a need for this word to be in the case of the subject; it has no nominative form. Also, the same forms are used for singular and plural subjects. If the subject is plural, this pronoun is considered plural.

Caesar se amat. *Caesar loves himself.*

Caesares se amant. *The Caesars love themselves.*

As with first and second person pronouns, the genitive is not used to indicate possession; it is used only in partitive or objective situations. A possessive adjective is available to mark that something is owned by the subject (**suus, sua, suum**).

si quis vestrum voluerit sua re causa facere, non illum pudeat.
If any one of you wants to do his business, it should not shame him.

nemo nostrum solide natus est.
No one of us was born solidly.

quinque dies acquam in os suum non coniecit.
For five days he did not put water into his (own) mouth.

quinque dies acquam in os suum non coniecerunt.
For five days they did not put water into their (own) mouths.

Remember that to indicate that a noun belongs to a third party, not the subject, the genitive of the demonstrative pronoun **is, ea, id** is normally used: **eīus**, *of him, her, its*; **eōrum/eārum**, *their, of them.*

quinque dies acquam in os eius non coniecerunt.
For five days they did not put water into his mouth.

tres iatraliptae in conspectu eius Falernum potabant.
Three masseurs were drinking Falernian wine in his (Trimalchio's) sight.

Intensive Adjective: **ipse, ipsa, ipsum**

In English, the same word *-self* is used in an intensifying role, not just as a reflexive. Although Latin uses a completely different word for this purpose, it is nonetheless useful for English speakers to review them together. Note the differences between the following sentences. In the first, there is a reflexive, while in the second *self* is an intensifying adjective (**ipse, ipsa, ipsum** in Latin).

dum versas te, nox fit.
While you are turning yourself around, it becomes night.
dum ipse versas, nox fit.
While you yourself are turning around, it becomes night.

quinque dies acquam in os suum non coniecit.
For five days he did not put water into his own mouth.
ipse quinque dies acquam in os non coniecit.
He himself did not put water into his mouth for five days.

nec medici se inveniunt.
Nor are the doctors finding themselves.
nec medici ipsi veniunt.
Nor are the doctors themselves coming.

Recall that **ipse, ipsa, ipsum** has an irregular genitive singular (**ipsīus**) and dative singular (**ipsī**). In the *Satyrica*, we also frequently find a colloquial superlative of this intensive, **ipsimus** or **ipsumus, -a, -um**. It usually is used by a slave of his master or mistress, and so means something like *the big man himself*, *her ladyship*, or *boss*.

Pre-Reading Review Sentences

1. statim scietis cui dederitis beneficium.

2. statim scivistis cui dedissetis beneficium.

3. statim scietis cui detis beneficium.

4. ego experiri volui, an tota familia cantaret.

5. ipse nescit quid habeat.

6. ipse nescit quid habuerit.

7. ipse nescivit quid habuisset.

8. ipse nesciebat quid haberet.

9. nemo curat quid annona mordet.

10. nescio quid nunc taceas.

11. nescio quid tacueris.

12. ego primum nesciebam ubi essem.

13. et quot putas illum annos secum tulisse?

14. nolunt sibi verum dicere.

15. nolunt verum ipsum dicere.

16. dicebat se oblitum esse porcum exinterare.

17. dicebat eam oblitam esse porcum exinterare.

18. ipsi mappas implevimus.

Post-Reading Activities

1. Transform sentences 9 and 11 of the review exercise into secondary sequence, and 4 and 12 into primary sequence while preserving the temporal relationship between the clauses.

2. In Latin, how is an indirect statement constructed differently from an indirect question? Consider the following sentence from chapter 7: *ego maiestate conterritus praetorem putabam venisse.*

3. Write a short riddle for your classmates about one of the characters we have met so far, using at least one intensive adjective, reflexive, and indirect question. Example:

Agamemnon melius me loquitur.
Puto iurem panem habere.
Ipse scio quis aves amet.
Quis sum?

Irregular Verb: **mālō, mālle, māluī,** *want more, prefer, choose*

INDICATIVE

Present	mālō	mālumus	
	māvīs	māvultis	
	māvult	mālunt	
Imperfect	mālēbam	mālēbāmus	
	mālēbās	mālēbātis	
	mālēbat	mālēbant	
Future	mālam	mālēmus	
	mālēs	mālētis	
	mālet	mālent	
Perfect	māluī	māluimus	
	māluistī	māluistis	
	māluit	māluērunt/māluēre	
Pluperfect	mālueram	māluerāmus	
	māluerās	māluerātis	
	māluerat	māluerant	
Future perfect	māluerō	māluerimus	
	mālueris	mālueritis	
	māluerit	māluerint	

SUBJUNCTIVE

Present	mālim	mālīmus	
	mālīs	mālītis	
	mālit	mālint	
Imperfect	māllem	māllēmus	
	māllēs	māllētis	
	māllet	māllent	
Perfect	māluerim	māluerimus	
	mālueris	mālueritis	
	māluerit	māluerint	
Pluperfect	māluissem	māluissēmus	
	māluissēs	māluissētis	
	māluisset	māluissent	

INFINITIVE

Present	mālle
Perfect	māluisse
Future	—

Vocabulary

addūcō, addūcere, addūxī, addūctus: *bring up, bring along*

admoneō, admonēre, admonuī, admonitus: *admonish, remind, warn*

bāsio, bāsiāre, bāsiāvī, bāsiātus: *kiss*

bene (adverb): *well*

cēna, cēnae, F: *dinner, a three-course meal*

comedō, comēsse, comēdī, comēsus: *eat up, consume*

dēbeō, dēbēre, dēbuī, dēbitus: *owe; be obliged to*

discumbō, discumbere, discubuī, discubitum: *recline, take one's place (at the table or in bed)*

ēbrius, ēbria, ēbrium: *drunk, inebriated*

ecce (interjection): *behold! lo! see!*

imitor, imitārī, imitātus sum: *imitate, copy*

ipsimus or **ipsumus, ipsumī**, M / **ipsuma, ipsumae**, F: *boss, master or mistress*

laudō, laudāre, laudāvī, laudātus: *praise*

mālō, mālle, māluī: *wish for more, prefer*

minimus, minima, minimum: (comparative of **parvus**) *smallest, least, youngest, very small*

mora, morae, F: *delay, pause*

moveō, movēre, mōvī, mōtus: *move, set in motion; stir, excite*

nōmen, nōminis, N: *name*

nūdus, nūda, nūdum: *nude, bare*

officium, officiī, N: *service, favor, duty, obligation*

pōtiō, pōtiōnis, F: *drinking; a drink*

prasinus, prasina, prasinum: *green; green team in chariot racing*

quōmodo (interrogative adverb): *how? in what way?*

surgō, surgere, surrēxī, surrēctum: *get up, rise*

temptō, temptāre, temptāvī, temptātus: *test, feel; attempt, try*

terra, terrae, F: *ground, land, earth*

ubi (interrogative adverb): *where? when?*

unguentum, unguentī, N: *ointment, perfume*

(utrum) . . . an / annōn (conjunction): *(whether) . . . or / or not?*

CHAPTER EIGHT:
INFINITIVES AND INDIRECT STATEMENTS

Latin has five infinitive forms in common use: the present active and passive, the perfect active and passive, and the future active. Recall that infinitives have no person or number—they are *infinite*, not finite—and thus they cannot under normal circumstances serve as the main verb of a sentence.

frangō, frangere, frēgī, frāctus: *break, shatter*

	ACTIVE	PASSIVE
Present	frangere	frangī
	to break	*to be broken*
Perfect	frēgisse	frāctus, -a, -um esse
	to have broken	*to have been broken*
Future	frāctūrus, -a, -um esse	—
	to be about to break	

The **present active infinitive** is a verb's second principal part. For most conjugations, the **present passive** is formed by changing the final -e into an -ī; however, for the third conjugation, including third i-stems, the final -ere as a whole is replaced with -ī:

ACTIVE	vocāre	habēre	agere	audīre
	to call	*to have*	*to do*	*to hear*
PASSIVE	vocārī	habērī	agī	audīrī
	to be called	*to be held*	*to be done*	*to be heard*

The **perfect active infinitive** is formed by adding -**isse** to the perfect active stem. As usual, the **perfect passive** is formed by using the perfect passive participle alongside the verb "to be," this time in the present infinitive form. This form is sometimes contracted, such as **amāsse** for **amāvisse**.

ACTIVE	vocāvisse	habuisse	ēgisse	audīvisse
	to have called	*to have had*	*to have done*	*to have heard*
PASSIVE	vocātum esse	habitum esse	actum esse	audītum esse
	to have been called	*to have been held*	*to have been done*	*to have been heard*

The **future active infinitive** is formed by placing the future active participle beside the present infinitive of **sum**. Note that although this makes it look passive, the participle and thus the infinitive are active.

vocātūrum esse	habitūrum esse	actūrum esse	audītūrum esse
to be about to call	*to be about to have*	*to be about to do*	*to be about to hear*

eum caedere debet.	*She ought to kill him.*
eum cecidisse debet.	*She ought to have killed him.*

caedi debet.	*She ought to be killed.*
se caedere debet.	*She ought to kill herself.*
ipsa caesa esse debet.	*She herself ought to have been killed.*

Infinitives of Deponent Verbs

Deponents have an infinitive of each tense—present, perfect, and future. Since there are passive forms for the present and perfect, these are used, but with active meanings (in keeping with the rules for deponent verbs). However, since only a future active infinitive form was in regular use, the deponent uses an active form for the future.

sequī, *to follow*	secūtum esse, *to have followed*	secūtūrum esse, *to be about to follow*

Indirect Statement

Indirect statements are to direct statements as indirect questions are to direct questions. Direct statements are quoted directly: "He went to the grocery store." Indirect statements are reported indirectly after verbs of speaking, thinking, seeing, perceiving, knowing, and the like: "I think that he went to the store." In English we usually use the subordinating conjunction "that" to introduce an indirect statement, although it can often be left out. In formal classical Latin, an accusative and infinitive construction is used for the statement provided indirectly. The subject from the direct statement is put into the accusative, and the verb is transformed into the infinitive. The tense of the infinitive is relative; that is, it expresses the temporal relationship between the event being stated indirectly and the main verb. Thus a present infinitive reports an event going on at the same time as the verb of speaking, a perfect infinitive an event prior to the main verb, and a future infinitive an event that will occur subsequent to the main verb.

ego putabam porcos portenta facturos esse.
I was thinking that the pigs were going to do tricks.

ego putabam porcos portenta fecisse.
I was thinking that the pigs had done tricks.

ego putabam porcos portenta facere.
I was thinking that the pigs were doing tricks.

ego puto porcos portenta facturos esse.
I think that the pigs are going to do tricks.

ego puto porcos portenta fecisse.
I think that the pigs have done tricks.

ego puto porcos portenta facere.
I think that the pigs are doing tricks.

ego putabam ab porcis portenta facta esse.
I was thinking that tricks had been done by the pigs.

ego putabam ab porcis portenta fieri.
I was thinking that tricks were being done by the pigs.

As discussed briefly in chapter 4, in later Latin the accusative and infinitive construction of indirect statement is increasingly replaced by **quia, quod,** or **quoniam** and the indicative. This construction occurs only a few times before Petronius, who thus provides some evidence that it was used first in colloquial speech.

Together, indirect statements and indirect questions make up what we refer to as *indirect discourse*. Keep in mind that questions and statements are reported indirectly using different constructions: questions take an interrogative and the subjunctive; statements use the accusative and infinitive construction.

Historical Infinitive

Within a narrative, the present infinitive is sometimes used in the place of the imperfect indicative. The subject remains in the nominative, unlike the subject of an infinitive in an indirect statement. The historical infinitive is relatively rare, but it is used repeatedly by some speakers in the *Satyrica*.

mihi anima in naso esse.
My heart was in my nose.

qui mori timore nisi ego?
What man died from fear if not I?

Pre-Reading Review Sentences

1. ego nullum puto tam magnum tormentum esse quam continere.

2. ego nullum puto tam magnum tormentum esse quam continuisse.

3. multos scio sic periisse.

4. multos scio sic perituros esse.

5. multos sciebam sic perituros esse.

6. intellexi illum versipellem esse.

7. intellexi illum versipellem fuisse.

8. non mehercules illum puto in domo canem reliquisse.

9. non mehercules illum putabam in domo canem relicturum esse.

10. puto omnia illa a diibus fieri.

11. scimus te prae litteras fatuum esse.

Post-Reading Activities

1. Transform Habinnas and Trimalchio's conversation about the other dinner party in chapter 7 (66–66.3) into indirect discourse in Latin.

2. Explain why clauses of purpose and result only rarely feature a subjunctive tense other than the present or imperfect. (Hint: consider the Sequence of Tenses.)

3. Draw a picture of the tomb that Trimalchio describes. Label as many parts as possible with Latin nouns and adjectives. Give it a caption that expresses your opinion of it.

4. (a) Find a few other Roman epitaphs, in Latin or translated. Compare what Trimalchio includes, and think about what is characteristic of a Roman epitaph, and where Trimalchio may go astray. What might a passerby expect to see on a Roman tomb? (b) Using the guidelines you have created, write an inscription in Latin commemorating a different character in the novel. Can your classmates guess whom you have selected?

Irregular Verb: **eō, īre, iī** or **īvī, itum,** *go*

Active		
INDICATIVE		
Present	eō	īmus
	īs	ītis
	it	eunt
Imperfect	ībam	ībāmus
	ībās	ībātis
	ībat	ībant
Future	ībō	ībimus
	ībis	ībitis
	ībit	ībunt

Irregular Verb: **eō, īre, iī** or **īvī, itum** (*continued*)

<table>
<tr><td colspan="3" align="center">Active</td></tr>
<tr><td colspan="3" align="center">INDICATIVE</td></tr>
<tr><td>*Perfect*</td><td>iī/īvī</td><td>iimus/īmus/īvimus</td></tr>
<tr><td></td><td>īstī/īvistī</td><td>īstis/īvistis</td></tr>
<tr><td></td><td>iit/īt/īvit</td><td>iērunt/iēre/īvērunt/īvēre</td></tr>
<tr><td>*Pluperfect*</td><td>ieram/īveram</td><td>ierāmus/īverāmus</td></tr>
<tr><td></td><td>ierās/īverās</td><td>ierātis/īverātis</td></tr>
<tr><td></td><td>ierat/īverat</td><td>ierant/īverant</td></tr>
<tr><td>*Future perfect*</td><td>ierō/īverō</td><td>ierimus/īverimus</td></tr>
<tr><td></td><td>ieris/īveris</td><td>ieritis/īveritis</td></tr>
<tr><td></td><td>ierit/īverit</td><td>ierint/īverint</td></tr>
<tr><td colspan="3" align="center">SUBJUNCTIVE</td></tr>
<tr><td>*Present*</td><td>eam</td><td>eāmus</td></tr>
<tr><td></td><td>eās</td><td>eātis</td></tr>
<tr><td></td><td>eat</td><td>eant</td></tr>
<tr><td>*Imperfect*</td><td>īrem</td><td>īrēmus</td></tr>
<tr><td></td><td>īrēs</td><td>īrētis</td></tr>
<tr><td></td><td>īret</td><td>īrent</td></tr>
<tr><td>*Perfect*</td><td>ierim/īverim</td><td>ierimus/īverimus</td></tr>
<tr><td></td><td>ieris/īveris</td><td>ieritis/īveritis</td></tr>
<tr><td></td><td>ierit/īverit</td><td>ierint/īverint</td></tr>
<tr><td>*Pluperfect*</td><td>īssem/īvissem</td><td>īssēmus/īvissēmus</td></tr>
<tr><td></td><td>īssēs/īvissēs</td><td>īssētis/īvissētis</td></tr>
<tr><td></td><td>īsset/īvisset</td><td>īssent/īvissent</td></tr>
<tr><td colspan="3" align="center">INFINITIVE</td></tr>
<tr><td>*Present*</td><td colspan="2" align="center">īre</td></tr>
<tr><td>*Perfect*</td><td colspan="2" align="center">īsse/īvisse</td></tr>
<tr><td>*Future*</td><td colspan="2" align="center">itūrus, -a, -um esse</td></tr>
<tr><td colspan="3" align="center">PARTICIPLES</td></tr>
<tr><td>*Present*</td><td colspan="2" align="center">iēns, euntis</td></tr>
<tr><td>*Perfect*</td><td colspan="2" align="center">—</td></tr>
<tr><td>*Future*</td><td colspan="2" align="center">itūrus, -a, -um</td></tr>
</table>

Vocabulary

beneficium, beneficiī, N: *favor, service*

causa, causae, F: *reason, pretext; situation, case;* **causā** (preposition + genitive): *for the sake of, because of*

contineō, continēre, continuī, contentus: *hold together; keep in; hold back, restrain*

contingō, contingere, contigī, contāctus: *contact, touch; happen, come to pass;*

(impersonal + dative) *it happens to,*
it befalls

dīligenter (adverb): *carefully, thoroughly*

dōnō, dōnāre, dōnāvī, dōnātus: *present;*
condone; give up

errō, errāre, errāvī, errātum: *wander; make*
a mistake

hōra, hōrae, F: *an hour; time*

iniūria, iniūriae, F: *injury, injustice, wrong*

līber, lībera, līberum: *free*

melior, melius: *better, kinder* (comparative
of **bonus**)

mors, mortis, F: *death*

nummus, nummī, M: *coin*

plōrō, plōrāre, plōrāvī, plōrātus: *mourn,*
cry over; wail, cry

pūblicus, pūblica, pūblicum: *public;*
common, ordinary

quemadmodum (adverb): *in what way, how;*
(conjunction) *just as, as*

relinquō, relinquere, relīquī, relictus: *leave,*
leave behind

respiciō, respicere, respexī, respectus: *look*
back at, gaze at, regard

satis (adverb): *enough, sufficiently;*
(indeclinable noun): *enough*

sedeō, sedēre, sēdī, sessum: *sit,*
remain sitting

subinde (adverb): *immediately afterward;*
from then on; from time to time

subitō (adverb): *suddenly, unexpectedly*

taceō, tacēre, tacuī, tacitus: *be silent,*
say nothing

testāmentum, testāmentī, N: *will, testament*

tot (indeclinable adjective): *so many, as*
many; **tot . . . quot:** *as many . . . as*

valdē (adverb): *greatly, very; yes, certainly*

vōx, vōcis, F: *voice, sound*

CHAPTER NINE:
CLAUSES OF PURPOSE AND RESULT, USES OF UT

haec omnia publico ut familia mea iam nunc sic me amet tamquam
mortuum.

I make all these things known so that my staff will love me as much now as
when I'm dead.

Trimalchio, ne videretur iactura motus, basiavit puerum.

Trimalchio, so as not to seem moved by the loss, kissed the boy.

These two sentences illustrate Latin **purpose clauses**. The action of the main verb
is performed *in order that* the subordinate clause occur: *I make things known* in
order that *my staff love me.* In order that *he not seem moved, he kissed the boy.*
Because the subordinate clause expresses a goal, intention, or aim rather than
stating a fact, its verb is in the subjunctive: **amet, videretur**. Because by definition
that event will always occur subsequent to the main verb, we find the present
and imperfect tense only in purpose clauses. In keeping with the Sequence of
Tenses, the present tense subjunctive occurs with a main verb in the present or a
future tense (that is, in primary sequence, **publico → amet**), the imperfect

subjunctive with main verbs in a past tense (in secondary sequence, **basiavit** →
videretur).

Purpose clauses are usually introduced by **ut** or **nē**, depending upon whether
they are positive or negative, and as with most subordinate clauses, they may come
before or after the main clause within the sentence.

Indirect Command

A command that is reported indirectly, rather than quoted directly, works exactly
like a purpose clause, and they both derive from a jussive noun clause. Indirect
commands are introduced by a verb of commanding, asking, begging, or similar;
are usually introduced by **ut** or **nē;** and have present tense subjunctive verbs in
primary sequence and imperfect subjunctive verbs in secondary sequence.

> catellam hortatus est ut ad rixam properaret.
> *He encouraged the puppy, that he might rush to the fight.*
> *He encouraged the puppy to rush to the fight.*

> te rogo ut secundum pedes statuae meae catellam fingas ut mihi contingat
>   tuo beneficio post mortem vivere.
> *I ask you to craft a puppy along the feet of my statue so that by your kindness it*
>   *will come about for me to live after death.*

Not all verbs of command use this construction, however; **iubeō, iubēre**, in
particular, takes an accusative and infinitive construction to describe what is
being commanded:

> puerum iussit supra dorsum ascendere suum.
> *He ordered the boy to climb up onto his back.*

Result Clauses

Result clauses are similar in construction to clauses of purpose, but the under-
lying idea is different. In a result clause, there is no purposeful intention—no
one performs the main verb *in order that* the subordinate clause happen. Instead,
the subordinate clause is an unintended result of some characteristic, quality, or
action in the main clause.

> miscebat Atellanicos versus ut tunc me etiam Vergilius offenderit.
> *He was mixing in Atellan verses with the result that then even Vergil*
>   *offended me.*

The performer is not trying to offend. On the contrary, his aim is to entertain, so this cannot be described as a purpose clause. Nevertheless, the result of his performance is to offend Encolpius. The characteristic, quality, or manner of acting in the main clause that results in the dependent clause is often (but not always) marked by an adjective or adverb of degree:

adverbs:	adjectives:
ita, *so*	**tantus, -a, -um**, *so great*
tam, *so*	**tālis, tāle**, *such, of such a sort*
sīc, *in this way, in such a way*	**tot**, *so many*
adeō, *so, to such a degree*	

nam tam bonae memoriae sum ut frequenter nomen meum obliviscar.
I am of such good memory that I frequently forget my own name.
My memory is so good that I frequently forget my own name.

venit galbino succincta cingillo ita ut infra cerasina appareret tunica.
She arrived tied up with a yellow sash in such a way that underneath her cherry-red tunic showed.

The Romans recognized the difference between a purpose and a result clause, as we can see in the way they are introduced. Although positive result clauses are introduced by **ut**, just like purpose clauses, the negative is introduced by **ut** with a **nōn** following later in the clause, rather than by **nē**.

Summary of the Uses of **ut**

The Latin word **ut** is used to introduce many subjunctive clauses. Here we have reviewed its use in purpose clauses, clauses of result, and indirect commands, and soon you will see it in fear clauses. You may also find it introducing subjunctive clauses of wishing, permitting, decreeing, cautioning, and so forth, much like its multivalent English equivalent, *that*. Keep in mind, however, that **ut** does not always signal a subjunctive. **ut** is often used with the indicative as a simple conjunction marking that two events happened at the same time.

Pre-Reading Review Sentences

Identify the type of subordinate clause in each sentence. Why are the verbs in these tenses and moods?

1. horologium in triclinio habet ut subinde sciat quantum de vita perdiderit.

2. horologium in triclinio habebat ut subinde sciret quantum de vita perdidisset.

3. ceterum ut pariter movimus dextros gressus, servus nobis despoliatus procubuit ad pedes.

4. dispensatorem in atrio aureos numerantem deprecati sumus ut servo remitteret poenam.

5. deinde ut respexi ad comitem, ille exuit se et omnia vestimenta secundum
viam posuit.

6. accessi ut vestimenta eius tollerem.

7. ego sic solebam ipsumam meam debattuere, ut etiam dominus suspicaretur.

8. haec ut audivi, operire oculos amplius non potui.

9. praeponam enim unum ex libertis sepulchro meo custodiae causa, ne in
monumentum meum populus cacatum currat.

Post-Reading Activities

1. Transform sentences 2, 4, and 6 into primary sequence, and 9 into secondary
sequence.

2. A dog who guards the exit recalls Cerberus in the underworld, and an
underworld with two gates refers to Aeneas' journey in the *Aeneid*, while Theseus escaped the labyrinth in Crete only with the assistance of the marks of Ariadne. Allusions to a variety of myths are embedded in these scenes. What are
their implications? Do they help to characterize Encolpius? How do they characterize other figures?

3. Chose a scene from chapter 9 to rewrite as a script for a film in English.
Include setting and stage directions, dialogue, camera angles, and the like.

4. Skim the passages in the next chapter for every use of the word **ut**. Identify
whether each is used with the indicative or subjunctive, and which if any introduce clauses of result, purpose, or indirect command.

5. Write a short one-act play in English of Trimalchio's dinner party that cap-
tures Petronius' main points. After comparing a few in class, watch the banquet
scene from *Fellini Satyricon*, the 1969 Italian film adapted from Petronius'
novel. How do Fellini's choices differ from yours? What has he chosen to
emphasize, and why?

Irregular Verb: **possum, posse, potuī,** *be able*

INDICATIVE

Present	possum	possumus
	potes	potestis
	potest	possunt
Imperfect	poteram	poterāmus
	poterās	poterātis
	poterat	poterant
Future	poterō	poterimus
	poteris	poteritis
	poterit	poterunt
Perfect	potuī	potuimus
	potuistī	potuistis
	potuit	potuērunt/potuēre
Pluperfect	potueram	potuerāmus
	potuerās	potuerātis
	potuerat	potuerant
Future perfect	potuerō	potuerimus
	potueris	potueritis
	potuerit	potuerint

SUBJUNCTIVE

Present	possim	possīmus
	possīs	possītis
	possit	possint
Imperfect	possem	possēmus
	possēs	possētis
	posset	possent
Perfect	potuerim	potuerimus
	potueris	potueritis
	potuerit	potuerint
Pluperfect	potuissem	potuissēmus
	potuissēs	potuissētis
	potuisset	potuissent

INFINITIVE

Present	posse
Perfect	potuisse
Future	—

Vocabulary

adeō (adverb): *so, to such a degree; indeed, for that matter*

aequē (adverb): *equally; justly*

āiō (verb in present and imperfect only): *I say, assert; I say yes, affirm*

amphora, amphorae, F: *amphora, a two-handled jar with a narrow neck used to transport and store liquid (Greek loan word)*

aperiō, aperīre, aperuī, apertus: *open, uncover*

cibus, cibī, M: *food, nourishment, fodder*

excipiō, excipere, excēpī, exceptus: *take out; rescue*

excitō, excitāre, excitāvī, excitātus: *awaken, arouse*

fidēs, fideī, F: *trust, faith, confidence*

frāter, frātris, M: *brother; companion*

fugiō, fugere, fūgī, fugitus: *flee, flee away*

gaudium, gaudiī, N: *joy, delight; cause of joy*

genus, generis, N: *birth, descent, origin; family; kind, sort*

iānua, iānuae, F: *door, entrance*

ideō (adverb): *therefore*

iungō, iungere, iūnxī, iūnctus: *join, join together*

iūs, iūris, N: *law, right, justice; juice, broth*

lūx, lūcis, F: *light, daylight*

morior, morī, mortuus sum (moritūrus): *die*

operiō, operīre, operuī, opertus: *cover, shut, hide*

ostendō, ostendere, ostendī, ostentus: *show, point out, reveal*

pār, paris: *equal, like; suitable, well-matched*

pār, paris, N: *pair, couple*

quaerō, quaerere, quaesīvī, quaesītus: *look for, seek; miss; ask, investigate*

reor, rērī, ratus sum: *reckon, think, suppose*

sentiō, sentīre, sēnsī, sēnsus: *feel, perceive, realize, think*

tālis, tāle: *such, of such a sort*

tangō, tangere, tetigī, tāctus: *touch*

tantus, tanta, tantum: *so great*

CHAPTER TEN: GERUNDIVES AND GERUNDS, PASSIVE PERIPHRASTIC AND SUPINE

Gerundives

The future passive participle is also referred to as the gerundive. As we reviewed in chapter 2, it is formed by adding **-nd** and first and second declension adjective endings to the present participial stem:

vocandus, -a, -um	habendus, -a, -um	agendus, -a, -um	audiendus, -a, -um
about to be called	*going to be held*	*having to be done*	*about to be heard*

Unlike the gerund, the gerundive is an **adjective.** Since it modifies a noun, it has the case, number, and gender of the noun it modifies. Gerundives thus occur in all cases, numbers, and genders.

Also unlike gerunds, gerundives are **passive;** that is, they describe an action that will be undergone by the noun they modify.

classis aedificanda bellum vincet.	*The fleet about to be built will win the war.*
classes aedificandae bellum vincent.	*The to-be-built fleets will win the war.*
vincemus classibus aedificandis.	*We will win by means of fleets about to be built.*
versum recitandum non audivi.	*I have not heard the verse about to be recited.*
versus recitandos non audivi.	*I have not heard the verses about to be recited.*

Gerunds

The gerund is a verbal noun, the act of doing something. It is formed by adding -**nd** and second declension neuter singular endings to the present participial stem:

vocandī, -ō, -um, -ō	habendī, -ō, -um, -ō	agendī, -ō, -um, -ō	audiendī, -ō, -um, -ō
calling	*the act of holding*	*doing*	*the act of hearing*

Unlike the gerundive, the gerund is a **noun**. Its case is thus determined by its role in the sentence. Moreover, it is a singular, neuter noun that occurs in only four cases—genitive, dative, accusative, and ablative. It is never the subject of a sentence, since the infinitive is used for that job instead.

The gerund is **active**. It denotes the performance of that action, and thus may take a direct object.

classem aedificando vincemus.	*We will win by means of building a fleet.*
classes aedificando vincemus.	*We will win by means of building fleets.*
ille est cupidus aedificandi classes.	*He is eager for the building (of) fleets.*
illos versus recitandum non audivi.	*I have not heard the reciting (of) those verses.*

Latin speakers tend to prefer the gerundive; English speakers tend to prefer the gerund. One may be easily transformed into another in the act of translation, but be wary of the difference between active and passive, nouns and adjectives.

Expressing Purpose

The gerund and gerundive are used to express purpose in two ways:

1. **ad** + accusative

ad legendos libros venit. *He came for the to-be-read books.*

ad legendum libros venit. *He came for the reading of books.*

} *He came to read books.*

2. genitive + **causā** or **grātiā**

> librorum legendorum causa venit. *He came*
> *for the sake of the books to be read.*
>
> libros legendi causa venit. *He came for the*
> *sake of reading books.*

} *He came to read books.*

Passive Periphrastic

You can hear in the English phrase *books to be read* not just the future and the passive qualities of this adjective, but also a sense of obligation or necessity: *they are to be read, they should be read, they must be read.* This same sense of obligation is expressed by the future passive participle or gerundive in Latin. By adding an appropriate form of **sum, esse** to the gerundive, a finite verb was created known as the *passive periphrastic.* The person, number, tense, and mood are expressed by the form of the verb **sum,** while the gerundive makes the verb passive and obligatory or necessary. As my elementary Latin teacher used to sing:

> The future passive participle plus the verb "to be"
> denotes obligation or necessity.

The person by whom the action must be done is put into the dative case (*dative of agent*).

> Encolpius Gitoni relinquendus est.
> *Encolpius is to be abandoned by Giton. / Encolpius should be abandoned*
>   *by Giton.*
>
> Encolpius Gitoni relinquendus erat.
> *Encolpius needed to be abandoned by Giton. / Encolpius had to be abandoned*
>   *by Giton.*
>
> Encolpius Gitoni relinquendus erit.
> *Encolpius will have to be abandoned by Giton. / Encolpius will need to be aban-*
>   *doned by Giton.*
>
> puto Encolpium Gitoni relinquendum esse.
> *I think that Encolpius should be abandoned by Giton.*
>
> scio quid Encolpius Gitoni relinquendus sit.
> *I know why Encolpius should be abandoned by Giton.*

Supine

The supine is yet another form of verbal noun in Latin, in addition to the gerund and infinitive, and by far the rarest. Formed from the fourth principal part (the perfect passive participle), the supine is active and a neuter noun that occurs in only two forms, the accusative singular (-**um**) and ablative singular (-**ū**). Each has a single distinctive use. The accusative is used with verbs of motion to express purpose. Unlike the gerund, the accusative supine does not require a preposition—the accusative supine is simply inserted into the sentence:

> praeponam enim unum ex libertis sepulchro meo custodiae causa ne in
>   monumentum meum populus cacatum currat.
> *I shall position one of my freedmen in front of my tomb as a safeguard so that*
>   *people do not run to defecate on my monument.*

The ablative supine is an ablative of respect, usually employed to qualify an adjective.

> non expectata electione nostra maximum porcum natu iussit occidi.
> *Our choice not having been awaited, he ordered the pig largest in regard to*
>   *being born to be killed.*
> *Our choice not having been awaited, he ordered the pig largest by birth to be*
>   *killed.*

Pre-Reading Review Sentences

1. Identify the gerunds in the following paragraph:

Singing is a difficult art. Despite training for many years, a singer may still be unable to make a living. He or she may go hungry for the sake of performing well. Although the singer is working, perhaps even by singing, she may not be earning enough to support herself.

The following sentences review gerunds, gerundives, and other forms that superficially resemble them in Latin but differ in meaning. In addition to preparing to translate each of the following, identify any gerunds or gerundives in the sentence and how you know which of the two you have.

1. ferrum emptum est.

2. ferrum emendum est.

3. ferrum emptura est.

4. isti ferrum emendum erit.

5. scio vota verenda.

6. scio votum verendum esse.

7. scio vota verendum.

8. numquam didicit, sed ego ad circulatores eum mittendo erudiebam.

9. cum sciamus nos morituros esse, quare non vivamus?

10. forte dominus Capuae exierat ad scruta expedienda.

11. valde enim falsum est vivo domos cultas esse, non curari eas, ubi diutius nobis habitandum est.

12. Rewrite #10 using a gerund.

Post-Reading Activities

1. Costas Panayotakis has called Encolpius' monologue at 81.3–6 a "pastiche of Homeric-Vergilian images" (1995, 115). How many can you and your classmates identify?

2. Create a storyboard of Encolpius' encounter with the soldier, like a comic book, with captions in Latin.

3. Express the following idea in Latin using at least three different syntactical constructions:

Venimus ad carmina cantanda.

4. What are the cultural expectations that underlie Eumolpus' story? What is expected of parents, of teachers, of a young man in the Roman province of Asia Minor? Where does the storyteller expect the reader to laugh, or to nod knowingly?

Regular Verb: **agō, agere, ēgī, āctus,** *do, drive, act*

	Active			Passive	
			INDICATIVE		
Present	agō	agimus	*Present*	agor	agimur
	agis	agitis		ageris/agere	agiminī
	agit	agunt		agitur	aguntur
Imperfect	agēbam	agēbāmus	*Imperfect*	agēbar	agēbamur
	agēbās	agēbātis		agēbaris	agēbaminī
	agēbat	agēbant		agēbatur	agēbantur
Future	agam	agēmus	*Future*	agar	agēmur
	agēs	agētis		agēris	agēminī
	aget	agent		agētur	agentur
Perfect	ēgī	ēgimus	*Perfect*	āctus sum	āctī sumus
	ēgistī	ēgistis		āctus es	āctī estis
	ēgit	ēgērunt/ēgēre		āctus est	āctī sunt
Pluperfect	ēgeram	ēgerāmus	*Pluperfect*	āctus eram	āctī erāmus
	ēgerās	ēgerātis		āctus erās	āctī erātis
	ēgerat	ēgerant		āctus erat	āctī erant
Future	ēgerō	ēgerimus	*Future*	āctus erō	āctī erimus
perfect	ēgeris	ēgeritis	*perfect*	āctus eris	āctī eritis
	ēgerit	ēgerint		āctus erit	āctī erunt
			SUBJUNCTIVE		
Present	agam	agāmus	*Present*	agar	agāmur
	agās	agātis		agāris/agāre	agāminī
	agat	agant		agātur	agantur
Imperfect	agerem	agerēmus	*Imperfect*	agerer	agerēmur
	agerēs	agerētis		agerēris/agerēre	agerēminī
	ageret	agerent		agerētur	agerentur
Perfect	ēgerim	ēgerimus	*Perfect*	āctus sim	āctī sīmus
	ēgeris	ēgeritis		āctus sīs	āctī sītis
	ēgerit	ēgerint		āctus sit	āctī sint
Pluperfect	ēgissem	ēgissēmus	*Pluperfect*	āctus essem	āctī essēmus
	ēgissēs	ēgissētis		āctus essēs	āctī essētis
	ēgisset	ēgissent		āctus esset	āctī essent
			INFINITIVE		
Present	agere		*Present*	agī	
Perfect	ēgisse		*Perfect*	āctus, -a, -um esse	
Future	āctūrus, -a, -um esse		*Future*	—	
			PARTICIPLES		
Present	agēns, agentis		*Present*	—	
Perfect	—		*Perfect*	āctus, -a, -um	
Future	āctūrus, -a, -um		*Future*	agendus, -a, -um	

Vocabulary

aeger, aegra, aegrum: *sick, diseased, weary*

altus, alta, altum: *high, tall, deep*

ambulō, ambulāre, ambulāvī, ambulātum: *walk, travel*

caveō, cavēre, cāvī, cautus: *guard against, beware of; be careful*

cervīx, cervīcis, F (often in plural with same meaning as singular): *neck, nape*

cēterus, cētera, cēterum: *the other, the remaining, the rest of*

dormiō, dormīre, dormīvī or **dormiī, dormītum**: *sleep*

emō, emere, ēmī, emptus: *buy, purchase*

ephēbus, ephēbī, M: *young man, Greek youth* entering manhood (18–20 years old) (Greek loan word)

ferrum, ferrī, N: *iron; sword*

gallus gallīnāceus, gallī gallīnāceī, M: *rooster*

Graecus, Graeca, Graecum: *Greek*

hospes, hospitis, M: *host, guest, stranger*

immo (adverb): (marking contrast) *rather, on the contrary;* (in confirmation) *quite so, indeed*

impleō, implēre, implēvī, implētus: *fill in, fill up*

īrātus, īrāta, īrātum: *angry, irate*

lacrima, lacrimae, F: *tear, teardrop*

libīdō, libidinis, F: *desire, pleasure; caprice, fancy; lust*

mūnus, mūneris, N: *service, duty, munificence*

patior, patī, passus sum: *experience, suffer, allow*

pectus, pectoris, N: *breast, chest; heart, soul*

perdō, perdere, perdidī, perditus: *ruin; waste; lose*

persuādeō, persuādēre, persuasī, persuasum: (with dative) *persuade, convince*

porticus, porticūs, F: *portico, colonnade; gallery*

praecipuē (adverb): *especially, chiefly*

proximus, proxima, proximum: *nearest, next, adjoining*

sermō, sermōnis, M: *conversation, talk*

verbum, verbī, N: *word; saying*

vereor, verērī, veritus sum: *revere, be in awe of; fear; be anxious*

voluptās, voluptātis, F: *pleasure, delight;* (in plural) *games, public performances*

vōtum, vōtī, N: *solemn vow, offering; prayer, wish*

CHAPTER ELEVEN: FEAR CLAUSES

timeo istos scholasticos, ne me derideant.
I fear those scholars, that they are laughing at me.

A verb communicating fear often introduces a dependent clause that expresses what is feared. Since such a clause describes a fear—by nature a possibility rather than a fact—its verb is in the subjunctive. The clause is introduced by **nē** (*that*) or **ut** (*that . . . not*), the reverse of the positive and negative of a purpose clause. Finally, since it is possible to fear that something has already happened, that something is happening right now, or that something may happen in the future, the full Sequence of Tenses is used in Latin to express this range of possibilities. This is our last review of the subjunctive Sequence of Tenses in this textbook.

Main Clause	Dependent Clause Occurs at Same Time as or After Main Clause	Dependent Clause Occurs Before Main Clause
Primary Sequence (Present, future, future perfect, perfect with present aspect)	Present subjunctive	Perfect subjunctive
Secondary Sequence (Imperfect, perfect, pluperfect)	Imperfect subjunctive	Pluperfect subjunctive

timeo istos scholasticos, ne me derideant.
subordinate clause verb **derideant** = present subjunctive = same time as or after main verb
I fear those scholars, that they are laughing at me.
I fear those scholars, that they may laugh at me.
I am afraid that those scholars will laugh at me.

timebam istos scholasticos, ne me deriderent.
subordinate clause verb **deriderent** = imperfect subjunctive = same time as or after main verb
I was afraid of those scholars, that they were laughing at me.
I feared that those scholars would laugh at me.

timeo istos scholasticos, ne me deriserint.
subordinate clause verb **deriserint** = perfect subjunctive = before main verb
I fear those scholars, that they were laughing at me.
I fear that those scholars laughed at me.

timebam istos scholasticos, ne me derisissent.
subordinate clause verb **derisissent** = pluperfect subjunctive = before main verb
I feared those scholars, that they had laughed at me.
I was afraid that those scholars had laughed at me.

Pre-Reading Review Sentences

1. Trimalchio veritus est ne mures vitalia tangerent.

2. Trimalchio veretur ne mures vitalia tangant.

3. Trimalchio veretur ne mures vitalia tetigerint.

4. Trimalchio veritus est ne mures vitalia tetigissent.

5. Timebo ne Trimalchio me ad cenam invitet.

6. Timui ne Trimalchio me ad cenam invitavisset.

7. Timebam ut Trimalchio me ad cenam invitaret.

8. Timeo ut Trimalchio me ad cenam invitaverit.

9. Giton veretur ut caedatur.

10. Giton veritus est ut caederetur.

11. Giton veritus est ut eum cecidisset.

12. nec diu tamen lacrimis indulsi, sed veritus ne Menelaus solum me in deversorio inveniret, collegi sarcinulas.

Post-Reading Activities

1. What modern film or literary genres strike you as similar to Eumolpus' stories about his seduction of the boy in Ephesus? How so? How are we meant to take this story? What do we learn about Eumolpus? What should Encolpius learn?

2. Complete the following phrases to describe where we are in the story at the end of this chapter:

Encolpius timet . . . .
Giton timebat . . .
Eumolpus verebatur . . .
Puto . . .

3. Skim the beginning of the passage in the next chapter (111.5–13) to find all of the subordinate clauses with verbs in the subjunctive. Note the person, number, tense, and voice of each, as well as why the subjunctive mood is being used.

Demonstrative Adjective: **ille, illa, illud,** *that*

SINGULAR

	Masculine	Feminine	Neuter
Nominative	ille	illa	illud
Genitive	illīus	illīus	illīus
Dative	illī	illī	illī
Accusative	illum	illam	illud
Ablative	illō	illā	illō

PLURAL

	Masculine	Feminine	Neuter
Nominative	illī	illae	illa
Genitive	illōrum	illārum	illōrum
Dative	illīs	illīs	illīs
Accusative	illōs	illās	illa
Ablative	illīs	illīs	illīs

Vocabulary

amiciō, amicīre, amicuī or **amīxī, amictus:** *wrap around, cover, clothe*

ancilla, ancillae, F: *slave girl, maid*

cella, cellae, F: *small room*

concupīscō, concupīscere, concupīvī or **concupiī, concupītus:** *long for, strive for*

conditōrium, conditōriī, N: *tomb; coffin*

convertō, convertere, convertī, conversus: *rotate, turn*

fēmina, fēminae, F: *woman, lady, female*

frequenter (adverb): *in crowds; frequently, commonly*

frequentia, frequentiae, F: *large group of people, crowd; population; abundance*

fūnus, fūneris, N: *funeral, burial*

genū, genūs, N: *knee*

igitur (adverb): *then, therefore, in short*

iterum (adverb): *again, a second time*

molestus, molesta, molestum: *annoying, troublesome*

ōs, ōris, N: *mouth, lip*

pariēs, parietis, M: *wall* (of a house or building)

praecō, praecōnis, M: *herald, public crier*

pudīcus, pudīca, pudīcum: *chaste, pure, modest*

reddō, reddere, reddidī, redditus: *give back; repay; repeat*

rīxa, rīxae, F: *fight, squabble*

saltem (adverb): *at least, in any event;* **nōn saltem:** *not even*

similis, simile: *similar, resembling, like*

somnus, somnī, M: *sleep, slumber*
spīritus, spīritūs, M: *breathing, breath; breeze*
stertō, stertere: *snore*
stō, stāre, stetī, statum: *stand; endure, last*
sūdor, sudōris, M: *sweat*

tempus, temporis, N: *time; season; occasion*
timidus, timida, timidum: *fearful, timid*
vincō, vincere, vīcī, victus: *conquer, defeat; convince*

CHAPTER TWELVE:
INDEPENDENT USES OF THE SUBJUNCTIVE

The subjunctive is found most commonly in subordinate clauses, but there are some constructions in which it occurs in the main clause. All are in keeping with the nature of the subjunctive to express or describe what is not fact, that is, what is possible or probable, a hope, wish, or command, what may happen or might have happened. The sense of most of these constructions can be gleaned from the context, but a quick review of the most commonly used independent subjunctive constructions is useful.

Hortatory and Jussive

The present subjunctive may be used in the first person to suggest or encourage some action (hortatory):

> veniamus!   *Let us come! Let's come!*
> coniciamus nos in balneum.   *Let's throw ourselves into the bath.*

A similar construction, the jussive, is found usually in the third person but sometimes in the second, and expresses a command, but not quite as forcefully as the imperative mood. The present is most commonly used.

> veniat.   *Let him come.*

The negative of both a hortatory and a jussive subjunctive is introduced by **nē**. In negative commands, the perfect tense may be found in lieu of the present.

Deliberative

To deliberate about a course of action either now or in the past, that is, to weigh one's options, Latin speakers employ either a present or an imperfect subjunctive. Frequently the deliberative subjunctive forms a rhetorical question. The negative is marked by **nōn**.

quid faciamus homines miserrimi?	*What should we miserable men do?*
quid faceremus?	*What were we to do? What should we have done?*
non venirem Romam?	*Should I not have come to Rome?*

Potential

To indicate that an action might possibly occur either now or in the future, Latin usually uses the present subjunctive, although sometimes the perfect is used. **Nōn** is used for negation.

Id non fecerim.
I would not do it. / I could not do it.

putes illum piper et cuminum non coniecisse.
You would think that he had not thrown in the pepper and cumin.

To cast this potentiality into the past, Latin uses the imperfect:

pantomimi chorum non patris familiae triclinium crederes.
You might have thought it was the chorus for a pantomime actor and not the dining room of a respectable homeowner.

Optative

Finally, wishes may also be expressed using the subjunctive mood independently. Such phrases are sometimes introduced by **utinam** or **ut** in the positive, and **utinam nē** or **nē** in the negative, particularly when the author wants to distinguish the optative from other possible uses of the subjunctive. What is conveyed by the tense is closely connected to the manner in which subjunctive tenses are used in conditions. To express a wish that may be fulfilled now or in the future, the present subjunctive is used, akin to *future less vivid* conditions:

(utinam) veniat.   *Would that he would come. / I wish he would come. / If only he would come.*

A wish that something were happening right now or that it had happened in the past obviously cannot be fulfilled. The tenses used here are the same as for present contrary-to-fact conditions (imperfect subjunctive) and past contrary-to-fact conditions (pluperfect subjunctive):

(utinam) veniret.   *Would that he were coming (but he's not).*
I wish he were coming. / If only he were coming.

(utinam) ne venisset.   *Would that he had not come. / I wish he had not come.*
If only he had not come.

Pre-Reading Review Sentences

Be prepared to explain why any verbs are in the subjunctive mood and what
their tenses communicate.

1. invitem Eumolpum?

2. invitarem Eumolpum?

3. Eumolpus invitandus est.

4. Eumolpum ne invitet.

5. utinam Eumolpus invitatus esset.

6. crederes Eumolpum timere.

7. credas Eumolpum timere.

8. ignoscet mihi genius tuus, noluisses de manu illius panem accipere.

9. vivorum meminerimus.

10. aedilibus male eveniat, qui cum pistoribus colludunt.

11. aliqua die te persuadeam, ut ad villam venias et videas casulas nostras?

12. hilaria mera sint, etsi timeo istos scolasticos.

13. dum illi balneum petunt, nos in turba exeamus.

14. puer ipse quem vult sequatur.

Post-Reading Activities

1. What is the impact or import of having the maid quote Vergil's *Aeneid* twice?

2. Using the passage in this chapter as well as earlier passages, make a list of at
least ten Latin words having to do with death and burial.

3. What is a "Milesian Tale"? Why might we consider the story of the Widow of
Ephesus an example? Is the story known from any other sources?

4. Based on those of Encolpius and Circe, what is the basic format of a Roman
letter? Compose one a few sentences in length to a character in the novel.

Irregular Verb: **nōlō, nōlle, nōluī,** *not want, be unwilling*

INDICATIVE

Present	nōlō	nōlumus	
	nōn vīs	nōn vultis	
	nōn vult	nōlunt	
Imperfect	nōlēbam	nōlēbāmus	
	nōlēbās	nōlēbātis	
	nōlēbat	nōlēbant	
Future	nōlam	nōlēmus	
	nōlēs	nōlētis	
	nōlet	nōlent	
Perfect	nōluī	nōluimus	
	nōluistī	nōluistis	
	nōluit	nōluērunt/nōlēre	
Pluperfect	nōlueram	nōluerāmus	
	nōluerās	nōluerātis	
	nōluerat	nōluerant	
Future perfect	nōluerō	nōluerimus	
	nōlueris	nōlueritis	
	nōluerit	nōluerint	

SUBJUNCTIVE

Present	nōlim	nōlīmus
	nōlīs	nōlītis
	nōlit	nōlint
Imperfect	nōllem	nōllēmus
	nōllēs	nōllētis
	nōllet	nōllent
Perfect	nōluerim	nōluerimus
	nōlueris	nōlueritis
	nōluerit	nōluerint
Pluperfect	nōluissem	nōluissēmus
	nōluissēs	nōluissētis
	nōluisset	nōluissent

INFINITIVE

Present	nōlle
Perfect	nōluisse
Future	—

PARTICIPLE

Present	nōlens, nōlentis

Vocabulary

amor, amōris, M: *love, affection; object of affection*

commodō, commodāre, commodāvī, commodātus: *bestow, grant, give*

crux, crucis, F: *cross; torture*

cubiculum, cubiculī, N: *room, bedroom, study*

dēlectō, dēlectāre, dēlectāvī, dēlectātus: *delight, charm*

fateor, fatērī, fassus sum: *confess, admit*

frīgus, frīgoris, N: *cold, chill, frost*

gemitus, gemitūs, M: *sigh, groan*

invītō, invītāre, invītāvī, invītātus: *invite, entertain*

invītus, invīta, invītum: *reluctant, unwilling*

licet, licēre, licuit (impersonal verb): *it is permitted, it is lawful*

lūgeo, lūgēre, lūxī, lūctus: *lament, mourn; be in mourning*

lūmen, lūminis, N: *light; lamp*

magnus, magna, magnum: *large, great*

mīror, mīrārī, mīrātus sum: *be amazed at, wonder at, admire*

moror, morārī, morātus sum: *detain, hinder; delay, loiter*

negō, negāre, negāvī, negātus: *deny; say no, refuse*

pāreō, pārēre, pāruī, pāritum: *appear;* (+ dative) *obey, yield to, satisfy*

pārō, pārāre, pārāvī, pārātus: *prepare, provide, acquire*

populus, populī, M: *the people, the public; crowd*

porrigō, porrigere, porrēxī, porrēctus: *reach out, stretch out, extend*

posterus, postera, posterum: *next, following, subsequent*

pudīcitia, pudīcitiae, F: *chastity, purity, modesty*

ratiō, ratiōnis, F: *calculation, reckoning; situation; reason, grounds; reasoning*

scrībō, scrībere, scrīpsī, scrīptus: *write*

sēcrētum, sēcrētī, N: *a secret, mystery*

sēcrētus, sēcrēta, sēcrētum: *separate, solitary, secret*

secundum (adverb): *after, behind;* (preposition + accusative) *beside, alongside; immediately after*

siccus, sicca, siccum: *dry; thirsty; solid, firm*

spectō, spectāre, spectāvī, spectātus: *watch, consider*

supplicium, suppliciī, N: *entreaty, prayer; punishment*

Dictionary

Numbers given in parentheses indicate the chapter in which the word occurs on the vocabulary list.

Words that occur only once in surviving classical Latin are marked with the term "hapax legomenon."

ā or **ab** (preposition + ablative): *from, away from; by, at the hands of* (3)

abdūcō, abdūcere, abdūxī, abductus: *lead away, take away*

abeō, abīre, abiī, abitum: *go away*

aberrō, aberrāre, aberrāvī, aberrātum: *wander, go astray, get lost*

abigō, abigere, abēgī, abāctus: *drive away*

ablātus: see **auferō**

abscīdō, abscīdere, abscīdī, abscīsus: *cut off, chop off; cut short*

abscondō, abscondere, abscondī, absconditus: *hide, conceal*

absēns, absentis: *absent; nonexistent*

absentivus: probably = **absēns** (hapax legomenon)

abstinax, abstinācis: *self-restrained, abstemious* (hapax legomenon)

abstinentia, abstinentiae, F: *restraint, self-control*

abstineō, abstinēre, abstinuī, abstentus: *withhold, restrain; refrain from; abstain*

abstulī: see **auferō**

abundāns, abundantis: *abundant, overflowing*

ac (conjunction): *and, and in particular; than, as* (3)

accēdō, accēdere, accessī, accessum: *approach* (4)

accersō, accersere, accersīvī, accersītus: *summon, call*

accidō, accidere, accidī: *happen, occur; happen to, befall*

accipiō, accipere, accēpī, acceptus: *take, receive* (2)

accumbō, accumbere, accubuī, accubitum: *take one's place at table, recline with*

accurō, accurrere, accurrī, accursum: *run up (to)*

acētum, acētī, N: *vinegar; sharp tongue*

acidus, acida, acidum: *sour, tart, harsh*

ācroāma, ācroāmatis, N: *entertainment; actor* (Greek loan word)

actus: see **agō**

acūmen, acūminis, N: *sharpness; cleverness*

acūtus, acūta, acūtum: *sharp, pointed; shrewd*

ad (preposition + accusative): *to, toward* (1); **ad summam:** *in short, in sum, to get to the point* (5)

adamō, adamāre, adamāvī, adamātus: *love deeply, fall in love with*

adcognoscō, adcognoscere: *recognize*

addūcō, addūcere, addūxī, adductus: *bring up/along* (7)

adeō (adverb): *so, to such a degree; indeed, for that matter* (9)

adhaereō, adhaerēre, adhaesī, adhaesum: *cling to, stick to*

adhibeō, adhibēre, adhibuī, adhibitus: *stretch out; apply, administer*

adhūc (adverb): *thus far; still; in addition* (5)

adiciō, adicere, adiēcī, adiectus: *add, increase; toss at; turn to*

aditus, aditūs, M: *doorway, entrance*

adiūtō, adiūtāre, adiūtāvī, adiūtātus: *help*

adligō, adligāre, adligāvī, adligātus: *bind, tie*

admīrātiō, admīrātiōnis, F: *admiration, wonder*

admittō, admittere, admīsī, admissus: *let in, admit, allow*

admoneō, admonēre, admonuī, admonitus: *admonish, remind, warn* (7)

admoveō, admovēre, admōvī, admōtus: *move up, bring near; promote*

adrādō, adrādere, adrāsī, adrāsus: *shave closely*

adspergō, adspergere, adspersī, adspersus: *sprinkle, scatter*

adulēscēns, adulēscentis, M: *young man*

adveniō, advenīre, advēnī, adventum: *arrive; approach*

adversārius, adversāria, adversārium: *opposed to, opposite*

adversus (preposition + accusative): *opposite to, against, compared with*

advocātus, advocātī, M: *helper, advocate*

aedicula, aediculae, F: *small room, shrine, closet*; (in plural) *small building*

aedificō, aedificāre, aedificāvī, aedificātus: *build*

aedīlis, aedīlis, M: *aedile, a magistrate in charge of public buildings and markets*

aeger, aegra, aegrum: *sick, diseased, weary* (10)

Aenēās, Aenēae, M: *Aeneas, hero of Vergil's Aeneid, son of Venus and Anchises*

aenigma, aenigmae, F: *enigma, riddle, puzzle*

aēnum, aēnī, N: *bronze vessel, copper pot*

aequē (adverb): *equally; justly* (9)

aequus, aequa, aequum: *equal; fair, even*

aerārium, aerāriī, N: *treasury*

aerārius, aerāria, aerārium: *(made of) copper, bronze*

aes, aeris, N: *copper, bronze; coin*

aestimō, aestimāre, aestimāvī, aestimātus: *appraise, value, esteem; think*

aestus, aestūs, M: *agitation, anxiety; heat*

aetās, aetātis, F: *lifetime, age; generation*

Aethiops, Aethiopis, M: *Ethiopian*

affābilitās, affābilitātis, F: *affability, courtesy*

afferō (adferō), afferre, attulī, allātus: *bring, carry* (2)

affīgō, affīgere, affīxī, affīxus: *fasten, attach*

afflīctō, afflīctāre, afflīctāvī, afflīctātus: *strike repeatedly, distress; be troubled*

affulgeō, affulgēre, affulsī: *shine; appear*

Āfrica, Āfricae, F: *Africa* (province—see map); *continent of Africa*

agaga, agagae, M: *pervert? pimp?* (hapax legomenon)

Agamēmnōn, Agamēmnonis, M: *Agamemnon*, leader of Greek forces at Troy; Encolpius' rhetoric teacher

agellus, agellī, M: *little field, plot*

ager, agrī, M: *field, soil, farm*

aggredior, aggredī, agressus sum: *approach; attack; undertake*

aginō, agināre, agināvī, aginātus: *scheme? cheat?* (hapax legomenon)

agō, agere, ēgī, actus: *do, perform; drive* (2)

āiō (verb in present and imperfect only): *I say, assert; I say yes, affirm* (9)

albus, alba, album: *white; bright* (5)

Alexandrīnus, Alexandrīna, Alexandrīnum: *from Alexandria*, a city in northern Egypt (see map)

algēns, algentis: *cold*

ālicula, āliculae, F: *light cape*

aliēnus, aliēna, aliēnum: *another's; foreign; strange*

alimentum, alimentī, N: *food, nourishment*

aliōquin (adverb): *otherwise, for the rest*

aliquandō (adverb): *sometime or other; ever*

aliquis, aliquid: *some; any* (1)

aliquot (indeclinable adjective): *some, several* (3)

aliter (adverb): *otherwise, else*

aliubi (adverb): *elsewhere*

alius, alia, aliud (gen. s. alterīus, dat. s. alterī): *another, other, different* (1); alius . . . alius / aliī . . . aliī: *one . . . another / some . . . others*

allātus: see afferō

alligō, alligāre, alligāvī, alligātus: *bind, tie*

alogus, aloga, alogum: *senseless, meaningless* (Greek loan word; hapax legomenon)

alter, altera, alterum (gen. s. alterīus, dat. s. alterī): *one (of two), the other, second, next* (2)

altilis, altile: *fattened, fat; rich*

altus, alta, altum: *high, tall, deep* (10)

amāsiunculus, amāsiunculī, M: *lover*

amātor, amātōris, M: *lover; friend*

ambulō, ambulāre, ambulāvī, ambulātum: *walk, travel* (10)

amīca, amīcae, F: *friend* (2)

amiciō, amicīre, amicuī or amīxī, amictus: *wrap around, cover, clothe* (11)

amīcitia, amīcitiae, F: *friendship*

amīcus, amīcī, M: *friend* (2)

amō, amāre, amāvī, amātus: *love, like* (2)

āmolior, āmolīrī: *remove, dispose of*

amor, amōris, M: *love, affection; object of affection* (12)

amphitheāter, amphitheātrī, M: *amphitheater*

amphora, amphorae, F: *amphora, a two-handled jar with a narrow neck used to transport and store liquid* (Greek loan word) (9)

amplexus, amplexūs, M: *embrace, caress*

amplius (comparative adverb): *any further; besides; more; more than* (6)

amplus, ampla, amplum: *large; strong* (6)

ampulla, ampullae, F: *small bottle, flask*

an (conjunction): *or, whether* (introduces the second part of a two-part question or indirect question) (3)

anathȳmiāsis, F: *a rising of vapors* (Greek loan word)

ancilla, ancillae, F: *slave girl, maid* (11)

angulus, angulī, M: *angle, corner, nook*

angustiae, angustiārum, F pl.: *narrow place, strait; difficulty*

angustus, angusta, angustum: *narrow, close*

anhēlitus, anhēlitūs, M: *panting, heavy breathing*

anima, animae, F: *air, wind; breath; life, soul* (6)

animadvertō, animadvertere, animadvertī, animadversus: *pay attention to*

animus, animī, M: *intellect, mind, thought; courage, will* (6)

annectō, annectere, annexuī, annexus: *tie, connect*

annōna, annōnae, F: *crop, grain; price of grain*

annus, annī, M: *year* (4)

ānser, ānseris, M: *male goose, gander*

ante (conjunction): *before, in the past, in front*; (preposition + accusative): *before* (3)

anteā (adverb): *before, previously*

antecēdō, antecēdere, antecessī, antecessus: *precede; surpass; excel*

antequam (conjunction): *before, sooner than*

antescholānus, antescholānī, M: *assistant teacher*

antīquus, antīqua, antīquum: *old, ancient*

ānulus, ānulī, M: *ring*

aper, aprī, M: *wild boar*

aperiō, aperīre, aperuī, apertus: *open, uncover* (9)

apis, apis, F: *bee*

apoculō, apoculāre: *leave, get out(?)* (only in the *Satyrica*)

apodixis (accusative s. apodixin), F: *proof, demonstration* (Greek loan word)

apophorētus, apophorēta, apophorētum: *to be taken away, serving as a party favor* (Greek loan word) apparātus, apparātūs, M: *equipment, gear*

appāreō, appārēre, appāruī, appāritum: *appear*

appellō, appellāre, appellāvī, appellātus: *speak to, call on*

appetō, appetere, appetīvī, appetītus: *try to reach, aim for*

applicō, applicāre, applicāvī, applicātus: *bring into contact, apply; lean on*

apud (preposition + accusative): *at, near; at the house of*

aqua, aquae, F: *water* (2)

Arātus, Arātī, M: *Aratus*, Greek author of a poem on astronomy

arbitrātus, arbitrātūs, M: *choice, inclination*

arca, arcae, F: *chest, box; coffin*

ārdeō, ārdēre, ārsī, ārsum: *burn, be on fire; be in love*

arduus, ardua, arduum: *steep; difficult*

argenteus, argentea, argenteum: *made of silver* (2)

argentum, argentī, N: *silver; money*

argūtō, argūtāre, argūtāvī: *argue childishly*

ariēs, arietis, M: *ram*

arma, armōrum, N pl.: *armor, defensive arms*

armārium, armāriī, N: *cupboard, chest*

arripiō, arripere, arripuī, arreptus: *seize*

artificium, artificiī, N: *trade, skill, profession*

artō, artāre, artāvī, artātus: *compress, limit, curtail*

ās, assis, M: *as, bronze coin, penny;* the base unit of the Roman monetary system

ascendō, ascendere, ascendī, ascensus: *climb*

Ascyltos or Ascyltus, Ascyltī, (Ascylton acc. s.) M: *Ascyltos,* one of Encolpius' companions; "Untroubled" in Greek

Āsia, Āsiae, F: Roman province *Asia;* continent of *Asia* (see map)

asinus, asinī, M: *ass; fool*

assentor, assentārī, assentātus sum: *always agree*

asservō, asservāre, asservāvī, asservātus: *preserve; watch*

assideō, assidēre, assēdī, assessus: *sit near*

assignō, assignāre, assignāvī, assignātus: *mark out, assign; confer on*

assurgō, assurgere, assurēxī, assurēctum: *stand up, rise*

asturcō, asturcōnis, M: *Asturian breed of horse, fine stallion*

astus, astūs, M: *cunning; trick*

at (conjunction): *but* (3)

Ātellānia, Ātellāniae, F: *Atellan farce* (a form of low comedy)

Ātellānicus, Ātellānica, Ātellānicum: *associated with Atellan farce, vulgarly comic*

Athāna, Athānae, F: presumably the goddess *Athena* (hapax legomenon)

Athēnae, Athēnārum, F pl.: city of *Athens* (see map)

āthlum, āthlī, N: *labor, task, feat* (Greek loan word)

atque (conjunction): *and also, besides, indeed* (3)

atquī (conjunction): *but yet; however*

ātriēnsis, ātriēnsis, M: *slave of the* atrium*, butler*

Atticus, Attica, Atticum: *Attic, from the region of Athens*

attineō, attinēre, attinuī, attentus: *hold; pertain to, concern*

attonitus, attonita, attonitum: *thunderstruck*

attrītus, attrīta, attrītum: *worn away, rubbed off; wasted; shameless*

attulī: see **afferō**

au (interjection): *ouch!*

auceps, aucupis, M: *bird-catcher*

auctor, auctōris, M: *author; expert*

audācia, audāciae, F: *boldness, daring*

audiō, audīre, audīvī, audītus: *hear, listen to* (6)

auferō (abferō), auferre, abstulī, ablātus: *take away* (2)

Augustus, Augustī, M: *Augustus,* the first emperor; generic term for an emperor

aureus, aurea, aureum: *golden, of gold* (4)

aureus, aureī, M: *a gold coin* worth 100 **sēstertiī**

auris, auris, F: *ear* (4)

aurum, aurī, N: *gold*

aut (conjunction): *or* (3)

autem (conjunction): *but, on the other hand, however* (marking a contrast); *moreover; now* (transitioning or picking up after aside) (3)

automatus, automata, automatum: *automatic; spontaneous; voluntary*

autopȳrus, autopȳra, autopȳrum: *whole meal, whole grain* (Greek loan word)

āvertō, āvertere, āvertī, āversus: *turn away, divert; retire*

avidus, avida, avidum: *earnest, greedy, vehemently desiring, longing for*

avis, avis, F: *bird*

āvocō, āvocāre, āvocāvī, āvocātus: *call away*

babae (interjection): *great! wonderful!*

babaecalus, babaeculī, M: *tycoon, fat cat,* slang for a *rich man* (from Greek loan words; hapax legomenon)

bacalūsiae, bacalūsiārum, F pl.: *stupid guesses?* (hapax legomenon)

bacciballum, bacciballī, N: *round berry? little peach?* (colloquial term for a woman, perhaps based on the word for "berry"; hapax legomenon)

bālātus, bālātūs, M: *bleating* of sheep

balineum or balneum, -ī, N: *bath, bathing place* (2)

balniscus, balniscī, M: *bath* (hapax legomenon)

barba, barbae, F: *beard*

barbaria, barbariae, F: *foreign country; rudeness, barbarity* (Greek loan word)

barbātus, barbāta, barbātum: *bearded*

bāro, bārōnis, M: *blockhead, idiot*

basilica, basilicae, F: *courthouse*

bāsio, bāsiāre, bāsiāvī, bāsiātus: *kiss* (7)

bāsiolum, bāsiolī, N: *little kiss, peck*

bāsium, bāsiī, N: *kiss*

beātitūdō, beātitūdinis, F: *happiness*

beātus, beāta, beātum: *happy, prosperous*

bellus, bella, bellum: *pretty, fine* (5)

bene (adverb): *well* (7)

beneficium, beneficiī, N: *favor, service* (8)

benemōrius, benemōria, benemōrium: *having good moral qualities, well-mannered(?)* (hapax legomenon)

bēsālis, bēsāle: *constituting two-thirds*

bēstia, bēstiae, F: *wild beast*

bēstiārius, bēstiāriī, M: *wild-beast fighter*

bēta, bētae, F: *beet*

bibō, bibere, bibī: *drink*

bifurcum, bifurcī, N: *crotch*

bīmus, bīma, bīmum: *two-year-old*

bīnī, bīnae, bīna: *two each, two at a time*

bipennis, bipenne: *having two edges, double-edged*

bis (adverb): *twice; doubly*

blanditia, blanditiae, F: *flattery, compliment*

blandus, blanda, blandum: *smooth; flattering*

bōlētus, bōlētī, M: *mushroom*

bonus, bona, bonum: *good* (1)

bōs, bovis, M: *ox, bull*

botulus, botulī, M: *sausage* (6)

bracchium, bracchiī, N: *arm, lower arm*

Bromius, Bromiī, M: *Bromius,* epithet of Bacchus/Dionysus

brūma, brūmae, F: *winter solstice, dead of winter*

bucca, buccae, F: *cheek; mouthful*

būcinātor, būcinātōris, M: *trumpeter*

bulla, bullae, F: *bubble*

burdubasta, burdubastae, M: *decrepit gladiator?* (hapax legomenon)

buxeus, buxea, buxeum: *made of boxwood*

bybliothēca, bybliothēcae, F: *collection of books; a library, study* (Greek loan word)

C: abbreviation of the name *Gaius*

cacō, cacāre, cacāvī, cacātus: (colloquial) *defecate, defecate on*

cadāver, cadāveris, N: *a dead body, carcass*

cadō, cadere, cecidī, cāsum: *fall*

cāducēus, cāducēī, M: *herald's staff, caduceus*

caedēs, caedis, F: *murder; bloodshed, gore*

caedō, caedere, cecīdī, caesus: *cut, hack; slay*

caelum, caelī, N: *the heavens, sky* (4)

calathīscus, calathīscī, M: *small basket* (Greek loan word)

calculus, calculī, M: *pebble; game piece*

caldicerebrius, caldicerebria, caldecerebrium: *hot-headed* (only in the *Satyrica*)

caldus, calda, caldum: *warm* (4)

caleō, calēre, caluī: *be warm, flushed; be busy*

calfaciō, calfacere, calfēcī, calfactus: *make warm; anger, rouse*

caliga, caligae, F: *army boot*

calva, calvae, F: *nut* with a smooth shell

calvus, calva, calvum: *bald*

calx, calcis, F: *heel, hoof; a kick*

camera, camerae, F: *vault, arched roof*

cancer, cancrī, M: *crab; cancer, disease, sore*

candēlābrum, candēlābrī, N: *lampstand*

candidus, candida, candidum: *white; glittering white, shining*

candor, candōris, M: *whiteness; radiance; clarity, candor*

canīnus, canīna, canīnum: *canine; snarling*

canis, canis, M or F: *dog* (4)

canor, canōris, M: *melody, song, sound*

canōrus, canōra, canōrum: *musical, singsong*

cantābundus, cantābunda, cantābundum: *chanting, singing*

canticum, canticī, N: *song; singing tone*

cantō, cantāre, cantāvī, cantātus: *sing*

capāx, capācis: *capacious, spacious, wide*

capillātus, -a, -um: *long-haired*

capillus, capillī, M: *hair, single hair*

capistrum, capistrī, N: *muzzle, halter*

Cappadox, Cappadocis, M: *a Cappadocian*, someone from central Asia Minor

Capua, Capuae, F: *Capua*, a city in south Italy

capulus, capulī, M: *hilt, handle*

caput, capitis, N: *head; top; main point* (2)

cardēlis, cardēlis, F: *goldfinch*

Carion, Carionis, M: *Carion*, a common Greek slave name

carnārium, carnāriī, N: *butcher's shop*

carnis, carnis, F: *meat*

carpō, carpere, carpsī, carptus: *pick, cut to pieces, carve*

Carpus, Carpī, M: *Carpus*, punning name of one of Trimalchio's servers

cārus, cāra, cārum: *dear, loving; expensive*

caryōta, caryōtae, F: *date, dried fruit* (Greek loan word)

castīgō, castīgāre, castīgāvī, castīgātus: *correct; reprove; restrain*

castus, casta, castum: *chaste, pure*

casula, casulae, F: *little hut, cottage*

cāsus, cāsūs, M: *a fall; downfall*

catastropha, catastrophae, F: *sensational act* (Greek loan word)

catella, catellae, F: *puppy*

catēna, catēnae, F: *chain, fetter*

catēnārius, catēnāria, catēnārium: *chained*

caupō, caupōnis, M: *innkeeper*

causa, causae, F: *reason, pretext; situation, case*; **causā** (preposition + genitive): *for the sake of, because of* (8)

causidicus, causidicī, M: *pleader, advocate*

cavea, caveae, F: *cage*

caveō, cavēre, cāvī, cautus: *guard against, beware of; be careful* (10)

cecīdī: see **caedō**

cecidī: see **cadō**

celeritās, celeritātis, F: *speed, quickness*

cella, cellae, F: *small room* (11)

cēna, cēnae, F: *dinner, a three-course meal* (7); **lībera cena**: dinner provided to a gladiator the evening before the games

cēnō, cēnāre, cēnāvī, cēnātus: *dine, eat together; dine on, eat*

cēnsus, cēnsūs, M: *census; income bracket, wealth*

centōnārius, centōnāriī, M: *clothes seller* or *someone who uses rags to put out fires, fireman*

centum (indeclinable): *hundred* (4)

centuria, centuriae, F: *military company, squad*

centuriōn, centuriōnis, M: *leader of a military squad, centurion*

cēnula, cēnulae, F: *light dinner*

cēpa, cēpae, F: *onion*

cerasinus, cerasina, cerasinum: *cherry-colored, cherry red* (only in the *Satyrica*)

cerebrum, cerebrī, N: *the brain*

certē (adverb): *certainly, surely*

cervīcal, cervīcālis, N: *pillow, cushion*

cervīx, cervīcis, F (often in plural with same meaning as singular): *neck, nape* (10)

cēterum (adverb): *but, still, for the rest, otherwise* (2)

cēterus, cētera, cēterum: *the other, the remaining, the rest of* (10)

chīramaxium, chīramaxiī, N: *handcart* (Greek loan word)

choraulēs, choraulae, M: *flute player* (Greek loan word)

chorus, chorī, M: *chorus, choir* (Greek loan word)

Chrȳsanthus, Chrȳsanthī, M: *Chrysanthus*, Greek name referring to the chrysanthemum

Chrȳsis, Chrȳsis, F: *Chrysis*, a name from the Greek word for gold; Circe's maid

cibāria, cibāriōrum, N pl.: *rations, provisions*

cibus, cibī, M: *food, nourishment, fodder* (9)

cicarō, cicarōnis, M: *small boy?* (only in the *Satyrica*)

cicer, ciceris, M: *chickpea, garbanzo bean*

cingillum, cingillī, N: *woman's belt, sash*

cingō, cingere, cinxī, cinctus: *encircle, surround, gird*

cingulum, cingulī, N: *sash, belt; sword belt*

cinis, cineris, M: *ashes; ruin, death*; (in plural) *cremated remains*

circā: (adverb) *around, in the vicinity*; (preposition + accusative) *around, about, near* (3)

Circē, Circae, F: *Circe*, name of the witch who turned Odysseus' men into swine; Encolpius' girlfriend

circēnsēs, circēnsum, M pl.: *races*

circulātor, circulātōris, M: *peddler; traveling performer*

circulus, circulī, M: *circle; group of people; bracelet, band*

circumeō, circumīre, circumīvī, circumitus: *go around; visit; surround*

circumferō, circumferre, circumtūlī, circumlātus: *carry around; spread around*

circummingō, circummingere, circumminxī: *urinate around*

circumscrībō, conscrībere, conscrīpsī, conscrīptus: *mark, limit, surround*

circumspiciō, circumspicere, circumspexī, circumspectus: *look around at; consider*

cirrātus, cirrāta, cirrātum: *curly-haired*

cito (adverb): *quickly, soon*

citrā (preposition + accusative): *on this side of, before, just short of*

citreus, citrea, citreum: *citrus, of citrus wood*

cīvis, cīvis, M or F: *citizen*

cīvitās, cīvitātis, F: *state, community; citizenry*

clāmō, clāmāre, clāmāvī, clāmātus: *shout*

clāmor, clāmōris, M: *shout; applause; noise*

clārus, clāra, clārum: *loud; bright, manifest; famous* (6)

classis, classis, F: *fleet* of ships

claustra, claustrōrum, N pl.: *lock, bolt*

cliēns, clientis, M or F: *client, dependent retainer*

clīvus, clīvī, M: *hill, incline; uphill struggle*

clūdō, clūdere, clūsī, clūsus: *shut, close*

coccin(e)us, coccin(e)a, coccin(e)um: *scarlet*

coctus, cocta, coctum: *cooked, roasted*

cocus, cocī, M: *cook* (2)

cōdicillī, cōdicillōrum, M pl.: *writing tablets; notes, letters*

coemō, coemere, coēmī, coemptus: *buy up*

coepī, coepisse, coeptus: (only in perfect) *begin* (1)

cōgitātiō, cōgitātiōnis, F: *reflection; plan, idea*

cōgitō, cōgitāre, cōgitāvī, cōgitātus: *consider, reflect on; think* cōgō, cōgere, coēgī, coāctus: *collect; compel*

cohaereō, cohaerēre, cohaesī, cohaesum: *stick together; be in agreement; be consistent*

coitus, coitūs, M: *meeting; sexual intercourse*

colaphus, colaphī, M: *punch, slap* (Greek loan word)

cōliculus, cōliculi, M: *small stalk, sprout*

collēctiō, collēctiōnis, F: *gathering, collection; inference*

collēga, collēgae, M: *colleague, associate*

colligō, colligere, collēgī, collēctus: *gather, collect*

collūdō, collūdere, collūsī, collūsum: *play together; be in collusion*

collum, collī, N: *the neck* (6)

colō, colere, coluī, cultus: *cultivate, care for, honor; adorn*

colōnia, colōniae, F: *colony, town*

colubra, colubrae, F: *snake*

columba, columbae, F: *dove*

columna, columnae, F: *column, pillar*

combūrō, combūrere, combūssī, combūstus: *burn up; consume*

comedō, comēsse, comēdī, comēsus: *eat up, consume* (7)

comes, comitis, M or F: *companion*

cōmissātor, cōmissātōris, M: *reveler*

commendō, commendāre, commendāvī, commendātus: *entrust, recommend*

commīlitō, commīlitōnis, M: *comrade in arms, fellow soldier*

commingō, commingere, commīnxī, commīctus: *urinate on, wet*

comminuō, comminuere, comminuī, comminūtus: *break into pieces, crush*

commissiō, commissiōnis, F: *beginning*

commissūra, commissūrae, F: *joint, hinge*

committō, committere, commīsī, commissus: *bring together; hand over*

commodō, commodāre, commodāvī, commodātus: *bestow, grant, give* (12)

commodum, commodī, N: *convenience, advantage; a good or useful thing*

commōnstrō, commōnstrāre, commōnstrāvī, commōnstrātus: *point out*

commundō, commundāre, commundāvī, commundātus: *clean thoroughly*

commūnis, commūne: *common, ordinary; public*

cōmoedus, cōmoedī, M: *comic actor* (Greek loan word)

comparō, comparāre, comparāvī, comparātus: *compare with, match*

compīlō, compīlāre, compīlāvī, compīlātus: *pillage*

complōdō, complōdere, complōsī, complōsus: *clap together*

complōrō, complōrāre, complōrāvī, complōrātus: *mourn (together)*

compōnō, compōnere, composuī, compositus: *put together; store up*

comprimō, comprimere, compressī, compressus: *press together; suppress*

computō, computāre, computāvī, computātus: *compute, count*

comula, comulae, F: *dainty hair, pretty hair*

conchȳliātus, conchȳliāta, conchȳliātum: *purple* (Greek loan word)

conciliō, conciliāre, conciliāvī, conciliātus: *bring together; win over*

concipiō, concipere, concēpī, conceptus: *take in; understand; conceive; hold*

concitō, concitāre, concitāvī, concitātus: *stir up, agitate; awaken*

conclāmō, conclāmāre, conclāmāvī, conclāmātus: *shout; call to; exclaim*

concordia, concordiae, F: *harmony, concord*

concrepō, concrepāre, concrepuī: *snap, clash*

concupīscō, concupīscere, concupīvī or concupiī, concupītus: *long for, strive for* (11)

concurrō, concurrere, concurrī, concursum: *run together; unite; crash*

concutiō, concutere, concussī, concussus: *bang together, shake*

condiciō, condiciōnis, F: *contract, arrangement; condition, terms*

condīmentum, condīmentī, N: *seasoning, spice*

condiscipulus, condiscipulī, M: *fellow student*

conditōrium, conditōriī, N: *tomb; coffin* (11)

condō, condere, condidī, conditus: *build; hoard; preserve*

condūcō, condūcere, condūxī, conductus: *bring together; rent, hire*

cōnfessiō, cōnfessiōnis, F: *confession, admission*

cōnficiō, cōnficere, cōnfēcī, cōnfectus: *make; do*

cōnfīnis, cōnfīne: *adjoining*

cōnfiteor, cōnfitērī, cōnfessus sum: *confess, acknowledge*

cōnfodiō, cōnfodere, cōnfōdī, cōnfossus: *dig up; stab; harm*

cōnfugiō, cōnfugere, cōnfūgī: *flee; appeal to*

coniciō, conicere, coniēcī, conectus: *throw together; cast, toss* (5)

coniungō, coniungere, coniūnxī, coniūnctus: *join together, unite*

conlībertus, conlībertī, M: *fellow ex-slave*

cōnor, cōnārī, cōnātus sum: *try*

cōnsiderō, cōnsiderāre, cōnsiderāvī, cōnsiderātus: *inspect; consider*

cōnsilium, cōnsiliī, N: *advice; plan; decision*

cōnsistō, consistere, constitī: *stop, pause; take one's stand; stand*

cōnsōlātiō, cōnsōlātiōnis, F: *consolation, comfort; encouragement*

cōnsonō, cōnsonāre, cōnsonuī: *sound together*

cōnspectus, cōnspectūs, M: *look, sight, view*

cōnspiciō, cōnspicere, cōnspexī, cōnspectus: *look at, spot; be conspicuous*

cōnstāns, cōnstantis: *constant, steady*

constitūtum, constitūtī, N: *agreement to pay, financial settlement*

cōnsuētudō, cōnsuētudinis, F: *custom, habit; social ties; sexual intercourse*

cōnsūmō, cōnsūmere, cōnsūmpsī, cōnsūmptus: *consume, use up*

cōnsurgō, cōnsurgere, cōnsurrēxī, cōnsurrēctum: *stand up, rise* (6)

contemnō, contemnere, contempsī, contemptus: *despise, disregard, treat with contempt*

contemptus, contemptūs, M: *contempt*

contentiō, contentiōnis, F: *exertion; competition; quarrel*

contentus, contenta, contentum: *content, satisfied*

conterreō, conterrēre, conterruī, conterritus: *terrify, frighten exceedingly*

contineō, continēre, continuī, contentus: *hold together; keep in; hold back, restrain* (8)

contingō, contingere, contigī, contāctus: *contact, touch; happen, come to pass; (impersonal + dative) it happens to, it befalls* (8)

continuō (adverb): *immediately; continuously*

contrā (preposition + accusative): *in opposition to, against; (adverb) on the other hand, conversely*

contrōversia, contrōversiae, F: *debate, controversy, subject for a debate*

contubernālis, contubernālis, M or F: *military comrade, army buddy; informal spouse of a slave*

contumāx, contumācis: *insubordinate, defiant*

contundō, contundere, contudī, contūsus: *crush, bruise; subdue*

conturbō, conturbāre, conturbāvī, conturbātus: *confuse; disturb*

convertō, convertere, convertī, conversus: *rotate, turn* (11)

convīcium, convīciī, N: *noise, outcry; altercation; abuse*

convictus, convictūs, M: *socializing, a social event*

convīva, convīvae, M: *guest, banqueter*

convīvium, convīviī, N: *banquet*

convīvō, convīvere, convixī, convictum: *live with; dine with*

cōpiōsus, cōpiōsa, cōpiōsum: *plentiful; rich*

cōpō, cōpōnis, M: *innkeeper*

coptoplacenta, coptoplacentae, F: *hard cake* (Greek loan word)

cor, cordis, N: *heart; mind*

corneolus, corneola, corneolum: *hard as horn, tough*

cornicen, cornicinis, M: *horn blower*

cornū, cornūs, N: *horn*

corōna, corōnae, F: *crown, garland*

corōnō, corōnāre, corōnāvī, corōnātus: *crown, wreathe; encircle*

corporālis, corporāle: *related to the body, physical*

corpus, corporis, N: *body; corpse* (1)

corripiō, corripere, corripuī, correptus: *take hold of; carry off*

corrumpō, corrumpere, corrūpī, corruptus: *burst, smash; ruin; corrupt*

corvus, corvī, M: *raven*

cōtīdiē (adverb): *daily*

crās (adverb): *tomorrow*

crēber, crēbra, crēbrum: *numerous, frequent*

crēdō, crēdere, crēdidī, crēditus: *trust, believe* (4)

crēscō, crēscere, crēvī, crētum: *come into existence, spring forth; grow, increase* (4)

crēta, crētae, F: *chalk*

crīnis, crīnis, M or F: *hair, lock of hair*

crispus, crispa, crispum: *curly-haired*

critica, criticōrum, N pl.: *literary criticism*

crocus, crocī, M: *saffron*

Croesus, Croesī, M: *Croesus,* Trimalchio's pet slave; the name of a famously wealthy king of Lydia

cruciārius, cruciāriī, M: *a man crucified or condemned to crucifixion*

crūdēlis, crūdēle: *cruel*

cruentus, cruenta, cruentum: *gory, bloody; bloodthirsty*

crūrālis, crūrāle: *of the shin*

crūs, crūris, N: *leg, shin*

crux, crucis, F: *cross; torture* (12)

crystallinus, crystallina, crystallinum: *(made of) crystal*

crystallus, crystallī, M: *crystal*

cubiculum, cubiculī, N: *room, bedroom, study* (12)

cubitōrius, cubitōria, cubitōrium: *suitable for using at dinner*

cubitum, cubitī, N: *elbow*

cubō, cubāre, cubāvī, cubitum: *lie down*

cucurrī: see **currō**

cui and **cuius:** see **quī, quae, quod** or **quis, quid**

culcita, culcitae, F: *mattress, cushion, pillow*

culīna, culīnae, F: *kitchen; cuisine*

cūlō, cūlāre, cūlāvī, cūlātus: *shove, thrust?* (hapax legomenon)

culpa, culpae, F: *fault, blame*

culter, cultrī, M: *knife*

cultus, cultūs, M: *refinement; high style of living*

cultus: see **colō**

cum (conjunction): *when, since, although;* (preposition + ablative) *with* (1)

cumīnum, cumīnī, N: *cumin, the spice*

cunctor, cunctārī, cunctātus sum: *hesitate, delay; be in doubt*

cūra, cūrae, F: *care, concern; attention; task*

cūriōsus, cūriōsa, cūriōsum: *careful, diligent*

cūrō, cūrāre, cūrāvī, cūrātus: *care for, pay attention to* (5)

currō, currere, cucurrī, cursus: *run over; run*

cursor, cursōris, M: *runner, courier*

custōdia, custōdiae, F: *protection; guard*

custōdiō, custōdīre, custōdīvī, custōdītus: *guard, protect*

Cyclōps, Cyclōpis, M: *Cyclops,* the one-eyed monster of Greek myth who trapped Odysseus in his cave

Dāma, Dāmae, M: *Dama,* a common slave name

damnō, damnāre, damnāvī, damnātus: *convict, condemn*

datus: see **dō**

dē (preposition + ablative): *from, out of; concerning* (3)

dēbattuō, dēbattuere: *thump, beat, bang, bonk*

dēbeō, dēbēre, dēbuī, dēbitus: *owe; be obliged to* (7)

dēcēdō, dēcēdere, dēcessī, dēcessum: *withdraw*

decem (indeclinable): *ten*

december, decembris, M: month of *December*

dēcernō, dēcernere, dēcrēvī, dēcrētus: *settle, decree, decide*

dēcidō, dēcidere, dēcidī: *fall down, drop*

dēcipiō, dēcipere, dēcēpī, dēceptus: *deceive*

dēclāmātiō, dēclāmātiōnis, F: *practice speech, theme*

dēclāmō, dēclāmāre, dēclāmāvī, dēclāmātus: *declaim, recite; practice public speaking*

dēcrepitus, dēcrepita, dēcrepitum: *decrepit, worn out*

dēcrētum, dēcrētī, N: *decree, decision*

decuma, decumae, F: *one-tenth; tithe*

decuria, decuriae, F: *group of ten; squad, division; town council; social club*

dedī: see **dō**

dēdūcō, dēdūcere, dēdūxī, dēductus: *lead down*

dēferō, dēferre, dētulī, dēlātus: *bring down; carry away; offer*

dēficiō, dēficere, dēfēcī, dēfectus: *fail; desert; die out*

dēfleō, dēflēre, dēflēvī, dēflētus: *cry for, lament; cry bitterly*

dēfōrmis, dēfōrme: *misshapen, ugly*

dēfraudō, dēfraudāre, dēfraudāvī, dēfraudātus: *rob, cheat*

dēfunctōrius, dēfunctōria, dēfunctōrium: *perfunctory, routine*

dēfūnctus, dēfūncta, dēfūnctum: *finished; dead*

dēiciō, dēicere, dēiēcī, dēiectus: *throw down*

dein = deinde

deinde (adverb): (of time) *then, afterward;* (of place) *from there, from that place* (3)

dēlābor, dēlābī, dēlāpsus sum: *slip, fall*

dēlātus: see **dēferō**

dēlectō, dēlectāre, dēlectāvī, dēlectātus: *delight, charm* (12)

dēleō, dēlēre, dēlēvī, dēlētus: *destroy*

dēlīberō, dēlīberāre, dēlīberāvī, dēlīberātus: *weigh, think over*

dēlicātus, dēlicāta, dēlicātum: *delicate, dainty, luxurious*

dēliciae, dēliciārum, F pl.: *delights, pleasures;* (often of a favorite slave) *pet, boy toy*

dēlinquō, dēlinquere, dēlīquī: *do wrong, commit an offense; be wanting, fall short*

dēmandō, dēmandāre, dēmandāvī, dēmandātus: *hand over, entrust*

dēmentia, dēmentiae, F: *insanity*

dēminuō, dēminuere, dēminuī, dēminūtus: *lessen, diminish; deprive of*

dēnārius, dēnāriī, M: *denarius,* a silver coin worth 4 **sēstertiī;** *money*

dēns, dentis, M: *tooth*

deorsum (adverb): *downward, down*

dēpendeō, dēpendēre, dēpendī, dēpensus: *hang down*

dēpendō, dēpendere, dēpendī, dēpensus: *pay*

dēpōnō, dēpōnere, dēposuī, dēpositus: *put down, put aside*

dēpraesentiārum (adverb): *here and now*

dēprāvō, dēprāvāre, dēprāvāvī, dēprāvātus: *distort, corrupt*

dēprecor, dēprecārī, dēprecātus sum: *pray against; pray for, intercede on behalf of*

dēprehendō, dēprehendere, dēprehendī, dēprehensus: *get hold of, catch*

dēprimō, dēprimere, dēpressī, dēpressus: *depress, push down*

dērīdeō, dērīdēre, dērīsī, dērīsus: *deride, mock; laugh off* (6)

dēscendō, dēscendere, dēscendī, dēscensum: *climb down; come down, fall*

dēsertus, dēserta, dēsertum: *deserted*

dēsideō, dēsidēre, dēsēdī: *sit idle*

dēsiderium, dēsideriī, N: *longing; need; request*

dēsinō, dēsinere, dēsiī, dēsitus: *cease, desist*

dēsistō, dēsistere, dēstitī: *stop, desist from*

dēsomnis, dēsomne: *sleep-deprived, sleepless*
(hapax legomenon)

dēspērātus, dēspērāta, dēspērātum: *desperate,*
hopeless; despaired of

dēspoliō, dēspoliāre, dēspoliāvī, dēspoliātus:
strip, plunder

dēstinō, dēstināre, dēstināvī, dēstinātus:
lash down, fix; determine

dētergeō, dētergēre, dētersī, dētersus:
wipe off

dētrahō, dētrahere, dētrāxī, dētractus:
draw down, drag down

dētulī: see dēferō

deūrō, deūrere, deussī, deūstus: *burn up*

deuro de: transliterated Greek "*(come)*
here!"— a command to a slave

deus, deī (nom. pl. dī or diī, dat./abl. pl. dīs
or diīs), M: *god, deity* (5)

dēversōrium, dēversōriī, N: *inn,*
cheap lodgings

dēvoveō, dēvovēre, dēvōvī, dēvōtus: *vow,*
sacrifice; consecrate; curse

dexter, dextera or dextra, dexterum or
dextrum: *right, right-handed*

dī or diī: see deus

dīcō, dīcere, dīxī, dictus: *say, speak* (1)

dictō, dictāre, dictāvī, dictātus: *say*
repeatedly; compose; suggest

didicī: see discō

dīdūcō, dīdūcere, dīdūxī, dīductus: *draw*
apart, open

diēs diēī, M: *daytime; a day* (1)

diffundō, diffundere, diffūdī, diffūsus:
spread, extend; cheer up, gladden

digitus, digitī, M: *finger*

dignitōsus, dignitōsa, dignitōsum:
dignified

dignus, digna, dignum: *worthy, proper*

dīligenter (adverb): *carefully, thoroughly* (8)

dīligentia, dīligentiae, F: *care,*
diligence; regard

dīmidius, dīmidia, dīmidium: *half of*

dīmittō, dīmittere, dīmīsī, dīmissus: *send*
away, dismiss; spread

Dionȳsus, Dionȳsī, M: Greek god *Dionysus,*
also called *Bromius, Bacchus,* or *Pater Liber*

discēdō, discēdere, discessī, discessum: *go*
away; separate, disperse

discipulus, discipulī, M: *student*

discō, discere, didicī: *learn* (4)

discolor, discolōris: *of different colors*

discordia, discordiae, F: *discord,*
disagreement

discumbō, discumbere, discubuī,
discubitum: *recline, take one's place* (at
the table or in bed) (7)

discurrō, discurrere, discucurrī,
discursum: *run in different directions,*
scurry about

discutiō, discutere, discussī, discussus:
smash, shatter; dispel, put aside

dispēnsātor, dispēnsātōris, M: *highest-*
ranking household slave or ex-slave, chief
of staff, steward

dissiliō, dissilīre, dissiluī: *fly apart, burst*

dissimulō, dissimulāre, dissimulāvī,
dissimulātus: *keep secret, pretend not to*
notice, ignore

distentus, distenta, distentum:
distended, bulging

diū: *for a long time* (3)

diūtius: *for a longer time* (3)

dīversus, dīversa, dīversum: *in different*
directions, opposite

dīves, dīvitis: *rich, wealthy*

dīvidō, dīvidere, dīvīsī, dīvīsus: *divide,*
distribute; break up

dīxī: see dīcō

dō, dare, dedī, datus: *give; grant* (1)

doceō, docēre, docuī, doctus: *teach*

dolor, dolōris, M: *pain, ache; anguish*

domesticus, domestica, domesticum:
domestic, familiar, private

domicilium, domiciliī, N: *residence, home*

domina, dominae, F: *mistress, owner* (1)

dominicus, dominica, dominicum: *belonging to the master, master's*

dominus, dominī, M: *master, owner* (1)

domus, domī or **domūs,** F: *house, home* (1);
domī (locative) *at home*

domūsiō, domūsiōnis, F: *private usage, household use*

dōnec (conjunction): *while; until*

dōnō, dōnāre, dōnāvī, dōnātus: *present; condone; give up* (8)

dormiō, dormīre, dormīvī or **dormiī, dormītum:** *sleep* (10)

dorsum, dorsī, N: *back* of the body

dubitō, dubitāre, dubitāvī, dubitātus: *doubt; consider; be uncertain; hesitate*

dubium, dubiī, N: *doubt, uncertainty*

ducentī, ducentae, ducenta: *two hundred*

dūcō, dūcere, dūxī, ductus: *lead, guide* (5)

dūdum (adverb): *a short time ago; once*

dum (conjunction): *while, as long as, until* (3)

duo, duae, duo: *two* (4)

dūpondius or **dūpundius, dūpondiī,** M: a coin worth double the **ās**

dupunduārius, dupunduāria, dupunduārium: *worth a* **dūpondius,** *worth two cents* (hapax legomenon)

dūrō, dūrāre, dūrāvī, dūrātus: *harden; toughen up; be tough*

dūrus, dūra, dūrum: *hard, tough; rude*

ē (preposition + ablative): *out of, from* (3)

ēbrietās, ēbrietātis, F: *drunkenness*

ēbrius, ēbria, ēbrium: *drunk, inebriated* (7)

ēbulliō, ēbullīre, ēbullīvī: *babble about; bubble up;* **animum ēbullīre:** *give up the ghost*

ecce (interjection): *behold! lo! see!* (7)

Echīōn, Echīonis, M: *Echion,* one of Trimalchio's dinner guests; in Greek myth, the name of Pentheus' father and of an Argonaut

edō, edere or **ēsse, ēdī, ēsus:** *eat*

ēdūcō, ēdūcere, ēdūxī, ēductus: *lead out, draw out*

efferō, efferāre, efferāvī, efferātus: *make wild, brutalize; exasperate*

efferō, efferre, extulī, ēlātus: *carry out; carry out to the grave, bury*

efflō, efflāre, efflāvī, efflātus: *breathe out, puff out*

effluō, effluere, effluxī: *flow out; slip away*

effringō, effringere, effrēgī, effrāctus: *break open, smash*

effugiō, effugere, effūgī: *escape*

effundō, effundere, effūdī, effūsus: *pour out* (2)

effusē (adverb): *far and wide, lavishly*

ēgī: see **agō**

ego, mihi (dat.), **mē** (acc. and abl.): *I, me* (1)

ēheu (interjection): *alas!*

ēiusmodī: ēius modī, *of that type*

ēlātus: see **efferō**

ēlēctiō, ēlēctiōnis, F: *choice, selection*

ēlēctus, ēlēcta, ēlēctum: *choice, select*

ēlegantia, ēlegantiae, F: *elegance, taste*

ēligo, ēligere, ēlēgī, ēlēctus: *pluck out; choose*

ēlūdō, ēlūdere, ēlūsī, ēlūsus: *elude, escape*

ēmendō, ēmendāre, ēmendāvī, ēmendātus: *correct, improve*

ēmentior, ēmentīrī, ēmentītus sum: *invent, fabricate; tell a lie*

ēminēns, ēminentis: *projecting*

ēmittō, ēmittere, ēmīsī, ēmissus: *send out; hurl; release, set free*

emō, emere, ēmī, emptus: *buy, purchase* (10)

emptīcius, emptīcia, emptīcium: *obtained by purchase, bought*

ēnatō, ēnatāre, ēnatāvī, ēnatātum: *swim away; get away with* something

Encolpius, Encolpī, M: *Encolpius,* the narrator of the *Satyirca,* whose name means "Crotch" in Greek

enim (conjunction): *for instance; yes, indeed; for, because* (3)

eō, īre, īvī or **iī, itum:** *go, walk* (4)

eō: see **is, ea, id**

ephēbus, ephēbī, M: *young man, Greek youth* entering manhood (18–20 years old) (Greek loan word) (10)

Ephesus, Ephesī, M: *Ephesus*, a city on the coast of Asia Minor (see map)

epidīpnis, epidīpnidis, F: extra *course* at the end of a meal, *dessert* (Greek loan word)

epulum, epulī, N: *banquet, feast*

eques, equitis, M: *cavalryman, knight*

equus, equī, M: *horse*

ergastulum, ergastulī, N: *prison, chain gang*

ergō (adverb): *therefore; as I was saying* (3)

ērigō, ērigere, ērēxī, ērēctus: *straighten; cheer up; excite*

ēripiō, ēripere, ēripuī, ēreptus: *snatch away; rescue; rob*

errō, errāre, errāvī, errātum: *wander; make a mistake* (8)

error, errōris, M: *wandering; uncertainty; error*

ērubēscō, ērubēscere, ērubuī: *blush, grow red*

ērudiō, ērudīre, ērudīvī, ērudītus: *educate, teach*

ervilia, erviliae, F: *vetch, herbs* (goat fodder)

ēsse: see edō

esse: see sum

essedāria, essedāriae, F or essedārius, essedāriī, M: *soldier* or *gladiator* fighting from a chariot

ēsuriō, ēsurīre: *be hungry, starve*

ēsurītiō, ēsurītiōnis, F: *hunger, famine*

et (conjunction): *and, even; however, but;* et ... et: *both ... and;* (adverb) *even; also* (1)

etiam (adverb and conjunction): *also, besides; yet, still* (3)

etsī (conjunction): *even if, although*

Euhius, Euhiī, M: *Euhius* or Bacchus

Eumolpus or Eumolpos, Eumolpī, M: *Eumolpus*, poet and fellow traveler of Encolpius; name meaning "Good Singer" in Greek; in myth, ancestor of a family of priests of the Eleusinian Mysteries

ēvādō, ēvādere, ēvāsī, ēvāsus: *pass by; escape*

ēveniō, ēvenīre, ēvēnī, ēventum: *come out; come to pass*

ēverrō, ēverrere, ēverrī, ēversus: *sweep out*

ēvertō, ēvertere, ēvertī, ēversus: *overturn*

ēvincō, ēvincere, ēvīcī, ēvictus: *conquer completely*

ēvītō, ēvītāre, ēvītāvī, ēvītātus: *avoid, escape*

ēvocō, ēvocāre, ēvocāvī, ēvocātus: *call out, summon; evoke; challenge*

ēvolō, ēvolāre, ēvolāvī, ēvolātum: *fly out/away*

ex (preposition + ablative): *out of, from* (3)

excandēscō, excandēscere, excanduī: *grow hot; burst into a rage*

excellēns, excellentis: *excellent, superior*

excelsus, excelsa, excelsum: *high; eminent*

exceptiō, exceptiōnis, F: *exception, limitation*

excidō, excidere, excidī: *fall, slip; be forgotten*

excipiō, excipere, excēpī, exceptus: *take out; rescue* (9)

excitō, excitāre, excitāvī, excitātus: *awaken, arouse* (9)

exclāmō, exclāmāre, exclāmāvī, exclāmātus: *exclaim, yell*

exclūdō, exclūdere, exclūsī, exclūsus: *exclude*

excōgitō, excōgitāre, excōgitāvī, excōgitātus: *think up, devise*

excūsātiō, excūsātiōnis, F: *excuse*

exemplar, exemplāris, N: *copy*

exemplum, exemplī, N: *example, precedent, model*

exeō, exīre, exīvī or exiī, exitus: *pass, cross; avoid; exceed; go out, depart* (6)

exerceō, exercēre, exercuī, exercitus: *exercise, train; practice*

exercitus, exercitūs, M: *army, infantry*

exhortātiō, exhortātiōnis, F: *encouragement*

exilium, exiliī, N: *exile; place of exile*

exinterō, exinterāre, exinterāvī, exinterātus: *disembowel, gut, clean* (5)

exitus, exitūs, M: *exit, departure, way out*

exonerō, exonerāre, exonerāvī, exonerātus: *unload, empty*

exopīnissō, exopīnissāre: *think, believe* (hapax legomenon)

exōrdior, exōrdīrī, exorsus sum: *commence*

exōrō, exōrāre, exōrāvī, exōrātus: *win over; beg for*

expectātiō, expectātiōnis, F: *expectation, anticipation, suspense*

expectō, expectāre, expectāvī, expectātus: *await, wait for; long for; wait expectantly* (5)

expediō, expedīre, expedīvī, expedītus: *put in order, settle; put up for sale*

expellō, expellere, expulī, expulsus: *drive out, expel*

expergīscor, expergīscī, experrēctus sum: *wake up; be alert*

experior, experīrī, expertus sum: *test, try; experience; endure*

expīrō, expīrāre, expīrāvī, expīrātus: *breathe out, exhale; expire, breathe one's last*

explicitus, explicita, explicitum: *disentangled; simple*

expōnō, expōnere, exposuī, expositus: *put out, expose, display; explain*

exprimō, exprimere, expressī, expressus: *press out, force; extort*

expugnō, expugnāre, expugnāvī, expugnātus: *assault, plunder; overcome*

exsolvō, exsolvere, exsolvī, exsolūtus: *loosen; release; pay*

extendō, extendere, extendī, extentus: *stretch out, extend; increase, prolong*

extinguō, extinguere, extinxī, extinctus: *extinguish, put out; kill; die*

extorqueō, extorquēre, extorsī, extortus: *wrench, wrest; extort*

extrā (preposition + accusative): *outside (of)*

extrahō, extrahere, extrāxī, extractus: *pull out, drag out*

extrēmus, extrēma, extrēmum: *extreme, last*

extulī: see **efferō**

exul, exulis, M or F: *exile, refugee*

exulcerō, exulcerāre, exulcerāvī, exulcerātus: *make sore, wound; exasperate*

exuō, exuere, exuī, exūtus: *take off; disrobe*

fābula, fābulae, F: *story* (5)

faciēs, faciēī, F: *face, appearance*

facilis, facile: *easy; ready; good-natured*

facinus, facinoris, N: *deed, act; crime*

faciō, facere, fēcī, factus: *make, do* (1)

facultās, facultātis, F: *opportunity; ability; means, resources*

Falernus, Falerna, Falernum: *Falernian, from the slopes of Mt. Falernus, between Latium and Campania, and famous for vineyards*

fallō, fallere, fefellī, falsus: *mislead, cheat*

falsus, falsa, falsum: *false; wrong*

fāma, fāmae, F: *talk, rumor; reputation; fame*

famēs, famis, F: *hunger*

familia, familiae, F: *household slaves, household* (1)

familiāris, familiāre: *domestic, personal; intimate*

familiāritās, familiāritatis, F: *close friendship, intimacy*

fāmōsus, fāmōsa, fāmōsum: *much talked of; famous; infamous*

fās est: *it is right/lawful/permissible*

fāscia, fāsciae, F: *ribbon, band; type*

fastīdiō, fastīdīre, fastīdīvī, fastīdītus: *disdain, despise*

fastīditum, fastīditiī, N: *distaste; squeamishness, disgust, snobbishness*

fātālis, fātāle: *fateful; fatal*

fateor, fatērī, fassus sum: *confess, admit* (12)

fātum, fātī, N: *fate, destiny*

fatuus, fatua, fatuum: *silly; tasteless*

favor, favōris, M: *favor, support; applause*

favus, favī, M: *honeycomb*

fax, facis, F: *torch*

fēcī: see **faciō**

fefellī: see **fallō**

fēlīcitās, fēlīcitātis, F: *fertility, luck, happiness*

fēlix, fēlīcis: *favorable, lucky, happy*

fēmina, fēminae, F: *woman, lady, female* (11)

ferculum, ferculī, N: *food tray, dish; course*

ferē (adverb): *approximately, nearly, almost*

fēriātus, fēriāta, fēriātum: *on holiday, taking it easy; dressed for a holiday*

ferō, ferre, tulī, lātus: *carry, bear, endure* (2)

ferrum, ferrī, N: *iron; sword* (10)

ferveō, fervēre, ferbuī: *boil, seethe; be busy*

festīnātiō, festīnātiōnis, F: *hurry, haste*

fēstus, fēsta, fēstum: *festive, joyous*

fēteō, fētēre: *have an offensive smell, stink*

fētus, fētūs, M: *young, offspring*

fictilis, fictile: *clay, terracotta*

fictus, ficta, fictum: *false*

fidēlis, fidēle: *faithful, loyal*

fidēs, fideī, F: *trust, faith, confidence* (9)

fīdus, fīda, fīdum: *reliable, trustworthy*

figūrō, figūrāre, figūrāvī, figūrātus: *shape, form*

filius, filiī, M: *son*

filix, filicis, F: *fern;* (colloquial) *worthless person, a no-good*

filum, filī, N: *thread; style* (of speech); *character* (of a person)

fimbriae, fimbriārum, F pl.: *fringe, tassels*

fingō, fingere, finxī, fictus: *shape, model; imagine, suppose*

finiō, finīre, finīvī, finītus: *limit, restrain; finish*

finis, finis, M: *boundary, end, limit*

fiō, fierī, factus sum: *be made; become, happen;* used as passive of facia (1)

firmitās, firmitātis, F: *firmness, stability*

fixus, fixa, fixum: *fixed, immovable; fitted (with)*

flagellum, flagellī, N: *whip, riding crop*

flātūra, flātūrae, F: *foundry; metal casting; caliber, quality* (of a person)

flectō, flectere, flexī, flexus: *bend*

fleō, flēre, flēvī, flētus: *cry for; cry*

flētus, flētūs, M: *crying*

flōrēns, flōrentis: *blooming, prosperous*

flūctus, flūctūs, M: *wave, turbulence, disorder*

fluō, fluere, fluxī, fluxum: *flow, drip; vanish*

folium, foliī, N: *leaf*

follis, follis, M: *bag, sack*

forāmen, forāminis, N: *hole, opening, crack*

forās (adverb): *out, outside*

foris, foris, F: *door;* (in plural) *double doors*

fōrma, fōrmae, F: *form, shape; beauty*

fōrmōsus, fōrmōsa, fōrmōsum: *shapely, beautiful*

fors, fortis, F: *chance, accident* (4)

forsitan (adverb): *perhaps*

fortis, forte: *brave, strong* (4)

fortūna, fortūnae, F: *chance, luck; prosperity; goods;* goddess *Fortūna*

Fortūnāta, Fortūnātae, F: *Fortunata,* wife of Trimalchio; *fortunate, prosperous*

forum, forī, N: *forum, marketplace*

fragmentum, fragmentī, N: *fragment, remnant*

frangō, frangere, frēgī, frāctus: *break, shatter*

frāter, frātris, M: *brother; companion* (9)

frequenter (adverb): *in crowds; frequently, commonly* (11)

frequentia, frequentiae, F: *large group of people, crowd; population; abundance* (11)

frīgidus, frīgida, frīgidum: *cold, numbed*

frīgus, frīgoris, N: *cold, chill, frost* (12)

frōns, frōntis, F: *forehead, brow*

frūnīscor, frūnīscī, frūnītus sum: *enjoy*

fruor, fruī, frūctus or fruitus sum: *have the benefit of, enjoy* (+ ablative)

frūstum, frūstī, N: *bit, scrap*

fuga, fugae, F: *flight, escape; exile; speed*

fugiō, fugere, fūgī, fugitus: *flee, flee away* (9)

fugitīvus, fugitīva, fugitīvum: *runaway, fugitive*

fuī: see sum

fulciō, fulcīre, fulsī, fultus: *prop up, support*

fulgeō, fulgēre, fulsī: *gleam, shine*

fullō, fullōnis, M: *fuller, launderer*

fūmōsus, fūmōsa, fūmōsum: *smoky; smoking*

fundō, fundere, fūdī, fūsus: *pour out*

fundus, fundī, M: *ground, soil; farm, estate*

fūnebris, fūnebre: *funerary; deadly*

fūnus, fūneris, N: *funeral, burial* (11)

furcifera, furciferae, F: *rascal*

furnus, furnī, M: *oven; bakery*

furō, furere: *rage, rave*

furor, furōris, M: *madness, rage, fury*

fūrtim (adverb): *secretly*

futūrus: see **sum**

Gāius, Gāiī, M: *Gaius*, common *praenomen* among Roman male citizens

galbinus, galbina, galbinum: *chartreuse, yellow-green*

gallicinium, galliciniī, N: *cockcrow*, about two hours after midnight in Roman timekeeping

gallus gallīnāceus, gallī gallīnāceī, M: *rooster* (10)

Ganymēdēs, Ganymēdis, M: *Ganymedes*, guest of Trimalchio; in myth, a beautiful Trojan prince seized by Zeus

gastra, gastrae, F: *large-bellied jar* (Greek loan word)

gaudeō, gaudēre, gavīsus sum: *rejoice at, be glad about* (+ ablative); *feel joy*

gaudimōnium, gaudimōniī, N: *joy* (hapax legomenon)

gaudium, gaudiī, N: *joy, delight; cause of joy* (9)

gausapa, gausapae, F: *felt; fleecy wool*

Gavilla, Gavillae, F: *Gavilla*, name of a new owner of a house in the *Satyrica*

gemitus, gemitūs, M: *sigh, groan* (12)

genius, geniī, M: *guardian spirit; natural inclination; talent, wit*

gēns, gēntis, F: *clan, family; people, race*

genū, genūs, N: *knee* (11)

genus, generis, N: *birth, descent, origin; family; kind, sort* (9)

geōmetrias, geōmetriae, F: *geometry*

gestiō, gestīre, gestīvī: *be delighted; be eager*

Gītōn, Gītōnis (acc. s. **Gītōna**), M: *Giton*, Encolpius' companion; "Neighbor Boy" in Greek

gizeria, gizeriōrum, N pl.: *giblets*

gladiātor, gladiātōris, M: *gladiator; ruffian*

gladius, gladiī, M: *sword* (6)

glāns, glāndis, F: *acorn, chestnut*

glebula, glebulae, F: *small lump; bit of land*

glōriōsus, glōriōsa, glōriōsum: *famous, glorious; boastful*

Glycō, Glycōnis, M: *Glyco*, Greek name meaning "Sweet"

grabātus, grabātī, M: *cot* (Greek loan word)

gradus, gradūs, M: *step, gait; stance*

Graeculus, Graecula, Graeculum: *thoroughly Greek; a dirty little Greek*

Graecus, Graeca, Graecum: *Greek* (10)

grandis, grande: *full-grown; large; important*

grassātor, grassātōris, M: *tramp; bully, hoodlum*

grātia, grātiae, F: *charm; service, favor, kindness;* **grātiās agere**: *thank, express gratitude* (4)

grātīs (adverb): *free, for nothing, gratis*

grātulor, grātulārī, grātulātus sum: *be glad, rejoice; congratulate; give thanks to*

gravis, grave: *heavy; serious*

gremium, gremiī, N: *lap; bosom*

gressus, gressūs, M: *step, footstep; course, way*

grex, gregis, M: *flock, herd; crowd*

gurges, gurgitis, M: *abyss, whirlpool; spendthrift*

gustātiō, gustātiōnis, F: *appetizer course*

gustātōrium, gustātōriī, N: *appetizer*

gustō, gustāre, gustāvī, gustātus: *taste, eat; dine; overhear* (6)

gustus, gustūs, M: *tasting; taste; small portion*

gymnasium, gymnasiī, N: *gymnasium, exercise ground, school* (Greek loan word)

gypsātus, gypsāta, gypsātum: *covered* or *sealed with gypsum, plastered*

habeō, habēre, habuī, habitus: *have, hold* (1)

Habinnas, Habinnae, M: *Habinnas*, a man's name possibly of Semitic origin

habitō, habitāre, habitāvī, habitātus:
  inhabit; dwell, live
hāc (adverb): *in this way*
harēna, harēnae, F: *sand; arena*
harundō, harundinis, F: *reed, cane*
hauriō, haurīre, hausī, haustus: *draw up;*
  engulf, swallow
hedera, hedera, F: *ivy*
hērēs, hērēdis, M or F: *heir or heiress*
herī (adverb): *yesterday*
Hermogenēs, Hermogenis, M: *Hermogenes,*
  Greek personal name
heu (interjection): *oh! ah!*
hic, haec, hoc: *this*
hilaris, hilare: *cheerful*
hilaritās, hilaritātis, F: *cheerfulness, mirth* (5)
hinc (adverb): *from here, hence*
Hipparchus, Hipparchī, M: *Hipparchus,*
  Greek name, including that of a famous
  astronomer
hircus, hircī, M: *goat*
Hispānus, Hispāna, Hispānum: *Spanish*
hodiē (adverb): *today, nowadays* (3)
homō, hominis, M or F: *a human being,*
  person (1)
homunciō, homunciōnis, M: *poor little guy,*
  mere human
honestus, honesta, honestum: *honored,*
  respected; well-born, of high rank
hōra, hōrae, F: *an hour; time* (8)
hōrologium, hōrologiī, N: *clock*
hortor, hortārī, hortātus sum: *exhort,*
  incite, encourage
hospes, hospitis, M: *host; guest; stranger* (10)
hospitium, hospitiī, N: *hospitality;*
  guest room
hūc (adverb): *here, to this place, to this point*
hūmānitās, hūmānitātis, F: *humanity,*
  kindness, courtesy; culture, refinement
hūmānus, hūmāna, hūmānum: *human,*
  humane, kind, cultured
humilis, humile: *low, short; humble,*
  low-born

hypogaeum, hypogaeī, N: *underground*
  burial vault (Greek loan word)

iaceō, iacēre, iacuī: *lie, rest, recline* (2)
iaciō, iacere, iēcī, iactus: *throw; set down;*
  build (2)
iactō, iactāre, iactāvī, iactātus: *throw, toss;*
  toss out, mention, brag about (2)
iactūra, iactūrae, F: *loss*
iam (adverb): *now, already; by then, soon,*
  next (3)
iānua, iānuae, F: *door, entrance* (9)
iātraliptēs, iātraliptae, M: *masseur, rubbing*
  physician (Greek loan word)
ibi (adverb): *there, in that place, at that point*
ictus, ictūs, M: *blow, strike, hit*
īdem, eadem, idem: *the same; also,*
  likewise (2)
ideō (adverb): *therefore* (9)
idōneus, idōnea, idōneum: *suitable, fit for*
iēcī: see **iaciō**
iēiūnium, iēiūniī, N: *fast, fast day* in honor
  of a deity
igitur (adverb): *then, therefore; in short* (11)
ignāvia, ignāviae, F: *laziness, idleness*
ignis, ignis, M: *fire*
ignōscō, ignōscere, ignōvī, ignōtum:
  overlook, forgive, pardon (one forgiven in
  dative) (5)
ignōtus, ignōta, ignōtum: *unknown,*
  strange; ignoble, base
iī or **īvī:** see **eō**
illāc (adverb): *in that way*
ille, illa, illud: *that, that famous*
illīc (adverb): *there, in that matter, in*
  that place
illinc (adverb): *from there; on that side*
illūc (adverb): *to that place, to that point; to*
  that one
imāgō, imāginis, F: *image, copy, likeness*
imitor, imitārī, imitātus sum: *imitate, copy* (7)
immineō, imminēre: *project; be near, be*
  imminent; threaten

immittō, immittere, immīsī, immissus: *send, guide; insert; let in*

immo (adverb): (marking contrast) *rather, on the contrary;* (in confirmation) *quite so, indeed* (10)

immortālis, immortāle: *immortal*

impendō, impendere, impendī, impensus: *weigh out, expend; apply; hang*

imperātor, imperātōris, M: *commander, general; emperor*

imperium, imperiī, N: *authority, power, command; realm; magistracy*

imperō, imperāre, imperāvī, imperātus: *order, demand; be in command*

impetrō, impetrāre, impetrāvī, impetrātus: *accomplish, achieve, bring about that (+ ut + subjunctive)*

impingō, impingere, impēgī, impāctus: *fasten to, force against, press*

impleō, implēre, implēvī, implētus: *fill in, fill up* (10)

impōnō, impōnere, imposuī, impositus: *place on, set on (+ dative)* (2)

imprecor, imprecārī, imprecātus sum: *call down (a curse), invoke; pray over, bless*

imprimō, imprimere, impressī, impressus: *press down, impress, thrust*

improbitās, improbitātis, F: *wickedness, depravity*

improbō, improbāre, improbāvī, improbātus: *disapprove*

improbus, improba, improbum: *inferior; shameless, perverse*

imprūdēns, imprūdentis: *unsuspecting, unwary, ignorant*

imprūdentia, imprūdentiae, F: *thoughtlessness; ignorance*

impūnē (adverb): *with impunity; safely*

impūrus, impūra, impūrum: *impure, unclean*

in (preposition + abl.): *in, on;* (+ acc.) *into* (1)

inaurō, inaurāre, inaurāvī, inaurātus: *gold-plate, gild*

incendium, incendiī, N: *fire, heat*

incensus, incensa, incensum: *inflamed, enraged*

inceptō, inceptāre, inceptāvī, inceptātus: *begin, undertake*

incipiō, incipere, incēpī, inceptus: *begin, start*

inclīnātiō, inclīnātiōnis, F: *leaning, inclination*

inclīnātus, inclīnāta, inclīnātum: *inclined; low*

inclūdō, inclūdere, inclūsī, inclūsus: *shut in; include; obstruct*

incumbō, incumbere, incubuī, incubitum: *lean on, lie down*

inde (adverb): *from there, after that*

indecenter (adverb): *improperly, indecently*

indēlectātus, indēlectāta, indēlectātum: *not delighted, displeased*

indemnātus, indemnāta, indemnātum: *unconvicted*

India, Indiae, F: *India and neighboring regions*

indicium, indiciī, N: *information, evidence*

indicō, indicāre, indicāvī, indicātus: *point out, reveal; betray*

indignor, indignārī, indignātus sum: *be indignant at, be displeased at*

indīligentia, indīligentiae, F: *carelessness*

indormiō, indormīre, indormīvī, indormītum: *fall asleep; grow careless*

indulgentia, indulgentiae, F: *indulgence, leniency*

indulgeō, indulgēre, indulsī, indulsus: *grant, concede to (+ dative)*

inedia, inediae, F: *abstaining from eating, fasting, starvation*

īnfācundus, īnfācunda, īnfācundum: *ineloquent*

īnfēlīx, īnfēlīcis: *unfruitful, unhappy, unfortunate*

īnfernus, īnferna, īnfernum: *lower; infernal, of the underworld*

īnferus, īnfera, īnferum: *lower; dead*

īnfirmitās, īnfirmitātis, F: *weakness; inconstancy*

īnflātus, īnflāta, īnflātum: *inflated, swollen*

īnfrā (adverb): *below, underneath;* (preposition + accusative) *below, under* īnfundō, īnfundere, īnfūdī, īnfūsus: *pour in/out/on*

ingemēscō, ingemēscere, ingemēscuī: *groan, sigh*

ingeniōsus, ingeniōsa, ingeniōsum: *clever, talented, ingenious*

ingenium, ingeniī, N: *nature, temper; natural ability, talent, genius*

ingēns, ingentis: *monstrous, vast, enormous* (5)

ingenuus, ingenua, ingenuum: *native, natural; like a freeman, noble*

ingerō, ingerere, ingessī, ingestus: *carry in; ingest*

ingrātus, ingrāta, ingrātum: *unpleasant, unappreciated*

ingurgitō, ingurgitāre, ingurgitāvī, ingurgitātus: *pour in; gorge, stuff*

inhaereō, inhaerēre, inhaesī, inhaesum: *cling to, remain attached to*

inhibeō, inhibēre, inhibuī, inhibitus: *hold back, curb; use, apply; inflict*

inimīcus, inimīca, inimīcum: *unfriendly, enemy*

iniūria, iniūriae, F: *injury, injustice, wrong* (8)

innocēns, innocentis: *innocent; upright*

inquam: *I say* / inquit: *he says, she says, one says;* defective verb used to introduce direct speech (1)

inquinō, inquināre, inquināvī, inquinātus: *defile, contaminate*

īnscrīptiō, īnscrīptiōnis, F: *inscribing, inscription, title*

īnsequor, īnsequī, īnsecūtus sum: *follow; attack; come next*

īnserō, īnserere, īnseruī, īnsertus: *insert, introduce; include*

īnsertō, īnsertāre, īnsertāvī, īnsertātus: *insert*

īnspiciō, īnspicere, īnspexī, īnspectus: *inspect; consider; comprehend*

īnstita, īnstitae, F: *band, strap, rope*

īnstrūmentum, īnstrūmentī, N: *instrument, tool*

īnsula, īnsulae, F: *island; city block, apartment building (urban island)*

īnsulsus, īnsulsa, īnsulsum: *unsalted, tasteless; coarse; silly*

intellegō, intellegere, intellēxī, intellēctus: *understand, realize; be an expert*

intemperāns, intemperantis: *intemperate; lewd*

inter (preposition + accusative): *between, among; during, within* (3)

interdiū (adverb): *by day, in the daytime*

interdum (adverb): *sometimes; meanwhile*

intereā (adverb): *meanwhile; nevertheless*

interim (adverb): *meanwhile; sometimes* (3)

intermittō, intermittere, intermīsī, intermissus: *interrupt, suspend; allow to pass; pause*

interpellō, interpellāre, interpellāvī, interpellātus: *interrupt, disturb*

interpōnō, interpōnere, interposuī, interpositus: *insert, interpose, introduce*

interpres, interpretis, M or F: *interpreter, translator*

interrogō, interrogāre, interrogāvī, interrogātus: *ask, question*

interventus, interventūs, M: *intervention*

intestīnum, intestīnī, N: *intestine, gut*

intonō, intonāre, intonuī, intonitus: *thunder*

intortus, intorta, intortum: *twisted*

intrā (preposition + accusative): *within, inside*

intrō, intrāre, intrāvī, intrātus: *enter, penetrate* (1)

intueor, intuērī, intuitus sum: *look at; consider*

īnvādō, īnvādere, īnvāsi, īnvāsus: *enter; undertake; invade*

inveniō, invenīre, invēnī, inventus: *find, come upon* (2)

inventor, inventōris, M: *inventor, author*

invideō, invidēre, invīdī, invīsus: *envy*

invidia, invidiae, F: *envy, jealousy*

invītō, invītāre, invītāvī, invītātus: *invite, entertain* (12)

invītus, invīta, invītum: *reluctant, unwilling* (12)

involō, involāre, involāvī, involātus: *swoop down on; steal from*

involūtus, involūta, involūtum: *wrapped up; complicated*

involvō, involvere, involvī, involūtus: *wrap up*

iō (interjection): *hurray! yo!*

iocor, iocārī, iocātus sum: *say in jest, joke*

iocus, iocī, M: *joke*

Iovis: see Iuppiter

ipse, ipsa, ipsum (gen. s. ipsīus, dat. s. ipsī): *-self, that very, precisely* (emphasizes noun) (2)

ipsimus or ipsumus, ipsumī, M / ipsuma, ipsumae, F: *boss, master* or *mistress* (7)

īrācundia, īrācundiae, F: *quick temper; wrath*

īrātus, īrāta, īrātum: *angry, irate* (10)

irrēpō, irrēpere, irrēpsī, irrēptum: *creep in, sneak in*

is, ea, id (gen. s. eīus, dat. s. eī): *this, that, the; he, she, it, they*

iste, ista, istud (gen. s. istīus, dat. s. istī): *that, that particular, that very; that despicable* (5)

istōc (adverb): *there, to where you are*

ita (adverb): *thus, so, in this manner* (3)

itaque (adverb): *and thus, and so; therefore, accordingly* (3)

iter, itineris, N: *journey; route, way*

iterātiō, iterātiōnis, F: *repetition*

iterō, iterāre, iterāvī, iterātus: *repeat, renew*

iterum (adverb): *again, a second time* (11)

iubeō, iubēre, iussī, iūssus: *order, bid, ask* (1)

iūdex, iūdicis, M: *judge, juror; critic, scholar*

iūdicium, iūdiciī, N: *evidence, proof; reward for giving evidence; court; judgment*

iūdicō, iūdicāre, iūdicāvī, iūdicātus: *judge, examine*

iugulum, iugulī, N: *throat*

iungō, iungere, iūnxī, iūnctus: *join, join together* (9)

Iuppiter or Iovis, Iovis, M: *Jupiter* or *Jove, king of the gods*

iūrō, iūrāre, iūrāvī, iūrātus: *swear, take an oath, vow*

iūs, iūris, N: *law, right, justice; juice, broth* (9)

iūssus: see iubeō

iūssus, iūssūs, M: *command, order*

iuvenis, iuvene: *young*

iuvō, iuvāre, iuvāvī, iuvātus: *help*

labōriōsus, labōriōsa, labōriōsum: *laborious, troublesome; hard-working*

labōrō, labōrāre, labōrāvī, labōrātus: *work at, produce; be worried about*

labrum, labrī, N: *lip; mouth*

labyrinthus, labyrinthī, M: *labyrinth, maze;* in Greek myth, the Cretan labyrinth held the Minotaur

lac, lactis, N: *milk*

lacernātus, lacernāta, lacernātum: *wearing a cloak*

lacerō, lacerāre, lacerāvī, lacerātus: *lacerate*

Lacōnicus, Lacōnica, Lacōnicum: *Spartan, from the Greek city of Sparta*

lacrima, lacrimae, F: *tear, teardrop* (10)

lactēns, lactentis: *milky; tender, juicy*

lacticulōsus, lacticulōsa, lacticulōsum: *unweaned, suckling*

laecasīn: (colloquial and derogatory) *have sex* (transliterated Greek present infinitive)

laesus, laesa, laesum: *harmed*

lāmellula, lāmellulae, F: *small sum of money*

lamna, lamnae, F: *thin sheet of metal, plate;* (colloquial) *cash, money*

lāna, lānae, F: *wool*

lānātus, lānāta, lānātus: *wooly*

lancea, lanceae, F: *light spear* or *lance*

languidus, languida, languidum: *weak, languid*

languōr, languōris, M: *weakness, listlessness*

lanisticius, lanisticia, lanisticium: *managed by a* lanista, a gladiator trainer

lanius, laniī, M: *butcher; executioner*

lanx, lancis, F: *dish, platter*

lapidārius, lapidāria, lapidārium: *stone*

lapidārius, lapidāriī, M: *stonemason, stonecutter*

lapideus, lapidea, lapideum: *stony, stone*

Lār, Lares, M: *Lar,* a household god; *home*

largiter (adverb): *abundantly;* used substantively with the genitive, *an abundance of*

largus, larga, largum: *abundant; generous*

larifuga, larifugae, F: *runaway* (hapax legomenon)

larva, larvae, F: *mask; ghost; skeleton*

lasanus, lasanī, M: *chamber pot* (Greek loan word)

lassitūdō, lassitūdinis, F: *tiredness, lassitude*

lassus, lassa, lassum: *tired, exhausted*

lātē (adverb): *widely, extensively*

lāticlāvius, lāticlāvia, lāticlāvium: *with a broad purple stripe* (worn by members of the senatorial class); *senatorial*

Latīnē (adverb): *in Latin, in proper Latin*

Latīnus, Latīna, Latīnum: *Latin, in Latin*

lātrātus, lātrātūs, M: *barking*

lātrō, lātrāre, lātrāvī, lātrātus: *bark*

latrō, latrōnis, M: *thief, bandit*

lātus: see **ferō**

latus, lateris, N: *side, flank; body; person*

laudō, laudāre, laudāvī, laudātus: *praise* (7)

lautitia, lautitiae, F: *luxury, high living*

lautus or **lōtus, lauta, lautum:** *washed; elegant* (1)

lavō, lavāre, lāvī, lautus or **lōtus** or **lavātus:** *wash, bathe* (4)

laxō, laxāre, laxāvī, laxātus: *extend; open up; relax*

lectīca, lectīcae, F: *litter*

lectulus, lectulī, M: *cot, small bed*

lectus, lectī, M: *couch, bed* (2)

legiō, legiōnis, M: *legion, large army unit*

lēgō, lēgāre, lēgāvī, lēgātus: *bequeath, leave in a will*

legō, legere, lēgī, lēctus: *read; choose*

lentus, lenta, lentum: *clinging; slow, reluctant*

levitās, levitātis, F: *lightness, levity, fickleness*

levō, levāre, levāvī, levātus: *raise up, lift*

libellus, libellī, M: *little book; notice, bit of writing*

libenter (adverb): *willingly, with pleasure* (4)

līber, lībera, līberum: *free* (8)

Līber, Līberī or **Līber Pater,** M: *Liber,* Italian fertility god identified with Bacchus

liber, librī, M: *book*

līberālitās, līberālitātis, F: *courtesy; generosity*

lībertās, lībertātis, F: *liberty, freedom*

lībertus, lībertī, M: *freedman, male ex-slave*

libet, libēre, libuit or **libitum est** (impersonal with dative): *it pleases, it is agreeable*

libīdinōsus, libīdinōsa, libīdinōsum: *willful; arbitrary; lustful*

libīdō, libidinis, F: *desire, pleasure; caprice, fancy; lust* (10)

libitīnārius, libitīnāriī, M: *undertaker*

lībra, lībrae, F: *scales, balance; pound*

licentia, licentiae, F: *license, freedom*

licet, licēre, licuit (impersonal verb): *it is permitted, it is lawful* (12)

lictor, lictōris, M: *lictor,* public attendant or bodyguard of a magistrate or priest

līmen, līminis, N: *threshold, doorway*

līneāmentum, līneāmentī, N: *line; feature; outline*

lingua, linguae, F: *tongue; speech, language*

linguōsus, linguōsa, linguōsum: *having a malicious tongue*

linteum, linteī, N: *linen*

lippus, lippa, lippum: *with sore eyes, blear-eyed*

liquēscō, liquēscere, licuī: *melt; decompose; grow soft*

līs, lītis, F: *quarrel, dispute; lawsuit*

littera or **lītera, -ae,** F: *letter of the alphabet;* (in plural) *letter, epistle; literature* (4)

lītus, lītoris, N: *seashore, beach*

locus, locī, M: *place, spot* (4)

longus, longa, longum: *long, tall, far*

loquor, loquī, locūtus sum: *speak,* especially in ordinary conversation (5)

lōripēs, lōripedis: *bowlegged*

lōrus, lōrī, M: *whip; leash*

lōtium, lōtiī, N: *urine*

lōtus: see **lautus**

lūceō, lūcēre, lūxī: *shine, glow; be clear*

lucerna, lucernae, F: *lamp*

lūcidus, lūcida, lūcidum: *bright; clear*

lucrum, lucrī, N: *profit, gain; wealth*

lūdō, lūdere, lūsī, lūsus: *play (with), amuse oneself* (6)

lūdus, lūdī, M: *game, play, diversion, joke* (6)

lūgeō, lūgēre, lūxī, lūctus: *lament, mourn; be in mourning* (12)

lūmen, lūminis, N: *light; lamp* (12)

lūna, lūnae, F: *moon*

lupātria, lupātriae, F: *she-wolf, whore* (hapax legomenon)

lupīnum, lupīnī, N: *lupine seed, legume, bean*

lupus, lupī, M: *wolf*

lūscinia, lūsciniae, F: *nightingale*

lūsī: see **lūdō**

lūsus, lūsūs, M: *game, play, amusement* (6)

lūx, lūcis, F: *light, daylight* (9)

lūxī: see **lūceō**

lūxī: see **lūgeō**

Lyaeus, Lyaeī, M: *Lyaeus,* another name for *Bacchus*

ma (indeclinable): *ma* (baby's first word)

Macedonicus, Macedonica, Macedonicum: *Macedonian, from* or *of Macedonia,* a region in the northern Balkans

Maecēnātiānus, Maecēnātiāna, Maecēnātiānum: *belonging to Maecenas,* one of Trimalchio's former owners, also the first emperor Augustus' patron of the arts

maestus, maesta, maestum: *sad, gloomy*

magis (comparative adverb): *more; rather* (2)

magister, magistrī, M: *teacher, adviser*

magistrātus, magistrātūs, M: *magistrate, local official*

magnitūdō, magnitūdinis, F: *magnitude, size*

magnus, magna, magnum: *large, great* (12)

māiestās, māiestātis, F: *majesty, dignity; authority*

māiestus, māiesta, māiestum: *majestic, dignified*

māior, māius (comparative of **magnus**): *bigger, greater; older*

maledīcō, maledīcere, maledīxī, maledictum: *speak ill of, slander, abuse*

mālicorium, mālicoriī, N: *pomegranate rind*

malignus, maligna, malignum: *spiteful, malicious; stingy*

mālō, mālle, māluī: *wish for more, prefer* (7)

mālum, mālī, N: *apple, fruit* (6)

malus, mala, malum: *bad* (6)

mālus, mālī, F: *apple tree* (6)

Mammea, Mammeae, M: *Mammea,* a man's name

mancipium, mancipiī, N: *movable property, especially a slave*

mandō, mandāre, mandāvī, mandātus: *hand over, consign; bury*

mandūcō, mandūcāre, mandūcāvī, mandūcātus: *chew, eat*

māne (adverb): *in the morning*

mānēs, mānium, M pl.: *spirits of the dead*

Manius, Maniī, M: *Manius,* Roman male name; colloquially, someone who has fallen on hard times

mantissa, mantissae, F: *sauce; trouble, fuss(?)*

manubiae, manubiārum, F pl.: *spoils; money from the sale of military booty or robbery*

manus, manūs, F: *hand; gang, group* (1)

mapālia, mapālium, N pl.: *African huts; a mess*

mappa, mappae, F: *napkin*

mare, maris, N: *sea*

Margarīta, Margarītae, F: *Margarita,* a name meaning "Pearl" in Latin

marītus, marītī, M: *husband*

marmoreus, marmorea, marmoreum: *marble, made of marble*

Mārs, Mārtis, M: *god Mars*

Massa, Massae, F: *lump* or *pile of cash*, here used as a slave's name

matauitatau (interjection?): *abracadabra?*

matella, matellae, F: *chamber pot*

māter, mātris, F: *mother, matron*

mātrōna, mātrōnae, F: *married woman*, especially a *noble lady*

mātūritās, mātūritātis, F: *maturity, ripeness; proper time; perfection*

matus, mata, matum: *drunk*

maximus, maxima, maximum (superlative of **magnus**): *biggest, largest, greatest*

mē: see **ego**

medicīna, medicīnae, F: *medicine*

medicus, medicī, M: *doctor* (4)

medius, media, medium: *middle, middle of* (2)

mehercules: *by Hercules* (a common exclamation used by men) (2)

mel, mellis, N: *honey*

melior, melius: *better, kinder* (comparative of **bonus**) (8)

Melissa, Melissae, F: *Melissa*, a woman's name that means "bee" in Greek

meliusculus, meliuscula, meliusculum: *a little better*

mementō: imperative of **meminī**

meminī, meminisse (perfect only): *remember*

memoria, memoriae, F: *memory, remembrance*

mendācium, mendāciī, N: *lie*

mendīcus, mendīcī, M: *beggar*

Menelāus, Menelāī, M: *Menelaus*, assistant of the rhetorician Agamemnon; in myth, the younger brother of King Agamemnon

menia, meniae, F: (meaning unclear) *nonsense? triviality?* (hapax legomenon)

Menophila, Menophilae, F: *Menophila*, "Moon-Lover," a well-attested Greek woman's name

mēns, mēntis, F: *mind; attitude; will; reason*

mēnsa, mēnsae, F: *a table; a course* (of a meal) (5)

mēnsis, mēnsis, F: *month*

mēnsūra, mēnsūrae, F: *measurement; size*

mentiō, mentiōnis, F: *mention*

mentior, mentīrī, mentītus sum: *invent, fabricate; lie, act deceitfully* (6)

mentum, mentī, N: *chin*

mercēs, mercēdis, F: *wages; bribe; reward*

Mercurius, Mercuriī, M: god *Mercury*

mereō, merēre, meruī, meritus: *deserve*

merīdiēs, merīdiēī, M: *midday, noon*

merus, mera, merum: *pure, unmixed*

mētior, mētīrī, mēnsus sum: *measure, estimate*

metus, metūs, M: *fear, anxiety*

meus, mea, meum: *my, belonging to me* (1)

mīca, mīcae, F: *crumb, morsel*

mihi: see **ego**

mīles, militis, M: *soldier* (2)

mīliārium, mīliāriī, N: *milestone*

mīlitia, mīlitiae, F: *army; war; the military, military service*

mīlle (singular), **mīlia** or **mīllia, mīlium** (pl.): *thousand* (4)

mīlvīnus, mīlvīna, mīlvīnum: *rapacious, like a bird of prey*

mīlvus, mīlvī, M: *kite, bird of prey*

Minerva, Minervae, F: goddess *Minerva*

minimus, minima, minimum: (comparative of **parvus**) *smallest, least, youngest, very small* (7)

minister, ministrī, M: *servant, helper, waiter*

ministrātor, ministrātōris, M: *assistant, helper; server*

ministrō, ministrāre, ministrāvī, ministrātus: *serve, wait on*

minor, minus (comparative of **parvus**): *smaller; less, inferior; younger*

minus (adverb): *less; not, by no means* (2)

minūtal, minūtālis, N: *bit, piece*

minūtus, minūta, minūtum: *small; petty*

mīror, mīrārī, mīrātus sum: *be amazed at, wonder at, admire* (12)

mīsceō, mīscēre, mīscuī, mīxtus: *mix, mingle*

misellus, misella, misellum: *poor little*

miser, misera, miserum: *pitiful, wretched*

misereor, miserērī, miseritus sum: *pity, feel sorry for*

miseria, miseriae, F: *misery, distress*

misericors, misericordis: *sympathetic, merciful*

missiō, missiōnis, F: *release; dismissal*

mītis, mīte: *ripe; calm, mild*

mittō, mittere, mīsī, missus: *send; throw; dismiss* (4)

mixcix: *given to half measures?* (hapax legomenon)

modicus, modica, modicum: *moderate; modest*

modius, modiī, M: *peck* (unit of measure)

modo (adverb): *only; just now; in a moment* (2)

modus, modī, M: *measure; mode, manner, style*

molestō, molestāre, molestāvī, molestātus: *disturb, annoy*

molestus, molesta, molestum: *annoying, troublesome* (11)

mollis, molle: *soft, tender; effeminate*

mōmentum, mōmentī, N: *motion; moment*

monimentum = monumentum

mōnstrum, mōnstrī, N: *portent; monster*

monumentum, monumentī, N: *reminder, memorial, monument* (2)

mora, morae, F: *delay, pause* (7)

morbōsus, morbōsa, morbōsum: *sickly; crazed;* morbōsus in: *crazy about*

mordeō, mordēre, momordī, morsus: *bite*

mordicus (adverb): *by biting, with the teeth*

morior, morī, mortuus sum (moritūrus): *die* (9)

moror, morārī, morātus sum: *detain, hinder; delay, loiter* (12)

mors, mortis, F: *death* (8)

mortiferus, mortifera, mortiferum: *deadly*

mortuus, mortua, mortuum: *dead* (2)

mōs, mōris, M: *custom, practice, manner* (6)

mōtus, mōtūs, M: *motion, movement*

moveō, movēre, mōvī, mōtus: *move, set in motion; stir, excite* (7)

mox (adverb): *soon*

mū: used to express a muttering sound

mucrō, mucrōnis, M: *edge, point; sword*

mufrius, mufriī, M: *blockhead* (hapax legomenon)

mūla, mūlae, F: *mule*

muliebris, muliebre: *feminine, womanly; effeminate*

mulier, mulieris, F: *woman; wife* (1)

muliercula, mulierculae, F: *little woman*

mūliō, mūliōnis, M: *mule driver*

mulsum, mulsī, N: *mead, honeyed wine*

multus, multa, multum: *many* (5)

mundus, munda, mundum: *neat, fine, sharp*

mūnus, mūneris, N: *service, duty, munificence* (10)

muria, muriae, F: *brine, pickling juice*

murmur, murmuris, N: *murmur, buzz, hum*

mūs, mūris, M or F: *mouse*

Mūsa, Mūsae, F: *Muse*, goddess of artistic inspiration; *talent*

mūsca, mūscae, F: *fly*

mustēlla, mustēllae, F: *weasel*

mūtō, mūtāre, mūtāvī, mūtātus: *change*

muttiō, muttīre, muttīvī, muttītus: *mutter, mumble*

mūtuor, mūtuārī, mūtuātus sum: *borrow, obtain*

mūtuus, mūtua, mūtuum: *mutual; borrowed*

nam (conjunction): *for; yes; on the other hand* (3)

namque (conjunction): *for in fact*

nancīscor, nancīscī, nactus sum: *get, obtain* (5)

nardum, nardī, N: *nard*, an oil scented with spikenard (Greek loan word)

nārrō, nārrāre, nārrāvī, nārrātus: *tell, relate* (4)

nāscor, nāscī, nātus sum: *be born, originate; occur* (5)

nāsus, nāsī, M: *nose; sense of smell*

nātālis, nātāle: *of birth, natal;* diēs nātālis: *birthday*

natō, natāre, natāvī, natātus: *swim (across); float*

nātūra, nātūrae, F: *nature, character*

nausea, nauseae, F: *sickness, nausea*

nāvigō, nāvigāre, nāvigāvī, nāvigātus: *sail across; sail*

nāvis, nāvis, F: *ship*

-ne (enclitic): attaches to the first main word of a clause and marks it as a question

nē (conjunction): *that . . . not, lest; that;* nē . . . quidem (adverb): *not . . . even* (3)

nec (adverb): *not;* (conjunction): *and not, nor* (3)

necdum (conjunction): *and not yet*

necesse (indeclinable adjective): *necessary*

neglegentia, neglegentiae, F: *carelessness, neglect*

negō, negāre, negāvī, negātus: *deny; say no, refuse* (12)

nēmō, nēminis, M or F: *no one, nobody* (1)

nēnia, nēniae, F: *ditty, little song; trifles, playthings*

nēquam (indeclinable adjective): *worthless, bad, good for nothing*

neque (adverb): *not;* (conjunction): *and not, nor*

nēquissimus, nēquissima, nēquissimum: *most worthless*

nēquitia, nēquitiae, F: *worthlessness; wickedness*

nervia, nerviōrum, N pl.: *sinews, tendons*

nervus, nervī, M: *sinew, muscle; strength*

nēsciō, nēscīre, nēscīvī or nēsciī, nēscītus: *not know, be ignorant of; not know how to* (6)

neuter, neutra, neutrum: *neither*

nēve (conjunction): *or not, and not*

Nīcerōs, Nīcerōtis, M: *Niceros,* guest of Trimalchio; "Lover of Victory" or "Victory of Love" in Greek

niger, nigra, nigrum: *black, dark; unlucky*

nihil (indeclinable) N: *nothing* (1); nihilō minus: *nonetheless*

nisi (conjunction): *if not, unless, except* (3)

nivātus, nivāta, nivātum: *cooled with snow*

nōbīs: see nōs

noceō, nocēre, nocuī, nocitum (+ dative): *harm*

nocturnus, nocturna, nocturnum: *nocturnal, at night, by night*

nōlō, nōlle, nōluī: *be unwilling, not want to* (2)

nōmen, nōminis, N: *name* (7)

nōmenclātor or nōmenculātor, nōmenclātōris, M: *name-reminder*

nōminō, nōmināre, nōmināvī, nōminātus: *call by name; make famous; denounce*

nōn (adverb): *not, no, by no means* (1)

nōndum (adverb): *not yet*

Norbānus, Norbānī, M: *Norbanus,* a man's name

nōs (nom. and acc.), nostrum (partitive gen.), nōbīs (dat. and abl.): *we, us* (2)

nōscō, nōscere, nōvī, nōtus: *get to know, learn;* (in perfect) *know, have learned* (4)

noster, nostra, nostrum: *our, belonging to us* (2)

nota, notae, F: *note, mark, sign*

notābilis, notābile: *notable, noteworthy*

nōtō, nōtāre, nōtāvī, nōtātus: *mark, note, observe* (5)

novendiāle, novendiālis, N: *ninth-day festival, funeral feast*

novus, nova, novum: *new, young; unusual*

nox, noctis, F: *night* (1)

noxius, noxia, noxium: *harmful; guilty*

nūdō, nūdāre, nūdāvī, nūdātus: *uncover, lay bare, strip*

nūdus, nūda, nūdum: *nude, bare* (7)

nūgae, nūgārum, F pl.: *nonsense, trivia, trash*

nūllus, nūlla, nūllum (gen. s. nūllīus, dat. s. nūllī): *no, none, not at all* (6)

numerō, numerāre, numerāvī, numerātus: *count, number; pay out; recount, relate*

numerus, numerī, M: *number; rank; part*
nummus, nummī, M: *coin* (8)
numquam (adverb): *never* (5)
numquid (adverb): signals a direct question, or *whether* for an indirect question
nunc (adverb): *now* (2)
nūptiae, nūptiārum, F pl.: *marriage, wedding*

ob (preposition + accusative): *before; on account of, for the sake of*
obdormiō, obdormīre, obdormīvī or **obdormiī, obdormītum**: *fall asleep*
obdūcō, obdūcere, obdūxī, obductus: *lead toward; extend; obstruct; close*
obeō, obīre, obīvī or **obiī, obitum**: *go to meet; travel; meet one's death, pass away*
obfutūrus: see **obsum**
obiter (adverb): *along the way, in passing*
obiūrgō, obiūrgāre, obiūrgāvī, obiūrgātus: *scold; correct; deter*
obligātus, obligāta, obligātum: *obliged*
oblīvīscor, oblīvīscī, oblītus sum: *forget* (4)
obscēnus, obscēna, obscēnum: *obscene, dirty, perverted*
obsōnium, obsōniī, N: *shopping items, groceries, food* (Greek loan word)
obsum, obesse, obfuī, obfutūrus: *be against, be harmful to*
occāsiō, occāsiōnis, F: *opportunity, chance*
occidō, occidere, occidī, occāsum: *fall; be ruined* (5)
occīdō, occīdere, occīdī, occīsus: *kill, murder* (5)
occupō, occupāre, occupāvī, occupātus: *occupy, seize*
Occupō, Occupōnis, M: *Occupo*, a god of opportunity(?) (hapax legomenon)
occurrō, occurrere, occucurrī, occursus: *run up to, meet, encounter*
ōcius (adverb): *rather swiftly; immediately*
ocrea, ocreae, F: *greave, shin guard*
oculus, oculī, M: *eye* (5)

ōdarium, ōdariī, N: *little song, ditty* (Greek loan word)
odor, odōris, M: *odor, smell*
oecārium, oecāriī, N: *little room* (Greek loan word)
offendō, offendere, offendī, offensus: *bump, strike; stumble upon; offend, annoy*
offēnsa, offēnsae, F: *offense, displeasure*
officium, officiī, N: *service, favor, duty, obligation* (7)
offla, offlae, F: *piece of food, bit of meat*
oleum, oleī, N: *olive oil*
ōlim (adverb): *once, once upon a time; at times*; **ōliōrum**: invented genitive plural (hapax legomenon), *time of times, once upon a times ago*
Olympius, Olympia, Olympium: *Olympian, of Olympus*, home of the gods
omnis, omne: *all, every* (1)
onager, onagrī, M: *wild ass*
onerō, onerāre, onerāvī, onerātus: *load, burden, pile on*
onus, oneris, N: *burden, load; trouble*
opera, operae, F: *trouble, pain; effort; attention*
operiō, operīre, operuī, opertus: *cover, shut, hide* (9)
Opīmiānus, Opīmiāna, Opīmiānum: *from the consulship of Opīmius*, 121 BCE; *wine* of this vintage
oportet, oportēre, oportuit: *it is right, it is proper*
oppessulō, oppessulāre, oppessulāvī, oppessulātus: *bolt, bar*
oppōnō, oppōnere, opposuī, oppositus: *put; oppose; expose*
opportūnus, opportūna, opportūnum: *opportune, convenient, useful*
opprimō, opprimere, oppressī, oppressus: *press down, pressure; overthrow, crush*
ops, opis, F: *power; help, aid*
optābilis, optābile: *desirable*
optimus, optima, optimum: (superlative of **bonus**) *very good, best, excellent* (4)

optiō, optiōnis, F: *option, choice*

optō, optāre, optāvī, optātus: *choose; wish for*

opus, operis, N: *work; achievement; task;*
opus est: *there is a need* (+ ablative of
thing needed)

ōrātiō, ōrātiōnis, F: *speech, eloquence; oration*

Orcus, Orcī, M: *Orcus, god of death; the
underworld; death*

ōrdinō, ōrdināre, ōrdināvī, ōrdinātus: *set
in order; govern*

ōrdior, ōrdīrī, ōrsus sum: *begin*

ōrdō, ōrdinis, M: *row; order; class, rank*

ōrō, ōrāre, ōrāvī, ōrātus: *beg, entreat*

ōs, ōris, N: *mouth, lip* (11)

os, ossis, N: *bone*

ōsculor, ōsculārī, ōsculātus sum: *kiss; make
a fuss over*

ōsculum, ōsculī, N: *kiss; mouth, lips*

ossuculum, ossuculī, N: *small bone*

ostendō, ostendere, ostendī, ostentus:
show, point out, reveal (9)

ōstiārius, ōstiāriī, M: *doorman*

ōvum, ōvī, N: *egg*

paene (adverb): *nearly, almost* (6)

paenitet, paenitēre, paenituit (impersonal
verb): *cause regret, displease*

palam (adverb): *openly, publicly;*
(preposition + ablative) *in the presence of*

pallium, palliī, N: wool *cloak* (Greek
loan word)

palma, palmae, F: *palm branch; victory
prize; victory*

palmula, palmulae, F: *oar blade; date* (fruit)

pānis, pānis, M: *bread* (2)

pannus, pannī, M: *rag, worn cloth*

Pānsa, Pānsae, M: *Pansa*, a Roman cognomen

pantomīmus, pantomīmī, M: *pantomime
actor*, someone who performed
scenes mutely with music and choral
accompaniment (Greek loan word)

papāver, papāveris, N: *poppy, poppy seed*

papilla, papillae, F: *nipple, breast*

pār, paris: *equal, like; suitable, well-matched*
(9)

pār, paris, N: *pair, couple* (9)

paralysis, paralysis, F: *paralysis, numbness*
(Greek loan word)

Parca, Parcae, F: goddess of *Fate*

parcō, parcere, pepercī, parsus (+ dative):
spare, use sparingly; treat mercifully

parēns, parentis, M or F: *parent, relative*

parentālia, parentāliōrum, N pl.: *Parentalia*,
festival in honor of dead ancestors

parentō, parentāre, parentāvī, parentātus:
*honor with a funeral service, celebrate at
the* **Parentālia**; *pay last respects; avenge*

pāreō, pārēre, pāruī, pāritum: *appear;*
(+ dative) *obey, yield to, satisfy* (12)

pariēs, parietis, M: *wall* (of a house or
building) (11)

pariō, parere, peperī, partus: *give birth
to, bear*

pariter (adverb): *equally; at the same time*

pārō, pārāre, pārāvī, pārātus: *prepare,
provide, acquire* (12)

parōnychium, parōnychiī, N: *hangnail,
inflammation of the fingernail;*
parōnychia . . . tollere: *lift the hangnails,
give a pedicure* (Greek loan word)

paropsis, paropsidis, F: *dish* (Greek
loan word)

parricīdālis, parricīdāle: *parricidal, murderous*

pars, partis, F: *part* (4)

parserō: from an overcorrected perfect stem
of **parceō**

partiō, partīre, partīvī, partītus:
share, distribute

parum (adverb): *too little, insufficiently*

parvus, parva, parvum: *small, young*

pāscō, pāscere, pāvī, pāstus: *feed*

pāssus, pāssa, pāssum: *spread out,
disheveled*

pataracinum, pataracinī, N: *large drinking
cup(?)* (hapax legomenon)

pater, patris, M: *father* (5)

patior, patī, passus sum: *experience, suffer; allow* (10)

patria, patriae, F: *fatherland, native land*

patrimōnium, patrimōniī, N: *patrimony, inheritance*

paucī, paucae, pauca: *few*

paulisper (adverb): *for a little while*

paulō (adverb): *a little, somewhat*

paululum (adverb): *a little, to some extent*

pauper, pauperis: *poor, not wealthy*

peccātum, peccātī, N: *error, mistake*

peccō, peccāre, peccāvī, peccātum: *make a mistake, slip*

pectus, pectoris, N: *breast, chest; heart, soul* (10)

pecūnia, pecūniae, F: *money, property*

pecus, pecoris, N: *herd of cattle; flock of sheep*

pēduclus, pēduclī, M: *louse*

pendeō, pendēre, pependī: *hang, be suspended; be uncertain*

pēnsum, pēnsī, N: *wool to be spun; work, task*

penthiacum, penthiacī, N: *hash* (in myth, King Pentheus was torn to shreds; hapax legomenon)

pepercī: see **parceō**

peperī: see **pariō**

per (preposition + accusative): *through* (3)

perbāsiō, perbāsiāre: *kiss thoroughly*

percoquō, percoquere, percoxī, percoctus: *cook thoroughly*

percutiō, percutere, percussī, percussus: *hit hard, strike, smash*

perdō, perdere, perdidī, perditus: *ruin; waste; lose* (10)

peregrīnus, peregrīna, peregrīnum: *foreign; strange; inexperienced*

pereō, perīre, perīvī or **periī, peritum:** *pass away, die, be lost, be ruined*

pererrō, pererrāre, pererrāvī, pererrātus: *roam around; survey*

perfodiō, perfodere, perfōdī, perfossus: *dig through, stab, pierce*

perfundō, perfundere, perfūdī, perfūsus: *drench; sprinkle*

Pergamum, Pergamī, N: *Pergamum,* a city in the Roman province of Asia (see map)

pergō, pergere, perrēxī, perrēctus: *continue, proceed*

perīclitor, perīclitārī, perīclitātus sum: *be in danger*

perīculum, perīculī, N: *danger, risk*

periscelis, periscelidis, F: *anklet* (Greek loan word)

peristasis, peristasis, F: *theme, topic* treated by a speaker (Greek loan word)

perlegō, perlegere, perlēgī, perlēctus: *scan, read through*

permittō, permittere, permīsī, permissus: *let through; give up; permit*

persequor, persequī, persecūtus sum: *follow; chase; imitate*

perseverō, perseverāre, perseverāvī, perseverātus: *persist in; persevere*

persuādeō, persuadēre, persuasī, persuasum: (with dative) *persuade, convince* (10)

pertinācia, pertināciae, F: *stubbornness*

pertineō, pertinēre, pertinuī: *reach; pervade; concern, pertain to*

pertrectō, pertrectāre, pertrectāvī, pertrectātus: *handle; examine in detail*

perveniō, pervenīre, pervēnī, perventum: *come to, reach; arrive*

perversus, perversa, perversum: *turned, awry, crooked, perverse*

pēs, pedis, M: *foot* (1)

pessimē (adverb): *worst, most wickedly, most unfortunately*

petauristārius, petauristāriī, M: *acrobat, trapeze artist*

petō, petere, petīvī or **petiī, petītus:** *make for, go to; seek, strive after; ask for, beg* (6)

Petraites, Petraitis, M: *Petraites,* famous gladiator of Nero's time

phaecasia, phaecasiae, F: *slipper* (Greek loan word)

phaecasiātus, phaecasiāta, phaecasiātum: *wearing* phaecasiae, *slippered*

phalerātus, phalerāta, phalerātum: *wearing medals, decorated* (Greek loan word)

Philargyrus, Philargyrī, M: *Philargyrus*, man's name meaning "Silver Lover" or "Fond of Money" in Greek

Philerōs, Philerōtis, M: *Phileros*, man's name meaning "Lover of Desire" in Greek, a common slave name

philosophus, philosophī, M: *philosopher* (Greek loan word)

pīca, pīcae, F: *magpie, jay*

pictor, pictōris, M: *painter*

pignus, pigneris, N: *pledge, security*

pigritia, pigritiae, F: *laziness*

pīla, pīlae, F: *pillar*

pila, pilae, F: *ball; ball game*

pilleātus, pilleāta, pilleātum: *wearing the cap of freedom, freed*

pilleum, pilleī, N: *felt cap* given to slaves as they were freed; *freedom*

pilus, pilī, M: *hair; a bit, trifle*; **nōn pilī facere**: *consider worthless*

pingō, pingere, pīnxī, pictus: *paint, depict*

pinguis, pingue: *fat*

pinna, pinnae, F: *feather; quill*

piper, piperis, N: *black pepper*

piscīna, piscīnae, F: *fish pond; pool*

piscis, piscis, M: *fish*

pīstor, pīstōris, M: *miller, baker*

pīsum, pīsī, N: *pea*

pittacium, pittaciī, N: *small bit of cloth; label* (Greek loan word)

pius, pia, pium: *dutiful; god-fearing*

placenta, placentae, F: *flat cake* (Greek loan word)

placeō, placēre, placuī, placitus: (+ dative) *please, satisfy, pleasure* (4)

placitus, placita, placitum: *pleasing; acceptable*

plācō, plācāre, plācāvī, plācātus: *calm, quiet, appease; reconcile*

plāga, plāgae, F: *blow, lash; cut, slit*

plānctus, plānctūs, M: *beating*

plānē (adverb): *clearly, certainly, quite* (2)

plangō, plangere, plānxī, plānctus: *beat; beat one's breast, lament*

planus, planī, M: *con man, grifter*

plaudō, plaudere, plausī, plausus: *slap, beat; clap, applaud*

plēnus, plēna, plēnum: *full* (4)

plērumque (adverb): *generally, mostly; often*

plōdō = plaudō

plōrō, plōrāre, plōrāvī, plōrātus: *mourn, cry over; wail, cry* (8)

plovō, plovere, plovuī: *rain*

plūrimus, plūrima, plūrimum (superlative of **multus**): *many, most, very much*

plūs, plūris: (comparative of **multus**): *more*; **plūs** (adverb): *more* (4)

poēma, poēmatis, N: *poem; poetry* (Greek loan word)

poena, poenae, F: *punishment, penalty*

polluō, polluere, polluī, pollūtus: *pollute, violate, dirty, soil*

Polyaenus or Polyaenos, Polyaenī, M: *much praised* in Greek, a common epithet of Odysseus in both the *Iliad* and *Odyssey*

polymitus, polymita, polymitum: *many-colored, woven of different colors* (Greek loan word)

pompa, pompae, F: *procession, parade*

Pompēius, Pompēiī, M: *Pompeius*, a Roman family name

pōmum, pōmī, N: *piece of fruit* (6)

pondus, ponderis, N: *weight; burden*

pōnō, pōnere, posuī, positus: *put, set, place* (1)

populus, populī, M: *the people, the public; crowd* (12)

porcellus, porcellī, M: *little pig*

porcus, porcī, M: *pig* (5)

porrigō, porrigere, porrēxī, porrēctus: *reach out, stretch out, extend* (12)

portentum, portentī, N: *portent, sign; abnormal event; trick, marvel*

porticus, porticūs, F: *portico, colonnade; gallery* (10)

pōscō, pōscere, popōscī: *ask for, request* (4)

possum, posse, potuī: *be able* (1)

post (conjunction): *after, behind, later;*
  (preposition + accusative) *behind, after* (5)

posteā (adverb): *afterward*

posterus, postera, posterum: *next, following,*
  subsequent (12)

postis, postis, M: *doorpost, door*

postquam (conjunction): *after, when* (3)

potentia, potentiae, F: *force, power*

potestās, potestātis, F: *power, ability, authority*

pōtiō, pōtiōnis, F: *drinking; a drink* (7)

pōtiuncula, pōtiunculae, F: *a little drink*

potius quam (adverb): *more than, rather than*

pōtō, pōtāre, pōtāvī, pōtātus: *drink*

prae (preposition + ablative): *before, in*
  front of

praebeō, praebēre, praebuī, praebitus: *offer*

praecēdō, praecēdere, praecessī,
  praecessum: *precede, lead; excel*

praeceps, praecipitis: *steep; swift, hasty*

praecīdō, praecīdere, praecīdī, praecīsus:
  lop off, cut, damage

praecipiō, praecipere, praecēpī, praeceptus:
  take before; admonish, advise; teach

praecipuē (adverb): *especially, chiefly* (10)

praeclūdō, praeclūdere, praeclusī,
  praeclusus: *close in front of, shut against*

praecō, praecōnis, M: *herald, public crier* (11)

praeda, praedae, F: *plunder, spoils; prey*

praedātor, praedātōris, M: *plunderer, looter*

praeferō, praeferre, praetulī, praelātus:
  hold out, carry in front; prefer

praepōnō, praepōnere, praeposuī,
  praepositus: *place; serve; entrust*

praesēns, praesentis: *present, in person, at hand*

praesidium, praesidiī, N: *protection, guard;*
  bodyguard, escort

praestō (adverb): *at hand, ready;* praestō
  esse: *be on hand (for), attend, aid*

praestō, praestāre, praestitī, praestitus: *be*
  superior to; display

praeter (adverb): *by, past;* (conjugation)
  besides, other than; (preposition +

accusative) *past, in front of, beyond; in*
  addition to; except

praetereā (adverb): *besides; hereafter*

praetereō, praeterīre, praeterīvī or
  praeteriī, praeteritus: *go past, skip;*
  escape notice of; overlook

praetextātus, praetextāta, praetextātum:
  wearing the toga praetexta (worn by
  magistrates and boys); *crimson-bordered*

praetextus, praetextūs, M: *show,*
  appearance; pretext

praetor, praetōris, M: *praetor, a high-ranking*
  magistrate often in charge of courts

praetōrius locus, praetōriī locī, M: *seat*
  of honor

praetulī: see praeferō

prandeō, prandēre, prandī, pransus: *eat*
  breakfast, eat lunch

prasinātus, prasināta, prasinātum: *wearing*
  a green garment (hapax legomenon)

prasiniānus, prasiniāna, prasiniānum:
  supporting the Greens (a chariot-racing team)

prasinus, prasina, prasinum: *green; green*
  team in chariot racing (7)

pretium, pretiī, N: *price, value; reward, bribe*

prex, precis, F: *prayer, request; curse*

Priāpus, Priāpī, M: *Priapus, a Roman*
  fertility god

Prīmigenius, Prīmigeniī, M: *Primigenius,*
  name meaning "Firstborn" in Latin

prīmitus (adverb): *at first*

prīmō or prīmum (adverb): *first, at first* (2)

prīmus, prīma, prīmum: *first, foremost,*
  front (2)

prīncipium, prīncipiī, N: *beginning; origin*

prior, prius: *previous, former, earlier;*
  first; preferable

prīvātus, prīvāta, prīvātum: *private, personal*

prō (preposition + abl.): *before, in front of;*
  on behalf of; instead of (5)

prōcēdō, prōcēdere, prōcessī, prōcessum:
  proceed

procella, procellae, F: *storm, squall*

prōclāmō, prōclāmāre, prōclāmāvī, prōclāmātus: *yell; exclaim, cry out that* (4)

prōcubō, prōcubāre, prōcubuī: *lie stretched out*

prōditiō, prōditiōnis, F: *betrayal; treason*

prōdō, prōdere, prōdidī, prōditus: *bring out, reveal, relate; surrender*

proelior, proeliārī, proeliātus sum: *battle, fight*

prōferō, prōferre, prōtulī, prōlātus: *bring forward, produce*

prōiciō, prōicere, prōiēcī, prōiectus: *throw out; abandon; exile; delay*

prōmittō, prōmittere, prōmīsī, prōmissus: *send forth; promise*

properō, properāre, properāvī, properātus: *speed up; be quick, rush*

propīn, N (nominative and accusative only): *drink, aperitif* (Greek loan word)

propinquus, propinqua, propinquum: *near, neighboring*

propinquus, propinquī, M: *relative, someone close*

propitius, propitia, propitium: *propitious toward, favorable to*

propter (preposition + accusative): *near, next to; on account of, because of* (6)

prōsequor, prōsequī, prōsecūtus sum: *escort; pursue, follow*

prōsiliō, prōsilīre, prōsiluī: *jump forward, rush out*

prōspectus, prōspectūs, M: *view; sight*

prōsum, prōdesse, prōfuī, prōfutūrus (+ dative): *be of use, benefit, profit*

prōtulī: see prōferō

prōvideō, prōvidēre, prōvīdī, prōvīsus: *see in the distance; foresee; look after, care for*

prōvincia, prōvinciae, F: *province; sphere of administration, public office*

prōvōcō, prōvōcāre, prōvōcāvī, prōvōcātus: *challenge; exasperate*

proximus, proxima, proximum: *nearest, next, adjoining* (10)

prūdēns, prūdentis: *foreseeing; aware; skilled; discreet*

pūblicō, pūblicāre, pūblicāvī, pūblicātus: *throw open to the public, publish*

pūblicus, pūblica, pūblicum: *public; common, ordinary* (8)

pudet, pudēre, puduit (impersonal): *it shames, it causes shame* (with genitive of the thing causing the shame, e.g., mē puerī pudet, *I am ashamed of the boy*)

pudīcitia, pudīcitiae, F: *chastity, purity, modesty* (12)

pudīcus, pudīca, pudīcum: *chaste, pure, modest* (11)

pudor, pudōris, M: *shame, modesty*

puella, puellae, F: *girl; girlfriend*

puer, puerī, M: *boy; slave* (1)

pugna, pugnae, F: *fight, fistfight, brawl*

pugnāx, pugnācis: *pugnacious, aggressive*

pugnō, pugnāre, pugnāvī, pugnātus: *fight, contend*

pulcher, pulchra, pulchrum: *beautiful*

pullārius, pullāriī, M: *chicken-keeper;* slang for *pederast*

pullus, pullī, M: *young, chick; chicken*

pultārius, pultāriī, M: *cooking pot*

pulvīnar, pulvīnāris, N: *cushioned couch*

pungō, pungere, pupugī, pūnctus: *prick, poke*

purgāmenta, purgāmentōrum, N pl.: *filth, trash*

purgō, purgāre, purgāvī, purgātus: *clean*

pūrus, pūra, pūrum: *clean, pure*

pusillus, pusilla, pusillum: *puny, petty*

puteus, puteī, M: *well; pit*

pūtidus, pūtida, pūtidum: *stinking, rotten*

putō, putāre, putāvī, putātus: *consider, weigh, imagine, think* (2)

pyxis, pyxidis, F: *small box, jewelry box* (Greek loan word)

quadrāgēsimus, quadrāgēsima, quadrāgēsimum: *fortieth*

quadrāgintā (indeclinable adjective): *forty*

quadrāns, quadrantis, M: *quarter, tiny coin* worth a quarter of an **ās**

quadrātus, quadrāta, quadrātum: *square, block*

quadringentī, quadringentae, quadringenta: *four hundred*

quaerō, quaerere, quaesīvī, quaesītus: *look for, seek; miss; ask, investigate* (9)

quaestiō, quaestiōnis, F: *inquiry, investigation*

quaestor, quaestōris, M: *quaestor,* magistrate in charge of the treasury or an assistant to a provincial governor

quālis, quāles: *what sort of? what kind of?; of such a kind, such as, as*

quam (adverb): *how? how much?; than, as* (in comparisons); *as . . . as possible* (with superlatives) (1)

quamdiū (conjunction): *as long as*

quamquam (conjunction): *although, though*

quamvīs (adverb): *however; ever so*

quandō (adverb): *when? at what time?*

quantō (adverb): *how much? by how much?*

quantum (adverb): *as much as, so much as; how much? how far? to what extent?*

quārē (adverb): *how, by what means; why; why? for what reason?* (4)

quasi (adverb): *as it were; nearly;* (conjunction) *on the grounds that*

quassō, quassāre: *shake, wave; smash*

quassus, quassa, quassum: *shattered, broken*

quater (adverb): *four times*

quattuor (indeclinable adjective): *four*

-que (enclitic conjunction): *and* (connects attached word or phrase to preceding word or phrase) (3)

quemadmodum (adverb): *in what way, how;* (conjunction) *just as, as* (8)

queror, querī, questus sum: *complain; lament*

quī, quae, quod (relative pronoun): *who, what, that;* (interrogative adjective) *which? what?*

quia (conjunction): *because* (3); (in later Latin) *that*

quicquam, cūiusquam (pronoun): *anything*

quicquid: see **quisquis**

quid (adverb): *how? why?;* (pronoun) *what?* (3)

quīdam, quaedam, quiddam (pronoun): *a certain person, a certain one, a certain thing* (4)

quidem (adverb): *indeed; at least; of course; for example* (1)

quiēs, quiētis, F: *quiet, rest, peace; sleep*

quīnam, quaenam, quodnam: *which, just which, just what*

quīnquāgintā (indeclinable adjective): *fifty*

quīnque (indeclinable adjective): *five*

quīntus, quīnta, quīntum: *fifth*

quis, quid (interrogative pronoun): *who? what?*

quisquam, quidquam (pronoun): *anyone, anything*

quisque, quaeque, quodque: *each* (4)

quisquis, quidquid or **quicquid**: *whoever, whatever, anyone who, anything that* (4)

quīvīs, quaevīs, quidvīs: *anyone, whoever you wish*

quō (adverb): *where? what for?;* (conjunction) *where, whereby*

quod (conjunction): *because; as for the fact that, insofar as, as far as*

quōmodo (interrogative adverb): *how? in what way?* (7)

quoniam (conjunction): *because, now that*

quoque (adverb): *too* (follows word it emphasizes) (3)

quot (indeclinable): *how many?; as many as*

quotiē(n)scumque (adverb): *as often as, however often*

quotus, quota, quotum: *which? what number?*

rapiō, rapere, rapuī, raptus: *seize, carry off* (2)

raptim (adverb): *hurriedly; suddenly*

ratiō, ratiōnis, F: *calculation, reckoning; situation; reason, grounds; reasoning* (12)

ratiōcinor, ratiōcinārī, ratiōcinātus sum: *calculate; keep accounts; reason* ratus: see reor

recēdō, recēdere, recessī, recessum: *go back, recede, give ground, depart*

recēns, recentis: *recent, fresh, young*

recipiō, recipere, recēpī, receptus: *keep back, bring back, retake, accept; undertake*

recitō, recitāre, recitāvī, recitātus: *read out, recite; appoint*

recreō, recreāre, recreāvī, recreātus: *restore, revive*

rēctā (adverb): *by a direct route, straight*

rēctē (adverb): *in a straight line; correctly, well*

recumbō, recumbere, recubuī: *lie back, recline*

recūsō, recūsāre, recūsāvī, recūsātus: *reject, refuse; be reluctant*

recutītus, recutīta, recutītum: *circumcised*

reddō, reddere, reddidī, redditus: *give back; repay; repeat* (11)

redeō, redīre, redīvī or rediī, reditum: *go back*

redimiō, redimīre, redimīvī, redimītus: *crown, wreath; encircle*

redimō, redimere, redēmī, redemptus: *buy back, ransom, pay off, atone for*

referō, referre, retulī, relātus: *bring back; reply*

reficiō, reficere, refēcī, refectus: *make again; repair; refresh*

regiō, regiōnis, F: *line; area, neighborhood*

relaxō, relaxāre, relaxāvī, relaxātus: *open, loosen, relax; cheer up*

relēgō, relēgāre, relēgāvī, relēgātus: *send away*

religiōsus, religiōsa, religiōsum: *pious; scrupulous; superstitious*

relinquō, relinquere, relīquī, relictus: *leave, leave behind* (8)

reliquiae, reliquiārum, F pl.: *remains, leftovers*

reliquus, reliqua, reliquum: *remaining, left over; subsequent*

remittō, remittere, remīsī, remissus: *send back; slacken; give up; pardon*

removeō, removēre, remōvī, remōtus: *move back, remove*

renovō, renovāre, renovāvī, renovātus: *renovate, restore, revive, repeat*

reor, rēri, ratus sum: *reckon, think, suppose* (9)

repente (adverb): *suddenly, unexpectedly*

repetō, repetere, repetīvī or repetiī, repetītus: *head back to; seek again; retake*

repleō, replēre, replēvī, replētus: *refill, fill; replace*

repōnō, repōnere, reposuī, repositus: *put back, replace; preserve*

repositōrium, repositōriī, N: *large serving dish, portable stand*

repugnō, repugnāre, repugnāvī, repugnātus: *fight back, oppose, disagree with*

repulsus, repulsa, repulsum: *rejected, spurned*

requiēscō, requiēscere, requiēvī, requiētus: *put to rest, calm down; rest, take a rest*

rēs, reī or rēī, F: *thing, matter, situation, job* (2)

rescrībō, rescrībere, rescrīpsī, rescrīptus: *write back, reply*

resecō, resecāre, resecāvī, resecātus: *cut back, cut short, trim*

resiliō, resilīre, resiliī: *spring back from, shrink from, resist*

respergō, respergere, respersī, respersus: *sprinkle, splash*

respiciō, respicere, respexī, respectus: *look back at, gaze at, regard* (8)

respondeō, respondēre, respondī, responsus: *answer, reply*

restis, restis, F: *rope*

restituō, restituere, restituī, restitūtus: *restore, revive*

resupīnō, resupīnāre, resupīnāvī, resupīnātus: *throw on one's back, throw down*

rētia, rētiae, F: *net*

retineō, retinēre, retinuī, retentus: *hold back*

retulī: see referō

reus, reī, M: *defendant, the accused*

rēvērā (adverb): *in fact, actually*

revertō, revertere, revertī or revertor, revertī, reversus sum: *turn back, come back*

revīvīscō, revīvīscere, revīvīxī,: *revive, recover*

revocō, revocāre, revocāvī, revocātus: *call back, recall; revive*

rēx, rēgis, M: *king*

rhētorica, rhētoricae, F: *rhetoric, public speaking* (Greek loan word)

ricinus, ricinī, M: *tick, parasite*

rīdeō, rīdēre, rīsī, rīsus: *laugh at, deride; smile* (4)

rīdiclus = rīdiculus

rīdiculus, rīdicula, rīdiculum: *funny, silly*

rigēns, rigentis: *stiff, rigid*

rīsus, rīsī, M: *laugh, smile*

rīxa, rīxae, F: *fight, squabble* (11)

rixor, rixārī, rixātus sum: *brawl, fight*

rogō, rogāre, rogāvī, rogātus: *ask, ask for* (4)

Rōma, Rōmae, F: city of *Rome;* goddess *Roma*

Rōmānus, Rōmāna, Rōmānum: *Roman*

rubor, rubōris, M: *redness; blush; shame*

rubricātus, rubricāta, rubricātum: *red-lined; legal* (law books had titles underlined in red)

rūga, rūgae, F: *wrinkle, crease, fold*

ruīna, ruīnae, F: *fall, collapse, catastrophe*

rumpō, rumpere, rūpī, ruptus: *break*

rūrsus (adverb): *back; in turn*

russeus, russea, russeum: *brownish red*

rūsticus, rūstica, rūsticum: *of the country, rustic, plain, coarse*

rūta, rūtae, F: *rue* (bitter herb)

sacculus, sacculī, M: *little bag, sack*

sacer, sacra, sacrum: *sacred, holy, consecrated*

sacrāmentum, sacrāmentī, N: *guarantee, oath*

sacrum, sacrī, N: *holy thing, sacrifice, rite*

saeculum, saeculī, N: *generation, lifetime, era*

saepe (adverb): *often*

saepius: *more frequently*

sagīnō, sagīnāre, sagīnāvī, sagīnātus: *fatten, feed, cram*

salāx, salācis: *fond of leaping; salacious, lustful, horny*

salīva, salīve, F: *saliva; taste, flavor*

salix, salicis, F: *willow tree*

saltem (adverb): *at least, in any event;* nōn saltem: *not even* (11)

saltō, saltāre, saltāvī, saltātus: *dance*

salūs, salūtis, F: *health, prosperity; greeting*

salūtō, salūtāre, salūtāvī, salūtātus: *greet, wish well*

salveō, salvēre: *be in good health, be well*

salvus, salva, salvum: *well, safe, unharmed*

sānē (adverb): *sanely, reasonably, very*

sanguis, sanguinis, M: *blood* (5)

sangunculum, sangunculī, N: *blood sausage* or perhaps *blood sauce* (hapax legomenon)

sānitās, sānitātis, F: *health, sanity*

sānus, sāna, sānum: *sound, healthy, sane*

sapiō, sapere, sapīvī: *have the flavor of, taste like; understand; have sense, be wise*

saplūtus, saplūta, saplūtum: *exceedingly rich* (Greek loan word; hapax legomenon)

sarcinulae, sarcinulārum, F pl.: *small bundles*

satagō, satagere, satēgī: *have trouble enough, have one's hands full*

satietās, satietātis, F: *sufficiency, satiety*

satiō, satiāre, satiāvī, satiātus: *satisfy, appease*

satis (adverb): *enough, sufficiently;* (indeclinable noun): *enough* (8); satis facere (+ dative): *make amends, make reparation, satisfy a debt*

satius est: *it is better, it is preferable*

satur, satura, saturum: *sated, well-fed*

Sāturnālia, Sāturnālium, N pl.: *Saturnalia,* festival of Saturn in December

saucius, saucia, saucium: *wounded; smashed; drunk*

scālae, scālārum, F pl.: *ladder*

scelus, sceleris, N: *crime, evil deed*

scholasticus, scholasticī, M: *rhetoric teacher, rhetorician* (Greek loan word)

scīlicet (adverb): *evidently, certainly, of course*

scindō, scindere, scidī, scissus: *cut*

scinīphēs, scinīphum, M pl.: *insects, bedbugs* (Greek loan word)

Scintilla, Scintillae, F: *Scintilla,* woman's name from the Latin word for *spark* or *flame*

sciō, scīre, scīvī or **sciī, scītus**: *know; know how to* (2)

scīscitor, scīscitārī, scīscitātus sum: *ask, consult*

Scissa, Scissae, F: *Scissa,* woman's name meaning "Shrill" in Latin

scītus, scīta, scītum: *neat, excellent*

scōpae, scōpārum, F pl.: *broom*

scriblīta, scriblītae, F: *cheese cake, cheese tart* (Greek loan word)

scrībō, scrībere, scrīpsī, scrīptus: *write* (12)

scrōfa, scrōfae, F: *sow*

scrūpus, scrūpī, M: *sharp stone*

scrūta, scrūtōrum, N pl.: *frippery, trash*

scrūtor, scrūtārī, scrūtātus sum: *scrutinize, look closely*

sculpō, sculpere, sculpsī, sculptus: *carve*

scūtum, scūtī, N: *shield, large quadrangular shield* used by Roman legionaries

Scylax, Scylācis, M: *Scylax,* dog's name meaning "Puppy" in Greek

scyphus, scyphī, M: *cup, goblet* (Greek loan word)

sēcessus, sēcessūs, M: *retreat, isolation, reflection*

secō, secāre, secuī, sectus: *cut, carve*

sēcrētum, sēcrētī, N: *a secret, mystery* (12)

sēcrētus, sēcrēta, sēcrētum: *separate, solitary, secret* (12)

secundum (adverb): *after, behind;* (preposition + accusative) *beside, alongside; immediately after* (12)

secūris, secūris, F: *axe*

secūtulēia, secūtulēiae, F: *follower; sycophant? stalker? groupie?* (hapax legomenon)

sed (conjunction): *but, but also* (1)

sedeō, sedēre, sēdī, sessum: *sit, remain sitting* (8)

Seleucus, Seleucī, M: *Seleucus,* one of Trimalchio's guests; name of a line of Hellenistic kings of Syria

semel (adverb): *once; ever*

sēmen, sēminis, N: *seed*

sēmēsus, sēmēsa, sēmēsum: *half-eaten*

sēmihōra, sēmihōrae, F: *half-hour*

sēmis, sēmissis, M: *half; half an* **ās**, *small coin*

sempiternus, sempiterna, sempiternum: *everlasting*

senecta, senectae, F: *old age, senility*

senex, senis, M: *old man*

sententia, sententiae, F: *opinion, intention, verdict*

sentiō, sentīre, sēnsī, sēnsus: *feel, perceive, realize, think* (9)

sepeliō, sepelīre, sepeliī, sepultus: *bury*

septuāgintā (indeclinable adjective): *seventy*

sepulchrum, sepulchrī, N: *grave, tomb*

sepultūra, sepultūrae, F: *burial*

sequor, sequī, secūtus sum: *follow* (5)

sērius, sēria, sērium: *serious, earnest*

sermō, sermōnis, M: *conversation, talk* (10)

sērō (adverb): *late, too late*

servīlis, servīle: *slave, servile*

serviō, servīre, servīvī or **serviī, servītum**: *be a slave, be obedient, serve* (4)

servitūs, servitūtis, F: *slavery; slaves*

servō, servāre, servāvī, servātus: *watch over, keep, preserve, protect* (4)

servulus, servulī, M: *young slave, little slave*

servus, serva, servum: *slave* (1)

sēstertiārius, sēstertiāria, sēstertiārium: *worth a* **sēstertius**, *worth little*

sēstertius, sēstertiī, M: *sesterce,* a small silver coin worth a quarter of a **dēnārius** or two and a half **assēs** and used as the

base unit in accounting; often used with
an understood **milia**, *thousands*

sevēritās, sevēritātis, F: *severity, seriousness*

sevērus, sevēra, sevērum: *severe; grim*

sēvir, sēvirī, M: *one on a board of six; priest
of the imperial cult*

sēviratus, sēviratūs, M: *office of a* **sēvir**

sexennis, sexenne: *six-year-old*

sī (conjunction): *if* (1)

sibi (dat.), **sē** (acc. and abl.): *oneself, himself,
herself, itself, themselves* (third person
reflexive) (4)

sīc (adverb): *thus, so, in this way; yes* (2)

siccitās, siccitātis, F: *dryness, drought*

siccus, sicca, siccum: *dry; thirsty; solid,
firm* (12)

Sicilia, Siciliae, F: *Sicily*

sīcut (conjunction): *as, just as, like*

**significō, significāre, significāvī,
significātus**: *show, indicate*

signum, signī, N: *sign, signal; figure, statue*

silentium, silentiī, N: *silence; inactivity*

sileō, silēre, siluī: *leave unmentioned;
be silent*

silva, silvae, F: *woods, forest*

silvāticus, silvātica, silvāticum: *of the woods*

similis, simile: *similar, resembling, like* (11)

simul (adverb): *together, at the same time*

simulō, simulāre, simulāvī, simulātus:
imitate; pretend

sine (preposition + ablative): *without* (3)

singulāris, singulāre: *single, alone, individual*

singulī, singulae, singula: *one at a time,
one each*

sinister, sinistra, sinistrum: *left, left-hand;
wrong, perverse, unfavorable*

sinō, sinere, sīvī, situs: *allow*

sinus, sinūs, M: *curve, fold; fold of a tunic or
toga, pocket; lap; crotch* (6)

sīve (conjunction): *or if, or* (3)

sōbrius, sōbria, sōbrium: *sober, temperate*

societās, societātis, F: *companionship;
association, partnership*

soleātus, soleāta, soleātum: *wearing slippers*

soleō, solēre, solitus sum: *be accustomed,
usual* (2)

solidus, solida, solidum: *solid, firm, whole*

sōlitūdō, sōlitūdinis, F: *loneliness,
solitude; wilderness*

sollemnis, sollemne: *annual; religious;
usual*

sollicitus, sollicita, sollicitum: *stirred up;
anxious, restless*

sōlum (adverb): *only, barely, merely;* **nōn
sōlum . . . sed etiam**: *not only . . .
but also* (3)

solum, solī, N: *bottom, floor; sole; foundation,
source, basis*

sōlus, sōla, sōlum (gen. s. **sōlīus**, dat. s.
sōlī): *only, sole, alone; lonely* (2)

solūtus, solūta, solūtum: *loose,
free, unrestrained*

solvō, solvere, solvī: *loosen, untie, free*

somnus, somnī, M: *sleep, slumber* (11)

sonō, sonāre, sonuī, sonitus: *utter, express;
ring, resound*

sonus, sonī, M: *sound, noise, tone*

sophus, sophī, M: *wise man, sage* (Greek
loan word)

sōpītus, sōpīta, sōpītum: *asleep, sleepy*

sordidus, sordida, sordidum: *dirty,
shabby, low*

spadō, spadōnis, M: *eunuch* (Greek
loan word)

spargō, spargere, sparsī, sparsus:
scatter, sprinkle

spatior, spatiārī, spatiātus sum:
stroll, walk

spatium, spatiī, N: *space, room; walk;
interval, moment of time*

speciōsus, speciōsa, speciōsum: *good-
looking; plausible*

spectāculum, spectāculī, N: *sight, spectacle;
public show*

spectō, spectāre, spectāvī, spectātus: *watch,
consider* (12)

speculum, speculī, N: *mirror*

spērō, spērāre, spērāvī, spērātus: *look for, expect, hope*

spēs, speī, F: *hope, expectation*

spīritus, spīritūs, M: *breathing, breath; breeze* (11)

spissus, spissa, spissum: *thick, dense; coming thick and fast*

sponda, spondae, F: *bed frame; bed, sofa*

spōnsiō, spōnsiōnis, F: *solemn promise; bet*

spōnsiuncula, spōnsiunculae, F: *a little bet*

sportella, sportellae, F: *a small basket* of food given by a patron to clients; *dole, present*

stabulum, stabulī, N: *stable; humble lodging; brothel*

stāminātus, stāmināta, stāminātum: *neat, not mixed with water*

statim (adverb): *at once* (3)

statua, statuae, F: *statue*

stēla, stēlae, F: *stele, block of stone; tombstone* (Greek loan word)

stercus, stercoris, N: *manure, dung*

sternūtō, sternūtāre, sternūtāvī: *sneeze violently*

stertō, stertere: *snore* (11)

Stichus, Stichī, M: *Stichus*, a common slave name

stigma, stigmatis, N: *mark, brand* (Greek loan word)

stīpendium, stīpendiī, N: *military pay; military service*

stō, stāre, stetī, statum: *stand; endure, last* (11)

stola, stolae, F: *dress*, outer garment worn by women, equivalent to male **toga**

stolātus, stolāta, stolātum: *wearing a* **stola**, *ladylike*

stomachus, stomachī, M: *stomach; taste; appetite* (Greek loan word)

strabōnus, strabōna, strabōnum: *squinty-eyed, cross-eyed*

strāgula, strāgulae, F: *covering, cloth*, especially a *shroud* for a corpse

strātum, strātī, N: *saddle, horse blanket*

strātus, strāta, strātum: *covered, spread with a cloth*

strepitus, strepitūs, M: *noise, crash, bang*

stringō, stringere, strīnxī, strictus: *draw tight, bind; draw a weapon*

studium, studiī, N: *enthusiasm, devotion;* (in plural) *academic studies*

stultus, stulta, stultum: *foolish, silly*

stupeō, stupēre, stupuī: *be amazed at; be stunned*

stupor, stupōris, M: *numbness, confusion, stupidity*

stuprum, stuprī, N: *immorality; illicit sex*

suāvis, suāve: *sweet, pleasant, agreeable* (6)

sub (preposition + ablative): *under; close to*

subdūcō, subdūcere, subdūxī, subductus: *draw or pull up, raise; steal; withdraw*

subeō, subīre, subīvī or **subiī, subitus**: *enter; approach; help; go up*

subiciō, subicere, subiēcī, subiectus: *throw up, fling up; expose; add*

subinde (adverb): *immediately afterward; from then on; from time to time* (8)

subitō (adverb): *suddenly, unexpectedly* (8)

sublātus: see **tollō**

subolfaciō, subolfacere: *perceive as if by smell, sniff out*

subōrnō, subōrnāre, subōrnāvī, subōrnātus: *equip, supply; dress*

subrīdeō, subrīdēre, subrīsī: *smile*

subsequor, subsequī, subsecūtus sum: *follow closely, pursue; support*

subsessor, subsessōris, M: *one who lies in wait for game; schemer*

subsistō, subsistere, substitī: *hold out against, stand up to*

subter (preposition + accusative): *underneath, beneath*

subtīlitās, subtīlitātis, F: *fineness; exactness*

suburbānus, suburbānī, N: *estate* or *farm* near the city

succingō, succingere, succīnxī, succīnctus: *tuck up, put on*

succinō, succinere: *chime in, accompany;*
recite in a droning voice
sūdārium, sūdāriī, N: *handkerchief, towel*
sūdor, sudōris, M: *sweat* (11)
sufficiō, sufficere, suffēcī, suffectus:
supply, yield
sufflō, sufflāre, sufflāvī, sufflātus: *blow up,*
blow on
sum, esse, fuī, futūrus: *be, exist* (1)
summus, summa, summum: *highest, last,*
greatest; ad summam: *in short, in sum, to*
get to the point
sūmō, sūmere, sūmpsī, sūmptus: *take up;*
wear; begin; eat
supellecticārius, supellecticāriī, M: *slave in*
charge of household furniture
super (adverb): *above, besides, in addition* (3)
superbus, superba, superbum:
arrogant, overbearing
supervacuus, supervacua, supervacuum:
superfluous
supplex, supplicis, M or F: *suppliant*
suppliciter (adverb): *suppliantly, humbly*
supplicium, suppliciī, N: *entreaty, prayer;*
punishment (12)
supprimō, supprimere, suppressī,
suppressus: *press down* or *under,*
sink, repress
suprā (adverb): *above, earlier, before;*
beyond, more (3)
suprēmus, suprēma, suprēmum: *last, final*
surgō, surgere, surrēxī, surrēctum: *get*
up, rise (7)
sūrsum (adverb): *upward, high up*
sūs, suis, M: *pig, hog*
suspectus, suspecta, suspectum: *suspect,*
mistrusted
suspiciō, suspiciōnis, F: *suspicion, inkling*
suspicor, suspicārī, suspicātus sum:
mistrust, suspect
sustineō, sustinere, sustinuī: *hold up* or
back; support
sustulī: see tollō

sūtor, sūtōris, M: *shoemaker*
suus, sua, suum: *his own, her own, its own,*
their own (owned by subject) (1)
symphōnia, symphōniae, F: *musical troupe,*
band (Greek loan word)
symphōniacus, symphōniacī, M: *musician*
(Greek loan word)

taberna, tabernae, F: *inn; hut*
tabula, tabulae, F: *board, tablet; painting;*
game board
taceō, tacēre, tacuī, tacitus: *be silent, say*
nothing (8)
tāctus, tāctūs, M: *touch, contact*
taeda, taedae, F: *pinewood, pitch*
taeter, taetra, taetrum: *offensive, hideous*
tālis, tāle: *such, of such a sort* (9)
tam (adverb): *so, so much, to such a degree* (3)
tamen (adverb): *yet, nevertheless, still* (3)
tamquam (conjunction): *as, just as, as much*
as; as if (3)
tandem (adverb): *at last, finally*
tangō, tangere, tetigī, tāctus: *touch* (9)
tangomenas facere: *drink one's fill* (only in
the *Satyrica*)
tantus, tanta, tantum: *so great* (9)
Tarentīnus, Tarentīna, Tarentīnum:
Tarentine, from the city of Tarentum in
south Italy
Tarentum, Tarentī, N: *Tarentum,* town on
southern Italian coast (see map)
Tarracīniensēs, Tarracīniensium, M pl.:
inhabitants of Tarracīna, a town on the
southwest coast of Italy (see map)
taurus, taurī, M: *bull*
tē: see tū
tempestās, tempestātis, F: *time, season,*
occasion; storm; disaster
templum, templī, N: *temple, shrine*
temptō, temptāre, temptāvī, temptātus:
test, feel; attempt, try (7)
tempus, temporis, N: *time; season;*
occasion (11)

tenebrae, tenebrārum, F. pl.: *darkness, night*

teneō, tenēre, tenuī, tentus: *hold, grasp; comprehend* (5)

ter (adverb): *three times*

terebinthinus, terebinthina, terebinthinum: *of the terebinth* or *turpentine tree*

Terentius, Terentiī, M: *Terentius*, a Roman family name

tergeō, tergēre, tersī, tersus: *wipe, scour, dry off; clean*

terra, terrae, F: *ground, land, earth* (7)

terribilis, terribile: *terrible, frightful*

tertiārius, tertiāriī, M: *one-third; gladiator* who takes on the winner after another has lost

tertius, tertia, tertium: *third*

tessera, tesserae, F: *token, game piece; die; ticket*

testāmentum, testāmentī, N: *will, testament* (8)

tetigī: see **tangō**

texō, texere, texuī, textus: *weave, braid*

textor, textōris, M: *weaver*

thēbaicus, thēbaica, thēbaicum: *of Egyptian Thebes; dry type of date fruit*

Thēbānus, Thēbāna, Thēbānum: *Theban, of Thebes*, the name of a city of Greece, Mysia in Asia Minor, and Egypt

thēsaurus, thēsaurī, M: *storehouse, treasure* (Greek loan word)

Thraex, Thraecis, M: *Thracian-style gladiator*, armed with a saber and small shield

thumatulum, thumatulī, N: *thyme-seasoned sausage* (only in the *Satyrica*)

thyrsus, thyrsī, M: *thyrsus*, a staff used in Bacchic ritual, a branch twined with ivy and vine leaves topped with a pinecone

tibi: see **tū**

tībia, tībiae, F: *shinbone; flute*

timeō, timēre, timuī: *fear, be afraid of* (5)

timidus, timida, timidum: *fearful, timid* (11)

timor, timōris, M: *fear, dread*

tinea, tineae, F: *moth*

tintinnābulum, tintinnābulī, N: *bell*

titulus, titulī, M: *inscription, label, tag*

Titus, Titī, M: *Titus,* common first name of Roman males

toga, togae, F: *toga,* outer garment of a Roman male citizen; diēs togae virilis: "day of the man's toga," male coming-of-age ritual

tollō, tollere, sustulī, sublātus: *take up, lift, raise* (2)

tōmentum, tōmentī, N: *pillow stuffing*

tōnstrīnum, tōnstrīnī, N: *barbering, trade of the barber*

topanta, N pl.: *everything, all in all* (Greek loan word; hapax legomenon)

toral, torālis, N: *coverlet, small blanket*

tormentum, tormentī, N: *torture*

torqueō, torquēre, torsī, tortus: *twist, turn; torment*

tortor, tortōris, M: *torturer*

tortus, torta, tortum: *twisted, plaited*

torus, torī, M: *bed, couch, mattress*

tot (indeclinable adjective): *so many, as many;* tot . . . quot: *as many . . . as* (8)

totiēns (adverb): *so often, so many times*

tōtus, tōta, tōtum (gen. s. tōtīus, dat. s. tōtī): *the whole, all, the entire* (4)

tractō, tractāre, tractāvī, tractātus: *touch, caress*

trādūcō, trādūcere, trādūxī, trāductus: *bring across; make a show of; disgrace, degrade*

tragoedia, tragoediae, F: *tragedy* (Greek loan word)

tragoedus, tragoedī, M: *tragic actor* (Greek loan word)

trahō, trahere, traxī, tractus: *draw, drag*

trāiciō, trāicere, trāiēcī, trāiectus: *throw across; pierce*

trānseō, trānsīre, trānsīvī or trānsiī, trānsitus: *cross, pass over*

trānsferō, trānsferre, trānstulī, trānslātus: *carry* or *bring across; copy*

trānsiliō, trānsilīre, trānsiluī: *jump over*

trecentī, trecentae, trecenta: *three hundred*

trecentiēs (adverb): *three hundred times*

tremō, tremere, tremuī: *tremble at; tremble*

trepidātiō, trepidātiōnis, F: *nervousness, trembling*

trepidō, trepidāre, trepidāvī, trepidātus: *be startled by; be nervous*

trēs, tria: *three* (4)

tribītārius, tribītāria, tribītārium: *subject to paying tribute, tributary*

tribūnal, tribūnālis, N: *platform, tribunal; magistrate's chair, seat of honor*

trīcae, trīcārum, F pl.: *tricks, nonsense*

trīclīnium, trīclīniī, N: *dining room* (1)

triduum, triduī, N: *three-day period, three days*

Trimalchiō, Trimalchiōnis, M: *Trimalchio,* name combining *tri,* three, and a Semitic root for "prince"

trīmus, trīma, trīmum: *three-year-old*

trīstis, trīste: *sad*

trīstitia, trīstitiae, F: *sadness; severity, sternness*

trītus, trīta, trītum: *worn, worn down, worn out*

trūdō, trūdere, trūsī, trūsus: *push, thrust*

trux, trucis: *savage, fierce*

tū, tibi (dat.), **tē** (acc. and abl.): *you* (sing.) (1)

tūber, tūberis, N: *lump;* **tūber terrae:** *truffle, exotic mushroom*

tubicen, tubicinis, M: *trumpeter*

tueor or **tuor, tuērī, tuitus** or **tūtus sum:** *look at, look after*

tulī: see **ferō**

tum (adverb): *then; next*

tumultuō, tumultuāre, tumultuāvī, tumultuātus: *make a disturbance, be in an uproar*

tumultus, tumultūs, M: *commotion, uproar*

tunc (adverb): *then; consequently*

tunica, tunicae, F: *tunic,* simple and standard short-sleeved, knee-length garment

turba, turbae, F: *tumult, uproar,* especially one caused by a crowd of people; *mob*

turbō, turbāre, turbāvī, turbātus: *throw into confusion, disturb; go wild*

turdus, turdī, M: *thrush*

turpis, turpe: *ugly, foul, deformed; shameful*

tūtēla, tūtēlae, F: *care, guardianship*

tūtus, tūta, tūtum: *safe; cautious*

tuus, tua, tuum: *your, of yours* (sing.) (2)

tyrannus, tyrannī, M: *monarch, tyrant* (Greek loan word)

Tyrius, Tyria, Tyrium: *Tyrian, Phoenician; purple* (from a famous Tyrian dye)

ūber, ūberis, N: *udder, nipple*

ubi (interrogative adverb): *where? when?* (7)

ubīque (adverb): *everywhere, anywhere*

ūdus, ūda, ūdum: *wet*

Ulixēs, Ulixis, M: *Ulysses,* Italian name for Odysseus

ūllus, ūlla, ūllum (gen. s. **ūllīus,** dat. s. **ūllī**): *any*

ultimus, ultima, ultimum: *farthest, most extreme, last*

ultrō (adverb): *beyond, on the other side; conversely; moreover*

ululō, ululāre, ululāvī, ululātus: *howl, ululate*

umbra, umbrae, F: *shade; shadow, ghost*

umerus, umerī, M: *shoulder, upper arm*

ūmor, ūmōris, M: *moisture; liquid*

umquam (adverb): *ever, at any time* (5)

ūnctus, ūncta, ūnctum: *anointed; sumptuous, extravagant*

unde (adverb): *from where, from which, from whom*

unguentum, unguentī, N: *ointment, perfume* (7)

unguis, unguis, M: *fingernail; claw*

unguō, unguere, ūnxī, ūnctus: *grease, anoint*

ūniversus, ūniversa, ūniversum: *all together, all*

ūnus, ūna, ūnum (gen. s. unīus, dat. s. unī):
    one, single, only (1)
urbānē (adverb): wittily, with sophistication
urbānitās, urbānitātis, F: city life,
    sophistication, wit
urbs, urbis, F: city
urceātim (adverb): by the pitcher, in buckets
    (hapax legomenon)
ursīna, ursīnae, F: bear meat
ursus, ursī, M: bear
ūsque (adverb): all the way; continuously
ūsus, ūsūs, M: use, using; enjoyment;
    custom; benefit; need (5); ūsū venīre: to
    happen in the course of life
ut: (conjunction + indicative) as, when;
    (conjunction + subjunctive) in order
    that, that (3)
utcumque (adverb): however; whenever; one
    way or another
uter, utra, utrum (gen. s. utrīus, dat. s. utrī):
    which of two; one of two, one or the other
ūter, ūtris, M: bag, skin
uterque, utraque, utrumque: each, both
utique (adverb): anyhow, at least; especially
ūtor, ūtī, ūsus sum: use, enjoy (+ ablative) (5)
utrum . . . an/annōn (conjunction): whether
    . . . or not? (7)
ūva, ūvae, F: grape
uxor, uxōris, F: wife, mate (6)

vacō, vacāre, vacāvī, vacātum: be empty; be
    without; be at leisure; be free from
vāh (interjection): ah! oh! wow!
valdē (adverb): greatly, very; yes, certainly (8)
valeō, valēre, valuī, valitum: be
    strong, be capable; farewell (used
    in saying goodbye)
valītūdō, valītūdinis, F: good health, state
    of health
valvae, valvārum, F pl.: folding doors,
    double doors
varius, varia, varium: variegated, of
    differing colors

vāsum, vāsī, N: dish; utensil, tool
-ve (enclitic conjunction): or
vehementer (adverb): vehemently
vehō, vehere, vexī, vectus: carry, convey;
    travel, ride
vel (adverb): even, actually; perhaps;
    (conjunction) either, or
vēlum, vēlī, N: sail
vēnābulum, vēnābulī, N: hunting spear
vēnālicium, vēnāliciī, N: slave sale,
    slave market
vēnālicius, vēnālicia, vēnālicium: for sale
vēnālis, vēnāle: for sale
vēnātiō, vēnātiōnis, F: hunt, hunting; wild
    beast show
vēnātōrius, vēnātōria, vēnātōrium:
    belonging to a hunter, hunter's
vēndō, vēndere, vēndidī, venditus: sell
vēneō, vēnīre, vēniī, vēnitum: go up for sale,
    be sold
venerātiō, venerātiōnis, F: veneration,
    deep respect
venerius, veneria, venerium: related to the
    goddess Venus, sexual, venereal
veniō, venīre, vēnī, ventum: come,
    arrive (1)
venter, ventris, M: belly, stomach
Venus, Veneris, F: goddess Venus
verber, verberis, N: whip; flogging; lash,
    slap, blow
verberō, verberāre, verberāvī, verberātus:
    flog, whip, beat
verbum, verbī, N: word; saying (10); verba
    dare: deceive, cheat; give the slip to
vereor, verērī, veritus sum: revere, be in awe
    of; fear; be anxious (10)
Vergilius, Vergiliī, M: Vergil, famous poet
    of the Aeneid
vermis, vermis, M: worm
vernāculus, vernācula, vernāculum: of
    home-born slaves, home-born; domestic
vernula, vernulae, M or F: little home-born
    slave, little pet; native

vērō (adverb): *in truth, certainly; even; however* (3)

versipellis, versipellis, M: *skin-shifter, pelt-changer; werewolf*

versō, versāre, versāvī, versātus: *spin, twist*

versus, versūs, M: *row, line* (of poetry)

vertō, vertere, vertī, versus: *turn, spin; change*

vērum (adverb): *yes, truly; but; yet, still* (3)

vērus, vēra, vērum: *true, real, fair* (2)

vervēx, vervēcis, M: *castrated hog; a pigheaded person*

vēsīca, vēsīcae, F: *bladder*

vester, vestra, vestrum: *your, of all of you* (2)

vestiārius, vestiāriī, M: *clothes-seller*

vestīgium, vestīgiī, N: *trace, track, vestige, outline, footprint*

vestīmentum, vestīmentī, N: *clothing* (5)

vestiō, vestīre, vestīvī, vestītus: *dress, clothe, attire*

vestis, vestis, F: *clothing, dress, covering*

vetō, vetāre, vetuī, vetitus: *forbid, veto, prohibit*

vetulus, vetula, vetulum: *little old, poor old*

vetus, veteris: *old, aged; well-established*

vetustus, vestusta, vestustum: *old, ancient, old-fashioned*

vexātiō, vexātiōnis, F: *shaking, tossing*

vexō, vexāre, vexāvī, vexātus: *shake, vex, annoy*

via, viae, F: *way, road, journey, method*

viātor, viātoris, M: *traveler, passenger; messenger*

vibrō, vibrāre: *wave around, hurl; vibrate, quiver*

vīcēnsimārius, vīcēnsimāria, vīcēnsimārium: *derived from the* **vīcēsima** *tax*

vīcēnsimārius, vīcēnsimāriī, M: *collector of the* **vīcēsima** *tax* (hapax legomenon)

vīcēsima, vīcēsimae, F: *twentieth (5%) tax* levied on the manumission of slaves

vīcīnia, vīcīniae, F: *neighborhood, vicinity*

vīcīnus, vīcīna, vīcīnum: *near, neighboring*

vicis (nominative does not occur), F: *change, alternation;* **in vicem**: *in turn, alternately*

victor, victōris, M: *victor*

vīcus, vīcī, M: *row of houses; street; ward*

vidēlicet (adverb): *clearly, of course*

videō, vidēre, vīdī, vīsus: *see;* (passive) *seem* (1)

vigil, vigilis, M: *night watchman, fireman*

vigilō, vigilāre, vigilāvī, vigilātum: *stay awake, be alert*

vīgintī (indeclinable adjective): *twenty*

vigor, vigōris, M: *vigor, liveliness*

vīlicātiō, vīlicātiōnis, F: *task of overseeing a farm*

vīlla, vīllae, F: *country home, farmhouse*

vīnārium, vīnāriī, N: *wine flask*

vinciō, vincīre, vīnxī, vīnctus: *bind, tie, restrain*

vincō, vincere, vīcī, victus: *conquer, defeat; convince* (11)

vinculum, vinculī, N: *binding, fetter; cord*

vindicō, vindicāre, vindicāvī, vindicātus: *lay claim to, protect; demand*

vīnea, vīneae, F: *vineyard, vine*

vīnum, vīnī, N: *wine* (2)

violō, violāre, violāvī, violātus: *treat with violence, violate, outrage, injure*

vir, virī, M: *man, hero, husband, lover* (5)

virīlis, virīle: *masculine, manly*

virtūs, virtūtis, F: *manliness, valor, excellence*

vīs, vīs (dat. **vī**, acc. **vim**, abl. **vī**; plural: **vīrēs, vīrium**), F: *power, strength, force* (5)

viscera, viscerum, N pl.: *internal organs, viscera, vitals*

vīta, vītae, F: *life; way of life; career*

vītālis, vītāle: *vital, alive, life-giving;* **vītālia, vītālium**, N pl.: *grave clothes, shroud* (euphemism)

vītis, vītis, F: *vine, vine branch*

vitium, vitiī, N: *fault, defect; weakness, vice*

vitreus, vitrea, vitreum: *glass, made of glass*

vitulus, vitulī, M: *calf; veal*

vīvō, vīvere, vixī, victum: *live, be alive, survive* (5)

vīvus, vīva, vīvum: *alive, lively* (5)

vix (adverb): *scarcely, hardly*

vōbīs: see vōs

vocō, vocāre, vocāvī, vocātus: *call, name, summon* (5)

volitō, volitāre, volitāvī, volitātum: *flit about, fly around*

volō, velle, voluī: *wish, want; be willing* (1)

volō, volāre, volāvī, volātum: *fly*

volpēs, volpis, F: *fox; craftiness*

voluptās, voluptātis, F: *pleasure, delight; (in plural) games, public performances* (10)

volūtō, volūtāre, volūtāvī, volūtātus: *roll around; (passive) wallow, luxuriate*

vomō, vomere, vomuī, vomitus: *vomit*

vōs (nom. and acc.), **vestrum** (partitive gen.), vōbīs (dat. and abl.): *you* (pl.) (2)

vōtum, vōtī, N: *solemn vow, offering; prayer, wish* (10)

vōx, vōcis, F: *voice, sound* (8)

vulgāris, vulgāre: *common, usual*

vulgātus, vulgāta, vulgātum: *common, well-known*

vulnerō, vulnerāre, vulnerāvī, vulnerātus: *wound*

vulnus, vulneris, N: *wound, blow*

vultus, vultūs, M: *face, expression, look, appearance* (4)

zēlotypus, zēlotypa, zēlotypum: *jealous* (Greek loan word)

Works Consulted

Ahern, Charles. 1991. "Notes on Word Order and Sentence Structure in Latin." *New England Classical Journal* 19: 20–23.

Andreau, Jean. 2009. "Freedmen in the *Satyrica*." Translated by Paul Dilley. In *Petronius: A Handbook*, edited by Jonathan Prag and Ian Repath, 114–24. Wiley-Blackwell.

Arrowsmith, William. 1966. "Luxury and Death in the *Satyricon*." *Arion* 5.3: 304–31.

Balme, M. G., and Petronius. 1973. *The Millionaire's Dinner Party: An Adaptation of the* Cena Trimalchionis *of Petronius*. Oxford University Press.

Bartsch, Shadi. 1994. *Actors in the Audience*. Harvard University Press.

———. 2008. "Narrative. 2. The Roman Novel." In *The Cambridge Companion to the Greek and Roman Novel*, edited by Tim Whitmarsh, 245–57. Cambridge University Press.

Beck, Roger. 1973. "Some Observations on the Narrative Technique of Petronius." *Phoenix* 27: 42–61. Reprinted in *Oxford Readings in the Roman Novel*, edited by Stephen J. Harrison (Oxford University Press, 1999), 50–73.

———. 1975. "Encolpius at the *Cena*." *Phoenix* 29: 271–83.

Bodel, John. 1994. "Trimalchio's Underworld." In *The Search for the Ancient Novel*, edited by James Tatum, 237–59. Johns Hopkins University Press.

Boyce, Bret. 1991. *The Language of the Freedmen in Petronius'* Cena Trimalchionis. Brill.

Bücheler, Franz, ed. 1862. *Petronii Arbitri Satirarum Reliquiae*. Weidmann.

Bulwer-Lytton, Edward. 1834. *The Last Days of Pompeii*. Richard Bentley.

Cameron, Averil. 1969. "Petronius and Plato." *Classical Quarterly* 19.2: 367–70.

Carver, Robert H. F. 1999. "The Rediscovery of the Latin Novels." In *Latin Fiction: The Latin Novel in Context*, edited by Heinz Hofmann, 214–28. Routledge.

Connors, Catherine M. 1998. *Petronius the Poet: Verse and Literary Tradition in the* Satyricon. Cambridge University Press.

Conte, Gian Biagio. 1996. *The Hidden Author: An Interpretation of Petronius'* Satyricon. Translated by Elaine Fantham. University of California Press.

Courtney, Edward. 2001. *A Companion to Petronius*. Oxford University Press.

Crompton, Louis. 1985. *Byron and Greek Love: Homophobia in 19th Century England*. Faber.

Eliot, T. S. 1922. *The Wasteland*. Horace Liveright.

Fellini Satyricon. 1969. Dir. Federico Fellini. United Artists. Film.

Fusillo, Massimo. 2008. "Modernity and Post-modernity." In *The Cambridge Companion to the Greek and Roman Novel*, edited by Tim Whitmarsh, 321–39. Cambridge University Press.

George, Peter A. 1966. "Style and Character in the *Satyricon*." *Arion* 5.3: 336–58.

Glare, P. G. W., ed. 1982. *Oxford Latin Dictionary*. Oxford University Press.

Goldhill, Simon. 2008. "Genre." In *The Cambridge Companion to the Greek and Roman Novel*, edited by Tim Whitmarsh, 185–200. Cambridge University Press.

Gruber-Miller, John, ed. 2006. *When Dead Tongues Speak: Teaching Beginning Greek and Latin*. Oxford University Press.

Habermehl, Peter. 2006. *Petronius, Satyrica 79–141: Ein philologisch-literarischer Kommentar*. Band 1: *Sat. 79–110*. Walter de Gruyter.

Hansen, Wells S. 1999–2000. "Teaching Latin Word Order for Reading Competence." *Classical Journal* 95: 173–80.

Harrison, Stephen J. 1998. "The Milesian Tales and the Roman Novel." *Groningen Colloquia on the Novel* 9: 61–73.

———, ed. 1999. *Oxford Readings in the Roman Novel*. Oxford University Press.

———. 2009. "Petronius' *Satyrica* and the Novel in English." In *Petronius: A Handbook*, edited by Jonathan Prag and Ian Repath, 181–97. Wiley-Blackwell.

Heinze, Robert. 1899. "Petron und der griechische Roman." *Hermes* 34: 494–519. Reprinted in *Beiträge zum griechischen Liebesroman*, edited by Hans Gärtner (Georg Olms, 1984), 15–40.

Highet, Gilbert. 1941. "Petronius the Moralist." *Transactions of the American Philological Association* 72: 176–94.

Hofmann, Heinz, ed. 1999. *Latin Fiction: The Latin Novel in Context*. Routledge.

Hope, Valerie M. 2009. "At Home with the Dead: Roman Funeral Traditions and Trimalchio's Tomb." In *Petronius: A Handbook*, edited by Jonathan Prag and Ian Repath, 140–60. Wiley-Blackwell.

Horsfall, Nicholas. 1989a. "'The Uses of Literacy' and the *Cena Trimalchionis* I." *Greece & Rome* 36: 74–89.

———. 1989b. "'The Uses of Literacy' and the *Cena Trimalchionis* II." *Greece & Rome* 36: 194–209.

Hoyos, B. Dexter. 1993. "Reading, Recognition, Comprehension: The Trouble with Understanding Latin." *JACT Review* 13: 11–16.

Jensson, Gottskálk. 2004. *The Recollections of Encolpius: The Satyrica of Petronius as Milesian Fiction*. Ancient Narrative Supplementum, 2. Barkhuis.

Joshel, Sandra R. 1992. *Work, Identity and Legal Status at Rome: A Study of the Occupational Inscriptions*. University of Oklahoma Press.

Keller, Andrew, and Stephanie Russell. 2004. *Learn to Read Latin*. Yale University Press.

Killeen, J. F. 1957. "James Joyce's Roman Prototype." *Comparative Literature* 9.3: 193–203.

Laird, Andrew. 1999. "Ideology and Taste: Narrative and Discourse in Petronius' *Satyricon*." In *Powers of Expression, Expressions of Power: Speech Presentation and Latin Literature*, 209–58. Oxford University Press.

Lawall, Gilbert, ed. 1995. *Petronius: Selections from the* Satyricon. 3rd rev. ed. Bolchalzy-Carducci.

Mahoney, Anne, ed. 2001. *Allen and Greenough's New Latin Grammar*. Focus.

———. 2004. "The Forms You Really Need to Know." *Classical Outlook* 81: 101–105.

Malamud, Martha. 2009. "Primitive Politics: Lucan and Petronius." In *Writing Politics in Imperial Rome*, edited by W. J. Dominik, J. Garthwaite, and P. A. Roche, 273–306. Brill.

Markus, Donka D., and Deborah Pennell Ross. 2004. "Reading Proficiency in Latin through Expectations and Visualization." *Classical World* 98: 79–93.

Morales, Helen. 2008. "The History of Sexuality." In *The Cambridge Companion to the Greek and Roman Novel*, edited by Tim Whitmarsh, 39–55. Cambridge University Press.

Morgan, J. R. 2009. "Petronius and Greek Literature." In *Petronius: A Handbook*, edited by Jonathan Prag and Ian Repath, 32–47. Wiley-Blackwell.

Müller, Konrad. 1983. *Petronius Arbiter: Satyrica*. Artemis.

———. 1995. *Petronii Arbitri: Satyricon Reliquae*. Teubner.

———. 2003. *Petronii Arbitri: Satyricon Reliquiae*. 4th ed., revised. Saur.

Oliensis, Ellen. 1997. "The Erotics of *Amicitia*: Readings in Tibullus, Propertius, and Horace." In *Roman Sexualities*, edited by Judith P. Hallett and Marilyn B. Skinner, 151–71. Princeton University Press.

Panayotakis, Costas. 1995. *Theatrum Arbitri: Theatrical Elements in the* Satyrica *of Petronius*. Brill.

———. 2009. "Petronius and the Roman Literary Tradition." In *Petronius: A Handbook*, edited by Jonathan Prag and Ian Repath, 48–64. Wiley-Blackwell.

———. 2010. "Petronius." *Oxford Bibliographies Online*, http:www.oxfordbibliographiesonline. com. Accessed December 30, 2010.

Parsons, Peter. 1971. "A Greek *Satyricon*?" *Bulletin of the Institute of Classical Studies* 18: 53–68.

Paschalis, Michael. 2011. "Petronius and Virgil: Contextual and Intertextual Readings." In *Echoing Narratives: Studies of Intertextuality in Greek and Roman Prose Fiction*, edited by Konstantin Doulamis, 73–98. Barkhuis.

Patimo, Valeria Maria. 2009. "Una seduta deliberante nel *Satyricon* (101.6–103.2)." In *Il romanzo latino: Modelli e tradizione letteraria; Atti della VII Giornata Ghisleriana di Filologia classica (Pavia, 11–12 ottobre 2007)*, edited by Fabio Gasti, 47–59. Collegio Ghislieri.

Paul, Joanna. 2009. "*Fellini-Satyricon*: Petronius and Film." In *Petronius: A Handbook*, edited by Jonathan Prag and Ian Repath, 198–217. Wiley-Blackwell.

Perry, B. E. 1967. *The Ancient Romances: A Literary-Historical Account of Their Origins*. University of California Press.

Petersen, Lauren Hackworth. 2006. *The Freedman in Roman Art and Art History*. Cambridge University Press.

Petersmann, Hubert. 1999. "Environment, Linguistic Situation, and Levels of Style in Petronius' *Satyrica*." Translated by Martin Revermann. In *Oxford Readings in the Roman Novel*, edited by Stephen Harrison, 105–23. Oxford University Press.

Petronius. 2000. *Satyricon*. Translated with notes and topical commentaries by Sarah Ruden. Hackett.

Petronius, *Satyricon*. Seneca, *Apocolocyntosis*. 1969. Translated by Michael Heseltine and W. H. D. Rouse. Revised by E. H. Warmington. Heinemann.

Petronius Arbiter and Martin S. Smith. 1975. *Petronii Arbitri Cena Trimalchionis*. Clarendon Press.

Plaza, Maria. 2000. *Laughter and Derision in Petronius' Satyrica: A Literary Study*. Almqvist & Wiksell.

Prag, Jonathan, and Ian Repath, eds. 2009. *Petronius: A Handbook*. Wiley-Blackwell.

Quo Vadis. 1951. Dir. Mervyn LeRoy. MGM. Film.

Reeve, Michael D. 1983. "Petronius." In *Texts and Transmission: A Survey of the Latin Classics*, edited by L. D. Reynolds, 295–300. Clarendon Press.

Reynolds, L. D., and N. G. Wilson. 1991. *Scribes and Scholars: A Guide to the Transmission of Greek and Latin Literature*. 3rd ed. Oxford University Press.

Richlin, Amy. 2009. "Sex in the *Satyrica*: Outlaws in Literatureland." In *Petronius: A Handbook*, edited by Jonathan Prag and Ian Repath, 82–100. Wiley-Blackwell.

Rimell, Victoria. 2002. *Petronius and the Anatomy of Fiction*. Cambridge University Press.

Roberts, Deborah H. 2006. "Petronius and the Vulgar Tongue: Colloquialism, Obscenity, Translation." *Classical and Modern Literature* 26.1: 33–55.

Roller, Mathew B. 2006. *Dining Posture in Ancient Rome: Bodies, Values, and Status*. Princeton University Press.

Romm, James. 2008. "Travel." In *The Cambridge Companion to the Greek and Roman Novel*, edited by Tim Whitmarsh, 109–26. Cambridge University Press.

Rose, K. F. C. 1971. *The Date and Author of the* Satyricon. Brill.

Ruebel, James S. 1996. "The Ablative as Adverb: Practical Linguistics and Practical Pedagogy." *The Classical Journal* 92: 57–63.

Sage, Evan T., and Brady B. Gilleland, eds. 1969. *Petronius: The Satiricon*. Appleton-Century-Crofts.

Sandy, Gerald, and Stephen Harrison. 2008. "Novels Ancient and Modern." In *The Cambridge Companion to the Greek and Roman Novel*, edited by Tim Whitmarsh, 299–320. Cambridge University Press.

Schmeling, Gareth. 1994. "*Quid attinet veritatem per interpretem quaerere? Interpretes* and the *Satyricon*." *Ramus* 23: 144–68.

———. 1994–95. "Confessor Gloriosus: A Role of Encolpius in the *Satyrica*." *Würzburger Jahrbücher für die Altertumswissenschaft* 20: 207–24.

———. 2003. "The *Satyrica* of Petronius." In *The Novel in the Ancient World*, rev. ed., edited by Gareth Schmeling, 457–90. Brill Academic.

———. 2011. *A Commentary on the* Satyrica *of Petronius*. Oxford University Press.

Schmeling, Gareth L., and Johanna H. Stuckey. 1977. *A Bibliography of Petronius*. Mnemosyne Supplement, 39. Brill.

Seneca the Elder. 1974. *Declamations, Volume II: Controversiae, Books 7–10. Suasoriae. Fragments*. Translated by Michael Winterbottom. Loeb Classical Library, 464. Harvard University Press.

Simpson, D. P. 1959. *Cassell's Latin Dictionary*. Macmillan.

Slater, Niall W. 1990. *Reading Petronius*. Johns Hopkins University Press.

Sochatoff, A. Fred. 1976. "Petronius Arbiter." In *Catalogus Translationum et Commentariorum: Medieval and Renaissance Latin Translations and Commentaries, Annotated Lists and Guides*, vol. 3, edited by F. Edward Cranz and Paul Oskar Kristeller, 313–39. Catholic University Press.

Stephens, Susan. 2008. "Cultural Identity." In *The Cambridge Companion to the Greek and Roman Novel*, edited by Tim Whitmarsh, 56–71. Cambridge University Press.

Suetonius. 1914. *Lives of the Caesars, Volume II*. Translated by J. C. Rolfe. Loeb Classical Library, 38. Harvard University Press.

Sullivan, J. P. 1968. "Petronius, Seneca and Lucan: A Neronian Literary Feud?" *Transactions and Proceedings of the American Philological Association* 99: 453–67.

———. 1985. "Petronius' *Satyricon* in Its Neronian Context." In *Aufstieg und Niedergang der römischen Welt* II.32.3, edited by Hildegard Temporini and Wolfgang Haase, 1666–86. Walter de Gruyter.

Swanson, Donald C. 1963. *A Formal Analysis of Petronius' Vocabulary.* Perine Book Co.

Tacitus. 1971. *The Annals of Imperial Rome.* Rev. ed. Translated by Michael Grant. Penguin.

Traupman, John C. 1966. *The New College Latin and English Dictionary.* 3rd ed. Bantam Books.

Vannini, Giulio, ed. 2010. *Petronii Arbitri Satyricon 100–115: Edizione critica e commento.* Beiträge zur Altertumskunde, Bd. 281. De Gruyter.

Wallace, Catherine. 1992. *Reading.* Oxford University Press.

Walsh, P. G. 1995. *The Roman Novel.* 2nd ed. Bristol Classical Press.

Whitmarsh, Tim, ed. 2008. *The Cambridge Companion to the Greek and Roman Novel.* Cambridge University Press.

Wohlberg, Joseph. 1964. *201 Latin Verbs.* Barron's Educational Series.

Zeitlin, Froma I. 1971. "Petronius as Paradox: Anarchy and Artistic Integrity." *Transactions and Proceedings of the American Philological Association* 102: 631–84. Reprinted in *Oxford Readings in the Roman Novel,* edited by Stephen J. Harrison (Oxford University Press, 1999), 1–49.

General Index

Achilles, 13, 34, 157

Aeneid, 13, 16, 19, 28, 35–36, 37, 93, 137, 145, 166, 167, 168, 240, 254

Agamemnon, character in novel, 5, 6, 28, 42, 55, 60, 70, 73, 78, 88, 107, 108, 110, 127, 133, 157, 173; mythical king, 28, 34, 41, 108, 100

Apuleius, 8, 12, 40, 46, 47, 49, 50

Ascyltos, 5–7, 12, 13, 18, 34, 37, 39, 42, 45, 50, 87, 88–89, 94, 100–101, 107, 134, 151, 163, 164, 165, 175–76

Atellan farce, 36, 37, 80, 145, 174

Augustales, 27. See also *Sevir*

Augustus (emperor), 16, 18, 24, 27, 35, 36, 74, 136, 150

Author of Satyrica, 9–11. *See also* Petronius

Banquet, 22–24, 60–62, 64–66, 66–82, 85–86, 87–88, 116

Baths, 6, 7, 23, 25, 55–56, 57–59, 87, 93

Christianity, 17, 18, 48

Cinaedi, 26

Circe, 5, 8, 35, 45, 105, 169

Claudius (emperor), 16, 17, 19, 32, 38, 44

Colloquialism, 32–33, 47

Contubernalis, 24, 75, 81, 137, 148, 175

Convivium. See Banquet

Croesus, 30, 76–77, 140. See also *Deliciae*

Croton, map, 5, 7, 12, 14, 24, 45, 169

Date of *Satyrica*, 10, 16–21

Declamation. *See* Oratory

Deliciae, 25, 29, 30, 56, 76, 80, 111, 140

Dining rooms, 22, 64–66. *See also* Banquet

Drama, 21, 36–38. *See also* Atellan farce; Mime

Elite status and attitudes, 9, 11, 13, 15, 17, 21, 22, 23, 28, 29, 36–37, 41, 115; of author, 11, 13; of senators, 9, 17, 20; toward education, 27–28, 33, 41, 44–45; toward Greek language, 28, 33; toward work, 27

Empire, history of, 15–21

Encolpius, character of, 3, 12, 13, 20–21, 28–29, 36, 37, 39; and Circe, 45, 105–106; and Giton, 5–8, 30–31, 37, 42, 50, 55, 74, 87, 88–89, 100–101, 105, 109; language of, 32–33. *See also* Narrator

Epic, 13, 19, 20, 28, 34–36, 38, 39, 46, 47, 49

Epicureanism, 44, 45

Ephesus, map, 29, 148, 166. *See also* Widow of Ephesus

Eumolpus, 5, 7–8, 12, 13, 19–20, 24, 29, 36, 38, 40, 42, 43, 44, 46, 48, 51, 98, 101, 159, 163, 165, 169

Family vs. *familia*, 24–25

Farce. *See* Atellan farce

Fellini Satyricon, 3, 11, 48, 50

307

Grammatical Index